**Jenny Holmes** has been writing fiction since her early twenties, having had series of children's books adapted for both the BBC and ITV.

Jenny was born and brought up in Yorkshire. After living in the Midlands and travelling widely in America, she returned to Yorkshire and brought up her two daughters with a spectacular view of the moors and a sense of belonging to the special, still undiscovered corners of the Yorkshire Dales.

One of three children brought up in Harrogate, Jenny's links with Yorkshire stretch back through many generations via a mother who served in the Land Army during the Second World War and pharmacist and shop-worker aunts, back to a maternal grandfather who worked as a village blacksmith and pub landlord. Her great-aunts worked in Edwardian times as seamstresses, milliners and upholsterers. All told stories of life lived with little material wealth but with great spirit and independence, where a sense of community and family loyalty were fierce – sometimes uncomfortable but never to be ignored. Theirs are the voices that echo down the years, and the author's hope is that their strength is brought back to life in many of the characters represented in these pages.

www.penguin.co.uk

*By Jenny Holmes*

The Mill Girls of Albion Lane
The Shop Girls of Chapel Street
The Midwives of Raglan Road
The Telephone Girls
The Land Girls at Christmas
Wedding Bells for Land Girls
A Christmas Wish for the Land Girls
The Spitfire Girls
The Spitfire Girls Fly for Victory
Christmas with the Spitfire Girls
The Air Raid Girls
The Air Raid Girls at Christmas

*and published by Corgi*

# THE AIR RAID GIRLS AT CHRISTMAS

Jenny Holmes

CORGI BOOKS

TRANSWORLD PUBLISHERS
Penguin Random House, One Embassy Gardens,
8 Viaduct Gardens, London SW11 7BW
www.penguin.co.uk

Transworld is part of the Penguin Random House group of companies
whose addresses can be found at global.penguinrandomhouse.com

Penguin
Random House
UK

First published in Great Britain in 2021 by Bantam Press
an imprint of Transworld Publishers
Corgi edition published 2021



A CIP catalogue record for this book
is available from the British Library.

ISBN 9780552177085

Typeset in 11.5/14pt New Baskerville ITC by Jouve (UK), Milton Keynes.
Printed and bound in Great Britain by Clays Ltd, Elcograf S.p.A.

The authorized representative in the EEA is Penguin Random House Ireland,
Morrison Chambers, 32 Nassau Street, Dublin D02 YH68.

Penguin Random House is committed to a sustainable
future for our business, our readers and our planet. This book
is made from Forest Stewardship Council® certified paper.

*For the bright stars in my night sky –*
*Lola, Jude and Evan*

# CHAPTER ONE

**November 1941**

'Home Sweet Home!' Connie Bailey and Pamela Carr stood back to admire the new banner they'd hung over the entrance to their air raid wardens' post.

'Very smart.' Connie blew into her cupped hands to warm them up. The letters on the white banner were painted a cheerful red. 'It'll stand out a mile, along with that Union Jack we scrounged.'

'Yes, it should give everyone a bit of a lift.' Pamela was satisfied with their efforts. The large flag fluttered from a makeshift flagpole jammed between two piles of sandbags that protected the entrance from bomb blasts. They were stacked to either side of the doorway of what had once been a cobbler's shop but was now converted into an Air Raid Precautions post for Kelthorpe docklands and the neighbouring area. Connie and Pamela had asked Bert Harrison, Connie's dad, for permission to hang the banner and fly the patriotic flag. As head warden of the Gas Street sector post, Bert had grudgingly given them the go-ahead.

'If you must,' he'd grumbled, his grizzled grey

head bent over paperwork as he began his Saturday afternoon shift. Bert's list of jobs had included making a telephone call to the central report and control centre and filling in an ARP/M1 form.

So the two off-duty junior wardens had borrowed a ladder, hammer and nails from Dixon's, a nearby builders' yard. Dressed in practical slacks and jumper, Pamela had advised against Connie shinning up the ladder in her tight skirt and nylon stockings and had volunteered to hang the banner above the doorway herself.

'Can you still read the blackout-time notice?' she'd checked.

'Plain as the nose on my face,' Connie had assured her. The large black clock dial was easily visible. 'Come down and take a look.'

'Home Sweet Home!' Passers-by smiled and gave the thumbs-up. 'That's the spirit, love,' one old man told Connie as he tottered by, a faded army beret from the Great War perched on his head at a precarious angle, eyes sunken in his lined face. 'Britain can take it, eh?'

'If we have anything to do with it,' Connie vowed, 'we' meaning all the volunteer wardens, rescue squads, fire watchers, ambulance drivers and first-aiders recruited into the town's Air Raid Precautions teams.

'"We've won it, we've done it. We've beaten 'em at last."' The skinny veteran broke into a chirpy rendition of the popular song, then gave a toothless grin as he went on his way.

'Not quite,' Connie muttered under her breath. Two years in and, despite Flanagan and Allen's music-hall bravado, the war against Hitler was far from won.

Why else would wardens like her still be patrolling Kelthorpe's streets, yelling at people to observe the blackout or shepherding terrified residents into communal shelters as sirens wailed? Though the Yorkshire coastal town seemed to have survived the worst of the Blitz, a sudden tip-and-run raid could happen without warning: a shower of Firebomb Fritz's incendiary bombs falling to earth in a spectacular cloud of white sparks that lit up the night sky. Children would wail and cry as they clutched at their mothers' skirts, while pale, haggard faces would gaze in horror at the unrecognizable wreckage of what had once been homes.

Pamela's buoyant mood held up in the face of Connie's sotto voce remark. 'That's not like you,' she chided. 'You're usually one of the "Up Housewives and At 'Em" brigade.'

'Less of the housewives, if you please.' Connie frowned. Seizing the ladder, she slung it over her shoulder. 'Here, grab the other end. I may be an old married lady – a widow, to be exact – but I could never be accused of being a stay-at-home housewife. Cleaning and polishing – pah! Washing and ironing – as little as possible, ta very much.' A breeze lifted her wavy mane of dark hair and swept it back from her animated features – sparkling brown eyes with heavy lashes, high cheekbones and full, smiling lips.

Pamela laughed as they returned the ladder to the builder's yard. 'No offence.'

'None taken.'

'Ta, girls.' A freckled, red-haired lad in faded blue overalls relieved them of the ladder. 'You didn't climb up it dressed like that, did you?' he teased Connie, secretly relishing the thought of shapely long legs leading to stocking tops and suspenders.

'What do you think?' she retorted with a toss of her head.

'I wouldn't put it past you, Connie Bailey.'

'She didn't, actually.' Pamela stepped forward and placed the hammer into the lad's outstretched hand. '*I* did.'

'Good for you.' He had to admit that the smaller, slighter one of the pair had her own attractions. Her big, wide eyes for a start – grey with a hint of green – and her light brown hair curled around her face the way some of those Hollywood film actresses wore it. She wasn't as lively as the taller one, though, so it was less easy to pull her leg.

'We'd best get a move on,' Pamela reminded Connie, leading her out on to Gas Street. 'We're due at St Joseph's in twenty minutes.'

Connie heaved a sigh and dragged her feet as they returned to the wardens' post to collect their coats and hats. 'Do we have to?'

'Yes, you promised Tom you would join the choir.'

'What choir?' Bert glanced up from his lists. 'Our Connie has never agreed to sing in public, has she?'

Pamela grinned. 'I'm talking about Mr Greenwood's Christmas choir,' she explained, accepting Bert's help with her coat. She slid her arms into the sleeves, then nodded her thanks. 'Today is our first practice session.'

'You don't say!' His look said it all – raised eyebrows, corners of his mouth turned down.

'All right, Dad!' Connie jammed on her red felt hat and threw him a challenging look.

He grinned to himself. 'I'm saying nowt.'

'You don't need to.' Ever since she was little, Connie's tin ear had given rise to much merriment. A confident child, she'd been able to run like the wind and shoot up her hand before other members of her class in any mental arithmetic test, but holding a tune had been beyond her.

'Has Doug Greenwood heard her sing?' Bert asked Pamela with a sly wink. He came out from behind his counter and accompanied them on to the street to adjust the hands on the blackout-time clock.

'No, but no one needs to audition,' Pamela assured him. 'It's all done in the best Christmas spirit. That's when we'll be carol singing in the streets, collecting money for St Joseph's.'

'Bye, Dad!' Connie grabbed Pamela by the hand and yanked her down the street before her father could get in any further digs. 'I'm only doing this because of Tom,' she muttered. Her sweetheart, Tom Rose, was the only person in the world who could have persuaded Connie to join the choir. 'He's been pestering me about the damned carol singing for ages. I'm warning you: I'm tone deaf.'

'Don't worry; it'll be painless.' How could someone as fearless as Connie in the face of bombs and burning buildings be scared about joining in with a few simple Christmas carols? Pamela wondered.

'"Once in royal David's city . . ."' Connie proved her point with a tuneless rendition.

'Hmm.' Pressing her lips together in a failed attempt not to laugh, Pamela spluttered. 'Oh dear, I see what you mean.'

'It's all right you smirking, but what am I going to

do?' Connie implored. The spire of St Joseph's church loomed ever nearer and she spotted Tom waiting for her at the entrance to the church hall, his bike propped against the wall. He waved eagerly when he saw her.

'Stand at the back and pretend?' Pamela struggled to control her amusement. 'Just mime the words – with a bit of luck no one will notice.'

'Are you sure you won't join us?' At the family bread shop on College Road, Lizzie Harrison had employed every charm she possessed to persuade Bill Evans to sing in the choir along with the rest of the gang; so far without success. She drew him into the windowless bakery behind the empty shop for one last try, sliding her arms around his neck and kissing him softly on the lips.

Bill reached for her hands and unclasped them. Lizzie had a rather fetching streak of flour on her cheek and her skin smelled of freshly baked bread. 'One hundred per cent certain,' he murmured. 'Traipsing the streets caterwauling Christmas carols is not for me. I leave that to Tom: he's the one with the decent voice.'

Lizzie moved in for another kiss. 'Just think of what you'll be missing.'

'Yes – getting frozen to the marrow, having doors slammed in my face, generally making a fool of myself.' Bill's objections emerged between flurries of quick pecks on his cheek. 'Give me storms at sea and the hard slog of a trawlerman's life any day of the week.'

Lizzie studied the mischievous curl of Bill's lips.

She loved his optimistic view of the world: never too serious, always bold and carefree. And boy, did she swoon and go weak at the knees every time she looked into those sparkling grey eyes!

'Scrumptious mince pies and hot toddies, sharing the run-up to Christmas with the rest of us,' she whispered in his ear.

Bill appreciated Lizzie's kisses but held his ground. 'You know I'd do most things you asked me to.'

'So, my sweetie-pie, my currant bun, why not this?' She made one last, teasing attempt. 'I'll be there and so will Con and Pamela, and Tom too, of course. We can all go to the pub after rehearsals.'

Laughing, Bill put his hands on her waist then backed her firmly towards the shop, where they would be on full display. All bread had been sold before midday – Saturday was half-day closing – so the shelves were empty except for a few jars of honey and lemon curd. 'I can always join you lot at the Anchor,' he promised, making for the door then changing his mind and going back for one last kiss. 'You're a hard girl to say no to, you know that?' Lizzie Harrison: the love of his life, with her glossy dark hair and wide brown eyes – the girl he wanted to spend the rest of his life with, roaming the world, footloose and fancy free. 'But I'm not keen on Christmas and that's the truth.'

'I didn't know that.' Bill's mood seemed suddenly thoughtful, so Lizzie was aware something must be up. 'How come?'

'It's nothing.' He brushed the question aside. 'I'll leave you to put up the closed sign. And I'll see you later?'

Lizzie wrinkled her nose. 'I can't, not tonight – I've promised to drive the new ambulance over from York. It's ready to collect.' In her role as ambulance driver for the Civil Defence team, she'd jumped at the chance to fetch the state-of-the-art vehicle.

Bill's face fell but he quickly rallied. 'Brand spanking new, eh?'

'Yes, no more make do and mend with our old Harrison's Bakery van.' This new ARP vehicle would be properly equipped; a Bedford straight from the factory, with an engine full of zip and an interior kitted out with stretchers, blankets and groundsheets. 'I'm free tomorrow morning, though. How about a ride along the coast to White Sands Bay? The weather's meant to be fine.'

'You're on.' Bill collected his crash helmet from the windowsill. 'I'll pick you up from Elliot Street at ten.'

The shop bell rang and he was gone. Lizzie pulled down the blind then fetched her coat and scarf. She hurried to lock the door. At this rate she'd be late for the first rehearsal and would receive a ticking-off from choirmaster Doug Greenwood. He was a Boy Scout leader and churchwarden – a stickler for the rules, by all accounts.

There was a problem with the boiler in St Joseph's church hall. The ancient radiators clicked and wheezed but remained steadfastly stone cold, so the two dozen carol singers kept on their coats as they stood nervously in a semicircle at one end of the dimly lit, unfurnished room. Exposed roof beams soared overhead, the polished wooden floor creaked and the upright piano in the corner seemed dwarfed by an arched window that let in a burst of late-autumn sunlight. Leaves from a giant beech tree – the last of the season – fluttered against the leaded panes as they spiralled down, covering mossy grave mounds in a glorious mosaic of gold, orange and crimson.

Doug Greenwood rested an elbow on the top of the piano and leaned forward to speak quietly with pianist Edith Carr.

'We owe you a big thank you, Mrs Carr . . . a great help . . . much appreciated.' Clean-cut, correct and polite, with a broad, solid build and a wide face, Doug came across as every inch the no-nonsense leader of Boy Scouts and upstanding servant of the Church.

'Not at all, Mr Greenwood, you're very welcome . . . all in a good cause,' was Edith's condescending reply.

Pamela rolled her eyes at Connie and Lizzie. 'Mum ought to have mentioned that she'd volunteered to play the piano for us,' she grumbled. 'It means I'll have to be on my best behaviour.' The relationship between mother and daughter was strained now that Pamela had flown the nest and was no longer at Edith's beck and call. Pamela had viewed her move into lodgings that spring as a bid for independence; Edith continued to interpret it as ingratitude.

'You hear that, Liz? No messing about.' Connie was aware of the piano teacher's strict, snobbish reputation – after all, Connie had lived close to the Carr family on Musgrave Street during the time she'd been married to John Bailey. And here was Edith, perched on her padded stool: stick thin, pinched and upright, not a dyed, dark brown hair out of place, wearing a lavender two-piece suit and a string of cultured pearls worth a week's wages for the average working man.

Struggling to concentrate on the matter in hand, Lizzie opened her hymn book at the section containing carols. This was going to be interesting, to say the least.

'I'm dreading this,' Connie confessed to Tom through gritted teeth. Her sweetheart stood next to her for moral support, head and shoulders taller than her, casually dressed in an open-necked shirt and dark blue pullover.

He reassured her with one of the quick, tender smiles that softened his angular features. 'You can't back out now – it's taken me long enough to get you here.'

'For good reason,' she muttered. It was all right for him: he opened his mouth and out came the loveliest baritone voice for miles around. She knew this from Tom's rendition of 'You Are My Sunshine', sung to her on her birthday back in August. Perched on his knee in the front room of the house in Elliot Street that she shared with her sister Lizzie and their dad, her beau had struck up an impromptu version of the bouncy popular song – 'You are my sunshine, my only sunshine, You make me happy when skies are grey . . .' It had been the best birthday present ever.

'Relax,' Tom murmured. 'Anyone can sing if they put their mind to it.'

'Says Tom Caruso Rose!'

'Attention, please!' Doug tapped the top of the piano with his conductor's baton. 'Thank you, everyone, for giving up your valuable time to be here. It's a decent turnout, considering that Christmas is bound to be a bit different this year.' The choirmaster had carefully thought out his opening remarks and had included this timely nod towards current black-out conditions and food rationing. 'I thought we'd start with a nice easy one that you'll all be familiar with – "Away in a Manger".'

'Oh, Lord!' Connie felt her heartbeat quicken and her mouth turn dry. Why, oh why, had she agreed to come?

'Play us in please, Edith.' Doug's instruction coincided with the raising of his baton and an encouraging smile at the rows of first-time choristers. Some were as young as eleven – members of his Fourth Kelthorpe Scout Group – sitting cross-legged in front of a smattering of doughty matrons from the WI who were well into their seventies. It seemed there was a full cross-section of the Kelthorpe community for Doug to work with.

'"Away in a manger, no crib for a bed . . ."'

Doug lowered his baton and tutted at the ragged, tuneless start. Edith stopped playing. 'No, no – let's begin again. You all know the words so look up from your hymn books,' he implored. 'Keep your eyes on me, if you please, and follow Mrs Carr's tempo.'

Tom winked at Connie. 'All right?'

'No!' A red flush had crept up her neck and threatened to suffuse her cheeks. Her throat was as dry as sandpaper.

'"Away in a manger, no crib for a bed,"' the choir began, accompanied once more by a background noise of creaking radiators.

Following Pamela's recommendation, Connie opened her mouth without emitting a sound.

'Sing up.' Tom dug his elbow in her ribs and winked a second time. Daredevil Connie was rarely at a loss and the sight of her struggling to join in brought tender feelings to the forefront. Later on, in the privacy of his lodgings on North Street, he would hug her and squeeze her half to death.

'"The little Lord Jesus lay down his sweet head."'

From her position at the far end of the row, Pamela sang sweetly. Next to her, Lizzie offered to share her tattered hymn book with Colin Strong, a Boy Scout and Civil Defence messenger whose job it was to brave the dark streets on his bicycle, carrying information between sector posts. He'd recently won a gallantry award for his efforts.

'Ta, but I know the words,' he told her as Doug brought them to a halt at the end of the first verse.

Connie shrank back as she felt the choirmaster fix a beady eye on her. Good God, was she about to be singled out?

But no, he addressed his remark to Tom instead. '"The cattle are lowing,"' he prompted. 'I'm sure you know how this goes on, Thomas. Please demonstrate how it should be done.'

Connie heaved a sigh of relief. Edith sat with slim fingers poised over the keys. All attention was on Tom, who took a deep breath then gave a perfect rendition of the second verse.

A glow of pride replaced Connie's panic. Goodness gracious, could Tom sing! You wouldn't think it to look at him: a tall, muscular fisherman who'd worked on the trawlers with Bill Evans since they'd left school at fourteen. Where was Bill, by the way? Connie must ask Lizzie later. Tom's shoulders were broad, his square, capable hands work-worn and his brown hair cropped short. Never the sort who wished to stand out in a crowd, he was modest and quiet, steady and unaffected. But when he sang, he puffed out his chest and his eyes came alive. He was perfect; just perfect!

'Very good.' Doug beamed. 'Now, if you all follow Tom's lead by lifting your heads and putting your shoulders back, then we might get somewhere.'

But when the choir attempted the third verse – 'Be near me, Lord Jesus, I ask you to stay . . . ' – what emerged was the same shaky sequence of wobbly tremolos, squeaky bass notes and tone-deaf grunts and groans as before.

A pained expression appeared on Edith's face. Her arched eyebrows knitted together and she pursed her lips. The radiators gave a loud gurgle, as if mocking the singers' latest attempts.

'Oh dear me.' Doug didn't try to hide his disappointment. 'That really was well below par. I fear this will take hard work on all our parts if we're to be ready in time for Christmas.'

One old girl close to the piano grumbled that she had joined up out of the goodness of her heart and didn't expect to be criticized. Colin and a fellow Boy Scout shifted uneasily from one buttock to the other. Lizzie felt a bubble of laughter rise from deep within.

'Don't start me off!' Pamela pleaded through clenched teeth.

But Lizzie couldn't help it. No doubt about it – the choir's efforts were dreadful. An old pair of fire bellows was more tuneful. She squirmed as the hysteria rose to chest level then into her throat. It came out as a stifled yelp that sent Pamela into stomach-churning paroxysms. Pamela pressed her hand over her mouth but it was no good: a snort of laughter forced its way out.

'That's quite enough!' With a slam of the piano lid Edith let it be known that her involvement with the St Joseph's carol singers was at a premature end. She was a highly trained classical pianist, not some end-of-the-pier, plinkety-plonk entertainer. Shooting a haughty look in her daughter's direction, she reached for her hat and coat. 'If certain people can't take this seriously, I'm afraid I want nothing more to do with it.'

Pamela clutched her stomach and wished she were dead. Colin and his pal fished in their shorts pockets for their handkerchiefs and stuffed them in their mouths. A rebellious mutter passed along the back row as Edith picked up her handbag, stalked the length of the hall and disappeared through a side door.

'Order!' A desperate Doug tapped the piano with his baton. 'Ladies and gentlemen, boys and girls, please!'

'Nay, this won't do.' Taking pity on the beleaguered choirmaster, Tom assumed control. 'Is there anybody here who can take over at the piano?'

A contrite Lizzie, still red in the face and exhausted from the struggle to suppress her giggles, shoved a shame-faced Pamela forward.

Before she knew it, Pamela was sitting on the stool recently vacated by her mother, rearranging sheet music and following Doug's instruction to play the opening chords of 'Good King Wenceslas'.

'"Good King Wen-ces-las looked out" – not "*Good King Wenslas last* looked out". There are three syllables in the king's name.' With a strained expression, Doug gritted his teeth and persevered. He was determined to get over this first hurdle; come hell or high water the Kelthorpe Christmas choir would be knocked into shape and ready to perform.

Pamela and Connie's route to the Anchor Inn took them along College Road, past Benson's music shop and Harrison's Bakery and on towards the old harbour.

'I don't know about you, but I need a stiff drink,' Connie confessed as they approached St Stephen's dock in the gathering dusk. Tom had already made his way to Gas Street, where he would begin a night shift as second in command under Kenneth Browning at the ARP post. Lizzie, meanwhile, had boarded a bus to York to collect her new ambulance.

Anderson's vast timber yard stood next to a grain mill overlooking the estuary. It dominated the harbour, with its tall cranes and stacks of logs rising twenty feet into the air. Protected by a high chain-link fence and connected to a railway line that transported Baltic wood, Swedish iron ore and other vital goods from Kelthorpe's docks to industrial centres in Leeds and Sheffield, it was a frequent target for Air Marshal Goering's Dorniers and Messerschmitts. Fat Hermann, as he was known, seemed to have it in for Anderson's, and it was a miracle that the red-brick office building and barn-like cutting shed were still standing while many warehouses and factories in the vicinity had been flattened. The last raid had taken place just a week earlier – a quick tip-and-run affair involving four bombers, two of which had jettisoned the last of their high explosives on the headland separating the old from the new town and demolished what was left of the bungalows on Musgrave Street.

As they passed a recently erected notice warning against looting – 'punishable by death or penal servitude for life' – Connie shuddered. She'd had her fingers burned over the issue of looting. Though innocent, she'd got much too close to that particular flame. 'Yes, a drink is definitely what the doctor ordered,' she repeated shakily.

Quick-thinking Pamela guessed the reason for Connie's sudden switch of mood. 'I'm on duty at Gas Street with you tomorrow,' she remarked brightly, linking arms and steering her friend away from the warning sign, along the dockside and out on to the small cobbled square where the fish market was held.

'Champion.' Connie gave a weak smile.

'If I emerge unscathed from Sunday dinner at my mother's house, that is.' Pamela was dreading her next encounter with Edith – she expected the cold-shoulder treatment at the very least. 'You've no idea what it's like to be on the receiving end of one of Ma's frosty looks.'

'Blame Lizzie,' Connie suggested. 'She's the one who set you off laughing. And point out to your ma that we're the worst choir in the world, so she's better off out of it.'

The girls crossed the market square arm in arm, then paused at the entrance to the Anchor.

'Whoever would've thought that being at war with Germany would mean that we'd run out of knicker elastic?' Pamela's remark came out of the blue. 'I went to three haberdashery shops today and I couldn't find any anywhere.'

'Eggs, onions, lipstick are all in short supply, and

now knicker elastic!' Connie put on a tragic expression. 'Boo-hoo!'

Pamela giggled. 'It's important. A girl depends on keeping her knickers up when she's out in public.'

'Not *all* girls.' Connie couldn't resist shocking her more innocent companion with a broad innuendo as she swung into the pub ahead of her.

'Oh, I say!' A rush of warm air greeted them. Luckily the small, low-ceilinged snug was dimly lit; the blackout blinds were already down and a single electric light cast a dim yellow glow, so Pamela's embarrassment went unnoticed.

Connie swept across the room, swinging her hips and enjoying the admiring stares of the fishermen types propping up the bar. 'Come on, Miss Pamela. You have to laugh, otherwise you'd cry.'

Christmas was coming and no geese were getting fat. The entire blacked-out nation lived in the dark or underground like moles. No one went anywhere because of the petrol shortage and an order had come down from on high that Christmas tree lights were to be prohibited this December. 'You can't let it get you down,' Connie declared, 'especially at this time of year.'

'I'm with you there.' Still blushing furiously, Pamela ordered the drinks then led the way to a table close to the fire. 'Christmas isn't cancelled – we won't give the Führer the satisfaction.' They raised their glasses – sherry for Pamela, whisky for Connie – then sipped. 'Which means we have to make the best of a bad job. We'll all get by with home-made cards and presents and we'll save up our coupons for a slap-up Christmas dinner.'

'Agreed.' The Scotch slid down nicely, thank you very much.

'And we must carry on carolling, whether we like it or not,' Pamela insisted, with a firm glint in her eye.

Connie gulped down the rest of her whisky. 'Oh, I'm not sure about that,' she objected shakily. 'I refuse to be cheated out of my Christmas, right enough, but "Ding dong Merrily on High" might be one step too far.'

# CHAPTER TWO

'You can borrow my long johns if you like.' When Bert learned that Lizzie planned a Sunday morning ride on the back of Bill's motorbike he made one of his typical quips.

'Ha ha, thanks but no thanks.' Across the breakfast table Lizzie gave her father's hand a playful tap. 'I'll be warm enough in two jumpers and a jacket.'

'Don't blame me if you freeze to death.' Bert often fretted over Lizzie. Connie had been the one who had bounced back better after their mother, Rhoda, died – Connie had been ten, Lizzie eight. Ever since, he'd regarded his younger daughter as the more tender shoot. 'How far is Bill taking you on that BSA of his?'

'Up to Raynard's Folly, then on to White Sands and back.' Lizzie described the twenty-mile circular route as she got up from the table and knotted a woollen head-scarf under her chin. 'He's due here any minute.'

'Tell him to slow down on those hairpin bends on the road up to the folly. When did he last check the brakes, by the way? And make sure the engine is topped up with oil before you set off.'

Lizzie made her escape with a click of her heels, a grin and a quick salute.

'In one ear and out the other,' Bert said with a sigh as Lizzie's young man pulled up outside the house. 'I worry about that sister of yours going off on that bike,' he confessed to Connie, who had come downstairs bleary-eyed and still in her pyjamas.

'No need.' Connie yawned and poured tea from the pot. 'Liz knows more about the BSA B1 engine than you and me put together.' Working with spanners, spark plugs and oil filters was something Lizzie had always been good at; odd for a girl before the war but more common now that the men had gone off to fight.

'Aye, but she's not tinkering with the innards – she's riding pillion, worse luck.' Bert feared that a young blood like Bill might be tempted to show off with bursts of speed and reckless overtaking. He heard the engine roar into life, then fade into the distance.

'Dad, stop mithering.' Connie drifted through to the front room to look out on the practically deserted terraced street. She tapped on the glass to attract the attention of young Colin Strong, who stood under a lamp post in his Boy Scouts uniform, apparently waiting for someone. She waved half-heartedly, worried that her father would give himself an ulcer if he went on like that. When her young cousin Arnold wheeled his bike out of an alley and he and Colin cycled off together, Connie wandered back into the kitchen. 'I've arranged to meet Tom in the Leisure Gardens in half an hour,' she informed Bert, patting his shoulder as she passed by. 'Is there anything I can get you while I'm out?'

Her father gave her a tired smile. 'Yes, you can fetch me my *Sunday Express*, if it's not too much trouble. I want to see what, if anything, Mr Churchill has to say about the sinking of the *Ark Royal*.'

Connie had read some recent newspaper reports. 'They're trying to point the finger at poor old Captain Maund, as if it had nothing to do with the dratted U-boat commander that fired the torpedo in the first place.'

'Well, it's a bad job, whichever way you look at it.' There was no denying that the sinking of the aircraft carrier was a sad loss to the Royal Navy and had caused a big dent in British morale; it was almost as shocking as the sinking of HMS *Hood* earlier in the year.

Connie assured Bert that it would be no trouble to bring him the paper, then she darted upstairs to the bedroom that she shared with Lizzie. She put on her duck-egg-blue blouse and black slacks, ran a comb through her unruly hair, then slipped into her red coat and hat. A quick lick of matching scarlet lipstick topped off the vibrant effect. She ran downstairs, calling goodbye to Bert and slamming the front door as she left.

Bert sat without moving, hands clasped and resting on the table, breakfast half eaten and pushed to one side. By Jove, he was weary. Up before dawn six days a week, hard at work in the bakery by half past five, clocking off from there in the early afternoon before hurrying on to fulfil his warden duties at Gas Street. It was only when he stopped for a rest that he had time to notice the toll such a routine was taking – aching limbs, hands a bit shaky, shortness of breath whenever he climbed the stairs. There was no getting away from it: he, Bert Harrison, wasn't getting any younger.

*

Connie and Tom strolled hand in hand through Kelthorpe Leisure Gardens on one of those rare late-November mornings when the sky matched the blue of Connie's blouse and only a few wispy white clouds trailed along the horizon. Leaves were crisp underfoot.

'I gather you had a quiet night last night?' Connie stopped by the bandstand to take in her surroundings – the duck pond was smooth and shiny as glass, the colonnade that ran the length of the park cast a dark shadow over the trampled grass and empty flower beds.

'Yes, the fire watchers on Maypole Street only spotted one nuisance raider stooging around over the headland. Nothing came of it, thank goodness.'

'Long may it continue.' Of course, every sighting of an enemy plane had to be reported to the town hall control centre, where it was duly logged. 'That's the eighth quiet night in a row, by my reckoning.'

Tom led Connie up the steps of the ornate octagonal bandstand and they sat down on a bench. He slid an arm around her waist and she responded with a kiss on his cheek. 'A couple of people on Tennyson Street missed the blackout deadline,' he reported.

'Let me guess: was one of them Eric Thompson, by any chance?'

'You've got it in one.'

Connie regretted that a spell in prison hadn't cured Thompson of his ugly behaviour. He still got drunk on a regular basis and wandered the streets at night, but at least his poor wife and kids were safe in a WVS shelter where he couldn't threaten and beat them or leave them locked in the house during air raids. 'Did he give you a mouthful?' Connie asked, remembering with a shudder the vicious attack that Thompson had subjected her to in the cellar of number 7 Tennyson Street. The whole nasty affair had been connected to the looting incident that Connie had been inadvertently caught up in – an episode that she would far rather forget.

Tom shook his head. 'There was no sign of him, so I just went into the house and switched off the lights. After that I had time on my hands so I went back to Gas Street and helped Kenneth sort out the storeroom, putting everything in its right place – anti-gas suits on the top shelf, eye shields and gloves on the next one down, torches and rattles on the one below that.'

Connie kissed him again, this time on the mouth.

'What was that for?'

'I love you, Tom Rose. That's what for.' Because he was one hundred per cent solid and trustworthy. Because he'd saved her life.

'Lord knows why.' Tom had always believed that Connie was out of reach of a quiet, steady chap like him – too glamorous by half and too outgoing and anyway married. It was only after she'd been widowed that he'd learned during their night-time patrols that her marriage to John Bailey had been far from perfect. Then he'd understood that there was more to Connie than met the eye – he'd discovered how determined she was, how she never felt sorry for herself and how seriously she took her duty as a warden.

'You do know why,' she insisted, snuggling against him.

Tom held her close. It was one of those occasions

when words were unnecessary, when in spite of everything going on around them, all seemed right with the world.

The loving silence was broken by the rattle of small stones against the side of the bandstand and by raucous shouts from two Boy Scouts who popped into view. Luckily for the young lovers, Arnold and Colin's aim with their home-made pea-shooters was less than perfect.

'Woo-hooh, we know what you're up to!'

'Ooh, Connie Bailey, wait till I tell Uncle Bert!'

Hearing the ping of stones against wrought iron, the courting couple jumped up and spun around.

'Just you wait, Arnold – I'll wring your bloody neck!' Connie cried.

Her cheeky cousin stuck his thumbs in his cheeks and waggled his fingers. 'Nah, nah – can't catch me!'

'Want to bet?' Tom vaulted over the railing and grabbed the culprit by the collar before he could mount his bike and pedal off.

'Colin, stay right where you are!' Connie went after the second junior marksman in similar fashion. She sent his broad-brimmed Scout hat flying into the mud.

'Ouch! Let go! Get off me!' The two boys squirmed and wriggled as they were dragged into the bandstand.

'I'm used to Arnold making a nuisance of himself, but I'm surprised at you, Colin.' Connie viewed the ARP messenger as a responsible, twelve-year-old lad going about his dangerous evening job with an earnest expression and a determination to do his bit.

'"Be prepared."' Tom sat both boys down on the bench and made an effort to keep a straight face.

'That's your motto, isn't it? Yes, well, I'd be prepared for a damned good hiding if I were you.'

Arnold wrestled free from Tom's grasp then straightened his neckerchief. 'You're not allowed to hit us,' he warned, with skin-deep bravado.

'No, I'll leave that to your dads,' Tom replied calmly.

'You can't. My dad's away in the Navy and his dad's dead.' As Arnold jerked his thumb towards Colin, he took satisfaction from witnessing Tom and Connie's shocked expressions. 'Tell 'em, Col. Your dad copped it in Egypt, didn't he?'

'It's true.' The mood plummeted and Colin's top lip quivered. Using the end of his neckerchief to wipe his nose, he mumbled an embarrassed apology for the prank then got up to go.

'No, wait.' Connie blocked his exit. 'I didn't know about your dad. It's us who should be saying sorry. How's your mum coping?'

'All right, I suppose. Maureen's come back home to live with us,' Colin mumbled reluctantly.

'Maureen is Colin's sister,' Connie explained to Tom. She didn't know much about the Strong family, only that they'd moved away from Musgrave Street and now rented a house in the new part of town close to the bus station, and that the mother, Nancy Strong, was a smart woman keen on keeping up appearances who worked as a telephonist at the North Street exchange. 'I didn't realize your sister had been living away.'

'No, and I wish she'd stayed away,' Colin said peevishly. 'She rows with Mum all the time. I hear them shouting after I've gone to bed.' Pushing past Connie, he went to retrieve his hat. 'I'm for it now,' he predicted miserably, inspecting the patches of wet mud on the crown.

Connie turned crossly to Arnold. 'I bet it was your idea to scare the living daylights out of me and Tom.'

'Keep your hair on. We were only having a lark.' Arnold's new uniform of bottle-green jumper emblazoned with a Fourth Kelthorpe Scout Group badge, khaki neckerchief and grey shorts was too big, emphasizing his skinny legs and scrawny neck. 'You won't really tell our mams, will you?'

Connie was the first to relent. 'I'll tell you what – if you two promise to do some extra waste-paper collecting, Tom and I will consider letting you off.' Up and down the land, teams of Scouts had been recruited to salvage waste paper for the war effort, as well as digging allotments and helping to build Anderson shelters. The local groups had amassed an impressive twenty tons of paper in six months in Kelthorpe alone. 'Oh, and Arnold,' she added pointedly, 'you'll be joining your Boy Scout pals at St Joseph's next carol-singing practice, won't you?'

'That's not fair,' Arnold whined. Joining a choir wasn't included in the list of Scouting duties that he'd signed up for.

'Shut your cake-hole,' Colin told him gruffly. 'I'll make sure he does it,' he promised Connie, relieved to be let off.

'On your way,' Tom told them, his serious expression relaxing into a smile as the boys made their escape, pedalling for all they were worth towards the park gates and the Savoy cinema beyond. He took Connie's hand and they walked together towards the colonnade. 'They're not bad lads really,' he said thoughtfully. 'Come to think of it, they remind me of me and Bill when we were that age.'

'What's the matter? You seem on edge.' Fred Miller had met Pamela as planned ten minutes before they were due to arrive for Sunday dinner at her parents' house, a recently built bungalow in the grounds of Sunrise, Hugh Anderson's imposing Victorian pile. The timber yard owner's house – all fancy gables and mock turrets – overlooked the sea and was much too big for a single occupant, now that Hugh's wife Peggy had been moved into a White Sands nursing home.

Fred had dressed smartly for today's occasion in a navy blue blazer and grey flannel trousers; he'd put a neat parting in his dark brown hair that shone with sweet-smelling Brilliantine.

'I am a little nervous,' she admitted, though her heart lifted as it always did at the sight of Fred, even after seven months of walking out together. A tingle of excitement ran through her as he took her hand and slipped it through the crook of his elbow.

'Why? What's happened?' Deciding that a quick stroll along the prom and some deep breaths of salty sea air might settle her nerves, Fred walked her in the direction of his own lodgings a few houses further along.

'Mum's gunning for me,' Pamela confessed. 'I showed myself up at yesterday's choir practice. I'll spare you the gory details, but she stormed out of the hall halfway through and I haven't spoken to her since.'

Fred squeezed her hand. Her downcast expression amused him – a slight crease had formed between her delicately arched eyebrows and she kept her eyes firmly fixed on the pavement. 'Leave your mother to me,' he suggested. 'I'll soon sweet-talk her out of her bad mood.'

It was true: Fred could charm the birds out of the trees. His manners were perfect and he was a good listener, not to mention his matinee-idol looks – dark hair cropped close to his head, a high forehead, straight eyebrows and a winning smile. Pamela brushed a stray lock of hair from her cheek then glanced out to sea, where two Royal Navy destroyers lay at anchor. 'But please don't try to persuade her to come back and play the piano for us.'

'I'll bear that in mind,' Fred promised. 'I don't know about you, but I'm starving. Shall we go and – er – face the music?'

Pamela smiled and there was a fresh bounce in her step as they turned back. As they entered the grounds of Sunrise, and Fred took in the clipped laurel hedges and well-behaved shrubberies, Pamela's Uncle Hugh emerged from a side door of the grand house. He greeted the couple and joined them in the short walk across the lawn to the bungalow.

'Your mother invited me to lunch,' he explained to Pamela, straightening his crimson bow tie then smoothing down his fawn waistcoat. 'She says she doesn't like to think of me rattling around in the old place all by myself. I hope you don't mind my joining you, Fred.'

'Not at all, sir.' Polite as ever, Fred adjusted his expectations. The presence of his boss – he was a junior clerk in the office at Anderson's timber yard – meant that he would have to mind his p's and q's even more than usual.

'We can drop the formalities. This is a purely social event, don't you know?' Hugh intended to put Fred at his ease, but he lacked the knack of casual conversation with his inferiors – any attempt came out as stiff and condescending. He cleared his throat, then tugged once more at the bottom of his waistcoat.

Pamela's nerves returned with a vengeance. In the few months since she'd got to know her uncle, she'd learned that there was a gloomy side to him and he was often awkward in company. In many ways he seemed unsuited to the rough and tumble of running the timber business that he'd inherited from his father. This meant that he relied a good deal on his foreman, Keith Nelson, as well as Pamela's steady, dependable father, Harold, who worked in the office.

As they approached the door of the bungalow, she opted for a bland remark: 'It's a lovely day, isn't it?'

'Very fine for the time of year,' Hugh agreed, stepping aside. 'Ladies first.'

Edith was hovering in the bungalow's small hallway, ready to greet them. She stared straight through Pamela and spoke instead to Fred – 'So nice to see you, Fred dear. How are you? Let me take your hat' – before leading him into the dining room.

Harold offered Pamela a warmer greeting: 'Come in . . . You look lovely . . . Is that a new dress? Take no notice of your mother,' he added in a whisper as he gave his daughter a hug.

Soon everyone was seated at a table set out with a Crown Derby dinner service, crystal glasses and silver cutlery from an earlier era.

'All courtesy of Hugh here,' Harold explained to Fred in a straightforward way. 'You recall that we lost all of our possessions in spring this year, during the air raid on Musgrave Street.'

'That was very generous of you, sir,' Fred acknowledged to his employer.

'Not at all – it could happen to any one of us, more's the pity.' Hugh unfurled his napkin while Edith, still pointedly ignoring Pamela, asked Harold to carve the chicken.

'I gather we won't be able to get hold of a turkey this Christmas – not for all the tea in China.' Mild-mannered Harold wielded the carving knife while Pamela offered to dish out the roast potatoes. Edith received hers with a stiff nod.

Fred began his charm offensive. 'I'm sure Mrs Carr will work her magic and produce something delicious nevertheless.'

Pamela smiled to herself. 'Nevertheless' was a good word to use on her mother – Edith would like its educated cadence. And it was typical of Fred, who had learned English as his second language after a childhood spent in Berlin, before his family had been forced to flee the Nazis. This accounted for the precise, grammatically correct flow of his sentences and set him apart from the crowd in a bustling, workaday fishing port like Kelthorpe.

'You'll come here to share Christmas dinner with us, I hope?' Distracted from her latest niggle over Pamela's conduct in the church hall, Edith graciously extended the invitation to Fred.

Harold served Pamela a slice of chicken accompanied by a knowing wink.

'Thank you, I will. And how have you been keeping, Mrs Carr? It seems a long time since we spoke.'

'I'm very well, thank you, Fred. Of course, I try not to pay too much attention to the wireless – I find the news too upsetting, in spite of Mr Churchill's attempts to keep us cheerful.'

'Quite right.' Fred soothed and flattered Edith until she practically purred. 'There's nothing any of us can do about world events other than to keep our heads down and follow the rules.'

'And you, Fred? I hope my brother recognizes your sterling efforts to modernize the office?'

'No talk of work here, if you please.' Hugh's curt interruption sent Fred off on a different tack.

'Perhaps you'll agree to play for us later, Mrs Carr – maybe Schubert or a little Bach.' He nodded towards the new grand piano visible in the drawing room.

Edith's smile conveyed a mixture of modesty and complacency. 'Oh, I'm sure the others would prefer a round of whist.'

'Not at all,' Hugh countered. Listening to his sister run through the classical repertoire on the instrument that he'd purchased for her required less effort than a game of cards.

Harold nudged Pamela. 'There's your cue,' he whispered.

'Yes, please play!' she declared. Fred's skill in buttering up her mother gave her the opportunity she needed to repair the previous day's damage. 'It would round off the afternoon beautifully.'

'Very well, Fred. Your wish is my command.' Edith glowed with pleasure. 'Pamela dear, pass me the gravy. And by the way, a little bird tells me that you've volunteered to step in and play the piano for the carol singers in my place.'

'That's true.' Pamela noted the 'dear' and smiled – Fred's mission was complete.

'Well, I wish you luck,' her mother said archly. 'I mention no names, but there are some in that line-up without a musical bone in their bodies.'

'Thank you,' Pamela told Fred as he walked her home. 'You dealt with Mummy beautifully, as per usual.'

The visit had been a success, with Edith at the piano, basking in compliments and being pleasant to everyone, Pamela included.

'Your hair looks very nice today, dear,' she'd said as they'd made tea to round off the afternoon. 'I do like to see you in a pretty dress with your hair done nicely rather than that unflattering warden's uniform. Why must the ARP put you in those nasty bluette overalls and tin hats?'

'We wear battledress these days, not overalls.' Pamela had laughed good-naturedly. 'Anyway, we'd be no good manning stirrup pumps or manhandling Redhill containers in skirts and stockings,' she'd pointed out, before glancing at her watch and informing her mother that she and Fred must soon be on their way. 'Fred is due to begin a stint at the report and control centre at five and I have to be at my sector post soon after.'

So the exit from what had promised to be an ordeal had been smooth, and now Fred and Pamela walked briskly towards her lodgings on King Edward Street. The good weather had held, though the sun was sinking behind the headland and a chilly breeze blew in off the sea.

'Your mother's bark is worse than her bite.' Fred

was happy to have helped ease the tension. 'That's what you say, isn't it?'

'We do. What is it in German?'

'*Ihre Rinde ist schlimmer als ihr Biss.* For all her faults, your mother is a very genuine person; she stands up for what she believes.' Fred never forgot that it was Edith who had helped him in his hour of need, when his German background had been uncovered by vigilantes and he'd been on the verge of being hounded out of Kelthorpe as a fifth columnist, an enemy alien. Throughout that difficult time, when accusations and threats had made him feel like a stag at bay, Edith had been unswervingly calm and supportive. 'And she's a cultured lady.'

'I'm grateful that you two get along so well.' They'd reached the harbour and negotiated the trawlermen's paraphernalia stacked on the quayside – coils of rope, lobster pots and fishing nets hung up to dry. The bottom of Pamela's street was in sight, rising steeply from the harbourside. 'You don't need to come any further,' she told him.

'No, but I prefer to see you to your door.'

'But I don't want to make you late.'

'Then we must kiss and say goodbye.' Fred made a sad face, then drew her close.

She glanced around before kissing him lightly on the lips.

'Is that it?' Those lips, that serious, innocent face! Even after all these months of walking out together, Fred was careful not to overstep the mark.

Pamela kissed him again. His mouth was warm and soft, his eyes were smiling. 'There, that's your lot,' she said with mock severity.

Then she was gone – hurrying away, with her coat caught by the breeze, taking her key from her pocket and turning it in the lock, disappearing from view.

'Jack of all trades – that's us ARP wardens.' Connie's orders for the evening were to check that all the telephone boxes on her patch were in working order before calling at individual houses to test gas masks, ensuring that they were airtight before updating the respirator census. Meanwhile Pamela's job would be to fill in the gaps in the Household Register – confirming how many people were resident in each dwelling, where each one slept, where they sheltered in the event of an air raid, and so on. It was a task that no warden liked to take on, smacking as it did of intrusion.

'I expect I'll be called a nosy parker and sent packing with a flea in my ear.' Pamela took items from the shelves in the tiny storeroom – first a torch, then a fire axe and finally a nozzle spanner that fitted into the loops on her sturdy canvas belt.

'Remind them that it's for their own good.' Connie slid her feet into a pair of size-six gumboots.

'The trouble is, we haven't had a raid for over a week now and people's memories are short – they're starting to forget what it's like.' The first helmet Pamela tried on was on the large side so she exchanged it for one that fitted better. She fastened the strap tightly under her chin.

'All set?' Connie asked.

Fully equipped and ready for action, the two wardens emerged from the storeroom to report to Kenneth. He was on the telephone to a fellow head warden so he simply nodded Connie and Pamela on their way.

They walked out under their cheery 'Home Sweet Home' banner, to be greeted by the toot of a horn from Lizzie in her shiny new ambulance.

Lizzie wound down her window and invited close inspection. 'Hello, you two. What do you think of this?'

Pamela made a full circuit of the shiny Bedford van, appreciating its hooded headlights, large Civil Defence logos and the word 'Ambulance' printed across front and rear.

Connie opened the back doors and gave her verdict on the roomy interior: 'Jolly nice.' There was ample space for six sitting-case casualties and a first-aid cupboard, as well as stretchers and harnesses for the more severely injured.

'I'm on my way to Maypole Street,' Lizzie informed them. 'Maisie Lawrence at number fifteen has gone into labour four weeks early. She needs to go to hospital.'

'Off you go, then, on your mission of mercy.' Connie slammed the doors shut, then waved Lizzie on her way.

But before she drove off, Lizzie had something else to impart to Connie. 'I left Bill at the King Edward Street depot with our favourite Boy Scout,' she reported with a wry smile.

'Do you mean Arnold?'

'Yes. Bill's training him and Colin in the basics of first aid. Apparently, Colin's had enough of being out on his pushbike as a messenger, dodging incendiary bombs and parachute mines. He's persuaded Arnold to train with him as a stretcher bearer instead.'

'But Arnold only just joined the Scouts.' Doubtful that their rascally cousin had what it took to carry out such a responsible job, Connie had visions of stretchers being dropped left, right and centre and of splints and bandages being randomly misapplied.

'Bill will soon knock the pair of them into shape,' Lizzie assured her as she pulled away from the kerb.

From inside the post, Kenneth barked at Pamela and Connie to get a move on. Small and neat, with a trimmed moustache and a clipped manner, he was not a man to be argued with, so they set off on their routine tasks.

They were ten minutes into their jobs when, without warning, the intermittent blare of sirens split the silence of the night. On-off, on-off; yellow alert meant that they had roughly ten minutes before yellow changed to red and imminent attack. Giant searchlights on the beach were switched on, their beams raking across the dark sky, lighting up the metal cranes that lined the docks to either side of the estuary and the cargo ships at anchor there. Anti-aircraft guns on the beach were manned by the 39th Brigade and ready for action.

Connie's stomach lurched at the dreaded wail, then she clicked into action. Out came the wooden rattle from her belt sling. She swung it vigorously to rouse any resident who might be sleeping through the siren. 'Hurry up, slowcoaches!' she cried to worried families emerging from their houses, all craning their necks and casting fearful glances at the dark, starless sky. 'No time to lose!'

On-off, on-off; sirens warbled and searchlights sought out enemy aircraft. 'Please, no parachute mines – not tonight,' Connie prayed. She could deal with incendiaries, which could be contained by quickly throwing a bucket of sand over them before they had time to explode, but she dreaded the sinister larger mines that floated gently to earth then exploded instantaneously, the blast of which was like the lash of a whip, ripping out roofs, windows and doors. 'Get a move on!' With fear tying her stomach in knots, she herded crying children and terrified mothers towards the communal shelter on College Road.

On-off, on-off. For a split second, panic threatened to overwhelm Pamela. She stood rooted to the spot on the corner of Valley Road, in the pitch-black shadow of the giant metal cylinder that gave Gas Street its name. Yellow alert. Perhaps it was a false alarm, or a tip-and-run raid involving only one or two planes? She hoped against hope that it wouldn't be a full-scale attack – the repetitive thud of dozens of high-explosive bombs dropping from the sky, the blinding flashes, the ear-splitting blasts that lifted you off your feet, the smell of cordite sharp in your nostrils, acrid smoke billowing from stricken buildings that were there one second and gone the next. And afterwards, the scrabble of rescue services through heaps of shattered concrete and bricks.

As the deserted street filled with fleeing residents, Pamela's training kicked in. Yellow alert meant that those who had been allocated space in a communal shelter had time to grab essentials such as blankets, coats, hats and scarves. They emerged from their houses equipped for the night and followed Pamela's instructions – hurry along, no torches, follow the white painted lines. *Keep calm, be steady,* she told herself, making a mental note that no one seemed to be in at number 18, the house belonging to the Russell family. She knew for a fact that the Russells had no Anderson shelter at the back of the house, so she would have to come back to check their whereabouts as soon as she'd ushered everyone else to safety.

A single, unbroken siren signalled red alert. *Imminent attack*. Lizzie had dropped off Maisie Lawrence at the Queen Alexandra hospital when the warning changed and she heard the drone of approaching aircraft. Could she make it back to the ambulance depot or should she sit it out in the grounds of the hospital? From her vantage point on the hill, she made out two enemy aircraft in the vanguard of the attack, caught in the glare of searchlight beams. There was a rattle of ack-ack guns from the ground – the aim from the cement pillboxes ranged along the beach was deadly accurate tonight and the two lean Dornier fighter planes went up in flames, shattering into hundreds of pieces that spiralled down into the sea. But they were soon replaced by three more, and after that a group of five heavy bombers, heading inexorably for the coast, flying in low and fast, machine guns rattling and spitting red-hot bullets, the deep-throated churn of their engines striking terror into Lizzie's heart.

*Get back to base.* She decided she was doing no good out here on a limb and with no telephone contact with her depot; it was a case of driving hell for leather and hoping for the best.

So she raced down the hill. Incendiaries rained down, showering sparks as they fell, then landing with a thud, lying inert for a few seconds before bursting into white-hot flames. Some would be tackled with buckets of sand or with Redhill containers, whereby you scooped the deadly cylinders into a long-handled dustpan before burying the container in a bucket of sand. Others would be dealt with by stirrup pumps belonging to firefighters identifiable by their white helmets, gas-mask cases slung across their chests as they pumped water out of red fire buckets. Extinguish the small fires first so that the possible second wave of Luftwaffe bombers was left with no markers – that was the drill. It had worked in the larger cities earlier in the year when the Blitz had been at its height.

'Where's the bloody fire guard when you need them?' Lizzie spoke through gritted teeth as she squealed to a halt close to three incendiaries lying dormant in the main town square. There was as yet no sign of any of the emergency services – no evidence of oilskin-clad fire teams standing by with trailer pumps, hoses at the ready.

Lizzie had seconds in which to act. She knew from the shape and size of the deadly metal cylinders that these were Magnesium Electrons: one kilogram's worth of explosive material contained within shiny aluminium-and-steel shells. She also knew that the bombs must strike the ground head-on to implode immediately – otherwise they would lie dormant until a sudden movement jarred them into action. These three must have landed on their sides. Jumping from the van, Lizzie heard the sinister hiss of the unexploded devices. She spotted a row of sand buckets stationed at the top of the town hall steps, and as she sprinted towards them a familiar figure – tall, slim and dressed in civvies – emerged from the building.

'Fred, give me a hand!' she yelled.

Following orders at the sound of the red alert, Fred had left his desk in the report and control centre and rushed outside to estimate the scale of the attack. Now, in his cool-headed way, he paused to assess the situation.

'Incendiaries!' Lizzie pointed to where the three sinister cylinders lay, threatening to explode at any moment.

Before they could act, there was a deafening boom and the dark sky lit up. A high explosive had hit its target: the rail depot close to Anderson's yard. Lizzie and Fred looked up in horror at the flare of mighty orange flame on St Stephen's dock followed by a pall of thick black smoke. Recovering from their shock and focusing on the incendiaries, they took hold of two fire buckets each and ran down the steps.

'Keep a safe distance,' Lizzie warned, her face illuminated by the lurid orange glare. 'Watch out for the one to your right!'

The incendiaries continued to hiss. Lizzie tipped a bucket of sand over the nearest but Fred's eyes had been slow to adjust and he accidentally disturbed the one that Lizzie had warned him about. He jerked back as it flared into life, causing him to stagger back and spill sand on the town hall steps. Within a split second Lizzie had acted to deaden the device.

Fred went down on his knees and frantically scooped sand back into his bucket.

'Over there – one more!' Lizzie pointed to the remaining incendiary.

He sprinted across, did what was necessary and waited for the hissing to stop. *Die Stille – Gott sei Dank!* Silence – thank God!

'Well done.' Lizzie sighed. Disaster had been averted, for now at least. 'Thanks for your help.'

'How many planes?' Fred's heart raced as he scanned the moonless sky. It had been a close call, but Lizzie had kept her head and they'd come through unscathed.

'At least eight – three fighters and five bombers – with more on the way, by the sound of it,' she reported.

A breathless Fred nodded, then carried the information back to his superiors inside the town hall.

Outside the imposing building, Lizzie inhaled deeply. A cloud of black smoke crept into the square from the nearby explosion, its tentacles curling around the base of Queen Victoria's toppled statue – victim of an earlier attack. *Will it ever end?* she wondered.

Fires blazed around the harbour and along the docks, on the headland and as far as the eye could see along the coast towards Raby. Did the pilots of the Dorniers and Heinkels spare a thought for the people of Kelthorpe as they released the deadly bombs from their cradles? Probably not, for how could a man follow the heartless orders of his superiors if he allowed the reality of what he was about to do to enter his brain? War was war in all its cruelty. Destruction and loss stretched across Europe, and over the Pacific and Atlantic oceans as far as Japan and America. No one was spared.

# CHAPTER THREE

*Keep calm, be steady*. Like a child memorizing items from a shopping list, Pamela repeated two crucial phrases to herself as she returned to Valley Road. With the exception of the residents at number 18, everyone was accounted for and safe in the shelter on College Road. Now she must track down the missing Russell family. As she made her way past two fire watchers stationed on the flat roof of Benson's music shop, one of the men gave a shrill blast on his whistle.

'Watch out – incendiaries ahead!' he yelled down at her.

Pamela hurried on, taking note of his warning and swerving to avoid two small bombs that had recently landed in a shower of sparks. The shiny, cylindrical devices lay close together in the middle of the road, hissing then suddenly flaring into life. A dustbin standing outside the nearby butcher's shop offered a solution – she seized the lid and covered the two small fires, extinguishing them in an instant.

'Good girl – quick thinking!' the fire watcher cried as Pamela rushed on.

A hundred yards ahead, the outline of the gasworks was silhouetted against an orange sky. Infernos raged.

Teams of firefighters tore along the street in commandeered vans and cars towing trailer pumps. With her heart in her mouth, Pamela watched the trailers sway and rock as they careered around a corner and disappeared from sight. Then a lad on a bike appeared, pedalling for all he was worth. He flew by, shouting to her above the roar of flames and incoming enemy aircraft that the water main had burst on Valley Road and there was not a drop of water to be had on Gladstone Square. The Auxiliary Fire Service urgently needed tenders to fight the blaze at the police station there – his job was to let the patrol officer know.

*Keep calm, be steady. Concentrate on finding the Russell family – Ben and Molly, plus an eight-year-old daughter.* Pamela came to the corner where Gas Street joined Valley Road. *So far so good.* She reached number 18, ran up the short path and tried to open the front door. No joy. She hammered loudly and waited. Blinds were down in all the windows. No one came to the door. What next?

'You're wasting your time there.' A middle-aged woman dressed in the tunic and peaked cap of the Auxiliary Police Corps had just rounded the corner. She wore white gauntlets and carried a cycle lamp with red glass, indicating that she had been on point duty on Gas Street, where it had been her job to direct the emergency services.

'Why's that?' Pamela was at her wits' end.

'I'm Molly Russell's sister, that's why,' the no-nonsense policewoman informed her. 'I know for a fact that she and Ben took their Eileen trekking up to Raynard's Folly tonight.'

'Without letting us know!' *Thoughtless so-and-sos!* Learning that the family had opted to sleep rough on the moor and so avoid the worst of any possible bombing, she was infuriated.

'That's Molly for you – she's got cotton wool for brains. And that husband of hers is no better – feckless as they come.'

'I'll have to report them,' Pamela told her through gritted teeth. Really and truly, it was beyond belief. 'I risked my neck coming back here, and all for nothing.'

A shower of sparks followed by a white flame from yet another incendiary reinforced her point. The police officer dealt with it by seizing the nearest sand bucket without fuss and dumping its contents on the device. 'I'll give Molly a piece of my mind next time I see her,' she promised grimly.

Feeling suddenly weary and deflated, Pamela beat a hasty retreat. She was forced to make a short detour to avoid a rescue party: a small Class B team with a two-wheeled handcart that had set about sealing off a damaged gas main at the end of College Road. The men, wearing gas masks and anti-spark goggles, had a long night ahead of them, digging holes with pick-axes and shovels to deal with damage to water and electricity supplies, as well as gas. Pamela didn't envy them – at least when she made it back to the communal shelter she would be able to take refuge there until the raid was over.

Slipping down a side alley, then following a narrow cinder track, she re-emerged on to the main street. She found herself ten yards from the entrance to the underground shelter, where Connie was stationed at ground level, clipboard in hand. When she saw Pamela she urged her to hurry.

'Any joy at number eighteen?' Connie asked as they descended the stone steps together. The wait for Pamela's safe return had been nerve-racking, to say the least.

Pamela shook her head. 'Wild goose chase.'

Down below ground, Connie and Pamela were greeted by the sight of families huddled together on benches and bunk beds in what had been until recently a public toilet. A smell of disinfectant lingered in the green-tiled cubicles and along the row of white urinals, which caused Pamela to hold her breath and turn away in embarrassment and distaste every time she saw them.

But beggars couldn't be choosers – without a cellar or an Anderson shelter of their own, the communal refuge was the safest bet for many local residents.

'What's happening up there – has Jerry done his worst?' A worried man in a flat cap and belted raincoat asked Pamela for an update.

A clamour of questions followed. Had any of the houses on Gas Street taken a direct hit? What about Maypole Street? Had Firebomb Fritz had another go at Anderson's?

Connie stepped in to quell the racket. 'We'll know more in the morning. For now, all we can do is sit tight.'

Minutes passed and resignation set in. A few women took out their knitting; some of the men began games of dominoes. Children, fully dressed and wearing woollen hats and mittens, fell asleep on the bunks.

*Sit tight.* Pamela repeated Connie's phrase. *Try not to let fear take over. Don't think of loved ones facing unknown danger. Put on a brave front and wait for the all-clear.*

Lizzie was within sight of the ambulance depot on King Edward Street when she hit a crater in the road. The front of her vehicle dipped suddenly and the sickening sound of the chassis scraping the ground told her immediately that the situation was serious. She swore as she was thrown forward against the dashboard and the ambulance came to a grinding halt, back wheels spinning in mid-air. 'Bloody hell, whatever next?'

Cutting off the engine, then scrambling down from the driver's seat to assess the damage, she feared the worst. *A brand-new Bedford, stuck in the middle of the road, tilting at an angle of forty-five degrees, with Jerry still raining down damned incendiaries like there's no tomorrow!*

Lizzie ducked at the sound and sight of a Heinkel defying ack-ack fire from the beach and flying low overhead, machine guns spitting fiery bullets. The rat-a-tat-tat of them ricocheting off nearby buildings forced her back into the ambulance, where she cowered beneath the steering column until the danger was past. She climbed out again in time to see the godsend of a flat-bed lorry emerging from the first-aid depot at the bottom of the hill and heading towards her stranded vehicle.

Bill drove like the devil towards Lizzie. As he squealed to a halt, positioning the lorry close to the rear of the stricken ambulance, he flung open the passenger door. 'Jump in!' he yelled at her.

Meanwhile, Walter Adams, a first-aider in Bill's team, leaped out of the back of the truck carrying a coil of thick rope.

'We'll tow you out,' Bill assured Lizzie.

'How did you know . . . ?' Lizzie could scarcely speak. *Bloody Heinkel!* Then, *Damn and blast, I've only gone and wrecked a brand-new vehicle!*

'You were gone for ages. I was wondering where on earth you'd got to.' There was no time for Bill to confess how he'd been on the point of saying, to hell with it, raid or no raid, he would search the streets of Kelthorpe until he found his beloved. 'Stay where you are,' he ordered.

Too shocked to argue, Lizzie watched the two men rapidly tie the rope to their tow bar and then to the back bumper of the Bedford. Then Bill returned to his cab and put the lorry into first gear. They edged forward and she felt the rope tauten and take the strain. Lizzie twisted round in her seat in time to see the ambulance slowly emerge, back end first, from the deep hole.

'A bit more!' Walter waved Bill on. 'Another couple of feet. Right you are!'

Bill pulled on the handbrake, then shouted another instruction: 'Take a quick look, Walt – what's the damage?'

The first-aider crouched to inspect the front of the ambulance. 'Not too bad. She'll need a new bumper and the left front wing will have to be straightened out, but the axle seems fine. I reckon she'll make it back to the depot under her own steam.'

'Champion. Get behind the wheel, will you? We'll see you back there.'

Gathering her wits, Lizzie drew breath. 'No – I'll drive it.'

'Are you sure?' Bill saw that she was trembling and her eyes were wide and dark in her pale face.

'Certain. This is my fault – I should have looked where I was going.'

'Come off it. You can't be expected to see in the dark, even with your hooded headlights switched on. It's no one's fault except Jerry's.'

'Even so.' Lizzie was determined. She was half out of the cab when Bill drew her back inside and whispered urgently, 'Swear you won't ever do that to me again.'

She felt his hand tight around her wrist. 'Do what?'

'Put yourself in harm's way.' Bill knew as he spoke that it was a futile thing to say, since every person in Kelthorpe – man, woman and child – diced with death on a daily basis. 'I couldn't stand losing you,' he added softly.

'You won't,' she promised, as the last of the Luftwaffe planes made a triumphant circuit of the town before heading out across the North Sea. 'I'm here, aren't I? You're stuck with me, Bill Evans; for better or worse.'

'Fritz knows what he's doing, all right.' Bert stood at the bakery shop window, gazing across the street at what was left of the *Kelthorpe Gazette* building. The entire front had been blown off during the previous night's raid, revealing desks, chairs, typewriters, telephones and hat stands half buried in bricks and plaster. A staircase had been ripped from the wall and the roof and upper storey threatened to collapse on rescue teams as they sifted through the rubble below.

'What do you mean?' Connie asked from behind the counter. It was five minutes to opening time and a short queue had already formed outside.

'He flies in low so his blasted bombs come in horizontally instead of from up above. They do more damage if they hit the lower floors. See?' Bert explained as Connie joined him.

True enough, the explosion had left the *Gazette* building's roof reasonably undamaged but unsupported. Half a dozen men dressed in overalls, their black helmets marked with an 'R', picked feverishly at piles of bricks. Bert and Connie watched as a policeman, helmet awry and with his sleeves rolled up to his elbows, raised a warning hand for the rescue team to stop work. Then he took off his helmet and lay on top of one of the heaps with his ear to the ground.

'It'll be a miracle if anyone has survived that lot.' A pessimistic Bert didn't wish to see more. He shook his head and shuffled back into the bakery, where Lizzie was taking sweet-smelling loaves from the ovens and transferring them to wire trays.

But Connie lingered to watch the rescue effort. She saw the policeman jump to his feet and order two of the men to carry on lifting bricks – carefully, one at a time. There was an air of tense excitement as every so often the officer told them to stop while he knelt to listen again.

'You in there, open up!' An impatient customer made Connie jump by rapping on the window. 'It's gone eight o'clock.'

Not twenty yards away someone's life hung by a thread, but for the harassed housewives of Kelthorpe it was business as usual. Connie unbolted the door, then took her place behind the counter. A small Hovis and two plain teacakes . . . a large white loaf, three sausage rolls, a custard tart . . . Customers placed their orders and paid their money while the rescue team raised a survivor from the rubble and stretcher bearers covered him in a grey blanket before carrying him to an ambulance. Connie caught sight of the injured man's face, thickly coated with plaster dust. There was a dark crimson gash down the right side, from temple to chin. He tried to raise his head. The policeman lit a cigarette and slid it between the rescued man's lips before the ambulance door was closed. God willing, a life had been saved.

Pamela wasn't sure why her Uncle Hugh had asked her to call in at his office. He'd made the request soon after their Sunday lunch, as Fred had helped Edith to sort through her musical scores. 'At your convenience,' Hugh had murmured, before being shushed by Edith, who was ready to begin.

Eager to know more, Pamela had decided to waste no time. First thing on Monday morning, as fires smouldered on the headland and teams of volunteers worked with block and tackle, pickaxe, jack and crane to restore mains services, she put on her best blue coat and hat then made her way to Anderson's timber yard. Why this summons? she wondered. Uncle Hugh had made it sound official, but then his voice always held that formal edge. Could it be connected with his ongoing efforts to make up for Old Man Anderson's cruelty towards her mother? Edith's father's opposition to her marriage thirty years earlier had been the spiteful act of a thoroughgoing snob and bully – Harold Carr's poor background and lack of prospects had put him beyond the pale in Anderson senior's books. Until the day he drew his last breath, he'd despised his daughter for marrying beneath her.

'Can I help you?' The bright and breezy sound of Betty Holroyd's voice interrupted Pamela's train of thought. Hugh's secretary – all blonde hair, lipstick smile and perfumed confidence – stood outside the ladies' cloakroom near the entrance to Hugh's office building. She greeted Pamela with a puzzled expression, as if trying to place her.

Pamela felt a flicker of resentment. Was she really as unmemorable as Betty made out? 'Yes, please. I've come to see my uncle – Mr Anderson.'

'Ah, of course – you're Harold's daughter.' Having put Pamela firmly in her place, Betty pretended to consult the large diary that she carried under her arm. 'Is Mr Anderson expecting you?'

At that moment a door on a landing at the top of the stairs opened and Fred emerged with a stack of buff-coloured envelopes. When he saw Pamela he ran downstairs and carelessly offloaded the envelopes on to Betty before seizing Pamela's hand and leading her outside, where he gave her a hug and beamed at her. 'To what do we owe the pleasure?'

Pamela glanced up at the first-floor windows. 'Uncle Hugh wants to see me.'

'What about?' Better not risk a kiss in case the boss was watching. Fred, too, glanced up at the building.

'I have no idea.' Activity in the yard cut across their conversation. A man in overalls shouted instructions to a crane driver and a big mechanical saw inside the cavernous cutting shed started up with a loud whine and a whir. The distinctive scent of resinous wood drifted towards them.

Fred gave Pamela's hand a playful squeeze. 'I mean what I say – it's a pleasure, a delight, a joy—'

'Stop!' she pleaded with a modest laugh.

'Not to mention a relief. Last night's raid was worse than anyone in the control room had envisaged. The plotting clerks had a heck of a job keeping up with developments. And you were out in the thick of it.'

'Not to worry – I came through without a scratch.' Conscious that Betty's gaze was trained on them, Pamela pulled her hand free. 'I admit I was a bit shaken up. Not like Connie and Lizzie – those two girls have nerves of steel.'

'Don't you believe it.' Fred shook his head. 'When that yellow alert blares out every one of us feels sick to the stomach, no matter how often we go through it. Some hide it better than others, that's all.'

'I suppose you're right.' Pamela appreciated Fred's reassurance. On learning that he was free that evening, she made an arrangement for them to meet outside his lodgings before remembering a prior commitment. 'Drat. I promised Mr Penrose that I'd fill in for Dorothy Morris at the Savoy tonight.'

He was disappointed. 'Can't you get out of it?'

'No – you know what he's like.' The cinema manager was a nit-picking and short-tempered man, a renowned Little Hitler who would sack an employee at the drop of a hat, so Pamela was always careful to keep on the right side of her irascible boss.

'Tomorrow night, then?'

'Yes – tomorrow.' Pamela backed away. 'I'd better go before Betty reports you for dawdling.'

'Pah!' Fred waved his hand dismissively, then rushed to hold the door open for her. As she slid by he stole a cheeky kiss, then strode towards a table to pick up the day's post. Betty still hovered, and he spoke to her coolly and without looking her in the eye. 'I was wondering, have you typed out the figures for last week's stock intake?'

'Keith hasn't handed them over yet,' Betty replied in a sexy, sugar-coated voice. *Give me half an hour in private with Fred Miller and I'll have him eating out of my hand*, she thought. She was willing to bet that if you dug beneath that clipped, well-mannered exterior, Fred would be as hot-blooded and malleable as the next man.

'Is that so?' As yard foreman, Keith Nelson knew perfectly well that the paperwork had to be on Mr Anderson's desk first thing Monday morning. Frowning, Fred decided to seek him out.

Meanwhile, Pamela went upstairs and knocked on her uncle's door – faintly at first, then a little louder.

'Yes?'

Hugh's curt response made her hesitate.

'Come in,' Hugh barked. He looked up to see his niece hovering uncertainly in the doorway.

'If this isn't a good time . . .' she faltered.

'Oh, it's you, Pamela. Come in and sit down.' Hugh's tone softened. Nattily dressed as always in a pinstripe, double-breasted suit, with his thick white hair brushed back and his grey moustache freshly trimmed, he set aside some paperwork. 'I'll come straight to the point. Edith has admitted to me that she doesn't approve of your being out on the streets at night. She feels it's not fitting.'

Pamela bristled and she sat forward on the edge of her seat. 'Mummy and I have never seen eye to eye about me volunteering for warden duty, but I've made it plain that I want to do my bit. I made up my mind and that's that.'

'Very commendable, I'm sure.' His niece's firm tone surprised Hugh: she was not so meek and mild, despite appearances. 'However, that's not the matter I wished to speak about.'

'No?'

'No. I understand that you're employed for three nights a week at the Savoy cinema?'

'That's true. I work in the ticket office.'

'And what would you say if I were to offer you three days a week here at the timber yard instead? No, no – before you give your answer let me explain in what capacity. It would be to work in the office as a junior secretary, helping Betty by writing letters under dictation and so on. You do type, I take it?'

'Not well,' she replied honestly. Her long-held ambition had been to train as a teacher at a college in York, but the war had forced her to postpone her plans. 'I've taught myself the basics.'

Hugh picked up a gold propelling pencil and made a note. 'Any shorthand?'

'I'm afraid not.'

'But you could soon pick it up. The wage would exceed what you earn at the cinema – I'd make sure of that. Well, what do you say?'

Pamela took her time to weigh up the pros and cons. One thing was certain: she wouldn't miss working for

Mr Penrose. And the daytime hours appealed, as did the prospect of seeing Fred and her father during tea and dinner breaks. The one drawback would be working alongside Betty Holroyd, whose disdain for Pamela oozed through her every pore.

'Well?' Hugh prompted.

'Junior secretary?' she repeated slowly. 'When would you want me to start?'

'The period before Christmas is always a busy time, so shall we say next Monday, the eighth?' Willing her to say yes so that he could report his success to his sister, Hugh tapped the point of his pencil on his desk.

Pamela made up her mind. 'Agreed.' Her heart skipped a beat as her uncle leaned forward and they shook hands. She couldn't wait to see the sour look on Mr Penrose's face when she handed in her notice or to watch Fred's glad expression as she gave him the news.

'Arnold Kershaw, take your hands out of your pockets and stand up straight.' Doug picked on the choir's most recent and, next to Connie, their most reluctant recruit. It was the third day of Advent and their second rehearsal, with Pamela at the piano and Connie skulking on the back row between Lizzie and Tom.

Arnold dug a savage elbow into Colin's ribs. 'It's your fault I have to be here,' he muttered as the choirmaster turned his attention elsewhere.

''Tisn't.'

''Tis.' Jab-jab went the sharp elbow.

''Tisn't – ouch!'

Connie leaned forward and ordered the boys to

stop mucking about. 'Not that I blame them,' she told Lizzie out of the side of her mouth. 'This is pure torture for some of us.'

'Not complaining, are we?' Tom whispered with a grin.

'No!' she fibbed, faking a cheery smile.

'Good King Wenceslas' was not going well. The choir staggered on as far as the poor man gathering winter fuel before Doug called an exasperated halt.

'"Brightly shone the moon that night,"' he repeated with slow emphasis on each syllable. '"Though the frost was cru-el, when a poor man came in sight, gathering winter fu-oo-el."'

They tried again.

'Better!' Doug encouraged. 'Now, "Hither page and stand by me . . ."' Baton raised, he guided them through the second verse.

Hither and thither they sang, through the dark night, through snow and wind, carrying flesh and wine to the peasant who lived a good league off by St Agnes' fountain.

'Thank the Lord!' Connie murmured as the choir stumbled to the end of the carol and she leaned against Tom with relief.

Doug lay down his baton. He made a point of praising the ladies from the WI and again picked out Tom as the example that everyone should follow. Then he turned his attention to Connie, who squirmed under his inquisitorial gaze. 'More effort is required in some corners,' he warned frostily.

Tom nudged her with his elbow. 'Caught red-handed,' he muttered under his breath, while Doug went on to scan his row of Boy Scout volunteers.

'Next time we must choose the soloist who will sing the first verse of "Once in Royal David's City", but for now we'll call it a day.'

The group broke up and left the church hall in dribs and drabs. Tom and Connie went on ahead to the Anchor, while Lizzie waited for Pamela to pack away her music. They took a shortcut across the dark, gloomy churchyard, out on to College Road, and it was here that they found Colin perched on a wall next to Barbieri's fish and chip shop making inroads into a bag of scraps.

'Hello, Colin. Doesn't your mother feed you?' Lizzie teased.

Scowling, the boy hung his head and looked away.

'Are you all right?' It struck Pamela that he had looked down in the mouth all evening.

As if in a rush, he screwed the greasy remains of his supper into a ball, threw it into a waste bin, then picked up his bike from the grass verge. 'Sorry, I've got to go,' he muttered.

'Hmm.' Lizzie was thoughtful as Colin cycled off full tilt. 'I hope he and Arnold haven't fallen out. Arnold can be a bit much at times.'

'Colin is probably just worn out. At school all day and then helping to dig Anderson shelters and what have you. And now he and Arnold are training as stretcher bearers, too – it's a lot to ask of a twelve-year-old.'

'I suppose so.' Lizzie followed Colin's progress along the unlit street, past heaps of rubble, demolished lamp posts and yawning craters, until he disappeared into the gloom. All was silent.

'What's this I hear about a new job at Anderson's?'

As the girls set off for the pub, Lizzie chose a more cheerful topic.

'Who told you that?' Pamela had wished to keep the news under her hat until after she'd received a letter of confirmation from her uncle.

'A little bird.' Lizzie tapped the side of her nose. 'Come along, Miss Pamela – I'm all ears.'

# CHAPTER FOUR

Kelthorpe's clear-up operation continued throughout the week. Demolition teams began to remove rubble from pavements, and an area on Valley Road was cordoned off to protect residents from an unexploded bomb. At the Gas Street sector post, Kenneth Browning commandeered shovels and a couple of lads from Dixon's yard and sent them out to help clear debris surrounding the *Gazette* building. A wireless set was retrieved from the wreckage, miraculously still in working order. It was dusted off and offered to Connie, who stood watching events from the doorway of the bakery shop.

'Ta very much.' Delighted, she hurried into the back room to show Lizzie and their dad.

'Marvellous! Now we'll be able to listen to the Home Service all day long – "Music While You Work", tra-la!' Lizzie gave the scratched and dented wireless a thorough dust, then perched it on a handy shelf and plugged it in before twiddling the knobs to find her favourite station. The valves whistled and warbled until she hit upon the right wavelength and jaunty big-band music filled the room. Grinning, the girls shimmied and twirled.

Bert was less enthusiastic. 'Your minds should be on your job, not Glenn Flippin' Miller,' he grumbled as he removed a batch of loaves from the oven. A blast of hot air filled the already stifling space. He tapped the bottom of the nearest loaf to check that it was properly baked. 'This lot is ready for you to take on your next round,' he informed Lizzie, using his apron to wipe beads of perspiration from his forehead. 'Get a move on, girls, it doesn't do to keep your customers waiting.'

So Lizzie loaded the van while Connie returned to the shop, humming to the tune on the wireless as her Aunty Vera came in for her daily loaf. They chatted about this and that – how Christmas would be upon them before they knew it and how Vera had left off trekking to Raynard's Folly since the weather had turned cold.

'It's no fun trudging up there every night, especially now that Doug Greenwood's Scout group has fitted out my cellar with bunk beds and an electric fire,' Vera explained as she watched Connie wrap her still-warm loaf in tissue paper. '"Be prepared" – that's what the Boy Scouts say, isn't it? It's good advice because no one knows when Fritz will pay us another visit.'

Connie accompanied her aunt to the door, then watched her plod down College Road – a somewhat shabby figure with the wiry Harrison build. Her head was forward, her shoulders hunched, and she looked worn down by life but doggedly determined to do her best for Arnold and her two little girls while her husband, Frank Kershaw, was away at sea.

'That was Aunty Vera,' Connie called through into

the bakery. 'She said to say hello.' There was no reply. Perhaps her father hadn't heard because of the music playing on the wireless. She raised her voice and repeated the message. Still no answer.

The shop bell tinkled and Connie served two more customers. Luckily, neither was as chatty as Aunty Vera, so Connie dealt quickly with them. 'Dad?' she called as she went through to the bakery.

Odd: he was nowhere to be seen. There was no back door and he certainly hadn't exited through the shop. The wireless played a version of 'Chattanooga Choo Choo' as she made a thorough search of the area where bins of flour were stored, then of the alcove containing the broom cupboard and finally the cramped space beyond the large ovens where they hung their outdoor clothes.

Bert had caught hold of his overcoat as he'd crashed to the floor. It had come off the hook and partly covered him, so that at first Connie saw only an untidy heap. But then the heap moved and there was a faint moan.

'Dad!' Shock rooted her to the spot. Her father's legs stuck out from under the coat, his trousers were hitched up to reveal thin ankles and wrinkled navy blue socks. One of his shoes had come off and had skidded across the concrete floor.

Bert stirred and groaned.

Clicking into action, Connie flew to lift the coat. Bert's thin face was white, pain etched into his narrow features. Unable to speak or to do more than lift his head, his eyes stared at her in undisguised terror.

Gently she raised him into a sitting position. 'It's all right, Dad – I'm here.' *Oh Lord, what's happened?*

*Whatever shall I do?* Panic threatened to scramble her brain as she crouched beside him in the dark, airless corner. 'Can you tell me what's wrong?' she pleaded.

A sound emerged from deep in Bert's throat – an incomprehensible, rasping groan.

She pressed an ear to his chest and heard a reedy, uneven heartbeat. *Dear God!* She must keep him warm and she must telephone for an ambulance. But she dare not leave him. At the sound of the shop bell out front she raised her voice and called loudly for help.

'What's up?' A bulky figure appeared in the narrow connecting doorway – it was Cyril Fielding, a regular customer and a lodger at number 21 Elliot Street.

*Damn!* Their idle, narrow-minded neighbour was the last person in Kelthorpe whom Connie would have appealed to for help. She cradled her father and called out nonetheless. 'Mr Fielding, we need an ambulance!'

'Has he had one too many?' Unmoved by the sight that greeted him, Fielding jumped to the wrong conclusion.

'No, he's not drunk! I think it's his heart. He needs to go to hospital. Please call 999 – quick as you can.' Connie's own heart raced as she pleaded for help.

Bert lay helpless in Connie's arms, locks of grey hair falling over his clammy forehead, his hands shaking uncontrollably. It was as if separate parts of his body were shutting down one at a time – his right foot, his leg, both of his hands, all went numb. And the pain in his arm – as bad as any he'd ever experienced – shot to his chest and formed a tight band that threatened to squeeze the life out of him.

His eyes flicked from Connie to Fielding, and he made the same groaning, desperate sound as before.

'There's a telephone next to the till. We need an ambulance.' There was a pause during which Connie despaired of getting through to Fielding. Reluctantly she lowered her father to the floor and arranged the coat over him. Every second was vital. 'I'll call for help myself,' she vowed.

'No, stay where you are – I'll do it.' At last Fielding took in the gravity of the situation. He heaved his bulk around, then crossed to the counter where he dialled the operator with clumsy fingers and told her what she needed to know – 'Send an ambulance to College Road . . . Harrison's Bakery . . . that's right, man laid flat out . . . probable heart attack . . . yes, right away.'

'If only I'd got him here sooner.' Connie couldn't forgive herself for the delay in bringing her father to hospital. She sat with Lizzie in a long corridor, outside the ward where Bert lay in a bed surrounded by doctors and nurses who fought to save his life.

Lizzie was silent, her gaze fixed on the brown lino beneath her feet. She'd finished her deliveries and returned to the bakery soon after midday, just in time to see an ambulance speeding away. Inside the shop she'd found Connie talking agitatedly to Aunty Vera on the telephone – please could she come and serve behind the counter while she, Connie, went to the Queen Alexandra . . . ? Dad . . . poorly . . . touch and go.

With only disjointed fragments of information to work on, and amid a flurry of frantic activity, it had taken Lizzie a while to make sense of events. But as soon as Vera had arrived she'd driven Connie to the hospital and now they sat side by side on tubular-steel and canvas chairs, scarcely able to breathe.

'I thought something was up, but the shop was busy at the time. And then I couldn't make Cyril Fielding understand what was happening . . .' Connie's voice trailed off. She felt completely drained and hopeless.

'Dad's been working far too hard,' Lizzie said faintly. 'That's what's brought this on.' Why was time passing so slowly? Why didn't someone tell them what was happening? How long would they have to sit here without knowing?

'You should have seen him; he was just a crumpled heap. And his face, Lizzie – it looked awful.'

'Hush.' Lizzie shuddered. Then, 'Did the ambulance men say anything?'

'Nothing. They were in too much of a hurry.' Fear had clutched at Connie's throat as they'd carried Bert out, then driven him away.

'So we don't even know if it's a heart attack?' Lizzie clasped her hands tightly together. 'It could be anything.' *Please, somebody come and tell us what's going on!*

Connie attempted to block out the memory of the terror in her father's eyes as he'd lain crumpled and helpless on the bakery floor. 'I listened to his heart,' she told Lizzie. 'It didn't sound right.'

A porter wheeled a trolley towards them and passed by without speaking. A nurse in a sister's uniform rushed out of the ward but kept her gaze averted as she hurried away.

'What else could it be?' The not-knowing was the

worst part. Lizzie stood up and took a few paces down the corridor. Stroke, epileptic seizure? Her first-aid training led her to other frightening possibilities.

'Miss Harrison?' A second nurse – younger than the first – came out into the corridor and spoke briskly to Lizzie.

'Yes, that's me.' Lizzie gestured for Connie to join them. 'This is Mrs Bailey.'

The nurse looked quickly from one to the other. 'You must be sisters. Come with me, please, both of you.'

She led them to a small, brightly lit side room where a doctor in a white coat sat behind a desk. His hair and moustache were grey and he bore a severe, military air as he gestured for Lizzie and Connie to sit down.

'How is he, Doctor?' Connie prepared herself for the worst.

Lizzie, too, steeled herself.

'We're doing everything we can to make your father comfortable,' he assured them. 'We've detected a pronounced disturbance of the heart rhythm, a myocardial infarction – in common parlance, a heart attack.'

Lizzie and Connie were mute, clinging to every word.

'An ECG will tell us in due course which of the arteries is blocked and how badly. Meanwhile, we're treating the pain with morphine.'

'But will he get better?' Connie spoke again. She was on the edge of her seat, leaning forward, desperate for an answer.

'I'm afraid it's too early to say.' After decades of dealing with relatives, not to mention serving on the

Western Front during the Great War, the doctor had trained the muscles in his face to give nothing away. 'Some patients recover well after a prolonged period of rest. Your father is otherwise fit for a man of his age – not overweight, with no underlying conditions.'

Connie: 'So what's brought it on?'

'Overwork, possibly. An attack happens when arteries have become partially blocked, leading to an inadequate supply of blood. Any undue strain on the heart can then lead to just such an attack.'

'I see. How long will our father have to stay in bed?'

'It's impossible to say. These next few days are critical. There must be absolutely no exertion during this first period of recuperation.'

'What does that mean?' Lizzie spoke for the first time.

'It means that we'll keep him here in hospital, initially for six weeks.' It was time to draw things to a close – the doctor had other urgent cases to attend to and he'd told the sisters everything he knew. 'It's best not to get too far ahead of ourselves. We'll know more tomorrow, after we've done the ECG.'

Certain words and phrases stayed with Connie and Lizzie after the nurse showed them out into the corridor. 'Morphine' was one of them and the mysterious initials, 'ECG'.

'Overwork,' Lizzie murmured.

'Six weeks.' Connie sighed. 'That means Dad will miss Christmas.'

'Can we see him?' Lizzie asked the nurse, her heart hammering at her ribs.

She took them into the ward and to Bert's bedside, warning them not to expect too much or to stay too long. 'Mr Harrison may be confused because of the medicine we've given him. And he's bound to be very tired.'

Their father lay with his eyes open and his head turned towards them. His throat was bare and scrawny, poking out of a pale green hospital gown. 'This is a fine to-do, eh, girls?'

'Ssh, Dad.' Connie placed her hand over his.

'Blow me. I thought I was a goner.' Bert had been certain of it. He'd collapsed to the floor of the bakery and experienced flashbacks to when Connie and Lizzie were young, had seen Rhoda's face, heard her voice – the lot.

'Hush.'

Lizzie stroked his pale cheek. 'The doctor says you have to rest to get your strength back.'

'Aye, I know.'

'You have to sleep as much as possible.'

Bert gave a long sigh. Lizzie and Connie's faces were blurred and their voices sounded a long way off. The pain in his chest was reduced to a dull ache and the peculiar sensation of floating and drifting off wasn't unpleasant. *What will be will be*.

'Do you hear, Dad – you're to do as you're told.' Connie squeezed his hand.

He sighed again.

The girls promised to bring pyjamas and a wash-bag next day and said not to worry about a thing; the doctors would make him better. Connie kissed him on the cheek. Lizzie stood at the end of the bed. They were miles away, drifting, fading . . .

'It's time to go,' the kind young nurse said.

*

Tom and Bill waited together at the hospital gate. It was a cold afternoon and Tom was due at the sector post, but on hearing the bad news about Bert he had swapped his shift with a warden from the Tennyson Street post.

'Connie won't let on how upset she is,' he predicted as he finished his second cigarette and ground it underfoot. 'But deep down she'll be feeling it.'

'Lizzie likewise.' Bill turned up his jacket collar and shoved his hands in his trouser pockets. He and Tom had unwelcome news of their own to impart to the girls, though now might not be the best time.

'I'll try to persuade Con to stay over at my place tonight.' Tom planned ahead – Connie and he could catch a number 11 bus to his lodgings on North Street. 'Maybe Lizzie could stay at yours?'

'She's not ready to do that yet, worse luck.' Bill dismissed the tempting idea and looked up at the starry sky. 'This is the sort of night for Jerry to take another pop at us,' he forecast gloomily. Absence of cloud cover and little wind combined to create ideal conditions for a Luftwaffe raid.

'So maybe I won't invite Connie after all,' Tom said out of consideration for Lizzie, who wouldn't like to be left alone at a time like this. 'And let's not tell the girls the latest bombshell. It's been a bad enough day for them as it is.'

Bill agreed not to say anything about the Admiralty letter that had landed on his mat that morning. He'd found it there when he'd returned home after a morning's fishing for cod within the thirty-mile limit and had opened it with a sinking heart. Then he'd shared its contents with Tom. They'd been drowning their sorrows at the Anchor when word about Bert had reached them and they'd come straight from there to the Queen Alexandra. 'But I'll make sure Lizzie is all right – Connie can still stay at yours if she wants.'

'Let's wait and see.' Tom offered Bill a cigarette. 'It's been a bloody rotten day,' he admitted. 'Hitler can't spoil our Christmas however hard he tries, but if the worst happens to Bert, none of us will be in the mood to celebrate.'

Bill struck a match with a steady hand and the flame lit up his regular, handsome features. Years of trawler work hadn't yet spoiled his smooth, healthy complexion. His forehead was unlined and his shoulders were broad: an Atlas who could bear the weight of the world if called upon. 'Here they come,' he warned as he flicked the spent match to the ground.

Connie and Lizzie emerged through the wide glass doors of the main entrance. They threaded their way between ambulances and cars towards their parked van. When they saw Tom and Bill they hesitated for a moment, then broke into a run.

'Well?' Tom was the first to speak. It was too dark to make out Connie's expression.

'Heart attack,' she confirmed breathlessly. The unexpected sight of Tom almost set her off crying but she fought back the tears.

Bill put his arm around Lizzie. 'What do the doctors say?'

'It's too early. We have to wait. Dad was woozy from the morphine.' Each sentence was an effort.

'What do you want to do now?' Tom asked them both. 'You can tell us to get lost and you can make your own way home if you'd rather – we'd understand.'

'Or we can stick around for a bit.' To Bill's surprise, Connie looked closer to tears than Lizzie did.

'Stay.' Lizzie slipped her hand into his. 'How did you get here – on your bike?'

'Yes. Would you like a lift back?'

Lizzie glanced uncertainly at Connie, who gave her a small push. 'Go,' Connie urged. 'I can drive the van.' Tom was the one she needed right this minute; his strength and steadiness would see her through.

'Are you sure you don't mind?' Lizzie checked.

'Of course not. Will it be all right with you if I stay at Tom's tonight?'

Lizzie nodded. She was almost dead with exhaustion – all she wanted to do was to lay her head on the pillow and sleep.

'I'll look after her,' Bill promised Connie.

Before long, Lizzie was perched on the BSA's pillion seat with her arms wrapped tightly around Bill's waist. He pulled away from the kerb, nodding at Tom and Connie, who stood hand in hand at the hospital gate.

Ten minutes later Bill turned into Elliot Street and pulled up outside number 12. Keeping the engine ticking over, he steadied the bike then patted Lizzie's clasped hands – a signal that it was safe for her to dismount. 'Shall I come in with you?' he asked.

'Yes please.' When it came to it, she couldn't face the idea of entering an empty house and seeing her father's slippers on the bottom step of the stairs.

Other reminders – his pipe rack and tobacco pouch on the front-room mantelpiece and his special teacup standing upside down on the draining board – might prove too much.

So Bill hitched the bike on to its stand while Lizzie turned the key in the lock. He followed her into the dark house, down a narrow corridor into the kitchen, where he reached for the kettle and filled it at the tap. 'Unless you want something stronger than tea?' he suggested.

'No – tea will do fine.' Still wearing her coat and hat, Lizzie sat down and rested her elbows on the table. Her head felt heavy, her shoulders were stiff and aching.

'Where do you keep your cups?'

'In the cupboard over the sink – top shelf.' Bill's movements as he accomplished the simple task soothed Lizzie's frayed nerves. He spooned sugar into her cup without asking, then sat down next to her, his shoulder touching hers.

'Neither Connie nor I saw this coming,' she confessed shakily. 'We both knew that Dad was working too hard, but it never occurred to either of us that he'd end up in hospital because of it.'

'What difference would it have made if you had?' The sight of her long fingers wrapped around the warm cup tempted Bill to reach across and stroke the back of her hand with his thumb. 'Even if you'd ordered Bert to slow down, I doubt that he would have listened. Your dad dashes at life full tilt – he can't help it.'

'You're right.' Lizzie put down her cup, then grasped Bill's hand. 'He will pull through, won't he?'

'I don't know, love. I hope so. We have to wait and

see.' There was no magic wand to wipe away Lizzie's misery; all Bill could do was to draw her closer and let her rest her head on his shoulder. 'I do know what it's like, though.'

She pulled away with a questioning look.

'My dad spent a couple of weeks in the Queen Alexandra before he . . . you know.' Harry Evans's death five years earlier wasn't something Bill liked to talk about. 'Mum wasn't around – she left us when I was three, so I don't remember much about her.'

'Left you? How?' This was news to Lizzie. Whenever she'd asked Bill what had happened to his mother, he'd scowled and changed the subject.

'Ran away, scarpered, buggered off – don't ask me where. Haven't I ever told you this?' Bill ran his hand across his mouth, as if wiping away a bad taste.

'No, you've never said a word. I remember hearing about your dad being poorly, though – it must have been a couple of years after you left St Joseph's.'

Bill nodded. 'I'd worked with Dad on the *Sea Knight* before he fell poorly. Tom joined us straight from school. Dad taught us all we know about trawler fishing and how to keep a boat in decent nick. It's stood us in good stead – until now.'

Lizzie picked up the hesitation. 'Has something happened?' she queried.

'No, nothing.' He brushed the question aside. 'Anyway, Dad was rushed to hospital on Christmas Eve and never came out. He had a growth in his throat – the worst kind of tumour – and he'd left it too late for the doctors to do anything about it. Dad passed away early in the New Year – a blessing really, because it was so quick.'

'I see. That's why I couldn't persuade you to join in with the carol singing . . . Christmas holds sad memories for you.'

'Why do they say passed away?' Bill's mind drifted off. 'Where to? Where do they go afterwards?'

Lizzie admitted that she didn't know. 'I wish I did,' she said with a sigh. 'Doesn't everyone?'

'But I'll tell you what, I swore to Dad that I'd keep *Sea Knight* shipshape for him and I've done that.' He forced himself back into the present. 'Listen to me going on about stuff when I'm meant to be looking after you.'

'No – I'm glad you told me.' Bill's trust in her formed a glue that bound them closer together.

'You look dead beat. I'd best be off.' Bill scraped back his chair, but before he stood up Lizzie spoke again.

'You don't have to go,' she said softly. 'You can stay here tonight if you like.'

Doubt flickered across his face. 'Are you sure this is the right time?' Perhaps fear of being alone had prompted the invitation – in which case, he ought not to take advantage.

'I'm sure.' She looked steadily into his eyes. 'I've wanted to for long enough.'

'And you won't regret it?'

For an answer she slowly took off her coat and shook her hair loose. Then she stood up and raised him from his chair. 'This will be my first time,' she said with a shy smile.

Bill wrapped his arms around her and held her close. Cheek to cheek, they swayed on the spot as if to the dreamy swell of violins. 'I didn't expect this.'

'We don't have to if you don't want to.' Lizzie felt the rough texture of Bill's jacket on her cheek. Had she got it wrong? Should she have waited for him to ask her?

'Of course I want to – you know that.'

'So,' she whispered, standing on tiptoe to kiss his lips. Inhibitions slipped away – now was the time to show Bill how much she loved him.

They'd reached the point of no return. He picked her up – her smooth skin against his rough cheek, her slender legs dangling, arms tight around his neck, supple and light – and carried her up the stairs, pausing on the landing until she pointed to the door on the left. He backed through it, then set her down on the floor between two single beds. There was no light on and Lizzie had to feel her way across the room to pull down the blackout blind. He waited in the dark for her to come back to him.

'There, that's better.' She switched on a bedside lamp and a dim yellow light revealed the contents of the room.

Bill noticed a pink petticoat and a blue cardigan strewn across the bed furthest from the window – Connie's. Lizzie's bed was clear of clutter. Two pairs of shoes peeped out from under it. The rug between the beds was worn in patches. There was no room for a wardrobe so dresses hung from a rail in a shallow alcove to one side of the chimney breast. There was wallpaper with yellow climbing roses, a small, cast-iron fireplace, striped curtains, and Lizzie unbuttoning her blouse with trembling fingers.

'You have no idea,' he breathed. No idea how long

he'd held himself back, how much self-control it had taken or how often he'd pictured this moment.

Lizzie slipped off her blouse and pulled him towards her. Shyness fell away when she felt his lips on her neck and shoulders, his hands on her hips and hers on his broad, smooth chest. She closed her eyes as a flood of sensations engulfed her and she lost herself in his embrace.

# CHAPTER FIVE

Daylight had not yet crept into the room but Bill was already wide awake. He lay quietly beside Lizzie, not wanting to disturb her. She was curled towards him in the narrow bed, her slim arm resting across his chest, and he could feel her warm breath on his shoulder. On any other day he and Tom would have already sailed out of the harbour and would be heading for the open sea in trusty old *Sea Knight*, their pride and joy. Not today.

Minutes ticked by on the small clock on Lizzie's bedside table. Damn the Admiralty letter ordering him and Tom to hand over *Sea Knight* to the Royal Naval Patrol Service for minesweeping duties. He hadn't had any time to let the news sink in – this very day patrol service men were due to come aboard the old girl to remove the trawl and fit her with a mechanical sweep and perhaps install a four-inch Lewis gun in her bow. You never knew; they might even come bang up to date and fit her with ASDIC sonar equipment, then send her out on anti-submarine duties.

'Harry Tate's Navy' – that's what they called the RNPS – a ramshackle outfit, a motley collection of trawlers, corvettes and motor launches press-ganged into protecting the approach to British harbours from U-boat attacks. In addition, they could be charged with neutralizing enemy mines strung out across the North Sea as far as Iceland and beyond. Or 'Sparrows' – that was another chirpy nickname, belying the fact that minesweeping was highly dangerous work. No end of ex-trawlermen had come under attack from German dive-bombers and torpedoes or had been killed by the mines that they were working on – young lads Bill knew personally had been blown sky high.

Unable to suppress a twitch of frustration, his leg jerked and Lizzie woke.

At first all was a daze. The room was dark and Bill lay beside her, his chest rising and falling and his skin warm under her fingertips. For a few magical seconds this was all she was aware of. 'What time is it?' she murmured, turning over and stretching out a hand to look at the luminous hands on the clock. 'Good Lord, it's six o'clock! Connie will be at the bakery, champing at the bit and wondering where on earth I've got to.' And surely Bill needed to get a move on too. 'We have to get up.'

Bill pulled her back towards him. 'Another five minutes,' he mumbled.

But Lizzie kissed him, then threw back the covers. Shy again, she fumbled for her underclothes before turning on the lamp.

He blinked in the light, then swung his legs over the side of the bed. 'No regrets?' he asked quietly.

'Not one.' Quite the opposite – Lizzie felt closer to Bill than ever before. Making love had been wonderful – slow and tender at first, then strong and passionate. In each thrilling moment she had felt safe and loved. Pausing, she studied his face. 'How about you?'

He didn't need to reply – the soft glow in his clear grey eyes told her everything.

'Won't you be late?' she asked.

'No, Tom and I are staying ashore today,' he said as casually as he could, grabbing his shirt and pulling it on over his head.

'I expect Connie will have telephoned the hospital by the time I get there.' Lizzie's thoughts raced ahead. 'The doctor told us that if we get through this first day or two, Dad's chances are good. He'll hate having to stay in hospital, though. The nurse said they won't even let him feed himself at first, let alone get out of bed.' She ran a brush through her hair. 'It's Friday. Why aren't you working?'

'I'll tell you later.' Sitting on the side of the bed, Bill avoided looking at her by bending forward to pull on his socks.

'But you and Tom never miss a day's fishing, fair or foul.' She paused with the brush in mid-air – it struck her that Bill was hiding something. 'Tell me,' she insisted.

'There isn't time. Come on – I'll run you down to College Road.'

'Bill!' Lizzie caught hold of his wrist. 'We're not meant to have secrets – not after last night.'

He sighed, then let it all out in a rush. 'All right then – the Royal Navy has got in on the act. They've requisitioned *Sea Knight* for minesweeping duties and Lord knows what else. There – now I bet you wish you hadn't asked.'

Lizzie's eyes narrowed. 'They want your boat?'

'And me and Tom as well. They say we're "essential" – that's the word – to maintain sea lanes and implement minesweeping operations. No one knows the waters around here the way we do; that's what they reckon.'

She took a sharp intake of breath. 'But what about your normal job? Who'll bring in the fish?'

Bill shrugged. 'That's all off for the time being – it's the same in Scarborough, Hull, Grimsby; you name it. Fleetwood over on the west coast is the main trawler port now.'

'It's not right,' Lizzie proclaimed indignantly. 'They can't make you.'

'They can and they have.' This was why Bill hadn't wanted to tell Lizzie in the first place – he knew how shocked and troubled she would be by the news. 'We're lucky they haven't nabbed us sooner, to be honest. It's because *Sea Knight* is smaller and older than most trawlers that they've waited this long.'

'Tell them you can't do it,' she pleaded. 'You're "essential" to Kelthorpe's Civil Defence team. You train first-aiders – you can't be spared.' Anything – *anything* – to stop the powers that be from forcing Bill to risk his life in this way!

'I'll have to give it up,' he told her quietly. 'I can't argue with the Navy, Lizzie. I have to do what they tell me.'

As the truth dawned, she pressed her hands to her mouth, then swayed on to her heels with a dizzying sense that everything had spun out of control. 'When?'

'As soon as they've fitted the sweep and taught us how to work it.'

'You and Tom?' Fear rose in her throat and threatened to choke her.

He nodded. 'We'll have a Royal Naval Reserve chap on board, a sub-lieutenant. He'll teach us how to cut the anchoring cables off moored mines so they float off to a safe distance. Then he's a crack shot with a rifle – you have to aim for the casing, apparently, not the contact horns.'

'Hush – don't say any more!' Lizzie's hands flew to her ears – she couldn't bear to hear the details. Her whole world had turned upside down. A minute ago she knew precisely the dangers that she, Bill, Connie, Tom, Pamela, Fred and all her ARP friends faced, and because she had experienced it she'd learned how to manage her fear. But now, suddenly, there was this enormous unknown – a dark, tumultuous sea, high winds, huge waves, sinister black mines bobbing on the surface, silent, invisible U-boats, deadly torpedoes . . . The list went on and on.

'I'm sorry, sweetheart,' Bill whispered. He held her and tried to comfort her. 'We'll pull through,' he promised. 'Fritz can't get rid of me that easily – I'm made of sterner stuff, and the Navy is right about one thing: I know these waters like the back of my hand.'

Connie followed the early morning bakery routine – exact amounts of flour, salt, yeast and water, length of time for proving the dough, temperature of the oven for various types of loaf. She could have done it blindfold if necessary. But where was Lizzie? Ought Connie to be worried or was it simply a case of her sister sleeping in? *It's not like her*, she thought as she dusted a board with flour, then pummelled and kneaded a third batch of dough. *Lizzie's always on time. Something must have happened.*

It was seven o'clock before Connie heard the telltale tinkle of the shop bell and Lizzie flew in, hatless and with her hair blown back from her face. The sound of Bill's motorbike outside the door told Connie everything she needed to know: Lizzie and Bill had spent their first night together.

'Aha!' she crowed knowingly, as Lizzie hung up her coat. 'At last!'

Lizzie slipped her calico apron over her head, then tied the strings tightly around her waist. 'Don't,' she said hastily. 'I'm not in the mood.'

Connie opened the oven door to take out a tray of Hovis loaves. 'My lips are sealed,' she promised, still with a twinkle in her eye.

'How's Dad?' Lizzie ignored her and began transferring cooled white loaves on to a wooden tray, ready for carrying through the shop to the van parked outside. 'I take it you've telephoned the hospital?'

Connie nodded. 'Yes, relax – they say Dad had a good night's sleep. We can visit him later, after he's had his ECG. They mentioned a few words I didn't understand – "ischemia", for one.'

'It means poor blood supply.'

'And remind me about "infarction".' Connie bowed to Lizzie's superior knowledge.

'Muscle damage. That's the thing – they have to find out if the heart muscle can heal itself.'

'Fingers crossed.' Connie slid the final batch into the oven. Her face was flushed from the heat and the hair at the nape of her neck was damp.

'It's true – Bill did stay at Elliot Street last night,'

Lizzie confessed as they carried loaves into the shop. 'I asked him to.'

'Good for you.' Connie waited to hear more.

'I'm glad I did,' Lizzie said with a touch of defiance.

'Yes – anyway, I'm hardly in a position to judge.'

'That's right, you're not. Besides, lots of girls do these days.' Lizzie's cheeks grew flushed.

'It's the war.' Connie steadily arranged loaves on shelves behind the counter. 'The old rules fly out of the window.'

'I love Bill so much it hurts.' Lizzie glanced at her and Connie's reflections in the dark window. Without warning she burst into tears. 'Oh, I can't bear to lose him!'

'Oh, love, why should you?' Connie put a comforting arm around her sister's shoulder, then fished in her apron pocket for a handkerchief. 'What's brought this on all of a sudden?'

'The RNPS – that's what.' Lizzie blew her nose hard. 'Why can't Bill and Tom carry on as normal? We need fish as much as we ever did.'

Connie stepped away with a puzzled frown. Alarm shot through her. 'What are you going on about?'

Lizzie let out a defeated groan. 'Didn't Tom tell you?'

'Tell me what?' What did the Patrol Service have to do with anything? It didn't make sense. Connie reached out and caught hold of Lizzie's arm. 'Come on, Liz – I'll shake it out of you if I have to.'

'The Navy has requisitioned *Sea Knight* for minesweeping duties,' Lizzie blurted out.

'Oh Lord, no!' *You might as well put a noose around*

*your own neck to save the hangman the trouble* – Connie didn't say this to Lizzie, but it was her first thought. 'When?'

'As soon as they fit the sweeps and teach Tom and Bill how to disable mines.'

Shaking her head, Connie retreated into the bakery and sat down heavily on a bench beside the coat rack. 'Tom didn't say a word,' she said with a sigh. They'd parted that morning in their usual way, with lingering kisses and murmured promises.

Lizzie sat down beside her. 'I expect he didn't want to add to your worries. I'm sorry, Con – I really am.'

'No, it's best that I know.' She took a deep breath, braced herself, then stood up with a dozen unanswered questions buzzing inside her head. 'I suppose it was bound to happen sooner or later.'

'Bill is worried about *Sea Knight*. He promised his dad he'd look after her.' It was a strange detail for Lizzie to dwell on in the midst of her other worries.

'Will it be just minesweeping or other things as well?'

'What other things?' What horrors were there that Lizzie hadn't already thought of?

'Sometimes the boats are used to bring in supplies from Sweden. Or for anti-submarine patrols, that kind of thing.' Connie had even heard of converted trawlers being sent out to pick up the bodies of drowned airmen. Then her thoughts shot off in another, more hopeful direction. 'Tom's in line for promotion to head warden,' she remembered. 'Kenneth is due to be transferred to Tennyson Street, leaving a vacancy at Gas Street.'

'Stop.' Lizzie shook her head. 'I've already clutched

at that straw. Bill said it won't make any difference – the Royal Navy can lord it over Civil Defence any day of the week.'

Sitting side by side, surrounded by the familiar fragrance of baking bread, Lizzie and Connie felt adrift in a stormy sea of troubles. *First Dad and now this*. It was only when dawn light filtered in through the shop window and they realized that they had less than half an hour in which to get ready for opening that they donned the life jacket of routine – more bread to take out of the oven, loaves to stack on trays, deliveries to be made.

'We'd best get a move on.' Lizzie surfaced first, consulting a list pinned to the wall. 'Let's see . . . how many loaves has Esther Cooke ordered? Today's Friday – that means one large white, one small brown and two teacakes.'

Connie, too, clicked into action. 'What's the use of worrying?' she said with a wry nod towards the words of an old song that was undergoing a revival. *Pack up your troubles in your old kit-bag and smile, smile, smile.* Even if your heart ached, even if it broke in two, the trick was to put on a brave face and soldier on.

It wasn't surprising that Connie and Lizzie hadn't seemed themselves over the weekend. On the Saturday night Pamela had shared a blessedly uneventful shift at the sector post with Connie and had caught up with her news – Bert was holding his own, thank goodness, but the doctors insisted on total rest for the foreseeable future. He was proving to be the worst kind of patient, already grumbling about the lousy food and itching to be up and back at work, but tests had shown muscle damage to one of the chambers of his heart – hopefully it would repair itself, but it would be a slow process and meanwhile Bert must stay where he was.

On Sunday Pamela had invited Lizzie to her lodgings. The day had been cold and foggy, and Lizzie had arrived on the doorstep looking pinched and worried – which was understandable once Pamela had learned what lay in store for Bill and Tom.

'It's one thing to go about your business trawling for cod,' Lizzie had said in an agony of apprehension. 'It's quite another for an enemy pilot to fly overhead and spot a minesweeper aboard *Sea Knight* – that makes her a legitimate target, as far as Fritz is concerned.'

Pamela had had little to offer except tea and sympathy. Privately she'd heaved a sigh of relief that no such prospect awaited Fred, whose night-time job in the report and control centre kept him relatively safe. Then she and Lizzie had diverted themselves by debating what to wear when the Christmas carol singers eventually ventured out into the streets. It would be chilly, so everyone would be well advised to don several warm layers under their coats, hats and scarves.

'Christmas!' Lizzie had heaved a sigh. It was under three weeks away but she'd never felt less like celebrating. Still, she'd rallied when Pamela had mentioned her new job at Anderson's.

'I'll be all fingers and thumbs with Betty watching my every move,' Pamela had confessed.

'Betty Holroyd – pooh!' Lizzie had made a swatting motion with the back of her hand. 'Believe me, you've got more brains than two of her put together.'

Pamela had enjoyed Lizzie's wickedly spiteful account of Betty briefly taking up with Bob Waterhouse, Lizzie's ex-fiancé. 'It was straight after Bob and I had called it off in spring this year. Betty moved in at lightning speed and bamboozled poor Bob into taking her out and buying her presents he couldn't afford. It didn't last long, though – she soon moved on to someone with deeper pockets.'

So, after a good gossip, Lizzie had been in better spirits when she and Pamela had parted, and Pamela had spent the evening deciding what to wear for her first day in the new job. She'd chosen a damson-coloured woollen dress with a gathered skirt and an interesting pleated panel on the bodice, finished off with a row of silver buttons down the front. She would wear her brown court shoes with a small heel – sensible and smart.

Now the time had come, and as Pamela presented herself to the gatekeeper at the timber yard at eight o'clock on Monday morning she was quaking in those smart, sensible shoes.

'Yes?' Jack Watkins scarcely glanced up from his copy of *Sporting Life*. A thin, hunched man dressed in a grey overcoat and flat cap with long features and a prominent nose over an old-fashioned walrus moustache, Watkins was ensconced in a small, draughty booth.

Pamela stated her name and purpose.

'Come again?' Reluctantly, Jack slid open the glass partition that separated them. 'Make it quick – it's blooming freezing.'

'I'm Pamela Carr. I'm starting a job as Mr Anderson's assistant secretary.'

The gateman grunted, then handed her a pale blue card. 'Fill this out. Clock in over there.' He pointed towards a large, glass-fronted machine with a dial and rows of identical cards outside the entrance to the office block, then he slid the window shut and went back to his paper. Licking the end of his pencil, he made a mark beside First Mate for the 1.30 at Ripon and What Larks for the 2.30 at York.

Inside the building, Pamela's case of the jitters worsened when Betty descended the stairs at a trot and whisked her off to the ladies' cloakroom, where she allocated Pamela a coat hook then warned her not to touch the bar of scented soap on the hand basin.

'We bring our own soap and towels.' Betty, dressed in a peacock-blue blouse and slim-fitting black skirt, cast a fashion-conscious eye over Pamela's demure outfit. 'We're the only two girls working here, so it'll be easy to keep track of who uses what.'

Pamela didn't have time to respond before she was whisked upstairs to the secretaries' office to be presented with an untidy stack of letters on a desk supporting a dusty black typewriter that could already be classed as an antique when compared with the sleek modern version on Betty's own desk.

'Those are all letters awaiting a reply,' Betty indicated with an airy waft of her manicured hand and no further instruction.

Pamela sat on an uncomfortable wooden chair and started to sift through the correspondence. Some were complaints about inaccurate invoices, others were excuses for non-payment. None seemed straightforward to a novice such as herself. She glanced up at Betty, expecting to see her hard at work. But no. Her fellow secretary had turned her back, taken out an emery board and was busy filing her nails. *The cheek of it! Thrown in at the deep end and left to sink or swim.* Very well. Pamela would seek advice from a friendlier source. Taking up a handful of letters, she quietly slipped from the room in search of her father, who worked in a larger office overlooking the yard and running the length of the building.

'Look who it isn't!' Harold greeted his daughter with a warm smile that dimmed when he spotted the worried look on her face. 'What's up, love?'

Pamela was explaining the problem when Fred came into the room. Soon all three were sorting through the letters. Ted Shaw of Shaw's Joinery Company was a notoriously late payer so Pamela should word her reply as a final warning. Morrison & Co. had definitely received their full order of pitch pine and was trying to wangle their way out of payment . . . and so on, with Pamela making careful notes. By nine o'clock she had worked out her responses and her mind was clear.

'Make sure you take them personally to Mr Anderson to be signed – don't let Betty do it because she'll take all the credit,' Fred advised as he accompanied her to the door.

Pamela gave his hand a grateful squeeze and arranged to see him at half past twelve in the canteen. She emerged into the corridor as Betty wafted her way towards their boss's room in a cloud of floral perfume.

'Our waste-paper basket is full to overflowing,' she reprimanded Pamela. 'Make sure it's emptied before I get back.'

What was she, a mind reader? Pamela bit her tongue and did as she was told. She kept her head down and spent the rest of the morning tapping away at her ancient typewriter. 'Dear Mr Shaw, In spite of repeated requests for payment of our invoice number 152 for the amount of £14/5/6d, due 17 September of this year, we have yet to receive a response. Please be advised that . . .'

She was interrupted now and then by curt commands from Betty – 'It's time to take Mr Anderson his cup of tea – a splash of milk, half a sugar', 'Run and find Keith Nelson in the cutting shed and point out the two mistakes that Fred found on this stock list', 'Order three new ribbons for my typewriter, Imperial Model 50'. On each occasion Pamela obliged, and before she knew it the clock on the wall said half past twelve.

'Well done! You survived your first morning.' Fred praised her as she flopped down next to him in the canteen. The bare, echoing room contained a long counter offering boiled beef and potatoes with overcooked cabbage. Trestle tables were set out next to steamed-up windows, and their conversation took place against a clatter of knives and forks and pots and pans, together with the general hubbub of men in overalls queuing at the counter.

'Why is Betty so mean?' she wanted to know. 'It's not as if I've done anything to her.'

'I expect she's jealous.' In fact, Fred had overheard Betty discussing Pamela with foreman Keith Nelson and gateman Jack Watkins as they'd waited together in the dinner queue. Fred had tagged on to the end of the line without them noticing.

'Hoity-toity little miss' had been Jack's snap verdict on Betty's new assistant.

'Pamela Carr only got given the job because she's the boss's niece,' Betty had announced snippily, while Keith had shrugged and said he didn't give a damn one way or the other.

'It's the jumped-up so-and-so who works in the main office with Harold who gets my goat,' he'd added. 'Fred Bleedin' Miller is who I'm on about, excuse my French. He's only been here five minutes when he starts throwing his weight around – "Do this, do that, do it my way or else!"'

Spotting Fred at the back of the queue, Jack had jabbed at Keith with his elbow and the hostile trio had fallen silent.

'Try not to mind about Betty,' Fred advised Pamela across the dinner table, though he was secretly worried for her after what he'd heard. 'I for one am glad you're here and so is your dad. And you deserve this chance, whatever Betty may think.'

Pamela toyed with the unappetizing food on her plate. 'I'll do my best,' she promised unconvincingly.

The mood lifted when Harold joined them at their table and the talk soon turned to Christmas.

'Your mother's busy unravelling old jumpers and using the wool to knit us all socks as presents,' Harold informed them with a wink. 'You included, Fred. Pamela will back me up – her mother is a fury with those knitting needles, so you may get two pairs if you're lucky.'

'What are you proposing to give her?' Fred asked.

'I'll probably buy her a record from Benson's – a nice classical one. You can help me choose.'

They moved on to discuss a morale-boosting Ministry of Information film that had just come out – *Christmas Under Fire* – in which traditions such as carol singing and pantomime productions were set against the backdrop of war. Men were shown cutting down small Christmas trees especially for cramped air raid shelters. 'Children will not be cheated out of Christmas!' the gung-ho narrator promised. 'Ding dong Merrily on High' chorused the choir from King's College, Cambridge.

When the klaxon sounded for the return to work, there was a hasty stubbing out of cigarettes and gathering of dirty crockery followed by a quick exit from the canteen. Seemingly deliberately Betty brushed against Fred in the bottleneck at the door. 'Oops!' She smiled and batted her lashes, making sure that Pamela had noticed.

'Beg your pardon.' Fred took a gentlemanly step backwards. 'After you.'

And Betty swept ahead in her shiny peacock blouse, laughing loudly at something Keith had said, swinging her hips as she crossed the yard before disappearing into the cloakroom to freshen up her lipstick and powder her nose.

No one was more surprised than Lizzie and Connie when their cousin Arnold turned out to be the sweetest singer of all the Boy Scouts press-ganged into Doug's Christmas choir.

'Who'd have thought it? The scruffy little devil has the voice of an angel!' Connie could hardly believe her ears.

Lizzie was speechless. Arnold had been the last to

attempt the opening verse of 'Once in Royal David's City' after a succession of lads had croaked their way through a couple of lines before the choirmaster had abruptly called a halt. Colin, bless him, had given it a go and had reached 'Mary was that mother mild' before Doug had signalled for Pamela to stop playing.

'That was a good effort, Colin,' he'd told the red-faced boy, before turning a sceptical eye on Arnold. 'I suppose we might as well give you a turn. If you please, Pamela.'

The piano had struck up again and Arnold, in his baggy shorts with his wrinkled socks around his ankles and his hair stubbornly refusing to lie flat, had opened his mouth to produce a pure sound that rose to the rafters of St Joseph's church hall and filled the space with magic, softening the hearts of all who listened. '"Where a mother laid her baby in a manger for His bed . . . Jesus Christ her little child."'

There was a moment's silence before the rest of the choir broke into spontaneous applause.

'He's the one,' Tom told Doug triumphantly. 'Arnold is our soloist, without a shadow of a doubt.'

'What if I don't feel like doing it?' Arnold scuffed his toes against the kerb. Rehearsal had finished and he was waiting for Colin outside Barbieri's fish and chip shop when Connie and Pamela stopped to congratulate him.

The girls had changed into their ARP uniforms and were setting off for Elliot Street to begin their shift. They'd already separated from Lizzie, who was on her way to the hospital to see Bert, and from Tom, who needed an early night before reporting to the custom house at six the next morning on what was to be his and Bill's important day of training for their new role on the refitted *Sea Knight*.

'Don't be daft, Arnold. Of course you want to sing the solo,' Connie chided. 'Mr Greenwood was mightily impressed by your singing – we all were.'

Arnold wasn't convinced. 'Will I have to wear one of those white nightie thingamajigs?'

'You mean a surplice?' Pamela failed to hide a smile. It must be admitted that the uncouth, sulky lad made an unlikely chorister. 'Not unless we're invited to sing in church on Christmas Eve.'

'Which I hope won't happen, by the way,' Connie chipped in. Ever since Doug had drawn attention to her shortcomings in an earlier rehearsal, she'd made an effort to mime more convincingly, and had thus succeeded in concealing her tin ear.

'It's more likely that we'll be singing in the streets with our coats on – knocking on doors and eating mince pies.' The way to a boy's heart was through his stomach, hence Pamela's enticing mention of the spiced Christmas treat.

'You'll do it, won't you?' Connie cajoled, before suddenly remembering that she'd left her gloves on a bench in the hall porch. 'Damn it – I'll be two ticks,' she muttered to Pamela as she hurried back to retrieve them.

She ran across the churchyard, glad of the full moon and a clear, starlit sky. As expected, the hall was already dark and deserted, securely locked up for the night. Now where exactly had she left the gloves? Not on the bench, after all. She was sure she remembered placing them there while she buttoned up her coat.

Perhaps they'd fallen on to the floor? Connie stooped to continue her search . . . no good; it was too dark to see a dratted thing, so she felt with her fingertips and came into contact with an unexpected object – something large and square, tucked away in the corner. Square but not heavy. It felt like a cardboard box – probably left there by the caretaker or one of the church flower arrangers.

Connie was about to straighten up. She must have left the gloves elsewhere. But then she heard a small sound coming from the box – a rustle, a breath, a whimper. At first she thought it might be an animal – a puppy or a kitten abandoned by its owners, perhaps. *Damned fools – it's far too cold to risk leaving the poor creature out on a night like this! I hope they've lined the box with plenty of straw, whoever it was,* she said to herself.

Torn between hurrying back to Pamela and checking on the mystery creature inside the box, Connie hesitated. There was another whimper, more movement and then a thin, human wail. This was no puppy, she realized. Quickly, she pulled the box from under the bench and felt inside. Her fingers touched a coarse woollen fabric then something warm, soft and silky-smooth. Without ceremony she dragged the box from the porch into the moonlight. A round face with tearful, dark eyes stared up at her – it was a small baby wrapped in a dark grey blanket.

Connie lifted the swaddled infant out of the box – gently and with disbelief. The baby opened its mouth and let out a high, plaintive cry.

'Oh my Lord!' Pamela had followed Connie back across the churchyard to find out what was taking her so long. Her stomach lurched to see Connie cradling a child, rocking it and holding it close. 'Wherever did that come from?'

'Hush now!' Connie stroked the crying baby's cheek. 'Someone has abandoned it. It could've frozen to death here in the porch.'

Pamela ventured closer as the infant sighed and settled against Connie's chest. 'Who could have done such a wicked thing?'

'Hush!' Connie murmured to the baby. 'A poor woman who is desperate, who has no one to turn to – that's who's done this.'

# CHAPTER SIX

Why the porch of the church hall? Why on a clear night with the temperature close to freezing? Why on earth would any mother be willing to take such a risk? Poor, innocent, unwanted child! 'Take a good look around,' Connie instructed Pamela. 'There may be a note, extra clothes – something that would give us a clue.'

Pamela searched the porch. 'Nothing,' she reported as she drew a blank.

The baby quickly fell asleep, soothed by the warmth of Connie's embrace.

'What now?' Pamela demanded helplessly. 'Do we go to the police? Or do we take it to the WVS centre? Surely someone there would know what to do.'

Connie struggled to think clearly. 'We're meant to be on duty. Kenneth will come down on us like a ton of bricks if we're late.'

'I have an idea. Lizzie's ambulance depot is on our way to Gas Street – there's bound to be a doctor or a nurse on duty there to offer first aid. Someone will be able to help.' Pamela led the way across the graveyard. Arnold was still waiting for Colin outside the fish and chip shop, but Pamela and Connie didn't stop to explain.

'Blimey, Connie – I never even knew you were expecting!' he called after their retreating figures.

Connie and Pamela ran through the dark, deserted streets, past sites of unexploded bombs and terraced houses whose fronts had been ripped off, leaving gas cookers, baths and beds exposed to the world. Skirting around a rescue team at work at the bottom of Tennyson Street, they headed for the disused brewery on King Edward Street that had been converted into an ambulance depot and first-aid post for the duration of the war. Here they found Walter Adams leaning against his ambulance, smoking a cigarette.

'Hey up!' Suddenly alert, Walter flicked his cigarette to the ground. 'What've you got there?'

'Would you believe it? Someone has ditched this child.' A breathless Connie was forced to pause.

'In the porch of St Joseph's church hall . . .' Pamela took up the thread but at the sight of the burly first-aider in his battledress and overcoat, complete with yellow armband, steel helmet and gas mask slung across his chest, her account tailed off. Walter was a market trader by day – unmarried and taciturn, with an intimidating presence for those who didn't know him well. 'Is there a nurse on duty?' she managed to stammer.

Walter glanced suspiciously at the bundle in Connie's arms. 'No nurse as yet,' he replied. 'Dr Moore started his shift ten minutes ago. It's just me and the doc at present.'

Pamela glanced beyond the row of ambulances at the tall brick building, a relic from Queen Victoria's reign. Its soot-blackened walls had a forbidding appearance – a wide archway led into a courtyard where a dozen empty barrels were carelessly stacked next to a rusty lorry. She sighed and gave Connie a doubtful shrug.

'Is it ailing?' Walter nodded towards the bundle. 'Does it need to see Dr Moore?'

'No, what it needs is its mother.' Connie didn't have time to waste. 'Pam, leave this with me. You run on and tell Kenneth what's happened; I'll stay here and sort it out.'

As Pamela went ahead with this plan, Connie side-stepped Walter and carried the infant into the courtyard, where the first-aid post was set up in a single-storey annexe to one side of the yard.

Walter followed her with another question. 'If it's not sick why not take it to the WVS rest centre next to the grammar school?'

'Because that's on the other side of town and I'm in a hurry,' Connie snapped back. She saw that the door to the annexe stood open and marched on. Inside she found a well-lit room lined with cupboards and shelves of first-aid equipment; an examination table had been set up in the middle. A doctor in a white coat stood with his back turned, studying a chart on the wall.

'Dr Moore?' Connie thought that she recognized the military set of the man's shoulders and his neatly combed grey hair and, sure enough, when he turned round to reveal his trimmed moustache and chis-elled, impassive features, she saw that this was the same doctor who was treating her father.

'Yes?' He seemed not to know her.

Connie launched into an explanation but was abruptly stopped in her tracks.

'Put it down here.' The doctor indicated the table that stood directly under a battery of bright lights.

The startled baby opened its eyes, blinked and let out a cry. Connie moved forward to comfort it.

'Stand back,' Dr Moore ordered. He quickly parted the coarse grey blanket to reveal the baby's clothes – a pale yellow knitted jacket with matching bootees. 'Well-nourished female,' he observed as he removed the clothing.

A scrap of paper fluttered to the floor and Connie stooped to pick it up. She read the few words scribbled in pencil: 'My name is Susan. Please love me.' Connie's heart was squeezed – the plain Christian name gave little away, but the mother's plea for the abandoned mite to be cherished touched her deeply. 'Hello, Susan,' she murmured.

'No skin rashes, no deformities. Around seven weeks old.' As the doctor continued his examination, a nurse entered the room. 'Ah, there you are, Nurse Ripley. Do we keep formula milk and feeding bottles here at the post?'

'Indeed we do, Doctor.' The nurse – a slim, dark-haired woman in a blue uniform, starched cap and stiff white collar – went straight to a cupboard and took out the required emergency items. She glanced at Connie, who had backed into a corner of the room, noticeably upset by the baby's crying.

'Apparently abandoned close to St Joseph's church.' The doctor gave his staccato version of events before pressing a stethoscope to the baby's chest. She wriggled under the touch of the cold metal, then gave a loud cry.

The nurse set a pan of water to boil on a portable gas

ring and scooped powder into a bottle. 'Are you the one who found her?' she asked Connie in a kindly tone.

'Yes.'

'Well done, you. Would you like to feed her?'

'Yes – no; I don't have time.' Already late for duty, Connie backed towards the door. 'What will happen to her now?'

'The police will have to be informed – I expect they'll try to track down the mother.' The nurse took the baby from the doctor, who had finished his examination and immediately left the room. 'They have a lot on their plate: protecting premises from looters, going after smugglers, leading rescue parties, and so on. Abandoned babies aren't a top priority. My guess is that she'll be taken in by the WVS and then put up for adoption in due course.'

'It says here that her name is Susan.' Connie showed Nurse Ripley the scrap of paper.

'It suits her,' the nurse decided. Resting the baby in the crook of her arm, she expertly slid the rubber teat into her mouth.

Susan sucked eagerly, her eyes fixed on the nurse's face.

'So small.' Connie took one last, lingering look. Tiny fingers with perfect fingernails, a head covered in soft, dark curls. Thick lashes, rosy cheeks.

It was a wrench for Connie to part from the Christmas baby who had been placed in a cardboard box rather than a manger, laying down her sweet head in a church-hall porch, of all places. Susan Who? Susan Why?

Questions drifted like snowflakes from a dark sky on to an indifferent earth that offered no answers.

*

Rumours about the abandoned child soon whirled around Kelthorpe. A baby didn't appear out of nowhere; there must be a mother (and a father, for that matter). Had a hard-pressed, poverty-stricken family found that they simply had one mouth too many to feed or, more likely, had an unmarried girl been taken advantage of by one of the many sailors who drifted in and out of the port? Morals were loose these days – witness the rise in the number of children whose fathers' names were left off birth certificates.

When Pamela clocked in at Anderson's on the day following the discovery of the infant, Betty pounced and dragged her off to the cloakroom.

'I hear you were a witness,' she began without preliminaries, 'so no holding back; tell me exactly what happened with this kid – when and where and who they think did the dastardly deed.'

'There's not a lot to tell.' Pamela took off her coat and hat, determined to resist Betty's attempt to turn the sad event into a kind of pantomime. 'Apparently the baby has been well cared for.'

'Yes, but surely one of your carol singers saw the mother lurking in the graveyard, waiting for a chance to ditch it. You can't all have gone around with your eyes closed.'

'It was dark,' Pamela reminded her.

'I also hear it's half foreign, with masses of dark, curly hair.' Betty shamelessly voiced one of the more salacious rumours.

*Oh, really!* A disgusted Pamela couldn't let this pass. 'And what if she is? What difference would that make?'

'Is she or isn't she?'

'She is not.'

Betty seemed amused by Pamela's indignation. 'I'm just saying there was a bunch of American marines hanging around Kelthorpe earlier in the year. And you know what they say about the Yanks: "Overpaid, oversexed and over here."'

'Don't be ridiculous.' Pamela made for the door but Betty got there first.

'Hold on, Miss Uppity – I'm your boss. You can't talk to me like that.'

Pamela flinched under Betty's sneering gaze. She hoped to draw a line by replying calmly, 'For the record, the baby is safe and well. Dr Moore gave her a clean bill of health and afterwards she was taken to the WVS rest centre to be looked after.'

But Betty refused to give ground. 'Come off it; your holier-than-thou act won't wash with me.'

'I'm sorry – that's all I know. Now, if you don't mind . . .'

'"Now, if you don't mind . . ."' Betty mimicked, before flinging open the door and standing aside. 'Funny that Connie Bailey was the one who found it,' she added. 'It couldn't be her brat, by any chance?'

'I'll pretend I didn't hear that.' Honestly and truly, Betty Holroyd was the limit! Anger propelled Pamela up the stairs and into their office, where she kept her head down all morning, avoiding conversation and looking ahead to when she could join her father and Fred at half past twelve.

In the canteen Fred took one look at Pamela and saw that relations between her and Betty hadn't improved. 'You know what I'm about to say,' he murmured with a glance across the crowded room to where Mr Anderson's secretary sat with her bosom buddies, Keith and Jack.

'Yes – you're going to tell me to ignore her,' Pamela said under her breath. 'But that's easier said than done.'

Fred nodded. 'Bullies soon become bored if they get no reaction. They move on to torment someone else.' Ever since fleeing from Berlin with his parents, he'd tried to live his life by this rule – don't draw attention, be compliant, take care not to put a foot wrong.

'Fred's right: put up and shut up is the way to go.' Harold wished for his daughter's sake that life was fairer, but experience told him that the opposite was often the case.

They ate in silence for a while. Today's mutton stew was no more appetizing than yesterday's boiled beef, and Pamela was uncomfortably aware that they were being talked about. When Keith picked up his empty plate and made his way towards the crockery trolley, he paused by their table for a word with Fred.

'Just to let you know: there was nothing wrong with that stock list you sent back yesterday,' he grumbled. 'If you'd have used your eyes you'd have seen the two extra items written on the back – ten boards of four-ply and twenty six-foot lengths of three by four.' Keith was his usual pugnacious self, sneering out from under jutting brows and squaring his shoulders as he spoke.

'Sorry about that.' Fred's apology was deliberately casual.

'It had better not happen again.' The yard foreman was determined to hang on to his well-paid job, so his remark contained thinly veiled menace. 'Otherwise Betty will make sure that the boss hears about your slapdash methods.'

'There'll be no repetition,' Fred assured him.

As Keith grunted then moved away, Pamela leaned over the table and whispered to Fred, 'He's lying. I know for a fact there was nothing written on the back of that stock list.'

'I know it too.' Fred speared a piece of mutton with his fork. 'Keith probably thinks he can get away with a little light pilfering – nothing too major. But it's as I said – best not to argue.'

Seeing Pamela's pained expression, Harold cut in more sharply than usual. 'No, love. I know – it's not fair. But believe me, Fred's right: it doesn't pay to get people's backs up.'

Pamela jumped at the sound of the klaxon, soon followed by the usual stampede for the door. Carried outside in the swell, she was greeted by a blast of bitterly cold, smoke-filled air. The sky over the headland was heavy with mustard-coloured clouds, and she noticed cranes lifting raw timber from the deck of SS *Francis Drake* – a recently docked coaster fresh in from Sweden. All was dirt, noise and dreariness. Was this to be her future? she wondered. A strong wave of nostalgia washed over her for the stories and stars of the silver screen – for Katharine Hepburn in *The Philadelphia Story* and for Laurence Olivier in *Pride and Prejudice*. How she'd loved watching those films, time and time again, from the projection room at the Savoy. *Come back, pedantic, paunchy, narrow-minded Mr Penrose – all is forgiven!*

Pamela gave a wry grin, then braced herself for the

cold walk across the yard. *There are people a lot worse off than me,* she reminded herself as her feet crunched over the loose cinder surface and workers swarmed by. She thought of wives who had lost husbands in Italy and Greece, of children whose fathers would never return, and of the baby named Susan abandoned by a desperate mother for reasons it was impossible to fathom.

'We set sail at nine.' Bill tried hard not to reveal the tension he felt as he and Lizzie prepared to part. Wednesday was to be his first day on patrol as one of Churchill's Sparrows; the training had been quick and efficient and *Sea Knight* was fully kitted out with a minesweep as well as a Lewis gun in the prow and depth-charge racks to port and starboard. 'Don't worry, we'll stick close to shore for the first few days,' he reassured her. 'With luck, we won't see much action.'

Sitting on the edge of his bed and slipping on her pale blue cotton nightdress, Lizzie went to the bedroom window and pulled up the blind. The sky glittered with stars and the moon shone a silvery light on the water in the harbour, where small boats bobbed and the few remaining trawlermen prepared to set sail for a day's fishing. 'Thank you,' she murmured, with her back turned to Bill.

He came up behind her and put his arms around her waist. 'What for?'

'For pretending.' She turned to kiss him. 'I know you're making light of the dangers for my sake.'

It was true; *Sea Knight* was one of four former fishing vessels that had been variously fitted with kites, rockets and machine guns. They had been instructed to patrol the approach to harbours stretching from Whitby in the north to Grimsby in the south. Anti-submarine duties came top of the list for the small fleet, a task that depended on somewhat primitive ASDIC systems that measured distance according to sound waves emitted from approaching underwater vessels. It was a major operation and Bill knew that it wouldn't be long before the small fleet attracted the attention of Kriegsmarine Command. He returned Lizzie's kiss enthusiastically. 'Promise me you won't spend all your time worrying about me.'

She managed to smile. 'No, just some of it.' During much of Bill's absence she would be busy with the bakery, first-aid duties, hospital visits and choir rehearsals. It would be the in-between parts, when she had time on her hands, that would prove more difficult to endure. 'How long will you be gone?'

'Five days.'

'I'll be counting the hours,' Lizzie said with a sigh, drinking in every detail of Bill's face: his smooth brow topped by a mass of dark waves, his firm jaw-line, the permanent upturn at the corners of his mouth and the dark lashes and straight eyebrows. Then she held him close and ran her fingers across his broad back. Their kisses were soft and long.

It was Bill who pulled away at last. 'You'll be in trouble with Connie again if you don't get a move on,' he said regretfully.

'I know.' Lizzie's sighs came thick and fast. Each moment together was precious, while every minute of separation would seem like forever. It was only Bill's mention of Connie that forced Lizzie to pull herself together – her sister had stayed overnight at

Tom's lodgings in North Street and at this moment would be saying a similar farewell. The two girls were in the same boat, and Lizzie felt she mustn't let Connie down today of all days. So she got dressed while Bill went down to make tea and toast, which she drank and ate quickly, without sitting down. Their final goodbyes were hasty, with only one lingering kiss.

'Until Monday.' Lizzie held her voice steady as she buttoned her coat and put on her hat.

'Monday,' Bill echoed.

The sky was still dark as she left the cottage and crossed the cobbled quay without looking back.

Nothing was said about the fond farewells but everything was understood between Connie and Lizzie as they began work for the day. Connie kneaded the dough with extra determination, silent as she pulled and twisted, thumped and pummelled, as if Hitler himself were on the receiving end. Meanwhile, Lizzie stared straight ahead as she set out on her rounds, avoiding the harbour for fear of seeing *Sea Knight* set sail on its five-day patrol and making a long detour to deliver bread to houses that lined the seafront, all the way to North Street in the new part of town. Here she encountered Colin trailing snail-like towards the bus stop, apparently on his way to school. She stopped to offer him a lift.

'I'm going your way, so why not hop in?' She leaned across to open the passenger door.

Colin reached the bus stop and checked with a smart, youngish woman whom Lizzie guessed must be his mother. The woman – slim with sleekly styled fair hair, dressed in a navy blue coat and matching hat – nodded brusquely and Colin got into Lizzie's van.

'Cheer up, it might never happen,' Lizzie said as they set off.

'It already has,' Colin said with a frown. He sat with hunched shoulders, looking peaky and with the stale, unwashed appearance of a lad who had crawled out of bed and into his grammar school uniform without looking in a mirror. He refused Lizzie's offer of a free bread bun and was silent all the way along the seafront and into the centre of town, where he suddenly said that this was where he wanted to be dropped off.

'Are you sure?' Lizzie knew they were still a good mile from the school.

'Yes. I said stop, didn't I?'

'Oh dear, someone got out of bed the wrong side,' Lizzie commented. Nevertheless, she pulled up beside the poor old bomb-damaged statue of Queen Victoria and waited for Colin to disembark. She lingered long enough to see him cross the square then set off up the hill, satchel gaping open and slung carelessly over his shoulder, his head down, dragging his feet.

She thought no more of it as she delivered the last of her orders, then returned to the bakery, where she offered to step in behind the counter to give Connie a break.

A grateful Connie turned down the volume on the wireless, then took off her apron. 'We *can* talk about it if you like,' she said pointedly against the background sound of Glenn Miller's swing version of 'Song of the Volga Boatmen'.

'What do you mean?'

'The elephant in the room: Tom and Bill setting out on their first patrol.'

Lizzie shook her head. 'I'd rather not.'

'Right – probably best not to dwell on it.' Connie reached for her coat. 'I'm slipping out for a breath of fresh air – round the block and back.'

Connie's hand was on the door handle when Lizzie turned off the wireless and spoke again. 'I'm scared stiff for them,' she confessed in a small voice, scarcely able to control the trembling of her fingers as she attempted to tie her apron strings.

'Me too,' Connie said softly. 'Last night I had a nightmare about U-boats creeping along underwater, turning into sea monsters that rose from the deep.'

'Don't – please,' Lizzie said with a shudder.

'Let's face it.' Connie's parting shot did nothing to calm her sister's nerves. Better to get things out in the open than to bury your head in the sand. 'We have no idea how bad it will be for Tom and Bill. But I do know one thing: these five days will be the longest we've ever known.'

'I'm afraid our hearts weren't in it,' Lizzie admitted to Pamela after carol singing practice that evening. 'I practically had to drag Connie here – for two pins she'd have given it a miss and gone straight to the hospital to see Dad.'

The rehearsal had been a scrappy, unenthusiastic affair. Doug had been dismayed to learn that the Royal Naval Patrol Service had robbed him of his best singer and had cast around for a substitute. No one had been a patch on Tom, so Pamela had promised to ask Fred if he would step in to fill the gap, although she was by no means certain that he would agree. Two of the WI ladies had also dropped out and Colin had mysteriously jumped ship, leaving a sulky Arnold without his main ally.

'I could tell your minds were wandering,' Pamela observed as she and Lizzie crossed the churchyard. Both wore knitted scarves and berets, together with thick tweed coats to protect them from the cold. 'And it's to be expected. Not hearing from Bill and Tom while they're at sea will be hard for you both.'

And so it proved, as a cold snap set in on the Thursday, bringing flurries of snow that quickly turned to slush underfoot and harsh winds driving in off the sea. Fierce waves at high tide lashed the harbour wall and whipped spray across the promenade: a reminder, if any were needed, that conditions at sea would be atrocious.

After work, Fred called in on Pamela at home on King Edward Street and she seized her chance to persuade him to take Tom's place in St Joseph's choir.

'For you – anything,' Fred teased, as he stepped inside. 'But seriously, we're rushed off our feet at the report centre, so I doubt that I'll be able to spare the time.'

'That's a shame. You'd improve the quality of our singing no end,' she told him gaily, as she invited him into the sitting room that she shared with three other lodgers.

'All right, then; let me think about it.' He blushed modestly.

Pamela made a special fuss of him, offering tea and home-baked ginger biscuits, then stoking up the fire before cuddling close on the lumpy chaise longue.

Fred didn't object to the kisses – it was rare for Pamela to make the first move. However, the cosy closeness was soon disturbed by the sound of the front door opening and female voices in the hallway. Pamela pulled away and was sitting demurely, cup and saucer in hand, when Joan Deering popped her head around the door.

'Oops!' Joan, who worked as a telephonist at the North Street exchange, occupied the room next to Pamela's on the first floor. 'I'm not interrupting, am I?'

Fred blushed and sprang to his feet. 'Not at all. It's time I was making a move anyway.'

'Not on my account.' Joan prepared to step back and close the door. 'I only wanted to show Maureen the sitting room. We can come back later.'

But Fred's polite insistence won the day. Saying goodbye to Pamela, he was gone before Joan could object further.

'Come in and meet a fellow lodger.' Joan ushered her unseen companion into the room.

It struck Pamela immediately that the two girls were chalk and cheese. Joan's full figure, auburn hair and smartly tailored camel coat contrasted with the new lodger's slight build, short brown hair and dowdy, belted raincoat. And while details of the telephone operator's appearance – the glint of a pearl brooch on her lapel, her matching earrings and her coral-pink lipstick – gave the impression of a young woman who was self-assured and completely at ease, her companion seemed to crave invisibility, almost shrinking into herself and preferring to stay hidden in Joan's shadow.

'Pamela, this is Maureen Strong. She'll be living here with us from now on.' Joan made a breezy introduction. 'As you see, Maureen, the sitting room is, shall we say, a touch old-fashioned.' She gestured towards the pink marble fireplace and an ornately framed oil painting depicting a Scottish mountain scene that hung on the chimney breast. The furniture was a dull brown, consisting of the horsehair chaise longue and two cottage-style wooden chairs, a small octagonal table supporting a tired-looking aspidistra and a bookcase in an alcove whose shelves bowed under the weight of volumes by Dickens, the Brontë sisters and H. G. Wells.

Maureen ducked her head and offered no response.

'I work alongside Maureen's mother at the exchange,' Joan explained to Pamela. 'When I heard that Maureen was looking for lodgings closer to town, I suggested the spare attic room here.' It had to be admitted that Joan was already regretting her good deed. She hadn't expected Maureen to be such a limp lettuce leaf; a complete contrast to her mother, Nancy, who was full of life – vibrant in the way she dressed and always immaculately turned out.

Pamela's instinct to protect the underdog shot to the fore. 'Don't be put off by the lack of modern amenities – we're a friendly bunch and that's what matters,' she told Maureen with an encouraging smile. The 'bunch' included herself and Joan, plus Kathleen Roberts and Winnie Margerison, who both worked as shop assistants in Bentley's department store on Valley Road. 'You're not related to Colin Strong, by any chance?'

'He's my brother.' Maureen kept her reply brief

and she looked as if she wanted the ground to swallow her up.

'Maureen has been living away,' Joan rushed on. 'Where was it now?'

'Axenby.' Maureen supplied the information in the same low voice.

Pamela racked her brains. 'Now, where is that exactly?'

'Just outside Leithley.' The awkward reply faded to nothing.

'So this is the sitting room.' Impatient to have the introductory tour over and done with, Joan took up the reins once more. 'I promised Mr Fairweather – he's our landlord, but he lives in Raby – that I'd show you your room. It's poky and there are no views out of the skylight windows, but that's the reason it's so cheap. Follow me.'

Listening to Joan and Maureen's footsteps on the stairs, Pamela resolved to look out for their mousy new lodger, who reminded her of herself when she'd been fresh out of school. She recognized the crippling shyness and uncertainty, the odd feeling of sadness that enveloped Maureen like a grey shroud. The girl was lonely and badly in need of a companion, and she, Pamela, was determined to be that friend.

# CHAPTER SEVEN

The sight of green screens around Bert's bed alarmed Lizzie and Connie the moment they walked into the ward. All heads – patients and visitors alike – turned towards the sisters.

'It's nothing – Dad probably just needed a bed-pan.' Determined not to panic, Connie came up with a practical reason for the presence of the screens.

Lizzie looked around anxiously for a nurse but none was in sight.

An elderly patient, bald and toothless, called out to them from a nearby bed. 'Your dad took a turn for the worse,' he informed them in a flat, matter-of-fact tone. 'The doc's with him now.'

There was a flurry of activity behind the screens. Voices murmured, trolley wheels squeaked and a muffled groan reached them.

'Oh, Lord!' Lizzie froze on the spot, while Connie felt a stab of fear under her breastbone.

A staff nurse emerged from behind the screens, holding a shallow metal dish at arm's length. When she saw Connie and Lizzie she motioned for them to follow her out into the corridor, where she deposited the dish in a sluice room then quickly returned to explain. 'It's bad news, I'm afraid. Dr Moore suspects that your father has suffered another heart attack. It happened a short while ago when Mr Harrison attempted to get out of bed – against doctor's orders, as you know.'

Lizzie pressed her lips together, scarcely daring to breathe. It was Connie who asked the inevitable question. 'How is he now, Nurse?'

'He's resting and his pulse is steady. Doctor thinks he's over the worst.'

Lizzie allowed herself to breathe again. 'When will we be able to see him?'

'That's up to Dr Moore.' Glancing through a window set into the wide door, the nurse informed them that the screens had been removed.

Connie and Lizzie caught a glimpse of their father's head propped up on pillows and the doctor wagging his finger and giving his patient a stern talking-to. Bert turned his head away to stare at the wall. Then the doctor took off his stethoscope, stuffed it into the pocket of his white coat and gave instructions to the junior nurse standing at the end of the bed, after which he strode the length of the ward and burst through the door into the corridor. When he saw Bert's visitors, he erased the frown from his face and in his mind prepared bland answers for any questions they might throw at him.

'Will he be all right, Doctor?' Lizzie jumped in first.

'Too early to tell . . . fortunately a relatively minor attack this time . . . in absolutely no circumstances must your father make any further attempts to get out of bed . . .'

'May we see him?' Connie asked.

'Ah, the ARP lady who rescues abandoned babies.' Moore had recognized her after all. He raised an eyebrow and noted again the similarity between the sisters: both tall, slim and attractive, with the same determined gleam in their dark brown eyes. 'Yes – I'll permit a short visit. No more than five minutes, mind you.'

Then he was gone, white coat flapping, and Lizzie and Connie ventured back into the ward. They approached their father's bed on tiptoe, with the staff nurse hovering in the background.

'Dad?' Lizzie whispered as they drew near.

Slowly and with an expression of total weariness, Bert turned his head towards his daughters. His eyes were yellow and sunk deep into their sockets, and lines were etched into his forehead and to either side of his mouth. 'Eh, girls,' he breathed. 'Here's a right carry-on.'

Connie reached for his hand and gently squeezed it. 'This is what comes of not doing as you're told.'

'Aye, but what's the point if I can't even get out of bed?'

'Not yet,' Lizzie explained carefully. 'You will be able to when you're better.'

'Not when but if,' Bert contradicted without self-pity. 'There's no guarantee. And what if I'm an invalid for the rest of my life? What then? I'll be no use to man nor beast.'

'Hush,' Lizzie implored. It cut her to the quick to see him laid up like this; the lively, caring dad who had taught her how to ride a bike and how to swim and had once, in the arctic winter of 1927, taken her and Connie ice skating on the frozen River Kell.

'Listen, Dad – we can't have you thinking that way.' Connie tapped his forearm insistently. 'You will be up and about again, but all in good time, you hear? In the meantime, Lizzie and I will keep the bakery going as best we can.'

'Mind you don't overbake those penny buns.' Bert revealed a flash of his old self. 'They only need twenty minutes at the most.'

'Yes, Dad. And guess what – Tom has been nabbed by the Royal Naval Patrol Service, so Connie's now first in line for head warden on Gas Street.' Lizzie conjured up the next subject that might focus their father's mind on life beyond his hospital bed. 'Kenneth will transfer to Tennyson Street on Monday, so there's a vacancy.'

'You don't say.' Bert smiled faintly.

'Yes, and the Union Jack and the "Home Sweet Home" banner are still there to cheer everyone up,' Connie added.

Lizzie kept up the flow of news. 'Oh, and you won't believe what Connie here found: a baby, abandoned by its mother – left out in the cold in a cardboard box.'

'Never.' Bert's eyelids began to droop and his voice faded.

'She's called Susan,' Connie said softly. 'You should have seen her, Dad – such a bonny wee thing.'

The staff nurse touched Lizzie's shoulder: it was time to leave. 'Let him sleep now,' she advised as she led them from the ward on soft-soled shoes and with a crackle of crisp, starched apron. 'And let's hope Mr Harrison does as he's told from now on – complete bed rest and no excitement is the order of the day.'

*

The Women's Voluntary Service rest centre stood on the western edge of town, opposite the Queen Alexandra Hospital and next door to Kelthorpe Grammar School.

'Shall we?' Lizzie asked Connie with a jerk of her head towards the rest home.

They'd left the hospital in two minds as to what to do next. Either they drove straight back to Elliot Street and got a well-earned early night or they called at the WVS centre to find out the latest news on little Susan.

Connie wasn't sure what good such a visit would do. Of course, thoughts about the baby's fate had drifted in and out of her head all week and she'd developed a habit of tightly crossing her fingers and hoping for the best possible future for the abandoned child – a warm bed, gentle hands and eventually a loving couple willing to adopt her – but Connie felt she had played her part in the rescue and had done all she could. Then again, what harm could come of dropping in?

'Come on,' Lizzie urged. 'I, for one, would love to see her.'

So they crossed the dark street together, their faces and fingers pinched by an icy breeze, past the school, built sixty years earlier as a fanciful mock-up of a medieval castle, with turrets and ornate stonework, complete with arched windows and an imposing entrance porch. The square, squat WVS house stood next to it: stone-built and relatively modest in scale and design, with only a small sign over the doorway to identify its function.

Lizzie rang the doorbell and waited. Connie hopped

impatiently from one foot to the other until at last the door was opened by a bespectacled, middle-aged woman in a green felt hat and overcoat, brightened up by a red hat band and by the red and white WVS badge sewn on to the right cuff.

'Yes?' the woman demanded. Then, without waiting for a response, she rattled off a list. 'If you've brought donations of sheets, nightdresses, pyjamas and suchlike, please come back tomorrow and ask to see Mrs Bridger. Likewise, if you wish to volunteer to work in one of our mobile canteens – in which case you must apply to Mrs Marlowe. And if it's about training as shelter marshals you're too late – we have as many as we need—'

'That's not why we've come,' Lizzie cut in. 'Anyway, my sister and I already work with the Civil Defence team – Connie's an air raid warden and I'm an ambulance driver.'

'You don't say.' The centre manager studied them more closely, her harassed expression relaxing as she did so. 'Haven't I seen you patrolling in the Gas Street sector?' she asked Connie, who answered with a nod. 'I thought so. I'm Gladys Smallwood and you are . . . ?'

'Connie Bailey and Lizzie Harrison. May we come in?' Connie replied.

Gladys shook their hands vigorously, then led them across a dimly lit hall into a small, cold room piled high with boxes, variously labelled with the words 'Blankets', 'Sheets' and 'Surgical dressings'. The walls were lined with shelves stacked with yet more boxes and in one corner there was a small table with a telephone, a lamp and a mountain of untidy paperwork.

'As you see, we're snowed under with donations,' Gladys apologized.

'You're busy.' Connie dug Lizzie in the ribs and rolled her eyes towards the door. This attempt to see baby Susan no longer felt like a good idea. 'Maybe we should do as you said and come back tomorrow.'

'Certainly not. I can always make time for our doughty Civil Defence gals.'

Connie pictured a thirteen-year-old Gladys playing centre-forward in a school hockey team, swinging her stick and whacking the ball into the net, or as a Girl Guide leader, rubbing sticks together to make fire – no-nonsense and putting the fear of God into her 'gals'.

'Now, how can I help?' Gladys asked.

'You took in a baby named Susan earlier this week.' Lizzie overrode Connie's reluctance.

'We did indeed.' The supervisor peered expectantly over the top of her heavily rimmed glasses. 'One of your ambulance drivers brought her in.'

'Connie was the one who found her in St Joseph's churchyard.'

'Ah, I see.' Disappointment flickered across the WVS woman's face, followed soon after by suspicion. 'I rather hoped that you'd brought information about the mother.'

'No, I'm sorry; we really only came to find out how Susan is doing,' Lizzie explained.

'The child is well.' Reverting to her former stiff manner, Gladys shared the basic information while still staring keenly at Connie.

Lizzie wasn't satisfied. 'That's good news, but we were hoping for a little more.'

'Our rest centre offers shelter to many infants. Most have been orphaned during air raids. However, sad to say, a few newborns have been deliberately abandoned by their mothers. In such cases our attempts to trace relatives usually fail.'

Unnerved by the switch of tone, Connie read disapproval into the WVS woman's piercing gaze. Good Lord, did Gladys Smallwood imagine that mixed motives lay behind this visit? Did she, in fact, suspect that she, Connie, was the guilty party – the mother who had abandoned her baby? Connie felt her cheeks burn and experienced a strong desire to turn tail and run.

'Could we see her?' Even as she asked the question, Lizzie knew what the answer would be.

'I'm afraid not. Lights are out in the nursery and all the babies are asleep.'

'Just a quick peep?' Lizzie wheedled.

'Impossible.' Gladys shook her head without shifting her gaze from a flustered Connie. 'But I can assure you that Susan will thrive while she's in our care. She's an exceptionally bonny child and if I'm any judge, there will be no shortage of people wishing to adopt her once the police have completed their investigations.'

'What is it about me? Why do people always think the worst?' Friday morning saw Connie with her sleeves rolled up, thumping and pummelling dough once more. 'You saw how that WVS woman looked at me, Liz – like I'd committed a crime.'

'You and your imagination.' Lizzie brushed past with a tray of freshly baked loaves.

'I'm not making it up. Gladys Smallwood has me

down as the villain of the piece. She most likely thinks I kept my pregnancy hidden for nine months and gave birth under a bush up by Raynard's Folly.' Connie glanced up to see that Lizzie had carried the tray through the shop and out on to the street. 'It's not as if I wanted to call in at the rest centre in the first place,' she muttered to herself as she twisted, then kneaded vigorously.

'Anyway, who's "people"?' Lizzie came back in and took up where they'd left off. 'If you mean the silly fools who judge a book by its cover, who gives a fig what they think?'

'What's wrong with my cover?' Connie made a fist and punched the dough.

Lizzie grinned at her sister's touchy response. 'Nothing – you have a lovely, colourful, shiny cover. That's part of the problem, Con – you can't help attracting attention.'

'I don't mean to,' Connie said sulkily.

'No, but you just do.' Lizzie had accepted this reality since she was little – Connie pirouetting and dazzling like the ballerina on top of a musical box while she, Lizzie, went about her business in a quieter way: studying hard at school, considering others and happy to let her older sister steal the limelight.

'It's a load of old cobblers,' Connie complained furiously. 'How could I have carried on with my warden duties all these months if I'd been expecting? And do I look like the type to ditch my own kid?'

'Mrs Smallwood didn't say you had,' Lizzie reminded her.

'No, but she thought it – I could tell by the way she looked at me.'

Lizzie opened the oven door to a blast of intense heat. She pulled out the second of the morning's bakes and slid the trays on to wire racks to the left of the oven. 'Anyhow, it's not me you have to convince.'

'No, it's the rest of the world.' Connie's sigh raised a cloud of flour from the board. She paused, then spoke with new determination. 'But there is one way I can do that.'

'Uh-oh.' Lizzie backed towards the shop, fearing where her sister's impetuosity might lead this time.

'Yes, it's simple.' It was as if a light had come on inside Connie's head. 'To clear this up, all I have to do is track down the real culprit. That's it, Liz. I intend to find Susan's poor, desperate mother.'

'Once Connie gets an idea into her head there's rarely any stopping her.' Lizzie called upstairs as she waited for Pamela in the hallway of her King Edward Street lodging house. She noted the missing stair rods and worn carpet as well as the cracked glass in the barometer hanging from the wall.

Pamela changed into her ARP uniform with the door to her room wide open. 'Why? What's she done now?' she called downstairs as she zipped up her trousers and fastened her jacket. Shoes at the ready, she slipped them on, tied her laces, then reached for her coat, cap and gas mask.

'Nothing yet. But she plans to turn detective – over the baby you two found outside the church hall. Typical Con: she's set her mind on identifying the mother, would you believe?'

Pamela emerged from her room. 'Yes, I can believe it.' And she understood the reason. It was a mystery that got under your skin and couldn't easily be shaken off – the question of who in their right mind would do such a thing on such a night, so close to Christmas.

'She's been going on about it all day; first off, she telephoned the registrar's office to ask about recent births. After that she was on the phone to St Joseph's to see if the vicar had baptized any babies named Susan in the past few weeks. Both were dead ends, but it won't stop Connie from taking it further.'

'What will she do if she finds the mother?' Pamela buttoned her coat as she joined Lizzie in the hallway.

'Ah – I'm not sure.' Lizzie hadn't thought that far ahead – and probably neither had Connie. 'Personally, I think it helps her to keep her mind off Tom and what he and Bill might be up against.' Suppressing a shudder, she followed Pamela out of the front door, where they almost bumped into the new lodger, Maureen Strong, who was lugging a suitcase along the pavement in the direction of the house.

'Here, let me help.' Pamela took one end of the case and lifted it over the doorstep, but her offer to carry it up the stairs was refused with an embarrassed smile.

'Thanks, but I can manage,' Maureen assured her. She wore the same drab raincoat as before and had the worn-down, weary air of someone much older than her years.

Lizzie tapped her wristwatch – time to get a move on – so Pamela told Maureen to be sure to let her know if there was anything she needed, then hurried to join her friend.

'I suppose no news is good news as far as Tom and Bill are concerned.' Lizzie's attempt to convince herself failed miserably. 'But honestly, I can't wait until they get back,' she confessed at the top of the street, where she and Pamela went their separate ways to start their night shifts. 'Neither can Con. So if, as I suspect, she asks you to be Dr Watson to her Sherlock Holmes over this baby business, it might be best to humour her for a while – at least until Tom has both feet back on dry land.'

'I'll do my best,' Pamela promised. She, too, would be glad of the distraction. Hurrying on towards the Gas Street post, she thought back over her first, difficult week in her new job. What made Betty so mean? Pamela had done her best not to provoke her; she'd worked hard for three days and done everything Betty had told her to, but still the jibes had fallen thick and fast. Why must Pamela make such a racket while she typed? Where had she 'hidden' the spare sheets of carbon paper? Pamela didn't know the first thing about shorthand and how could she, Betty, be expected to put up with such a dunce? The atmosphere in the canteen had also gone from bad to worse when, during the Wednesday dinner break, Fred had rebuffed a blatant attempt by Betty to flirt with him in front of Pamela.

'You don't mind if I sit down next to you . . . So tell me, Fred, what's Father Christmas bringing you this year?' (*Honestly!*) 'Have you seen *Kiss the Boys Goodbye* at the Savoy? Mary Martin was wonderful as a chorus girl – those legs!' *(Oh, please!)*

'Not my kind of film, I'm afraid,' Fred had replied in an even tone. 'Earlier this year Pamela and I went to see *Citizen Kane* with Orson Welles in the title role – now, that really was an excellent film.'

'Stuck-up so-and-so.' Pamela had overheard Betty's catty remark to Jack and Keith shortly afterwards, and Keith had followed it with a comment that Pamela had chosen not to repeat to Fred.

'Not to worry – it won't be long before Fred Miller gets his comeuppance,' he'd muttered.

What had Keith meant by that? Perhaps it had been an empty threat or maybe there was more to it. Pamela had decided to keep her eyes and ears open on Fred's behalf. Meanwhile, she intended to follow her father's advice to put up and shut up.

Arriving at the sector post, Pamela was greeted by Connie with the words, 'Do you want the good news first or the bad news?'

'Wait! Don't tell me – you've discovered the name of Susan's mother.'

Connie drew her inside. 'No such luck. Anyway, it's nothing to do with that. Give her my good news,' she prompted Kenneth, who stood behind the counter with the telephone receiver in his hand.

'HQ has confirmed Connie's position as the new head warden here,' he reported. 'She takes over on Monday night, after I move on to Tennyson Street.'

'It's true.' Connie allowed herself a satisfied smile. 'The news just came through.'

'I put in a good word.' Kenneth was keen to let them know that he'd played his part. 'I said Connie Bailey has her faults but when push comes to shove she's one of the best ARP wardens in Kelthorpe.'

'Congratulations!' Was hugging allowed whilst on duty? Pamela wondered. Dash it, yes – Connie's promotion merited a quick embrace.

'Steady on!' Connie protested as she disentangled

herself and straightened her ski cap. 'The bad news is that a message came through from report and control. Tell her about that, Kenneth.'

'Yes. Not good, I'm afraid.' Kenneth dialled a number that would connect him to David Drake, head warden on North Street. 'Weather outlook tonight is set fair. There'll be little or no cloud cover. Jerry's bound to take advantage.' He waited until David lifted the receiver at his end. 'Gas Street here,' Kenneth said briskly. 'We're on high alert. I repeat: high alert. Enemy aircraft have been spotted a hundred miles offshore, heading this way.'

# CHAPTER EIGHT

Gloves, rubber boots, eye shield, rattle . . . Pamela made ready for her night-time patrol.

Torch, first-aid supplies, gas mask . . . Connie hastily followed suit.

At his desk, Kenneth ordered a messenger to pedal like hell to warn the fire watchers posted on roofs around his sector that Jerry was on his way; number and types of aircraft as yet unknown. Heinkel He 111s, Dornier Do 317s, Focke-Wulfs or the dreaded Messerschmitt Me 262s; the list of deadly possibilities went on and on.

In the back room, Pamela and Connie quickly strapped on their helmets, hoping against hope that the Luftwaffe would give Kelthorpe a miss tonight.

'Not that it would be fair to wish an attack on any other poor beggars,' Connie said through gritted teeth.

'True,' Pamela agreed. The butterflies in her stomach refused to settle as she followed Connie out on to the street. Kenneth's orders were for them to patrol the area from Gas Street, along Park Road and on through the old town as far as St Stephen's dock. They were to stick together and in the event of an incident, one was to report back to the sector post without delay. The other was to stay at the scene and direct operations until a trained incident officer arrived.

'You remember what the old ARP recruitment poster said? "Serve to Save".' Connie's face was unusually serious as she and Pamela set off along Park Road, skirting the edge of the famous Leisure Gardens. It was a wide road, with iron railings and a high laurel hedge to the park side and a row of superior, three-storey terraced houses to the other, all observing the blackout and showing no signs of life. So far there was no siren and still no certainty that Kelthorpe was the intended target. 'Well, we did what the poster said; we volunteered, and look where it got us: tramping the streets in the pitch dark in the dead of winter, ready to be blown to bits or burned to a cinder by Firebomb Fritz.'

'You're not saying that you wish you hadn't signed up?' Pamela couldn't believe Connie was serious. True, there was no glamour attached to the job of air raid warden and they received little thanks for the routine, day-to-day work they undertook – from gas mask fitting to the digging of Anderson shelters and enforcing the blackout. And yet their role during an incident was vital. Connie must know this better than most, having shepherded countless local families to safety in various underground shelters and on one occasion having saved the life of a fire watcher trapped inside a burning building – the old municipal swimming baths on Elliot Street, to be exact. 'Come off it, Connie – you don't mean it.'

Connie craned her neck to scan the star-spangled

skies to the east. There was still no sign of enemy planes and the searchlights stationed along the beach remained switched off. There was an eerie silence and stillness; a sense of dread that mounted with each passing minute. 'No, don't mind me. It's been a bad week,' she said with a wistful sigh. 'I just long for the time when there'll be no need for any of this. I wish with all my heart that the lights could go on again all across poor old Blighty and we could have a normal Christmas.' Most of all, though she didn't say it, Connie wished that *Sea Knight* was safely anchored in the harbour and Tom was home in one piece.

'Yellow alert!' Pamela reacted to the sudden warbling sound of the siren as if she'd been stung.

Connie shrugged off her lethargy and leaped into action. They'd reached the park gates and there was a choice to be made – either to retrace their steps along Park Road to marshal residents and lead them to the nearest shelter on Gas Street or else to carry straight on to deal with dozens of panic-stricken cinemagoers who currently poured through the doors of the Savoy on to the pavement. 'The cinema first,' she decided. People were running around like headless chickens, darting off in every direction in search of shelter.

Taking out their rattles and swinging them mightily to make the loudest possible racket, Pamela and Connie raced to the rescue.

'Don't run. Stay together!' Connie instructed at the top of her voice. 'We have plenty of time.'

Pamela dashed after a small group of jittery girls and ordered them to rejoin the crowd at the cinema entrance. They jostled and cried out, clasping hands and infecting each other with their fear. 'Stay together!' Pamela repeated Connie's instruction. 'The office supplies warehouse next door has a cellar that we can use as a shelter – there'll be room for everyone.'

On-off, on-off; the siren warned of an imminent raid. The searchlights on the beach flashed on and their beams pierced the dark sky, criss-crossing and lighting up the bulk of the headland that loomed over the town.

*Yes, the cellar next door!* Connie instantly acted on Pamela's idea. She ran into the cinema's foyer, where she found the manager behind the glass partition of the ticket booth, frantically scooping the night's takings into a canvas bag. 'The key to next door, Mr Penrose – where is it kept?'

Penrose, with his tie askew and his jacket hanging open, seemed scarcely to know what was happening. He took up the bag of cash and looked around, wild-eyed, like a burglar seeking an escape route.

'The key!' Connie repeated. She recalled from her time as an usherette here that the office supplies foreman had agreed to allow access to his cellar in just such an emergency.

Penrose patted his empty waistcoat pocket with podgy, trembling fingers.

'Open the till, Mr Penrose!' Pamela had joined Connie in the foyer. 'That's where the key is kept.'

The petrified manager followed her instruction. Darting into the ticket booth, Connie snatched the key from his trembling fingers, then both girls sprinted back across the foyer to the assembled crowd.

'Follow me!' Connie directed her torch towards the warehouse and led the way.

Bringing up the rear, Pamela ushered the frightened group towards the windowless building. The wail of the sirens was still intermittent, meaning the countdown to red alert was continuing. When the same small group of terrified girls tried to make another run for it, Pamela went after them.

'Come along now,' she said as sternly as she could. The girls looked to be no more than fifteen or sixteen years old and all were dressed in light, brightly coloured jackets and high-heeled shoes that were the height of fashion but unsuited to the December weather. They shivered and skittered but fortunately did as they were told.

Meanwhile, Connie opened the warehouse door with the large iron key. Inside was a cold, cavernous space stacked high with metal shelving containing everything from typewriters and Xerox copiers to boxes of carbon paper, rulers, staplers and paper clips. Remembering a plan of the building's layout that she'd once been shown, Connie reckoned that the entrance to the cellar lay straight ahead. 'Single file,' she yelled as she unbolted the door, to be greeted by the fusty smell common to all cellars – a mixture of cold, damp stone, coal dust and decay. Fumbling for the switch, she turned on the light. 'One at a time, no need to push.'

She aimed this sharp reprimand at Penrose as he shoved from behind and tried to elbow his way past the bunch of frightened girls.

'You must wait your turn.' Connie pulled him to one side, recalling the pettiness he'd displayed when he'd been her boss. *Smarten yourself up, Mrs Bailey.*

*You're two minutes late. What's this I find – discarded sweet wrappers under the seats in Row E!*

Obedient courting couples filed by, followed by a few doddery Darby and Joans, then four strapping lads, all looking anxiously over their shoulders.

'What happens if Jerry flattens this building and the whole bloomin' lot comes crashing down on top of us?' One of the youths croaked a common fear.

'Bloody hell, we'll be buried alive!' His pal, a small, tough-looking lad with cropped hair and a pock-marked complexion, was about to turn tail until Pamela grabbed him by the collar.

'This is our best bet,' she advised. 'The cellar roof will withstand the blast from a high explosive and if the worst does happen and the building comes down, they'll send a rescue team to dig us out. All we have to do is sit tight.'

'Do as she says – she sounds like she knows what she's talking about.' And the nervous youth was dragged down the cellar steps by his mates.

The terrified girls followed, clutching each other's hands and stumbling as they went.

'Right; on you go.' Connie could scarcely control her contempt as she let go of Penrose's arm. 'But I'd keep that cash out of sight if I was you.'

The cinema manager stuffed the bulging bag into his jacket pocket. He was breathing heavily and his face was shiny with sweat, his owlish glasses slipping from the bridge of his nose as he descended the steps.

Connie and Pamela drew breath. They'd stayed calm and done a good job, but there was still work to be done. 'One of us should go back out and check that we didn't miss anyone, while the other takes a list of names,' Connie decided.

'You make the list.' Pamela was quick off the mark. She ran back through the dark warehouse and out on to the empty street, to the wail of sirens but as yet no sign of enemy aircraft. Then suddenly, seemingly without reason, the sirens ceased. Silence hung heavy in the air. The searchlights on the beach were switched off. All was dark and still.

Then a boy on a bike rode into view. He burst through the park gates, helmet low over his forehead, gas mask slung across his chest, going hell for leather and yelling at the top of his voice: 'All clear! All clear!'

Pamela's heart skipped several beats as she waved him down.

He squealed to a halt. 'False alarm!' he gabbled, his features alive with self-importance. *Listen to me! I bring glad tidings!* 'Good news – Jerry changed his mind!'

'Who says so?' Pamela could scarcely believe her ears, yet the thick silence of the night told her it was true.

'Report and control,' the boy informed her. 'They saw 'em on the radar heading north towards Whitby, every last one of 'em.' The triumphant messenger was eager to spread the good news. 'All clear!' he repeated as he set off from the kerb, pedalling for all he was worth and calling out in a high-pitched voice, 'False alarm, everyone! False alarm! All clear!'

'It happens sometimes,' Fred told Pamela. 'Our controller acted on the information coming in from the

Raby sector. Raby had picked up enemy aircraft on their radar and were obliged to alert us. It was their boys who charted the enemy advance. We couldn't afford to take any chances; it had to be yellow alert for thirty miles up and down the coast. Then we crossed our fingers and hoped for the best.'

He and Pamela were in her parents' sitting room, busily putting the finishing touches to Edith's Christmas tree – the job had been delegated to them because brushing against the pine needles brought her out in a rash. Edith and Harold, meanwhile, were in town shopping for coloured crêpe paper to make streamers to hang from the ceiling.

Pamela stood on a stool to thread lengths of silver tinsel between the prickly branches. 'It was panic stations outside the Savoy,' she reported. 'No one knew where the nearest shelter was until I remembered the cellar next door.'

Fred held her by the waist to steady her – an action that both knew wasn't strictly necessary. Feeling the sway and twist of her slender body, he was tempted to pull her off balance and into his arms.

'Hand me the star for the top of the tree, please.' She pointed to the box of decorations on a small table by the door.

'Oh, little star of Bethlehem,' he crooned as he gave her the glittery star. 'Are you sure you can reach?'

'I think so.' The stool wobbled as Pamela stood on tiptoe and she overbalanced – perhaps on purpose. Fred darted in to save her. And that was how they found themselves in a close embrace, his arms around her waist, her arms around his neck, pressed together in the gap between the tree and the bay window.

Their kiss was long, hesitant at first then deeper as he held her tighter still. It was a feeling that neither wanted to end.

'You know that I love you.' Fred was the first to speak, his lips against her cool, smooth cheek. 'Maybe too much,' he murmured.

She kissed away his last remark, then smoothed the frown line between his brows. 'I feel the same.'

'I always promised myself that I wouldn't let this happen; that I would steer clear of affairs of the heart for as long as the war lasted.'

'Until you met me,' Pamela said with a sweet smile followed by a shower of fresh kisses.

'Yes; in the end I couldn't resist.' He'd tried his best to keep his distance when Pamela had rented a room at his old lodgings on Elliot Street. The armour of politeness – please; thank you; after you; no, after you – had offered limited protection, however. Their eyes had kept on meeting over landlady Thora Mason's cold, lumpy porridge or during one of fellow lodger Cyril Fielding's drunken rants about Johnny Foreigner. And during air raids, before Pamela had joined the Civil Defence team, Fred had made sure that she was first into the cellar, where the landlady and her lodgers would see out the night playing draughts or games of gin rummy.

Over the weeks, the ice-cool civilities had thawed, especially when Fred and Pamela had discovered a shared love of reading. Then joint trips to the library had strengthened their bond and their conversations had become more intimate. He'd grown fascinated by her shy, demure smile and quick gestures – the light way she brushed her short curls from her cheeks when the wind caught them and the way colour suffused her cheeks when she was embarrassed or uncertain. One Sunday, when the scarlet tulips had been in full bloom, he'd invited her to walk in the Leisure Gardens with him, then a few days later they'd gone on a cycle ride up to the folly. It was there they had shared the inevitable first kiss that had come as no surprise to either of them. And that was it – what was the English phrase? Fred Miller had fallen hook, line and sinker for Pamela Carr.

He loved her and she loved him.

'There's something I have to tell you.' Stepping back from the Christmas tree, and making the delicate glass baubles shake and tremble as he brushed against its branches, Fred drew Pamela into the middle of the room. The flickering fire cast shadows across her eager face – soft lips, warm cheeks, bright and beautiful eyes. And now he must spoil that with his latest piece of news.

'Let me guess – you can't spare the time to sing carols with us after all?' Knowing how busy Fred was, this was a disappointment that Pamela was prepared to bear.

'Well, I'm afraid that's true.' Another frown creased his forehead. 'But that's not it.'

'What then?' If not the carol singing, then perhaps he wished to back out of the ordeal of the Carr family Christmas dinner, or perhaps it was connected with Fred's important work at the report and control centre? Various dark clouds appeared on Pamela's sunny horizon.

'I received another note,' he mumbled, as simply and directly as he could. There; he'd said it. He broke hands with her and looked down at the floor.

Not carol singing, not Christmas dinner, not Civil Defence work. A note! The short word bore a heavy weight.

'I found it on my desk at Anderson's,' he went on, eyes stubbornly down, refusing to look up. 'Unsigned, of course.'

'Ignore it, for goodness' sake!' Pamela's petulant tone made Fred turn away, but she caught his hand and tugged at it. 'I'm sorry. You caught me off guard. But try to follow your own advice: don't let it bother you.'

'Do you want to know what it said?' It had been yesterday, straight after the dinner break, that Fred had found the piece of paper. Something about the look of it had made him wary – the torn scrap had been carelessly folded and his name had been written with a blunt pencil in capital letters. Just 'MULLER' – the German form of his name – and nothing else until he'd opened it up and placed it flat on his desk, then read the words he dreaded: 'WE KNOW WHAT YOU ARE – YOU'RE A DIRTY GERMAN SPY. GET LOST OR ELSE!!'

'No.' Pamela dashed away hot tears with the back of her hand. 'I don't care what it says. *No one* cares.'

'On the contrary,' Fred sighed, 'the person who wrote the note obviously cares a great deal.' The misery on Pamela's face cut him to the quick. 'I'm so sorry, my love.'

'Don't be. It's not your fault. Anyway, what difference does it make?' She and Fred had dealt with such notes before – accusations of treachery, threats of violence. 'Uncle Hugh knows that you have a bona fide tribunal card from the Home Office. It states when your family came to England and how the Nazis destroyed your father's business in Berlin. Uncle Hugh vouched for you.' Pamela remembered the exact wording on the card – 'Muller bears an excellent character and there is no doubt as to his loyalty to this country. The Committee regards the alien as a genuine racial refugee whose being at liberty in no way constitutes a danger to the State.'

'I'm not afraid of losing my job at the timber yard,' Fred assured her. 'What bothers me is that some unknown person who works for your uncle still has it in for me. They want to get rid of me.' GET LOST OR ELSE! It was a pathetically worded threat, but dangerous all the same.

Pamela recalled with a sharp stab of fear what she'd heard Keith Nelson say about Fred getting his comeuppance. She blurted out her suspicion. 'Perhaps it's Keith. He objected when you challenged him over the stock list discrepancies.'

'Or one of his sidekicks.' Fred thought through the possibilities. 'He and Jack Watkins spend a good deal of time together.'

'And Betty as well,' Pamela reminded him.

'No – not Betty.' The clumsy handwriting didn't fit. 'The point is: this might only be the start. We both know that plenty of folk in Kelthorpe would turn against me if this were to get out. There's a well-organized group of vigilantes dedicated to rooting out fifth columnists, as they call them.'

'But why single you out?' Pamela clenched her hands into tight fists, trying to control the storm inside her head. 'You volunteer in report and control to help this country, for heaven's sake. And don't they realize that you hate the Nazis for what they did to your family and what they still do to Jews in the ghettos!'

'People don't need reasons.' Here was trouble, straight and fast as an arrow, headed Fred's way. 'Collar the lot!' had been Churchill's policy when the question of enemy aliens had been the hot topic at the start of the war. Many German Jewish refugees had been interned on the Isle of Man, as they had been during the Great War. A few had even been lined up in front of firing squads – take Corporal Josef Jakobs as recently as August this year: rounded up by MI5, convicted of being a Nazi spy, then shot. 'Once an idea takes hold, there's no logic behind what men – or women – will do.'

'Then we should tell Uncle Hugh,' Pamela decided. 'He'll put a stop to it right away.'

'If only it were that simple.' Fred had had time during a sleepless night to examine the problem from many different angles. True, one bad apple in the Anderson barrel could be tracked down and given fair warning – if further threats occurred, the culprit would be sacked. But a whispering war could be waged: rumours carried between zealots to whom any sniff of a German national in their midst was anathema. Word would travel beyond the confines of the timber yard – to dock workers, market traders and fishermen – then throughout Kelthorpe and beyond (perhaps it already had).

'Then what shall we do?' she pleaded. *Please, not again!* Memories of Fred's last attempt at flight flashed through her mind – a night attack, a red alert. Fred had parted from her at the entrance to the College Road shelter as bombs had dropped, setting fire to the town and turning the sky orange. Pamela relived her fear that he was gone for ever. And worse – those dreadful hours when the railway station had taken a direct hit and Fred had been buried alive under tons of rubble, unable to move, scarcely able to breathe, until a rescue team had heard his cry for help, then removed the debris brick by brick. Fred's face coated in a thick layer of dust; dirt and blood under his fingernails, with a shattered leg, but his will to live unbroken.

'There's nothing we can do except wait,' he said, opening his arms and inviting the comfort of an embrace.

She hugged him and closed her eyes to shut out the fire in the hearth, the box of glittering glass decorations and the outline of the Christmas tree against the fading light.

The relieved townspeople of Kelthorpe had woken to a crisp, clear morning. There was no wind and the sea was calm. The early morning bustle and raucous racket of the Saturday fish market had given way to a quieter hum of shoppers going about their business in the town centre – with less than two weeks to go before Christmas Day there was a run on bottles of sweet sherry at Varley's off-licence on Gladstone Square and on Airfix kits at Hodgson's toy shop on College Road. War games were also proving popular, along with tin helmets and soldiers' uniforms for patriotic little boys and nurses' outfits for girls.

By early afternoon, Pamela was out and about with Maureen, on the lookout at Pamela's insistence for warm underwear from Bentley's department store on Valley Road.

At first Maureen had resisted the invitation to go shopping, but her excuses had fallen on deaf ears. 'Of course a girl needs warm underthings – if you're not careful you'll freeze to death up in that attic room. And if you've run out of coupons, I have a few to spare. Bentley's is the place to go for winceyette pyjamas and liberty bodices, but we must be quick about it. Kathleen says that they're in short supply and are being snapped up fast.' Pamela had whisked Maureen out of the house, chattering all the while. 'Have you met Kathleen and Winnie yet? They share a room on my landing, directly below you – very nice girls once you get to know them. You already know Joan, of course.'

In fact, Pamela was relieved to be busy. The knot of anxiety she'd felt after the morning's conversation with Fred had stayed with her and she hoped the diversion of shopping with Maureen would take her mind off the latest threat. Besides, the new lodger brought out the mother hen in Pamela: the girl seemed so nervous and unsure of herself, determined to mask her undeniably pretty features with a flat, unbecoming hairstyle – a severe side parting anchored in place by several kirby grips – and bulky, mud-coloured clothes that did nothing for her.

'Branching out on your own can be frightening,' Pamela acknowledged as she and Maureen completed the purchases in Bentley's, then re-emerged on to Valley Road. 'I did it myself earlier this year – the first few days in your new lodgings are the worst: wondering if you can manage, whether or not you've done the right thing, and so on.'

A bus trundled by, followed by a man on a motorbike, then by an ARP rescue squad on their way to shore up what remained of the *Gazette* building on College Road. Three of the men hung out of the back of their lorry and waved and whistled at Pamela and Maureen as they passed by.

Embarrassed, Maureen tucked herself in behind Pamela.

'Tell me, where do you work?' Pamela pressed ahead with a topic that she hoped would draw Maureen out of her shell.

'Nowhere. I've applied for a job at the Corner Café on Gladstone Square.'

'I know the one.' The café was one up from a greasy spoon, used by off-duty PC Plods from the police station and by retired dock workers and traders from the fish market.

'I'm looking for other jobs too,' Maureen said with a hint of defensiveness, as if aware that the waitressing job was beneath her.

'Anything to keep the wolf from the door, eh?' Finding themselves at the end of College Road, Pamela fished for more information. 'What did you do before? How old are you, by the way?'

'I was at school. I'll be sixteen in February.' The brief answers were expressionless.

'Which school?'

'St Joseph's.'

'The same as me. I must have left before you arrived. Lord, that makes me feel old!'

Just then two familiar figures cycled into view – Arnold ahead in his Boy Scouts uniform, with Maureen's brother Colin bringing up the rear. Each had a pile of old newspapers strapped to the back of his bike – they were on their way to the paper collection depot on Maypole Street.

Pamela flagged them down. 'Don't forget carol singing practice this evening – five o'clock sharp,' she reminded them. 'We only have a few more sessions and we're nowhere near ready. Mr Greenwood is relying on you to be there, Arnold.'

'"Once in royal David's city".' He warbled his way through the first few lines to prove that he didn't need any coaching. '"Where a mother la-la-la!"'

'And you too, Colin.' Pamela remembered that he'd been absent from recent rehearsals. 'Promise you'll come.'

Colin narrowed his eyes and shot an uneasy glance at his sister. He seemed about to blurt something out but changed his mind. 'Get a move on,' he said roughly to Arnold, giving him a shove from behind.

So the boys cycled on without a word exchanged between brother and sister, which Pamela thought odd. Not for the first time, she wondered if there had been a bust-up over Maureen leaving home. Never one to pry, she tactfully avoided the subject until they came to Harrison's Bakery, where she suggested stopping for a chat with Connie and Lizzie. 'You'll like them,' she assured her companion, before tapping on the shop window without giving her time to object.

'Too late!' Connie exclaimed as she opened the door an inch. 'It's half-day closing, don't you know?' Jokingly she made as if to shut the door again, then she flung it open and allowed them to enter. 'Look what the wind blew in!' she called to Lizzie in the back room.

'Is there any news of Tom and Bill?' Pamela asked as Lizzie joined them.

'No, but no news is still good news as far as that goes.' Connie, like Lizzie, was permanently on edge. *Sea Knight* was due to dock at daybreak on Monday, depending on tides and weather conditions.

'And your dad?'

'No change there.' Lizzie glanced at Pamela's companion and tried to place her. The girl looked ill at ease, shifting from one foot to the other, clutching a parcel bearing the Bentley's logo and doing her best to fade into the background.

'Poor Fred has received another note.' Pamela spilled out her worries while Connie wiped down the counter and Lizzie emptied money from the till. 'The same nonsense as before: accusing him of being a spy – not signed, of course.'

'Oh, dear me.' Lizzie scooped coins into a bag. 'What will he do about it?'

'What *can* he do?' Pamela gave an exasperated sigh. 'I expect he'll try to ignore it, unless it happens again and then we might have to reconsider.'

'It's not fair after what he's already been through.' Aware of Pamela's restless companion hovering by the door, Connie indicated with a roll of her eyes that introductions were necessary.

'Oh, yes!' Pamela blushed at her lack of manners. 'Sorry. Connie Bailey, meet Maureen Strong. Lizzie Harrison . . . Maureen.'

Hands were shaken, details exchanged.

'Connie is due to take over as head warden of the Gas Street post.' Pamela filled an awkward silence. 'She'll be dishing out the orders and keeping us all in line. Lizzie drives an ARP ambulance and knows engines inside out, though you wouldn't think so to look at her.'

Maureen shook visibly under their scrutiny. Her face was pale and her hazel eyes held a silent plea for them to ignore her and to carry on their conversation as if she wasn't there.

'Will you be at carol practice this evening or are you on duty?' Pamela asked Lizzie.

'No, I'm free. Count me in.' Lizzie closed the till drawer.

'Sorry, I can't make it,' Connie said with a smile and a wink that showed she wasn't at all sorry. 'Duty calls.'

'Seriously?'

'I'm afraid so. And before that I want to find out from the WVS what's been happening as far as baby Susan is concerned. I was thinking of going up there in person rather than making a phone call. You can come with me, Pam, and protect me from Gladys Smallwood's baleful stare.'

Pamela was in no rush to accept Connie's invitation. 'Have there been any developments?'

Connie shook her head. 'Not a sausage. The affair is still a complete mystery – no one at the town hall had registered a baby girl of that name and likewise there were no Susans baptized at St Joseph's.'

'I know – Lizzie told me as much.'

'I even tried St Michael's in Raby and St Robert's – the Catholic church in White Sands Bay. It was no-go there as well.'

Three-quarters of the way through Connie's speech Maureen took a faltering step backwards. She leaned against the door, dislodging the 'Closed' sign from its hook and letting her parcel drop. Her heart thudded to a halt then fluttered back into life and raced unevenly. Her breath came short but she was desperate not to attract attention. 'No-go there as well' was the last phrase she heard before she stammered the words, 'No, please . . .' and slid to the floor in a dead faint.

Connie, Lizzie and Pamela had their backs turned. It was only when Lizzie glanced over her shoulder that anyone realized what was going on.

'What the heck . . . ?' Lizzie flew to Maureen's aid, crouching beside her and turning her on to her side before calling for a glass of water. 'And fetch my coat while you're at it,' she told Connie as she felt for a pulse. 'The poor girl is freezing and she looks half starved. Why, she's practically skin and bone. When did she last have something to eat?'

Pamela watched Connie place Lizzie's coat over a senseless Maureen. 'I saw her have half a slice of toast for breakfast – she said she wasn't hungry.'

Curled on her side, Maureen's eyelids flickered open and then shut again. She groaned softly, and a tear rolled down her pale cheek.

'Stand by with the water,' Lizzie murmured to Connie. 'Pamela, let's try to get her into a sitting position – gently does it.'

Slowly the two girls raised Maureen from the tiled floor. Lizzie placed the glass to her lips and encouraged her to drink while Pamela rearranged the coat around her shoulders.

Maureen sipped and tried to speak.

'Hush – nice and slow,' Lizzie cajoled.

The shock of cold water trickling down her throat made Maureen open her eyes wide. Three blurred faces stared at her. The room was bright and warm. Who were these people and where was she? She pushed away the glass, then raised her hands to her wet cheeks. Why was she crying? Snatches of memory like scattered shards of a broken glass slowly reassembled in her mind. The WVS had been mentioned, and so had 'mystery'. More words came back – 'name', 'baptized' and finally 'baby Susan'. With a despairing groan, Maureen moved her hands to cover her mouth.

'Oh, I say!' Realization dawned first for Connie, who took two steps back and shook her head. 'Surely not!'

Frowning, Pamela stood up slowly. Her mind followed where Connie's had led. Instinct told her it had to be true but reason argued differently. Maureen was a child – not yet sixteen. It wasn't possible.

*Ah yes. I see!* Without saying a word, Lizzie sat on the floor beside Maureen and put an arm around her shoulder. They need look no further for the mother of the abandoned baby – here she sat, pale as death, with tears streaming down her face, as desperate, lonely and forsaken as Connie had foretold.

# CHAPTER NINE

'My name is Susan. Please love me.' The note, the cardboard box, the cold, deserted porch – all made sense to Connie, Pamela and Lizzie as they gazed at Maureen and prepared to protect her from a hostile world.

Gently they put it to her and she didn't deny it: you must be Susan's mother. Sitting on the stool that Connie fetched from the back room and accepting more water, Maureen allowed Pamela to dab her tears with a clean handkerchief as if she lacked a will of her own.

'Better now?' Lizzie asked.

*Not better. Hollow. Numb. Lost deep in the Valley of Desolation.* Maureen bowed her head and closed her eyes to shut it all out – her fainting then coming round, the three blurred faces with dark, staring eyes, followed by the sharp torment of remembering the cardboard box that she'd placed in the porch and now the shocked expression of the tallest of the women as she made the glaringly obvious connection.

'You don't have to explain anything,' Connie assured her. 'And remember, we're not here to judge.'

'All we want to do is help,' Pamela added earnestly.

As Lizzie gestured for them to back away to allow

Maureen space to breathe, Pamela and Connie retreated behind the counter and watched anxiously.

'Connie's right – there's no need to explain.' Lizzie's voice was soft and low. 'We want you to know that you're not on your own, that's all.'

'Don't,' Maureen pleaded.

'Don't what?'

'Be kind.'

'Why ever not?'

'I don't deserve it.' Fresh tears came. 'I'm a bad girl. God won't forgive me.'

*What does God have to do with it?* At a warning glance from Lizzie, Connie bit her tongue. But she was angry at the sanctimonious so-and-so who had put this notion into the girl's head. Bloody unfair – she was little more than a child herself. Some unknown man – not to put too fine a point on it, most likely an unfeeling, unprincipled bastard – had taken advantage and ruined her, then walked away without a backward glance.

'Not bad, but very unhappy because of the fix you found yourself in,' Lizzie contradicted in the same soft tone. She began to understand why Maureen might have abandoned her baby in the grounds of the church. Burdened with guilt and feeling worthless, she must have decided to put her trust in the Almighty – praying that God would protect the tiny, innocent mite from harm. Suffer little children to come unto me – wasn't that what the Bible said? 'Was there no one to help you?'

Maureen sighed and shook her head.

'What about her mother?' Connie muttered to Pamela. After all, there was one in the frame – Nancy

Strong from the telephone exchange. 'Where is she in all of this?'

'I'm very sorry that you had to cope alone.' Lizzie squeezed the girl's hand. 'But you did your best to look after Susan until it all became too much – isn't that right?'

'No. They wouldn't let me look after her.' Maureen's face was contorted with misery. 'They said I couldn't – I wasn't old enough, and I was too stupid to know what to do.'

'Who's "they"?' Finding it impossible to stay quiet a moment longer, Connie came out from behind the counter and began to pace the floor.

'I'm not allowed to say. And you mustn't tell anyone.' A sudden panic replaced the pain of moments before. Maureen's eyes were wide with fear. 'Promise me you won't tell.'

Once more, Lizzie raised a hand to warn Connie not to interfere. 'We promise,' she said simply.

'People mustn't find out that it was me. I wouldn't be able to stay in Kelthorpe if everyone knew.'

Connie drew Pamela into the bakery, where they would be out of earshot. 'Something doesn't add up,' she said in a low, angry voice. 'How come there's no mention of a father? Why is Maureen taking all the blame?'

'It's obviously what she's been taught to believe – we all know it's the easiest thing in the world to make the girl the guilty one. Look at Adam and Eve – it's been happening for thousands of years. And Maureen's so young.'

'And impressionable, wouldn't you say?'

'Yes,' Pamela agreed. 'I wanted to take her under my wing the moment I saw her.'

'Picture the terrible state she must have been in.' Connie shuddered. 'Can you imagine dressing your precious little one in her knitted jacket for the last time and wrapping her up in a blanket, tucking her up in a cardboard box, writing a note and leaving her – walking away for good?'

Pamela fought back tears. 'No, I can't.'

'Maureen obviously cares about her baby.' Connie considered the tragic situation. 'Perhaps she gave Susan up even though she loved her because she wanted the bairn to have a better life than the one she could offer, given that her mother was no bloody help. Or maybe Nancy Strong or even the father forced her to do it – we just don't know.'

Pamela too grew thoughtful. 'We have to win Maureen's trust,' she decided. 'That means being patient and not pressing too hard for answers.'

Connie sucked air through her teeth. 'Patience isn't my strong point,' she pointed out.

'The first task is to get Maureen safely back home to King Edward Street. Do you think she's strong enough to walk?'

'No, but Lizzie can drive her there in the bakery van.' Connie sounded distracted. 'Do you know what else bothers me? Maureen talks about a mysterious "they" – "they said I was too stupid", and so on. That means there was more than one person telling her what to do.'

'Maybe the baby's father and Maureen's mother both played a part?' Pamela suggested.

'Perhaps, but my guess is that the father was long gone by then.' *Tinker, tailor, soldier, sailor . . .*

'The other question I want an answer to is: where

did Maureen live during the time she was pregnant?' Pamela tried to fill in the gaps. 'Did her mother keep her locked up in the house on North Street to avoid prying eyes?'

Pamela's question jogged Connie's memory. 'Wait a minute – don't I remember her brother saying that Maureen had been away but was back home and having endless arguments with their mother?' Yes, she was sure of it – when Connie and Tom had collared the little pests in the bandstand that day, this had definitely been one of Colin's sulky grumbles. 'I wish she'd stayed away' – those had been his very words.

'So Colin could tell us more if we ask him.' Then again, the lad had been behaving out of character lately – witness his absence from rehearsals. Pamela frowned at yet another conundrum.

The silence that followed was broken by Lizzie, who came into the back room to tell them that Maureen had accepted a lift home. 'She's not giving much away,' she admitted with a worried frown. 'In fact, she's clammed right up. But she promises to have something to eat when she gets home. I've popped a couple of teacakes in a bag for her.'

'I'll toast them and make sure she eats them with plenty of butter.' Pamela resolved to hand over the rest of her week's ration to help ensure that Maureen got her strength back.

For now it was the best they could do. So Pamela rode in the van with Lizzie and a silent Maureen, while Connie shut up shop for the day.

On the doorstep to the lodging house, Maureen hesitated. 'Remember – you promised not to tell,' she insisted as Pamela turned her key in the lock.

‘Not a word,’ Pamela agreed, while Lizzie made a U-turn and went back the way she’d come.

Maureen glanced up and down the street, trembling like a deer who had outrun a pack of hounds and was about to take cover in a thicket of thorns. Her eyes were wide, her breathing rapid and shallow.

‘Your secret is safe with me.’ Pamela led the way. The door closed behind them with a satisfying click. ‘I’ll make us a cup of tea and a toasted teacake,’ she said brightly. ‘Take off your coat and go into the living room where it’s nice and cosy. Read a magazine, make yourself at home.’

A grateful smile flickered across Maureen’s face. Her doubts and fears receded. Home was a sitting room with lumpy furniture, a threadbare carpet and a painting of mountains hanging in its gold frame on the chimney breast. Home meant warm underwear, hot tea and the miracle of kind words after months of insult and blame. She opened the door to a warm fire crackling in the grate, went to the window and pulled down the blind. Safe at last.

‘“Ding dong merrily on high, in heaven the bells are ringing . . .”’ *Not bad,* Pamela thought as she listened to the carol singers’ latest efforts. Despite several gaps in their line-up, they sang with gusto and more or less kept time.

‘That’s much better!’ Doug, too, was encouraged. Lizzie, in particular, had stepped up to the mark, her rich contralto rounding out the reedier notes of the ladies of the WI. ‘A few of you stumbled over “Gloria”, which is tricky, I admit.’ He tapped out the number of notes with his baton. ‘“Gl-o-o-o-o-o-o-oria”.’

A bored Arnold picked his nose. 'While Shepherds Watched' had kept him interested for a while, especially when he'd sneakily inserted his own version – 'While shepherds washed their socks by night' – and made his Boy Scout pals secretly titter. Now he sat cross-legged at the front and longed for merciful release.

But Doug was a hard taskmaster. 'Let's try one more time – if you please, Pamela.'

She played them in. '"Ding dong merrily on high . . ."' Her fingers flew over the smooth keys while her mind returned to Maureen, now quietly resting on her bed in her attic room. She'd seemed calmer when Pamela left, promising to get some sleep and not to venture out again until she felt stronger. '"Verily the sky . . . Hosanna in excelsis!"'

Doug conducted his singers through three difficult verses. His broad face was red with the effort and his baggy black jacket billowed, then spread like crows' wings as he raised his arms and waved his baton. '"Io-io-io . . . Glo-o-o-o-o-o-o-oria in ex-cel-sis!"' At the end of the carol he beamed with satisfaction. 'Thank you very much, one and all,' he said, reaching for a handkerchief and mopping his brow. The church hall boiler was pumping out a good deal of heat for once. 'I'm confident that we'll do St Joseph's proud this Christmas.'

'Can we go now?' Arnold was first to scramble to his feet while the grown-ups quietly congratulated one another and discussed the time for the next rehearsal.

Lizzie tapped her cousin on the shoulder. 'What's young Colin up to these days?' she enquired. 'This is the third practice in a row that he's missed.'

Arnold shrugged. 'How should I know?'

'All right, there's no need to bite my head off.' Lizzie collected her hat and coat from the stand by the door, then walked outside with Arnold. A freezing yellow fog lent a ghostly, gloomy aspect to the ancient graveyard, whose square black tombs and crooked crosses loomed through the mist as they made their way towards the gate. 'Has something happened at Colin's house?' she asked more pointedly.

Quick footsteps coming up from behind made them turn around.

'It's only me,' Pamela said as she hurried to catch up. 'Did I hear mention of Colin's name?'

Arnold gave an exasperated pop of his lips. 'Why's everyone so interested in 'im all of a sudden?'

'No reason,' Lizzie assured him. 'We're just a bit worried, that's all. He's normally so reliable. And you were with him earlier this afternoon – I thought you might know why he didn't turn up this evening.'

'No, I don't bloody know – all right!'

'Methinks the lad doth protest too much.' Overlooking the swear word, Lizzie adapted a phrase from Shakespeare and blocked her cousin's exit from the graveyard. 'Come on, Arnie – spill the beans.'

'All right, if you must know – Colin's mum won't let him out after it gets dark. She stopped him being a messenger cos it was too dangerous, and now she says he can't be a stretcher bearer neither. She locks him in his room to make sure.'

'Does she now?' Lizzie glanced at Pamela, who stepped in with another question.

'I take it Colin isn't happy about that?'

'He hates her,' came the blunt reply. 'He bunked off school to get his own back.'

This fitted well with what Lizzie knew. She remembered giving Colin a lift and him insisting on being dropped off in the centre of town. 'How often does he do that?'

'I 'aven't got a clue.' Arnold had said all he wanted to say. Now Barbieri's chip shop and a free bag of scraps beckoned. 'I'm starving,' he told them, sidestepping Lizzie and squeezing past her with his usual cheeky grin. 'See you later, alligator!' Ding-a-ling went the shop bell. 'In a while, crocodile!'

That night, unlike the one before, there was no false alarm. Connie was on solo patrol along St Stephen's dock when the red siren went off – no yellow warning had been given. *Surely not!* The fog tonight was a real pea-souper, with visibility down to just a few yards; Jerry wouldn't risk an attack on a night like this. Then again, this might give him the element of surprise.

She saw searchlights along the beach flash on and fail to penetrate the thick, smoke-clogged mist. Soldiers from the 39th Brigade were at the ready with their out-of-date anti-aircraft guns, waiting for the first bombs to drop. Two fire watchers sprinted along the dockside, scarcely breaking stride to warn her.

'Hit-and-run!' one yelled. 'A bleeding Dornier, spotted over Raby, heading this way.'

'Happy Christmas to you too!' The other man's ironic cry was swallowed up in a sudden roar of the approaching fighter plane's engines.

Connie clenched her fists in an effort to control the

rising panic. The best shelter lay some fifty yards ahead – a concrete bunker at the edge of Freeman's grain store yard. As she was deciding whether or not to follow the two men, Fritz released his canister of incendiaries. The container was designed to break open in mid-air and spill its stick bombs over a wide area. They fell in a deadly shower before Connie could reach the bunker . . . and still she hesitated, uncertain what to do. A dozen of the blasted things dropped near by, all hitting the ground at the right angle and erupting in sizzling white flames that would have been bright enough to blind her if she hadn't had the presence of mind to reach for her goggles to protect her eyes. Bravely she kicked the nearest bombs over the edge of the jetty into the water below, where they landed with a splash and fizzled out. But there were too many for one person to deal with, and by now the sky was lit up – flames had erupted from the roof of the grain store, leaving Connie and the fire watchers powerless.

There was a pause as the unseen enemy plane circled overhead. Waiting for it to return was almost worse than dodging the incendiaries – the lone pilot would undoubtedly fly in low, guns blazing, ready to release his high explosives over the dock. Connie was still stranded in the open, caught midway between the timber yard and the grain store. What to do? Which way to run?

'Follow us, love!' The fire watchers retraced their steps, dragging her with them. 'The bugger is dropping phosphorus pellets – they'll burn deep into your flesh if you cop one of them!'

The Dornier's engines grew louder – though they couldn't see him, they knew he was almost directly overhead. A hail of machine-gun bullets rattled against the metal side of Anderson's cutting shed and brick office buildings.

'Get down!' The leader of the fire watchers yanked Connie to the ground and made her lie face down on the cobbled jetty. The force of his action sent her helmet flying and she watched it roll out of reach. Terrified, she covered her bare head with both arms. Then there was an ear-splitting explosion. A blinding yellow light engulfed them. The water itself seemed alight and the ground was shaken as if by an earthquake. A hundred yards from where they lay, the grain store took a second direct hit. Bricks, steel girders and glass exploded in every direction, raining down on the jetty and into the water, missing Connie and the fire watchers by inches.

She lay inert for several seconds, only looking up when one of the fire watchers shakily raised himself to his knees. In the fierce blaze of a nearby stick bomb she saw through the slit in her goggles that the man's face was covered in soot and sweat and his helmet bore a deep dent from where a piece of shrapnel had struck. Bending over, he offered her his hand, then raised her to her feet and dusted her down. 'This'll be one to tell your grandkids,' he said with a wry grin. '"The night I survived Firebomb Fritz's scalded cat raid by the skin of my teeth."'

In the ops room at the town hall, Fred sat on his hard wooden chair amid the smell of fusty ledgers, wax polish and dust. There was a constant trill of telephones and the buzz of conversation as reports of the latest incident came in – Freeman's grain store had taken two direct hits from a lone raider. A single canister of incendiaries had resulted in widespread fires and severe damage to property. There was no report of casualties so far. On the wall behind Fred, a detailed map of the area was brought up to date by his controller, ARPO Ronald Atkinson. Across the small, crowded room, Hilda Fielding, the controller's second in command, filled in a siren report, recording earliest notice of the current attack while another girl leaned over her shoulder to identify St Stephen's dock as the exact location.

'Has there been any disruption of utilities?' In this atmosphere of intense concentration, Atkinson barked his question at Fred. 'Telephone lines, water mains, gas, electric?'

'No, sir.' Fred was confident of his reply. He'd been the one designated to intercept a messenger out at the front of the building and had been handed the area warden's detailed report. 'The only service we need to deploy is a fire crew.'

'What's access like?' Atkinson picked up a phone and shot another question across his desk.

'Difficult at the best of times,' Fred replied. He knew that the fire crew would have to approach via a narrow lane leading out of the market square. The only other access to Freeman's yard was by the privately built railway line shared with Anderson's that provided a direct link between the dockside and the major north–south rail network.

Nodding, Atkinson dialled a number. 'Send three small fire trailers to St Stephen's dock,' he ordered down the line. 'And get a fire boat down from Raby, just in case we need to tackle the blaze from the harbour.'

As measures to cope with the incident were swiftly

put in place, Fred sat forward in his chair in a state of high alert. He kept his hands hidden under his desk to control a sudden attack of the jitters and reminded himself to take several deep breaths.

'Is everything all right, Fred?' Violet Parsons, a telephonist who sat near by, swivelled in her chair to study his face.

'Perfectly all right, thank you.' Damn – his hands wouldn't stop shaking and he had to clench his teeth to stop them from chattering. A cold sweat had broken out on his forehead.

'You don't look it.' Violet was the motherly sort – the type who wore high-necked floral blouses and eau de cologne, and whose mousy brown hair was carefully permed and pinned back from her homely face. 'Why not take a quick break? I'll tell Mr Atkinson that you weren't feeling well.'

'No need, thank you, Violet. I'm quite well.' Desperate not to attract more attention, Fred managed to look busy by shuffling papers around his desk. Finding a badly written, pathetically worded threat on his desk at Anderson's had been troubling, but discovering another note here in the report and control centre, right in the heart of things, was altogether more serious.

He'd found it at the height of tonight's incident – typewritten on a pristine sheet of A4 paper. The wording had burned itself into his memory.

> MI5 is on to you, Muller. You may have fooled the Home Office but you can't fool us. Make no mistake – your days in Kelthorpe are numbered. Get out if you know what's good for you.

It had happened during the brief period when he'd been ordered outside to intercept the messenger's report. That was when the note had appeared – prominently positioned on his desk so it couldn't be missed. This meant that someone in this room was responsible.

Fred found that he was holding his breath as he stole surreptitious glances at the row of telephonists, all except Violet with their headsets on and their backs turned, then at Atkinson's deputy, Hilda Fielding, smart in her Civil Defence uniform with three narrow bars denoting her rank. But why should it necessarily be one of the women? Representatives for the police and the various rescue services also worked in the control room, in charge of coordinating the response to major incidents but at present gathered in a corner, twiddling their thumbs. These were men whom Fred scarcely knew – mostly older, self-important types, who were Kelthorpe born and bred; tradesmen and small business owners who sat on the town council. To a man, they took their voluntary Civil Defence work seriously, often vying for promotion within their various teams – Casualty, Engineer, Rescue, Police and Fire. Fred swallowed hard. Who in this group was capable of making such a threat? Or was it indeed one of the women? He transferred his gaze back towards the telephonists hard at work at their switchboards. One thing was certain – the threat to his safety was mounting.

# CHAPTER TEN

'"Deck the halls with boughs of holly,"' Lizzie trilled as she climbed a stile ahead of Connie and Pamela. '"Fa, la, la, la, la, la, la, la, la!"'

The previous night's fog had lifted and, in an attempt to put their troubles to one side, the three girls had made the most of a fine, clear Sunday morning to gather Christmas holly from the copse below Raynard's Folly. On the way up the steep, frosty hill, where trekkers still trudged on a nightly basis, Connie had recounted details of her narrow escape. 'It was just me and two fire watchers against a Dornier Do17,' she told them. 'Jerry was flying blind. He came straight at us out of the fog – our boys on the beach didn't have a hope in hell of bringing him down. Luckily for us he targeted the grain store, not the dock itself, which is where we found ourselves stranded.'

'I read in the *Daily Express* that Hitler's plan is to starve us into surrender by destroying our grain supplies.' Pamela was the next to climb the stile. She'd dressed for the bracing cold in a bright green knitted hat and scarf, teamed with her warm tweed coat and fur-lined boots. 'The Führer still believes he can break our spirits, but I heard on the wireless that it's not plain sailing for him. We sank another two Italian cruisers off the coast of Tunisia earlier this week.'

'I've stopped listening to the wireless on a Sunday,' Connie declared as she vaulted the stile and landed with a crunch in a frozen puddle. 'All you get is dreary music and gloomy sermons.'

'You should try Radio Hamburg.' Pamela made a beeline for the nearest holly bush laden with bright red berries, much to the annoyance of a territorial robin that flew off with a discordant chatter. 'I've been listening to Lord Haw-Haw recently and having a good laugh at his expense. Honestly, you've never heard anything so silly.'

'You mean the Humbug of Hamburg – he's supposed to be Hitler's secret weapon!' Connie poured scorn over the toffee-nosed traitor. Though the frost nipped at her fingers and she could see her breath emerging as clouds of steam, it felt good to be out in the fresh air making preparations for Christmas. 'Do you think Tom would appreciate me decorating his halls with boughs of holly?' she asked with a suggestive wink.

'Hush!' Lizzie gave her a hefty shove sideways. 'There are innocents abroad.'

'Why, what's wrong with that?' Connie was suddenly all wide-eyed innocence. 'We can both fill the mead cup and drain the barrel once Tom and Bill get back – fa, la, la, la! – that's all I'm saying.'

Pamela took Connie's playful teasing with good grace. 'I bet you can't wait.'

'They'll be home in less than twenty-four hours.' Lizzie, like Connie, was focused on their return. 'I say, why don't we all get together tomorrow night – me and Bill, Connie and Tom, you and Fred?'

'Yes. By the way, where is Fred? I thought he was meant to come with us this morning.' Connie got to work with a pair of secateurs, choosing sprigs with the most berries. The sharp tool from their father's allotment shed made a satisfying snip each time it sliced through a woody stem.

'He backed out at the last minute.' Pamela had been surprised by a knock on the front door at eight o'clock. She'd run downstairs to answer it. 'You're early,' she'd told Fred with an embarrassed smile – she hadn't brushed her hair and was without a scrap of make-up. 'But don't wait outside in the cold. Come into the sitting room.'

'No, I won't, thank you.' He'd looked awkward and had avoided her gaze. 'I'm sorry. I have to give back-word for this morning – I'm afraid something came up.'

He hadn't offered any further explanation and Pamela had felt let down. 'Never mind. It can't be helped,' she'd said a touch huffily, and they'd parted company on that unsatisfactory note.

Looking back, she wished she'd dug deeper. Fred's behaviour had unnerved her, and now that she thought about it, this was exactly how he'd been when the first round of threatening notes had dropped on his doormat. Had something else happened since he'd found the recent one on his desk at work? Naturally he'd been worried but he had at least included her and they'd managed to talk it through. He certainly knew that she would stand by him through thick and thin. So what was different this morning? Why had he been so unforthcoming?

'Is he poorly?' Connie asked, stepping back to examine the higher branches of the holly bush. The glossy, dark green leaves gleamed in the sunlight and clusters of berries shone scarlet against an achingly blue winter sky.

'I don't think so.' Pamela's frown was uncertain but she gave herself a shake, then got down to business.

Soon the girls had gathered as much holly as they could carry. They divided the prickly bunches equally, then tied them up with string. By mid-morning they were heading down the hill with their seasonal spoils before splitting up at the edge of town – Connie intending to visit Bert at the Queen Alexandra, while Pamela hurried home to keep Maureen company and Lizzie headed for Bill's harbourside cottage. 'To deck the halls,' she called cheerfully as they said their goodbyes.

Lizzie's route took her past St Joseph's church, where worshippers trickled out after the morning service. Spotting Pamela's mother in her fur-trimmed coat and hat, she gave a friendly wave that was returned in queenly fashion. Among the congregation there was a smattering of older townsfolk whom Lizzie also recognized – three elderly Christmas carollers from the WI and Gladys Smallwood with a companion, both dressed in their green WVS uniforms. As the two women shook hands with the vicar, Terence Ibbotson, in the church porch, Lizzie caught a glimpse of Doug in his churchwarden's role, busily gathering hymn books and stacking them on the back of a pew just inside the church door.

'I say – Miss Harrison, isn't it?' Gladys approached in a determined manner.

Lizzie waited for her to march down the path and through the lychgate, leaving her companion trailing behind.

'I have news for you about the abandoned child that your sister brought to us,' Gladys declared as she emerged on to the pavement.

'Good news, I hope?' It seemed from Gladys's self-satisfied expression that this was the case.

'Excellent, in fact. Barring any untoward hitches, such as the discovery of Susan's biological mother, a couple with no children of their own and currently living in White Sands Bay has expressed an interest in adopting her.'

'Oh, you don't say.' Lizzie hoped that her face didn't convey the disappointment she felt. She forced a pleasant smile, all the while dreading how Maureen would react to the news.

'Yes, very respectable people – he works as a pharmacist in a chemist's shop in Easby, and she's a housewife and a member of White Sands Bay WI. They've been on our list of would-be adoptive parents for quite some time.'

'I'll let Connie know,' Lizzie promised.

'There are still i's to dot and t's to cross, but it looks promising.' Gladys had hoped for a more enthusiastic response. 'It's a perfect match,' she insisted. 'Not all abandoned babies are so fortunate.'

'I'm glad for her.' *But sad beyond words for Maureen*. It was impossible for Lizzie to pretend otherwise.

Lizzie's muted reaction resurrected Gladys's earlier suspicions. 'Your sister . . .' she began, then hesitated.

'What about her?' Straight away Lizzie's guard was up.

'Does she really know nothing of Susan's origins?'

'Of course she doesn't,' Lizzie snapped back. 'It was pure chance that she came across her.'

A frowning Gladys redoubled her efforts. 'Perhaps she had a friend who'd got herself into trouble?' The stress on the word 'friend' was heavy with insinuation.

*Too much!* Lizzie fizzed with fury. 'Girls don't get themselves into trouble, Mrs Smallwood – men queue up to do that for them,' she said bluntly. 'In any case, it doesn't seem to have occurred to you that my sister deserves thanks for what she did that night. If it hadn't been for her, the baby might have frozen to death.'

'Quite so.' Stepping back from confrontation, Gladys beckoned to her colleague. 'Let's agree that all's well that ends well and leave it at that.'

Lizzie was still fuming as she watched the two women walk away. She hadn't had time to recover before Colin came down the path accompanied by a fair-haired woman wearing a purple coat that was nipped in at the waist and a brimless black hat with a delicate veil that covered her eyes and forehead. Ah, yes – Lizzie recognized the well-dressed woman from the bus stop on North Street.

Seeing Lizzie, Colin fell two steps behind until his mother grabbed him roughly by the jacket sleeve and shoved him ahead of her.

'Don't dawdle, Colin. You're getting in people's way.' She smiled apologetically at Doug, who had hurried after them and almost crashed into them.

'Mrs Strong, the very person!' Doug's tone was hail-fellow-well-met. He spoke firmly and confidently. 'A little bird tells me that you've been keeping young Colin away from choir rehearsals.'

Nancy Strong bristled but didn't deny it. She let go of her son's sleeve to fix her shiny black handbag more firmly in the crook of her arm. 'That's true, Mr Greenwood. I trust the same little bird informed you that I'm keeping him at home as a punishment.'

The warden pressed his lips together in an obvious attempt to remain civil. 'That's a great pity. We were relying on Colin to swell the ranks. What has he done wrong, if I may ask?'

'You may not.' Nancy didn't bother to return the courtesy. 'I intend to keep him in and that's that.'

*Now there's a woman I wouldn't want to cross.* Lizzie imagined describing the scene later to Connie and Pamela. *An iron fist is hidden beneath that velvet glove of hers.*

'I see.' Doug was down but not out. Spying Lizzie on the pavement, he beckoned for her to join them.

'Hello, Doug. Hello, Colin – long time, no see.' Lizzie breezed up to the small group, ignoring the sullen look on the boy's face and his mother's pent-up irritation.

'I was wondering if, between us, we might persuade Mrs Strong to reverse her decision banning Colin from carol singing next week.' Douglas banked on his own bombast and on Nancy Strong's reluctance to make a scene.

Lizzie's response was wary. 'What do you want me to say?'

'Best to keep out of this,' Colin's mother muttered out of the corner of her mouth. Her voice was light and narrow, with little evidence of a Yorkshire accent.

'Perhaps you could vouch for the boy's impeccable behaviour during rehearsals.' Doug's confidence started to falter. 'Then perhaps Mrs Strong might relent.'

'Then again, she might not.' Nancy stood her ground and treated Lizzie to a defiant glare. *Argue with me at your peril.*

'Does Colin still want to come carol singing?' Lizzie thought to ask. *No, he wishes he was invisible, more like.* The boy's round face was partly hidden behind a thick woollen scarf, but a deep red flush crept on to his cheeks as the discussion continued.

'What Colin wants has got nothing to do with it. What I say goes in our house.'

Lizzie was in no doubt that this was the case. After all, this was a woman who'd refused to help her daughter in her hour of greatest need. 'Fair enough,' she conceded quietly. 'I'm sure Mrs Strong has her reasons.'

Doug blinked back his disappointment. 'As you wish,' he murmured.

'You may as well know that I'll be taking Colin out of the Scout group as well.' Nancy's gaze didn't waver. 'I insist that he concentrates on his schoolwork from now on.'

'That's commendable, I'm sure. But Colin is one of our best Scout messengers. Why, he recently won a gallantry award.'

'Precisely.' Nancy raised her chin and squared her slight shoulders. Her thin veil fluttered as she spoke. 'What you and your like don't seem to realize, Mr Greenwood, is that this is a man's war, not one that should be fought by boys,' she insisted coldly. 'I've lost my husband to the war effort and I refuse to risk my son's life too.'

*Fair enough again.* In spite of Lizzie's unfavourable

first impressions, she had to admit that Nancy Strong had a point.

Bowing his head in defeat, Doug retreated to the church porch, where he joined the vicar in earnest discussion of the morning's sermon – 'Not too long, I hope?' 'By no means; most concise and to the point.'

'We carol singers will miss you, Colin.' Lizzie poured oil over troubled waters as she accompanied him and his mother through the gate. 'But be a good boy and do as your mum says, do you hear?'

He shot her a look. They were doing *Julius Caesar* at school – *Et tu, Brute?*

Nancy, however, had the grace to thank her unexpected ally. 'You may consider me harsh, Miss . . . ?'

'Harrison – Lizzie.'

'Miss Harrison, but my son must learn his lesson the hard way,' she said with a sigh. 'It's difficult enough trying to make ends meet on my telephonist's wage and a small widow's pension, without having to worry myself sick about what Colin gets up to behind my back.'

'It's a lot to cope with,' Lizzie agreed. They walked slowly along the street, past the church hall and on along College Road. Nancy held her head in the air, seemingly oblivious to the bombed buildings and signs warning of danger; meanwhile, Lizzie stole quick glances at a silent Colin.

'Do you have children?' Nancy asked conversationally. 'No, of course not – you're far too young.'

*I'm seven years older than your daughter, and look what's happened to her*. The thought darted to the forefront of Lizzie's brain but she managed to keep it to herself. 'I have a sweetheart,' she confessed.

'Of course you do – you're a pretty girl. You must have boys falling at your feet. What's his name?'

'Bill Evans. He's a trawlerman, but his boat has recently been requisitioned by the Patrol Service.'

'Bill Evans? I knew his mother, May Barlow as was.' Nancy stopped opposite Lizzie's bakery shop, outside the ruins of the *Gazette* building, to indulge in a few moments of nostalgia. 'May and I were in the same class at school – and there's no need to look so surprised.'

Lizzie added up the years. Bill was twenty-five, and even if his mother had had him early, it put Nancy's age at well above forty – much older than she looked. Only on close inspection did Lizzie see that the judiciously positioned veil covered a few shallow worry lines on her forehead and wrinkles at the corners of her blue eyes.

It was as if Nancy had heard the click of abacus beads. 'I married much later,' she explained. 'Bill was already ten years old when I had Maureen, and by then May and Harry Evans were long divorced.'

Lizzie took a quick, sharp intake of breath. Nancy's voluntary mention of her daughter's name had created an opening that couldn't be ignored. 'Maureen has found lodgings with a pal of mine on King Edward Street,' she said as casually as she could.

'So I believe.' Nancy raised her eyebrows at Lizzie, then stared into space. 'She's been living away from home for quite some time.'

'In Axenby, I believe?'

'You believe correctly.'

Lizzie swore later that she heard the key turn in the lock and the no-entry sign go up. 'I mentioned the village where Maureen had been living and that was it – I knew for a fact that I wouldn't get another peep out of her.'

'What else did you want to know?' Pamela would ask.

'Where exactly in Axenby? Why there?' Lizzie would reel off a whole list of queries. 'Maureen refuses to talk about it so I was hoping her mother might.'

'Not a cat in hell's chance.' Connie would hit the nail on the head as usual. 'Young Colin might, though, if we play our cards right.'

Lizzie and Connie rose before dawn the next day, then walked from Elliot Street to the harbour. Neither had eaten a scrap of breakfast.

'Nervous?' Connie asked as they seated themselves on the bench outside Bill's cottage. *Silly question – we're both on tenterhooks here.*

'As a kitten,' Lizzie confessed. She'd scarcely slept for thinking of this moment. The dark night had crawled by, punctuated in the early hours by the rattle and whir of an electric milk float along the cobbled street and the clink of bottles delivered to the doorstep.

Their Aunty Vera and her best friend Ivy Cooper had been persuaded to look after the bakery in their absence. 'It'll only be for a few hours,' Connie had assured them. Ivy had baking experience, having worked for Bert before her marriage, and Vera was rock-solid in her loyalty to her brother and his two girls. '*Sea Knight* is due to dock at eight o'clock. We should be back at work by midday.'

'Pooh – take your time.' Vera had swiped the air nonchalantly with the back of her hand.

Ivy had followed it up with, 'Yes, why not have the whole day off?'

Lizzie and Connie had replied with a rapid and excited, 'Ta, that would be champion,' and a simultaneous, 'The whole day it is, then!'

So now the sisters sat and shivered on the chilly bench as a weak sun rose with a pale pink glow over the watery horizon and black-headed gulls wheeled and shrieked over the harbour. A few silent trawlermen transferred nets and lobster pots from jetty to boats and vice versa – gnarled, stooped sailors in their sixties and seventies dressed in oilskins and rubber boots. They went about their daily grind as they had for decades, ignoring the restless brown waves that rocked their sturdy wooden boats and slapped continuously against the stone jetty. Further out to sea, toy-sized battleships criss-crossed the bay.

For Connie, the days of separation from Tom had been grim but bearable. She'd only had to picture him in her mind's eye to calm her nerves. Yes, life at sea was harsh and the dangers of minesweeping were all too real, but if Connie had concentrated hard she'd been able to visualize Tom's clear gaze and to hear his deep, soothing voice; to recall as if he were there in the room his fond way of looking at her and catching her by the hand before enclosing her in a warm, strong embrace – her Tom, the settled centre of her world.

For Lizzie, on the other hand, Bill's departure on his minesweeping mission had filled her with a dread that had continued to plague her. Most of the time she'd lived on her nerves, jumping at every little sound and finding it hard to concentrate as she'd driven the bread van and delivered orders. Constantly in her mind was *Sea Knight* ploughing through mighty waves with depth-charge racks to port and starboard, a mechanical sweep towed behind. And always, during every minute of Bill's absence, there had been the possibility of his boat suddenly encountering a sinister U-boat or sighting a deadly contact mine – its black orb bobbing towards the boat, knowing that one fatal touch of those horns and all would be over.

Her father's relapse hadn't helped matters – yet again Lizzie's stomach had tied itself in knots as they'd waited for the doctor's verdict. As for poor Maureen's pitiable situation – Lizzie's natural cheerfulness had been badly dented by what she'd observed. To be so alone and desperate, to be cast out and left to fend for yourself by a cold-hearted mother and to have to hide the truth from an unforgiving world – surely it was a burden that was too hard for any girl of fifteen to bear.

Now, though, Lizzie's whole focus was on the horizon. As bands of light cloud gathered over the headland, she fixed her gaze far out to sea, where the choppy water glinted restlessly in the sunlight. She was startled by a motor launch making a noisy exit from the harbour. Its engine coughed into life and it cut through the dark water, leaving a narrow white wake behind. Then an old-fashioned, flimsy biplane – possibly a Gipsy Moth – flew clumsily across the bay from south to north, put to shame by the effortless acrobatics of the gulls as they used air currents to soar and dive.

'There!' Connie said suddenly. She pointed to a

small flotilla rounding the headland to the north. It was led by a fully armed Royal Navy destroyer with HMS *Intrepid* emblazoned along its prow, a much larger and more imposing vessel than the two trawlers in its wake. The *Intrepid* and one of the fishing boats followed a straight course across the bay; the other split away and headed for Kelthorpe harbour.

'It's them!' Connie cried.

*At last!* Lizzie jumped to her feet and ran along the jetty. Yes, it was brave little *Sea Knight*; and there was Bill, waving with all his might, with Tom next to him and the Royal Naval Reserve man at the wheel. The same wind whipped around Lizzie and Connie, practically lifting them off their feet. They felt the sting of cold, salty spray on their faces and hands.

The chug of the engine grew louder; Bill's face was grinning broadly as he and Tom stood ready, mooring ropes in hand.

'Welcome home!' Connie cupped her hands around her mouth. Her heart leaped as a gust of wind tugged at the woollen scarf around her neck. Tom waved back – a single, slow sweep of his arm. Joy, pure and simple.

'We brought back a load of Swedish ball bearings disguised as butter.' Tom entertained Connie with one of the less hair-raising aspects of his five-day tour of duty. 'I know; it beggars belief.' They sat on the rug in front of a roaring fire in his North Street digs, saying little but savouring every moment. She kept touching his face to prove that he was really there.

'Why ball bearings?'

'Lord knows. There must be a shortage and they're

classed as vital supplies.' What Tom didn't tell Connie was that their small fleet had been subjected to three separate dive-bomber attacks. On one occasion, Bill had been at the wheel, calling for full steam ahead while he played cat and mouse between fifteen-foot waves to avoid cannon shells fired from a Focke-Wulf 190. They'd survived thanks to Bill's skill, but the next day one boat in their convoy had taken a direct hit: a shell had splintered her wooden hull and she'd sunk like a stone before the crew had time to take to their lifeboat. Luckily, *Sea Knight* had been able to fish two of them out of the drink but two other poor devils had drowned.

'In the old days it was whisky and rum that they smuggled in, not ball bearings.' Connie snuggled closer to him.

'I know; not very romantic, eh?' Tom thrilled to the feel of her soft hair as she leaned forward to tend to the fire and a long strand brushed against his cheek. 'Not like this is.' He meant the warm fire, Connie's face glowing in the firelight, the cosy nest of his room that she'd decorated with sprigs of Christmas holly, and most of all the weight of her body resting against him.

She turned her face towards him and stared at him for a long time. Every contour was familiar – the sweep of his cheekbones, the deep set of his grey eyes, the high forehead and the square angle of his jaw. He was all she needed, all she desired.

'How about you?' he murmured between kisses. 'What have you been up to?'

'Oh, you know, the usual: baking, visiting Dad, patrolling the streets.'

'Have you rescued any more abandoned babies?'

'No – one is more than enough for the time being.' Connie kept her word to Maureen by not revealing the identity of Susan's mother.

'And what about the choir?'

'Limping on without its star singer. Doug wants us to start proper carolling this Wednesday, on the streets of the old town. Will you be able to join us?'

Tom shook his head. 'No, I'll be back out at sea with the RNPS.' Seeing her look of alarm, he went on quickly. 'But home again in time for Christmas.'

Connie's heart missed a beat, then settled into its normal rhythm. 'We'd better make the most of our time, then.'

Her face was so close to his that he could only see her indistinctly. 'What do you propose?'

She slid her arms around his neck. 'We've got a whole day ahead of us before I start my shift at Gas Street.'

'Well then,' he murmured, 'let's celebrate your promotion to head warden.'

Connie frowned. 'I prefer not to go out. I'd rather stay here with you.' Close to the flickering fire, with the blind pulled down and with their arms and legs entwined.

'Who said anything about going out?' Tom shifted his weight until he lay on top of her, then he kissed her tenderly before pulling his head back. 'Yes?'

'Yes.' A hundred, a thousand times yes. She kissed him back. They had both courted danger and were safe in each other's arms. War held them in its grasp but their hearts and bodies were whole.

*

'Have you ever been in love before?' Lizzie was nervous about Bill's answer. 'No, wait – do I really want to know?'

'Why ask me, then?' She was a funny girl – skittish as a colt, prone to sideways jumps then heading off in a direction Bill least expected.

'All right – you can tell me.' She turned from staring out of his living-room window at the fishing boats sailing in and out of the harbour to look directly into his eyes.

'You go first.' Bill was confident that it was him she loved now and that was all that mattered. He was in the mood to tease her and watch her blush. 'You must have been in love with Bob Waterhouse – you were engaged to him for Lord knows how long.'

'That was different.'

'How?' Here came the blush and the averted gaze, right on cue.

'It just was.' Lizzie stared out of the window once more. 'I'd known Bob since we were at school.'

'"Romeo, Romeo . . ."' Bill kept his distance and bided his time. Five days at sea hadn't altered his feelings. If anything, they'd made him love Lizzie more.

'It *was* different,' she insisted. 'Bob didn't treat me as if I was his equal. He wanted to make all the decisions and he could be a bit of a stick-in-the-mud. But he wasn't unkind.'

Bill came up behind her and lowered his head until his chin rested on her shoulder. 'You're off the hook – I'm only kidding.'

'I want you to know something.' Lizzie turned towards him. 'Bob and I . . . we never . . . you know . . .'

'I do know.' He stopped her with a kiss. 'All right, since we're being serious, the answer to your question is no, I never loved a girl before I met you. I went out with plenty but none of them meant much to me. And don't look at me like that – I never led any of the girls on or pretended that I was going to marry them or anything.'

'So you loved them and left them? Bill Evans, you ought to be ashamed, leaving a trail of broken hearts from Raby to White Sands Bay.'

The tables were turned: the teaser had become the teased. 'Not on purpose. The thing is, this feeling is new to me. I'm not sure how to deal with it.' He'd thought about the subject a lot, during snatched hours aboard *Sea Knight* when he should have been resting. Lizzie had got in the way of sleep – either he'd lain half awake in his narrow bunk, worrying about her in case she drove the Bedford into another crater, or else he'd nodded off and seen her in his dreams, in one of her floaty summer dresses, with bare legs and arms, her dark hair loosely tied back as she walked a cliff path or sat by a rock pool on the beach. 'I don't know what's happening to me,' he confessed.

'No, but it feels right, doesn't it?' Lizzie didn't know how else to describe it. Easy and relaxed? Yes. Thrilling, painful at times to be this much in love, but full of happiness and hope? Yes. It was like living a heightened existence, like being the main characters in a romantic film where every gesture and every glance spoke volumes.

'You mean the world to me, Lizzie. You know that?'

She answered him with a lingering kiss.

'Do you ever look ahead to what we might do after the war has ended? Would you still want to get away from Kelthorpe?'

She thought long and hard before she answered. 'It's not so much the getting away – I love this town and I love Dad and Connie too, so I would always want to come back. It's what there is to see and explore out there in the rest of the world that draws me.'

'Australia, Canada, America, the South Seas.' Bill began an ambitious list of his dream destinations.

'Niagara Falls, the Grand Canyon, the Rocky Mountains.'

'Do you think we'll ever get there?' he asked wistfully.

'We could always work our passage.' Turning a dream into a reality wasn't impossible when you did it with the person you loved. 'Dad and Aunty Vera have a brother called Arthur who stowed away on the *Queen Mary* and sailed to America in the twenties. It was the Depression; he made a new life for himself in Chicago. Now he has a wife and three children.'

'Wouldn't it be grand?' A brighter, more colourful future beckoned.

'Yes, and what's to prevent us?' Once the world had stopped fighting and harmony was restored.

'Nothing.' Bill held Lizzie close. 'Not if we went with your family's blessing by travelling as man and wife.' Had he meant to say it this way? Did it sound how he intended? Should he have gone down on one knee? 'If you wanted to, that is.'

Lizzie broke free and stared at him in wordless astonishment.

Damn; he ought to have phrased it better and not sprung it on her without warning. What if she said no? Bill tried again. 'Will you marry me, Lizzie Harrison? Say yes and make me the happiest man alive.'

# CHAPTER ELEVEN

'What's up, love?' Harold took Pamela to one side. He'd been watching her all morning, noticing how on edge she'd seemed when she'd come into the main office with a query about a tricky piece of correspondence and how little she'd had to say for herself during their dinner break. Fred, too, had been unusually uncommunicative. 'Is it a lovers' tiff, by any chance?'

'No, nothing like that.' They left the canteen and crossed the yard along with a dozen other workers hastening back to work. Fred had gone ahead to sort out another muddle over an invoice with Keith. Pamela brushed aside her father's question with feigned casualness. 'It's the Monday morning blues, that's all.'

Harold knew his daughter too well to believe her. Peering over the top of his glasses with a sceptical look, he gave her hand a squeeze before they parted. 'Well, you know where I am . . .'

Sighing deeply, Pamela returned to the office she shared with Betty, bracing herself for the usual nit-picking criticisms.

Sure enough, she was greeted with, 'Where's the

book of first-class stamps I asked you to buy last Wednesday?'

Betty had done no such thing, but Pamela saw little point in arguing. 'I'm sorry, it must have slipped my mind,' she answered meekly. 'If you like, I can go to the post office on my way home tonight.'

Betty had a way of flaring her nostrils when annoyed. 'What good is that, pray, when there are five letters here on my desk, each urgently in need of a stamp?'

'I'm sorry,' Pamela repeated. Since starting work at Anderson's she'd upped her game in the clothes department. Connie had insisted on lending her a tailored blue dress with white piping around the collar and cuffs, while Lizzie's contribution to Pamela's smart new image had been a pair of black court shoes. The newly sophisticated Pamela had drawn catty, sideways glances from Betty and a wolf whistle or two from workers in the cutting shed. 'Shall I go now?'

'No need.' Having searched through a drawer stuffed with an assortment of used envelopes and crumpled sheets of carbon paper, lo and behold, Betty produced a book of stamps. Making a show of licking each one and pressing it precisely into place, she redoubled her attack on Pamela's efficiency. 'Just make sure you remember to follow instructions in future.'

Pamela's task for the afternoon was to write more reminders about late payments. At one point her uncle put in an appearance to ask Betty about the damaged railway line: how soon would the rescue teams clear the rubble from the grain yard, who would bear the cost of repairing the lines, when would they be able to load the goods wagons and transport timber out to their customers, et cetera. Betty used information meticulously gathered by Pamela first thing that morning to provide answers that were quick and precise – the grain yard was already clear, thanks to sterling work by rescue teams from Gas Street, the cost would be shared equally with Mr Freeman, the expectation was that goods would start moving out again on Wednesday or Thursday at the latest. A preoccupied Hugh left the office without a glance in Pamela's direction.

Five o'clock couldn't come fast enough. At the sound of the klaxon, Pamela was on her feet, first out of the door and down the stairs to the cloakroom to collect her hat and coat. Then she waited impatiently in the reception area for Fred.

He came down after what felt like an age and they were the last to leave the site, clocking off under Jack Watkins' beady eye.

'Goodnight, Jack.' Fred made a point of acknowledging the gateman as they passed his booth. Straight ahead, dockside cranes stood idle in the darkness. One cargo ship lay at anchor, its grey bulk looming over them, while black water lapped below.

Buttoned up against the cold, Pamela and Fred walked in silence around the harbour's edge, then across the empty market square; together yet separate. Arriving at the junction where they must part ways – he to his lodgings on the seafront, she to hers on King Edward Street – she felt a physical wrench.

'It's no good, Fred!' she exclaimed. 'You must tell me if I've done something wrong, otherwise I shan't sleep a wink.'

Fred stood on the corner with his hands shoved deep into his coat pockets, his face hidden by the brim of his trilby hat. 'It's not you,' he insisted.

'Then why didn't you come to the folly yesterday? And why are you being like this with me now?'

'I'm sorry,' he said through clenched teeth. 'You know what I'm like when I have something on my mind.' Closed as a clam on the murky seabed, temperamentally unsuited to sharing his troubles.

*Not good enough*. 'I thought we agreed not to do this,' Pamela protested. 'You must tell me everything if we're to make a go of things.'

'It's not easy for me,' he admitted, against the background growl of buses and cars. 'It goes against the grain.'

'But think about it,' she pleaded. 'Maybe it was right to keep matters to yourself when we didn't really know each other. Back then, in spring, you weren't sure that you could trust me.'

'Being secretive is second nature,' Fred said miserably.

'Come home with me so we can talk it through.' Pamela ignored his excuses. 'Come along,' she insisted as she linked arms and hurried him up King Edward Street to her lodgings.

The house was empty save for Maureen, who immediately gave up the sitting room to them and retreated to her attic.

'That girl looks poorly.' Fred hovered just inside the door, frowning at the Scottish mountain scene above the fireplace rather than looking Pamela in the eye. 'Oughtn't you to go after her to see that she's all right?'

‘Not now.’ Pamela stuck to her guns. ‘You don’t look well yourself. Take off your hat and coat. Come closer to the fire. Sit down and tell me what’s wrong.’

‘You already know.’ He sat reluctantly on a wooden chair, aware that his stubborn streak had pushed itself to the fore. ‘What’s the point in talking about it?’

She drew up the second chair and sat so that their knees were touching. ‘Very well, go ahead and do what you did last time,’ she challenged. ‘Push me away. Refuse to let me help.’

‘If you must know, I’m tired out.’ Fred let his head sink on to his chest in a gesture of defeat. ‘Exhausted. *Ermudet*.’

‘All the more reason to let me help you.’

Glancing up to see tears welling up then trickling down her cheeks, Fred was stricken with remorse. ‘My dear, don’t let me drag you down. You don’t deserve it.’

‘Listen to me: we knew from the beginning that some people were against you because of where you were born. I’ve always said that it made no difference; I love you for who you are, which is a true and honest, brave and good man. Nothing has changed.’

‘I’m not brave.’ Quite the opposite – ever since receiving the second note, Fred had felt a gnawing fear in the pit of his stomach. ‘It scares me that keeping my head down isn’t enough,’ he explained in chopped, broken sentences. ‘The enemy is always out there. Again, on Saturday night – another note. On my desk at the control centre.’

So that was it! Pamela grasped his hands. ‘Fred, we must find out who wrote it.’

‘No.’

‘Why not? What did it say?’

*MI5 is on to you, Muller . . . Get out if you know what's good for you.* Fred shook his head and stayed silent.

Pamela's thoughts galloped on. 'Then it can't have been Keith, can it? So who works with you at the town hall and might bear a grudge? Could it be one of the telephonists? Cyril Fielding's sister works there, and we know for a fact that Cyril was all for shipping you off to the Isle of Man as a fifth columnist. Perhaps his sister feels the same way.'

'Pamela, please stop,' Fred pleaded. 'Don't you see? it doesn't make any difference. For every Keith Nelson there's a Jack Watkins or an Eric Thompson or a Cyril Fielding. And for every Hilda Fielding there's a Betty Holroyd – small-minded, bigoted people, full of suspicion and hatred. We can never beat them.'

The sudden passion in his voice silenced her. She stood up and began to pace the room. 'What then?' she said at last.

He closed his eyes as a way of delaying what he needed to say, then opened them again and met her gaze. 'There's nothing else for it; I have to move on, start again.'

'Where to?' Panic rose like a murmuration of starlings, whirling overhead. It swept Pamela's thoughts this way and that.

'It doesn't matter where.'

'I'll come too,' she vowed with total conviction.

'No, you must stay here.'

'Why must I? I want to be with you.' Nothing else mattered. Pamela was willing to give up her job, to say goodbye to everything and everyone she knew.

'It wouldn't be safe,' Fred explained from his fireside chair. 'You must see that.'

'I don't care.' In her mind, her suitcase was already packed. She was on the train with Fred, travelling through the night to Liverpool, Bristol or Edinburgh.

'Oh, but I do.' Overcoming his weariness, he stood up and waited for her to come to him. 'Sooner or later this war will end,' he promised as he enfolded her in his arms. 'Germany and Britain will no longer want to fight. Berlin or London – it won't matter where I was born. Then we will be together, you and I.'

'Bill has asked me to marry him and I said yes!' Lizzie felt she would burst with joy as she dropped her news in Connie's lap in the bedroom they shared on Elliot Street.

Anticipating her first shift as head warden, Connie had one arm in the sleeve of her battledress jacket, complete with three new yellow stripes sewn on to the cuff. She stopped dead and stared, open-mouthed.

'Say something.' Lizzie tingled from head to foot. She could hardly fasten the buttons of her driver's tunic.

'Am I imagining things or did I just hear you say a sentence containing the words "Bill", "ask" and "marry"?'

'You're not and you did.' Lizzie's smile was so broad it practically split her face in two.

Connie clicked back into action, sliding her other arm into her jacket before perching on the edge of her bed to tie her shoelaces. 'Blimey, here was me thinking that I was the one who rushed headlong into things.'

'Congratulate me!' Lizzie demanded as she pulled Connie back on to her feet. She'd said yes to Bill without a moment's hesitation – yes, yes, yes! They were engaged to be married. 'The sooner the better,' he'd suggested. 'There's no reason to hang around, is there?'

'Congratulations.' The announcement had left Connie feeling dazed. 'I admit I didn't see that coming – not this soon, at any rate.'

'Why not? Bill loves me and I love him. He said he thinks about me every waking moment – those were his very words. Isn't it wonderful?'

Sparks of happiness lit up the dingy room. They quickly enveloped Connie in their warm glow, so that she soon overcame her surprise and beamed back at Lizzie. 'Come here, you – let your big sister give you a hug.'

They embraced breathlessly as Connie fired questions at Lizzie: when was the big day, was there a ring, would it be church or register office?

No date yet and no ring. 'I'd like us to get married in St Joseph's.' The words were new and strange to Lizzie's ears. 'And I want Dad to give me away.'

Connie nodded, then crossed her fingers. 'He'll be pleased as Punch when you tell him.'

'I hope so. I'll go to the hospital tomorrow. Will you be my maid of honour?'

'Of course I will.' Once Christmas was over there would be flowers to order, dresses to make, invitations to be sent out. Aunty Vera would no doubt help with a wedding cake. The exact timing would depend on how soon their father was allowed out of hospital.

'Bill plans to ask Tom to be his best man. Picture it, Con – the two of them standing at the front of the church in their best suits, nervous as kittens, waiting for you, me and Dad to walk down the aisle.' The day would be fine and sunny. Ruby-red and sapphire-blue rays would filter in through the stained-glass window behind the altar. The organ would play 'Here Comes the Bride'.

Connie hugged her again. 'Marvellous,' she breathed. 'Tell Bill from me that he's a lucky man.'

'Carnations were Mum's favourite flower.' Lizzie went off at an apparent tangent.

'Yes – pink ones.'

The flowers added the final touch to Lizzie's picture of what would be the happiest day of her life. 'A simple spray of pink carnations – that will be my bridal bouquet.'

To Fred it had been obvious: he and Pamela had no choice; for the time being they must live apart.

'If you love me you will let me go.' He'd presented her with this ultimate paradox.

His reasons: number one, it would be far simpler and easier if he were to leave Kelthorpe and start a new, anonymous life without her. Number two, her mother and father would be heartbroken if she were to vanish from their lives without a trace. Number three, whereas he was well rehearsed in disguise and subterfuge, Pamela might be caught off guard. A careless word from her would ruin everything.

'For how long?' she'd demanded, fighting back her tears. What had become of their unspoken, loving exchange beneath the Christmas tree?

'Until it's safe for us to be together.' It was the only way forward. Everything else would end in disaster.

Pamela's resistance had crumpled at last. 'Will you send me an address so that I can write to you? We can use false names if you'd prefer.'

'Perhaps it will be possible,' Fred had conceded without any certainty.

In the end she'd promised to endure the separation. She loved him more than the world and would bear any sacrifice for his sake.

Fred had steeled himself to walk away – out into a dark world where recently bombed buildings tilted at impossible angles, disgorging their contents on to the street. He stepped over a mangled baby's pram and around vehicles buried in rubble. He would not look back, knowing that Pamela would still be standing in her doorway, willing him to change his mind.

Reaching the bottom of King Edward Street, he crossed the market square, then took a shortcut down the side of the Anchor leading to a narrow, exposed footpath that would take him around the headland. Misery turned Fred in on himself so that he failed to pay attention to three men smoking and drinking outside the entrance to the pub. *In the end Pamela will see that I'm right,* he convinced himself as he walked, head down in the inky blackness. A sudden wind blasted in from the sea, tearing at his coat and forcing him to hold on to his hat as he approached the bottom of Musgrave Street. *There's no future for us here and no safety for her if she were to come with me.* At work tomorrow he would explain as much to Harold, who would surely see the strength of Fred's argument. Then, with regret, he would hand in his notice with as little fuss as possible before slipping away.

Footsteps followed Fred around the headland but still he ignored them.

Harold and Edith would take care of Pamela after he left. Fred hoped she would stay in her job at

Anderson's and learn to stand up to Betty. Her voluntary work as a warden had proved a sticking point – all too aware of the dangers, he had tried to persuade Pamela to give it up but she'd refused. 'The uniform makes me feel as if I'm doing something worthwhile,' she'd insisted. 'The ARP needs people who can keep calm in a crisis and I've proved my worth in that respect.'

He would have to live with her decision, just as she would have to live with his.

Quick, heavy footsteps gained on Fred and he prepared to stand to one side of the path to allow the men who followed to overtake. There was an overhang of rock above his head, casting a shadow that blocked out what little moonlight there was.

The three men broke into a run as Fred pressed himself against the rough rock face. But instead of passing by, they surrounded him. Without warning or provocation, one struck out with his fist, causing Fred to duck sideways to avoid the blow.

'Dirty Nazi spy!' The insult came from a second man who landed a high kick to Fred's ribs, spinning him into the arms of the third attacker. 'This is what we do to traitors.'

Fred bent double and staggered forward. The kick was the first of many – the men booted him to the ground and didn't stop, landing one swift, thudding blow after another on their defenceless victim. Then one took out a bicycle chain and whipped it across Fred's back, cutting into the flesh of his neck. The inside of his head rang with searing pain.

As the blows rained down, Fred willed himself not to cry out.

'Take that, filthy Fritz!' A foot thudded into his ribs.

The strongest of the three hauled Fred on to his feet then ordered the others to pin their victim's arms to his sides. Fred caught a glimpse of the man's face beneath the peak of his cap – its expression was what he'd expected: mindless, brutish and cruel. But it was not a face he recognized.

'Go on, give it to him good and proper!' his accomplices urged.

Their leader wrapped both hands around Fred's throat, throttling him as he shoved his head against the rock. Fred fought for breath and pushed back but the odds against him were too great. Time seemed to slow down and he grew acutely aware of the crash of waves on to the beach – possibly the last sound he would ever hear. He smelled tobacco smoke and beer on the men's breath and the sweat of their unwashed bodies.

The strongest, roughest of the three drew back and clenched both fists. He seemed to be in no hurry.

'Go on, Tommo. Finish the bugger off!'

The leader sneered. 'Admit it, Muller – you tip off your Nazi bosses every chance you get.' His fist hovered in the air, threatening to smash into the side of Fred's jaw. 'They've caught you doing it.'

'Who has?' Fred resisted with all his might, writhing in desperation.

'Never you mind. You've been heard whispering into your phone, telling Fritz what's what.'

The absurd accusation was so vague that it seemed almost funny. 'Liars, whoever they are.' Fred went on struggling to break free but it was no use. So instead, he twisted his body to kick out at the man with the chain, forcing him to loosen his grip. Managing to snatch the makeshift weapon, Fred lashed out, only for his heavyweight opponent to spring into action and land the threatened punch square in his solar plexus. Fred jackknifed forward and fought for breath as his assailants wrested back the chain. Then all three landed rapid flurries of kicks and punches that drove him to the ground once more. Collapsing sideways, he curled into a ball, hardly registering the pain. Waves broke on the shore. He knew no more.

It was unfair; it wasn't right! Pamela hardly knew what to do with herself. She shouldn't have let Fred go home without putting up more of a fight.

Up in her room she stared at her reflection in the mirror and fought back the tears. *Don't give in! Find a way forward that doesn't involve us having to part.* She picked up a brush and ran it fiercely through her fine, wavy hair, then she changed into her uniform – hopefully a night shift at Gas Street would give her a different focus and time to clear her head. *Don't give in!* she repeated as she jammed on her ski cap and slung her gas mask over her shoulder. *Talk to Connie – she's bound to come up with a different solution.*

As she rushed downstairs, she crossed paths with Kathleen and Winnie, who were coming in through the front door after a long day serving behind the counters at Bentley's. Instead of exchanging greetings with Pamela, they gave her odd looks before ducking into the sitting room. Too preoccupied to wonder about it, Pamela hurried on. *It's Connie's first shift as head warden – she might be too busy to advise me,* she realized as she threaded her way down back streets and through alleyways towards the sector post. Pamela decided that it would be best to wait before asking her friend for help, but then again tomorrow might be too late. Knowing Fred, he would put his plan into action straight away. Pamela's stomach churned. How could she concentrate on patrolling bomb sites or reorganizing gloves, boots, eye shields and whistles in the stockroom, or bringing the incident ledger up to date? And God help her if the sirens sounded tonight. How would she cope then?

Reaching her destination, she saw that the Union Jack fluttered outside the sector post and the banner reading 'Home Sweet Home' hung above the entrance as if nothing had changed.

'What's up?' Stationed behind the head warden's desk, surrounded by maps, two telephones and endless lists, and trying not to feel daunted by her new responsibilities, Connie saw at once that Pamela was in a flap.

'Nothing,' Pamela fibbed, though anxiety welled up and threatened to choke her.

'A new consignment of helmets has arrived,' Connie reported in a businesslike way. 'They're in a cardboard box at the bottom of the stairs. Can you sort them into sizes and stack them on the shelves, please? And there's a box of ARP penknives next to the helmets. They came without lanyards so they're no earthly use. I'll have to send them back.'

Gritting her teeth, Pamela went through to the storeroom to begin her task.

'Oh, and Lizzie and Bill are engaged,' Connie threw in casually as three more wardens arrived for duty. 'Needless to say, she's over the moon. Eddie, the Ministry has issued this new Tactical Training Manual.' She pushed a leaflet across the counter towards one of the new arrivals. 'Have a quick read, then pass it on to Simon and Alf, please.'

'Engaged?' Pamela emerged from the storeroom with a look of disbelief. 'As in, engaged to be married?'

'What else, you silly goose? Bill and Tom set sail again the day after tomorrow. I expect Bill wanted to slip in his proposal before then.'

'Well, that's marvellous.' The surprise news shook Pamela's mind free of the hook of her present worries.

'Lizzie has beaten us both to it,' Connie observed with a shrewd, inquisitive glance at Pamela. She hadn't forgotten the fact that Fred had failed to show up for Sunday's holly-gathering expedition.

Pamela was about to retreat into the storeroom without responding.

'By the way, this arrived, addressed to you.' Connie held up a white envelope. "Miss Pamela Carr, care of Gas Street Sector Post". You don't have a secret admirer, by any chance?'

'Not that I know of.' Pamela took the envelope with a worried frown. 'I'll open it later,' she added, about to slip it into her top pocket.

'Don't keep me in suspense,' Connie teased. 'Open it now.'

So Pamela turned over the mysterious, typewritten envelope. She tore it open and pulled out the contents, assuming that the letter might be connected with her ongoing inter-service training. But in that case it would have arrived in an official, buff-coloured envelope. KRAUT WHORE! she read, before gasping then letting the sheet of paper flutter to the floor.

Connie came out from behind the counter to pick it up and read silently.

*KRAUT WHORE! You know what the French do to collaborators – they shave their dirty heads and tar and feather them. So watch out – you're next.*

She screwed the unsigned note into a ball, then threw it down and stamped on it in disgust.

Pamela reeled backwards, to the consternation of Eddie Fraser, who managed to sit her on a stool before she collapsed. His younger brother Simon brought her a glass of water.

'I'll deal with this,' Connie told them. 'Eddie, it's time to start your patrol on Maypole Street. Simon, you take Tennyson Street, and Alf, stay local on Gas Street.'

The mystified junior wardens followed orders, leaving Connie to tend to Pamela.

Connie crouched to speak quietly and earnestly. 'Deep breaths,' she insisted. 'In and out, nice and slow.'

Pamela tried to stand but her legs refused to hold her weight. The word *whore* pierced her pure heart. She felt defiled and dirty, shocked to her core.

'It's nonsense – you mustn't let it bother you.' Connie placed her hand firmly around Pamela's wrist. 'Remember, sticks and stones . . .'

'Who?' Pamela gasped. 'Why?'

'Some silly idiots with bees in their bonnets. Don't give them a second thought.'

The gorge rose in Pamela's throat. She swallowed it back, then stood up to clear her head and think through her next move.

'Breathe in,' Connie repeated as she surreptitiously retrieved the poisonous note and shoved it in her trouser pocket. Had Pamela read the whole thing? And had she seen the ugly swastika symbol at the bottom?

'Don't tell Fred,' Pamela pleaded with Connie. 'He mustn't find out.'

'Very well.' Slowly, Connie acquiesced.

'Don't tell anyone. Mum, Dad, Uncle Hugh. Not even Lizzie.' Pamela would rather die than have their view of her contaminated by the dreadful accusation. 'I haven't – Fred and I . . .' The words 'made love' refused to pass her lips.

'I know,' Connie murmured. 'They're talking rubbish.' But the threat was real and she understood that she must do everything in her power to protect her friend. 'We should inform the authorities,' she said more firmly. 'There's an Aliens department at the Home Office – they might be able to tell us what to do.'

Pamela scarcely heard. She understood now what Fred had meant when he'd warned her that the enemy was always out there – innumerable prying eyes and suspicious minds driven by an ugly, twisted version of patriotism. 'What am I to do?' she groaned.

One of the phones on Connie's counter rang loudly. Hurrying to answer it, she gestured for Pamela to stay where she was. Connie picked up the receiver and listened intently. 'Yes, she's here,' she answered, flashing a concerned look in Pamela's direction. 'Yes, I'll tell her.'

Putting down the phone, she returned to Pamela's side. 'That was your father,' she told her softly. 'He's asked that you sit tight until he gets here.'

# CHAPTER TWELVE

Hugh Anderson's sleek grey car pulled up outside the sector post. It was driven by Harold, who hurriedly pulled on the handbrake then jumped out and ran across the pavement to be intercepted by Connie.

'Is she still here?' Harold had left the house without hat or coat and driven as fast as the blackout allowed to fetch his daughter.

'Yes. I persuaded her to wait in the restroom.' Connie led the way up a narrow staircase to a small room containing a few old easy chairs, a card table and a dartboard.

Pamela sat in one of the chairs, scarcely daring to breathe. At the sight of her father's worried expression, she jumped to her feet and rushed towards him. 'What is it, Daddy? What's happened?'

'Sit down.' Gently, Harold guided her back to the chair. 'It's bad news, I'm afraid.'

Pamela's body was rigid with fright. She closed her eyes and held her breath.

The words stuck in Harold's throat, so Connie stepped forward and prompted him. 'Whatever it is, Pamela needs to know,' she counselled.

'You're right.' His voice was not much above a whisper. 'Fred has been injured.'

*Injured, not dead.* Pamela clung to a shred of hope.

'He was set upon by three men.'

'What on earth . . . ?' Exasperated, Connie struck the wall with the side of her fist. First Pamela's note, now this.

'Fred was making his way home around the headland. The men knocked him unconscious. When he came round, there was no sign of his attackers.'

'Who found him?' Connie demanded.

'No one. He managed to crawl along the footpath until he reached the promenade. How he did it I'll never know.' Harold studied his daughter's reaction – every flutter of her eyelids, every twitch at the corners of her mouth. 'He made it on his hands and knees as far as Uncle Hugh's house.'

Connie wasn't certain how much of the information was getting through to Pamela. 'Where is Fred now?' she asked.

'Still at Sunrise. He refuses to go to hospital.'

'How badly is he hurt?'

Pamela gripped the arms of the chair until her knuckles turned white as Harold shaped his answer.

'No bones are broken as far as we can tell, but the poor lad is covered in cuts and bruises. There's some concussion, some grogginess . . .'

'Right – this is what we'll do . . .' Connie made a plan. 'Pamela, Fred needs you. I'm relieving you of your duties for the rest of the night. I'll inform the control centre and they'll organize a replacement. You must go back to Sunrise with your father.'

*Fred needs me.* As if in a trance, Pamela stood up and

allowed Harold to take her hand and lead her down the stairs.

*Thank you*, Harold mouthed at Connie as they departed.

'Give Fred my love,' she called after them. What else could she say? *Wish him well and tell him to get better soon. I hope they lock up the culprits for a good long while*. What was the world coming to when it turned against decent, honourable men like Fred Miller and innocent girls like Pamela Carr; when neighbours were at each other's throats and the streets of Kelthorpe were home to gang violence?

Connie backed away from the door. Pamela might be relieved of her duties but she, newly promoted head warden Connie Bailey, wasn't. Reports must be updated then sent by messenger to the control centre. Then she needed to find six volunteers to act as casualties in a training exercise scheduled for early in the New Year. Plus, information had reached her about a number of untrained civilians interfering with the work of demolition squads, which was a roundabout way of saying that looting was taking place. Immediate follow-up was required. And then there was the matter of the out-of-date household register for Valley Road. And so it went on, well into the night, against an intermittent call of 'Put that light out!' from wardens on patrol and the constant ring of the telephone.

*Roll up your sleeves and get on with it,* Connie decided. *Put one foot in front of another, take pride in your job, and whatever you do, don't let the side down*.

Fred lay under an eiderdown on the sofa in Hugh's large sitting room. Light came from a tall standard lamp in the far corner of the room and from the low fire in the grate. Objects drifted in and out of focus – a wireless on a small table by the window, rich emerald curtains hanging from a brass pole, a stylized figure of a female dancer fashioned in bronze that stood on a plinth in one of the alcoves. Every time he moved he felt excruciating pain.

Pamela hovered outside the door with her mother. 'We tried our best to persuade him to go to hospital,' an exasperated Edith whispered.

It was an hour since Hugh had fetched her and Harold from the bungalow. He'd knocked on their door in quite a state, jumbling his words. Fred – been knocked about by three assailants – bad – bleeding – what to do? Edith, too, had flapped, but Harold had kept his head. He'd run across the lawn to the big house to find Fred curled up on his side in the front porch. His coat and shirt were ripped and his face was bleeding and covered in cuts. Harold had raised him with difficulty, then aided him, limping and groaning, into the sitting room before removing his coat and calling for warm water, cotton wool and disinfectant. Then Harold had driven to find Pamela, and Edith had stepped into the role of nurse, swabbing away the dirt and grit, with Hugh all the while hovering anxiously in the background.

'How bad is it?' Pamela steeled herself to go into the room.

'See for yourself,' was all Edith said, as she pushed open the door.

Pamela tiptoed in. It took a few seconds for her eyes to grow accustomed to the low light, but then she made out Fred lying motionless on the sofa. He turned his head towards the sound of footsteps, then looked away again.

'Fred, it's me.' She went to him and knelt beside him. His handsome face was scarcely recognizable: disfigured and swollen, with cuts above his eyes and deep grazes down one side. A strong smell of Dettol came from the metal basin on a low table next to the sofa. 'What can I do?' she asked softly.

He swallowed, then let out a small groan before shaking his head.

'Let me do something. Do you need more cushions? Another blanket?'

'Nothing,' he whispered. He hated for Pamela to see him like this – bruised, battered and defeated. *Besiegt*. And it hurt so much to move, even to talk.

She rested a hand lightly on top of the blanket. 'Your poor, poor face,' she murmured.

Fred blinked but didn't reply. He felt her breath on his cheek. *Meine liebster Liebling. My dearest darling.*

'Some of the cuts are deep – they might need stitches.'

'No.'

'Why not?'

Slowly he reached for her hand – it was warm and soft. 'No,' he repeated.

'My love.' She kissed his grazed knuckles. 'I am so sorry.' *That this has happened, that none of it was your fault, that men's minds can be so poisoned by hate*. She experienced a moment of panic – what had happened to the letter that she'd received at the sector post? Connie had crumpled it, then stamped on it. What message had followed on from 'Kraut whore'? What if one of the other wardens had picked up the paper and read it? The two humiliating words were etched permanently on her brain.

Fred kept tight hold of Pamela's trembling hand. 'Try not to worry,' he said, despite the pain. In time his cuts would heal and the swelling would disappear.

Pamela gazed at him through a blur of tears. 'Do you need to rest?' she whispered.

'No – stay with me.' The waves had crashed on to the shore, the men had kicked him to the ground and left him for dead, and the last vision Fred had seen before he'd blacked out had been of her lovely, heart-shaped face and those tender, grey-green eyes.

Edith joined Harold and Hugh in the dining room. They spoke in low voices, even though there was little chance of being overheard.

'Shall we call the police?' Edith wondered out loud. After all, justice demanded that the culprits be caught and punished.

'I'm not sure. Would Fred want us to?' Hugh had been badly shaken by events and sought to calm his nerves with a stiff whisky. 'Can I pour one for you?' he asked the others.

'No, thank you; not for me,' Edith replied. Alcohol didn't help anyone to think more clearly – quite the opposite. She stayed on her prim perch, soberly pecking away at the problem before them.

'Yes, I'll join you if I may,' Harold decided. 'You're right, Hugh – let's not rush into anything. We must ask Fred what to do. From what I gather, he has no clue as to the identity of these three louts.'

'Perhaps he won't want to draw attention to the incident.' Hugh's view was shrewder than Harold or

Edith had expected. 'That would certainly happen if we involved the police.'

'I see what you're saying.' Harold took his brother-in-law's point.

Edith wasn't convinced. 'But is he the best judge?' she demanded. 'The poor boy is in a state of shock and perhaps unable to see what's best for him.'

'Let's sleep on it.' Harold offered a compromise. 'I assume Fred can stay here tonight?' he asked Hugh between sips of whisky.

'Certainly.' Hugh Anderson had taken to Fred from the moment the young man had presented himself for interview at the timber yard, immaculately dressed and with perfect manners. He'd struck Hugh as extremely bright and with a good head for figures, a quality that would be invaluable in clearing up some outstanding income tax returns that lay both on Hugh's desk and on his conscience. The candidate had also been modest, personable and above all honest, making no bones about his status as a Category C alien. Hugh had been quickly convinced that Fred was a genuine Jewish refugee 'whose being at liberty in no way constituted a danger to the State', as stated on the back of his tribunal card. And his judgement had proved correct – at work, Fred had never put a foot wrong and more recently, as Pamela's sweetheart, he'd been a welcome addition to their social circle. 'I've grown fond of the boy,' he confessed as he drained the bottom of his glass. 'Fred can stay at Sunrise for as long as he wishes. And for the time being it's probably best that we tell no one of his whereabouts.'

'Agreed,' Harold said immediately. 'Who knows what those thugs might do next?'

Edith concurred. 'I'll fetch a pair of Harold's pyjamas from the bungalow,' she said, hurrying off and only pausing to glance into the sitting room to see Fred's hand clasped around Pamela's and Pamela's head resting on the cushion next to his.

'How many hours' kip did you get?' Lizzie buzzed about the bakery, a bundle of non-stop energy as she took trays from the oven, turned out freshly baked loaves and prepared to set out on her first round of deliveries. Love floated her high on cloud nine and made her heart sing. Connie, meanwhile, moved at a slower pace.

'A measly three,' Connie replied. Her shift at Gas Street had finished at two in the morning, leaving her just enough time to go home and get her head down for some much needed rest. She'd arrived at the bakery looking solemn and bleary-eyed. 'How about you?'

Lizzie had spent the night at the harbourside cottage. 'I wasn't counting,' she admitted. 'Bill and I were too busy talking,' she added with a smile. Talking, dreaming of the future and making love – trying to ignore the fact that their short time together would soon come to an abrupt end.

'Lucky you.' Connie pinched her cheeks to wake herself up. 'Did you call the hospital?'

'Yes. Dad is doing as he's told, for once.' Lizzie spoke from the shop, where she arranged teacakes and Hovis buns under the glass counter. 'The nurses are pleased with him; he's become quite a favourite.'

'Who, Dad?' Connie handed a tray of fresh scones to Lizzie. 'Are you sure they've got the right man?'

Lizzie's smile broadened. 'Yes. Butter wouldn't

melt, apparently. By the way, did you tell Pamela about my engagement?'

A small frown appeared on Connie's face. 'Yes. She said for me to congratulate you.'

'Why the glum expression? No, save it for later – I don't have time to gossip. Anyway, I'm hoping to see Pam at rehearsal this evening. I want to ask her if she'll be my bridesmaid.'

'I wouldn't bank on her being there, if I were you.' Connie fussed with Lizzie's display of teacakes. 'I had to arrange a stand-in for her last night after Fred was beaten up.'

'Good Lord! What do you mean?'

Connie shook her head. 'I don't know the details – only that Pamela's dad came to Gas Street and told her that Fred had been knocked unconscious by a gang of thugs. Somehow he ended up at Hugh Anderson's house.'

'Have you heard from Pamela since?'

'No, not a dicky bird.' Connie wasn't sure what the silence indicated.

'Maybe I'll call in at King Edward Street,' Lizzie said thoughtfully. 'There's a chance I'll catch her there.'

'No, it's Tuesday – Pam will be at work.'

Lizzie had picked up the van key and was on her way out. 'I'll knock on her door anyway,' she decided. 'And if she's not there I'll call back later.'

True to her word, as soon as Lizzie had finished her round she made a detour to Pamela's lodgings, only to knock on the door and find no one at home. Connie was right: Pamela had gone to work.

She was returning to the van when she glanced along the street to see Colin approaching on his bike. He seemed to be in a hurry and didn't notice Lizzie, simply ditching his bicycle at the edge of the kerb before racing up the worn stone steps and knocking on the door. This time it was answered quickly and Colin disappeared inside, leaving the door slightly ajar.

Lizzie seized her opportunity to follow him into the house. She intended to write Pamela a quick note saying how sorry she was to hear about the attack on Fred, but as she searched in her pockets for pencil and paper, she heard shouting coming from the top landing.

'You never should of done it in the first place!' Colin's accusation was loud and vehement. 'Now look – I'm not allowed out of the 'ouse except to go to school. She locks me in.'

'I know – you don't have to keep going on about it.' Maureen's voice was fainter than her brother's and she was obviously in distress.

'And it's not fair neither. None of it was my fault.'

'I know it wasn't. I'm sorry, Colin.'

'I'm not supposed to speak to you ever again. I shouldn't even be 'ere now.'

'Hush – keep your voice down.'

As Maureen peered over the banister to check that no one could overhear the row, Lizzie ducked into the living room and out of sight. Embarrassed to be snooping, she was fascinated nevertheless.

'I only came to tell you what's happened to the baby so you'll stop nagging me.'

'Go on!' Maureen begged.

'It got taken to that place on the hill – near the grammar school.'

'I already know that!' For the first time Maureen raised her voice in exasperation.

'So it got put on a list where couples ask to take babies home with them. Well, Miss Know-it-all, yours has been picked.'

Maureen gave a long, low wail – a sound of pure misery.

'What are you blubbing for? I thought that's what you wanted.' Now that he'd delivered the message, Colin was intent on a quick getaway.

'I do. I did.' The wail was followed by loud sobs.

'Isn't that why you left it at the church in the first place?' Puzzled by his sister's tears, he shifted uneasily from one foot to the other.

'She's not an "it"; she's a "she"!' A perfect little girl with soft, pink skin and curled fingers and toes. *Her* perfect little girl.

Lizzie couldn't bear to hear more. She stepped out into the hallway and called up to them. 'Maureen, Colin – it's me, Lizzie Harrison. Can I do anything to help?'

The boy gave a guilty start, then thundered down two flights of stairs. He cannoned straight into Lizzie, who grabbed him and refused to let him go.

'Why aren't you at school?' she demanded as he squirmed in her grasp. Strange that this was the question that popped out first.

'I'm poorly, that's why.' Colin grew red in the face with the effort of lying at the same time as trying to escape. 'Mam said I could stay off.'

Maureen looked over the banister. 'Let go of him,'

she said in a state of high agitation. 'Colin hasn't done anything wrong.'

So Lizzie loosened her grip, allowing the boy to dart through the open door on to the street. Then she quickly mounted the stairs to try to calm Maureen, who had retreated into her room and slammed the door. Lizzie heard her slide the bolt.

'Go away!' Maureen whimpered.

'I will, as soon as I've made sure you're all right.' Lizzie spoke slowly and calmly. 'Won't you please open the door?'

'No – go away.'

'Maureen, I won't cause any trouble – I want to help.'

'You can't. No one can.' There was a rustling noise, as if the fugitive had slid to the floor with her back to the door.

'I can tell you more about the couple who want to adopt Susan.' Lizzie held her breath as she waited for a response. There was a fumbling and a slow pushing back of the bolt before the door opened.

Lizzie was shocked by what she saw. Maureen shook from head to foot and her face was ghostly pale. There were dark shadows under her eyes. Her hair was unwashed and her plain dark brown dress hung sack-like from her thin body. 'You're not well,' she gasped.

'Just tell me what you know, then leave me alone.' As Maureen swayed backwards her hand slipped from the door handle. She lost her balance and would have fallen if Lizzie hadn't moved swiftly to catch her.

Lizzie steadied her, then sat her down on the bed. A glance around the cold attic room told her that

Maureen had made no attempt to make a home for herself. There was nothing here except a bed and a bare mattress with Maureen's coat thrown across it – no other furniture and no rug to cover the bare boards. Her suitcase lay on the floor, spilling out its meagre contents. The damp walls were bare, with patches of mould. Dusty cobwebs hung from the sloping ceiling.

Taking off her own coat, Lizzie draped it around Maureen, then sat down beside her. 'This is what I've heard: the couple who want to adopt Susan don't have any other children. The husband works in a chemist's shop. The wife stays at home.'

'Do they live in Kelthorpe?' Maureen asked the question as if her life depended on Lizzie's answer.

Lizzie shook her head and Maureen let out a long sigh, seemingly of relief.

'Good. I don't want to bump into them by accident. But will they look after Susan properly?'

'Yes, they will. The WVS will make sure of it.' Pity rose up and choked Lizzie, and she could say no more.

'Better than I could.' Maureen's voice was almost inaudible. 'She'll have a proper family.'

'But what about you?' Sniffing back tears, Lizzie risked reaching out to touch Maureen's thin hand. 'How will you cope?'

The miserable, guilt-ridden girl seemed not to hear. 'A baby needs a proper, respectable family. Girls like me can't do that.'

'What do you mean, girls like you?' Lizzie kept her hand where it was.

'Bad girls. Girls who should know better.'

'Who says so?'

'Everyone – the matron in the home – all the girls who got sent there.' Maureen's voice was hollow and her lips quivered. 'We all knew we weren't fit to be mothers.'

'You went to stay at a home?' Lizzie prompted. 'What kind of a place was it?'

'For mothers and babies.' Maureen stared at Lizzie's hand over hers as if wondering why it was there. 'In a big house in the country, run by the Church. They look after you there until you've had your baby.'

Lizzie knew vaguely about such homes. They were often houses that had been built as reformatories or workhouses, carrying that old, Victorian stigma with them into the modern world. Dark and dank, hidden away in remote places and specifically catering for mothers whose infants would be born out of wedlock, they were one of the few alternatives open to unfortunate girls whose families refused to support them through their pregnancies. 'What's the home called?' she asked cautiously.

Maureen pressed her lips together and was silent.

'All right. It was in Axenby, at any rate. Was it the matron there who told you that you were bad?'

'Yes, and that's why our babies had to be given up. We girls were selfish if we said we wanted to keep them. We had to do the scrubbing and cleaning. We had to fetch the coal.'

'Even when your baby was due?' Such brainwashing and harsh treatment in the name of religion outraged Lizzie.

Maureen barely nodded. 'I didn't know what would happen. We never learned anything about it at school. The home made us work. In the morning we had a strip wash in a big washing area, then we had a church service. I was in the chapel when my waters broke and I was frightened because I didn't know what was wrong with me. They made me wear a baby's nappy and carry on working until the pains got worse.'

'Good God in heaven, that's barbaric!' Lizzie couldn't stop herself from jumping up.

'I didn't know any better. No one told me anything.' Maureen seemed bemused by Lizzie's anger. 'Afterwards they let me feed Susan but I wasn't allowed to see her in-between. The babies slept in their own dormitory.'

'For how long?' Lizzie calmed herself and sat down again.

'For six weeks. You weren't supposed to cuddle your baby – they didn't like it if you did because it makes it harder for you to give them away. Some of the girls didn't care – when it came to it they handed them over and they didn't even cry – but I knew I would.'

'So what did you do?'

'I counted the days. Six times seven is forty-two. I knitted a matinee jacket, bonnet and bootees. You had to dress your baby in them when the day came – they didn't tell you exactly what time.' Maureen paused and her eyes grew dark and deeply troubled. 'It was then that I did the really bad thing.'

# CHAPTER THIRTEEN

'Hark the Herald' was Tom's all-time favourite. He stood tall between Connie and Lizzie in the church hall and belted it out for all he was worth. 'Peace on earth and mercy mild . . .'

*If only,* Connie thought. Peace and mercy had been in short supply lately, not to mention joyful nations and sons of righteousness. As usual she mimed the words, content to stand beside the man she loved and to hear his voice soar above the rest.

Lizzie, meanwhile, felt her spirits lift at last. Her conversation with Maureen earlier in the day had left her feeling helpless and dispirited. She'd done her best to ease the situation – lending Maureen her warm coat while she went to fetch fresh bread, some margarine, a few ounces of cheese and a pint of milk. The girl had seemed grateful and begged her not to worry. *Fat chance!* Afterwards, Lizzie had gone around with a dark cloud hanging over her that had only dissipated when the singers raised the roof with the rousing carol.

Doug conducted with his usual gusto, then congratulated his singers heartily. 'Well done, everyone. Tomorrow is our big night. Young Arnold is ready for his solo and we must all do our best to make up for Tom's absence.' He cast a rueful glance in his most talented singer's direction. 'Hopefully Miss Carr will be able to rejoin us tomorrow evening?' he enquired of Connie and Lizzie as he laid his baton on the top of the piano. 'She sings as well as she plays and is an invaluable member of our little group.'

The sisters were in the dark as far as that went. Neither had heard a whisper from Pamela since news of the attack on Fred had broken, so they could only suppose that she'd been too caught up in looking after him to get in touch. In any case, Lizzie had been preoccupied with the Maureen problem and Connie had twisted herself into knots wondering what to do about the blasted note addressed to Pamela that was still crumpled up inside the pocket of her battledress. On top of which, the hours slid by and the time that the sisters had left to spend with Tom and Bill dwindled minute by minute. Tick-tick-tick went the clock. *Sea Knight* would sail from the harbour tomorrow morning at seven o'clock precisely.

'St Joseph's wishes to thank you all most sincerely in advance,' Doug went on in his self-important way. 'Rest assured that whatever money we collect through our carol singing will go directly into the fund for church repairs.'

The choir shuffled and coughed. Doug had rehearsed them longer than usual and many were cold and tired.

'Wrap up well tomorrow night,' he advised, oblivious to any mutterings. 'The weather forecast is for a light snowfall around about six o'clock.'

'Merry flippin' Christmas to you too,' a retired

trawlerman grumbled under his breath as he shuffled from the room.

Several Boy Scouts – Arnold among them – overtook the old sailor, elbowing each other to be first out. Tom, Connie and Lizzie were also in a hurry. They exchanged friendly farewells with other carol singers before crossing the churchyard together.

'It's starting to really feel like Christmas.' Connie tried to remain upbeat as the trio made their way through town. Darkness had fallen but the sky was clear and frost was in the air, with no sign of the snow predicted for the following day.

'Nine days to go.' Lizzie had made an advent calendar out of stiff white card decorated with red and gold glitter and was opening the tiny doors in the countdown to the Nativity. 'Tom, I take it you're all ready and shipshape for tomorrow?' She faced the elephant in the room with a brave smile.

'As I'll ever be.' Tom held Connie's hand more firmly. 'Don't worry, Bill and I will be back, getting under your feet and cramping your style again before you know it.'

'The sooner the better!' Lizzie declared as she picked up her pace. They were on their way to meet Bill at the Anchor and she was eager to get there.

'Hold your horses.' Connie had to trot to keep up, while Tom merely lengthened his stride. 'What's the rush, as if I didn't know?'

They'd reached the town square before Lizzie was forced to pause for breath.

'You haven't told me what happened when you dropped in on Pamela earlier,' Connie reminded her.

Lizzie loosened her scarf and opened the top

button of her coat. 'She wasn't in, like you said, but Maureen was.'

'And?'

Lizzie gave a sorrowful shake of her head. 'You can't begin to imagine what that girl's been through.'

'Try me.'

'That mother of hers stuck her in a Christian home for unmarried mothers. By all accounts it was like the workhouse, only worse. That was where Maureen got it into her head that she wasn't fit to be a mother. But the matron didn't take the babies away straight after they were born – oh, no siree! The girls were allowed to bathe and feed them for six weeks – six whole weeks to grow fond of them and have their hearts broken when they were forced to part.'

'Don't tell me – when it came to it, Maureen couldn't bear to give Susan away?'

'Bull's eye – you guessed it.'

'She took the baby and ran away from the home?' It was what Connie herself would have done in the circumstances.

'Yes – on the day of the handover – or rather, the night before. Maureen set off in the dark and walked for miles across country with baby Susan and only the clothes she stood up in. By some miracle she headed in the right direction, across the moors towards the coast. When it grew light she managed to get her bearings. She trudged the last few miles to Kelthorpe on the back roads, dead beat and desperate not to be seen.'

The harbour was in sight and the salt tang in the air told the girls that they were approaching the sea. 'Maureen told you all this?' Connie asked.

Lizzie nodded. 'Can you believe it – she talked as if she was the one who'd committed a crime. That's how the matron at the home made her feel – like a piece of dog dirt stuck to the sole of her shoe. Anyway, Maureen told me the whole story, including the fact that when she arrived at her mother's house with the baby, desperate for help, she had the door slammed in her face.'

'I say, that's a poor show.' Tom's muttered understatement was accompanied by a deep frown.

'So how come Colin reckoned that the pair were at each other's throats the whole time?' Connie clearly remembered the boy saying as much.

'It seems Nancy quickly had second thoughts. The last thing she wanted was for the neighbours on North Street to see Maureen carrying the baby – think of the shame, the disgrace.'

'Hang the disgrace.' Connie's curt interruption spoke volumes.

'Anyway, Nancy dragged her and the baby inside. She said Maureen wasn't to show her face; she was to stay out of sight until she, Nancy, had made up her mind what to do.'

'And how long did that take her, pray?' Connie was indignant.

'I'm not sure. I do know that Maureen was made to feel like a pariah by her own mother and that Colin was piggy in the middle. If he tried to stick up for his sister he got shouted at and smacked – likewise if he paid the baby any attention. Finally it got too much for Maureen to bear.'

'And that's how little Susan ended up in a cardboard box in the church-hall porch.' Connie felt sick at heart to hear how events had unravelled.

'But why there?' Tom wondered. 'St Joseph's is a long way from North Street.'

'That's true.' Lizzie hadn't considered this. 'Perhaps because it's where the family has always gone to church? They lived on Musgrave Street before they moved, which is nearer to the centre of town.'

'That makes sense.' Connie was more interested in the people involved than the places. 'Did Maureen mention anything about the baby's father? Do Nancy and Colin know who he is?' Sailor, dock worker, shopkeeper, tinker, tailor . . .

'No, not a word. And I didn't press her on that point. It felt as if that would be the straw that finally broke the camel's back.'

'Fair enough.' As they came to the empty fish market, with the Anchor to one side and the row of fishermen's cottages to the other, Tom paused. Despite it being a Tuesday, the pub was busy, with drinkers spilling out of the door. 'What say we switch to a more cheerful subject?'

But Connie wasn't quite done. 'How did you leave Maureen?' she asked.

'Upset,' Lizzie admitted. 'She tried to be glad about the couple coming forward to adopt Susan, but I could tell her heart was breaking all the same.'

Connie grunted. It wasn't often that she felt this stumped.

Tom squeezed her hand. 'Leave it for a bit,' he suggested.

Right on cue Bill came out of his cottage and strode towards them just as a customer was ejected from the pub by the landlord. The crowd by the door parted as the drunkard was thrust forward, swearing and staggering into the cobbled square, where he sank to his knees then collapsed in a heap.

'That's Eric Thompson up to his old tricks,' Bill commented as he put his arm around Lizzie's waist and guided her towards the door. 'Drinking himself into a stupor, then refusing to stump up for what he owes.'

Thompson lay face down at their feet, making no attempt to get up. His jacket was filthy and torn, his long hair matted.

Bill and company gave him a suitably wide berth – Connie, in particular, stayed as far away as possible from her old enemy. Two men broke free from the group by the door and raised Thompson from the ground, slinging his arms around their shoulders and hauling him to a nearby bench.

'Rather them than me.' Tom's comment was dismissive. 'This round is on me. Bill, is it your usual? Connie, Lizzie – what'll you have?'

Pamela had done everything possible to make Fred comfortable. She saw to it that soft cushions bolstered his aching joints and that blankets and hot-water bottles kept him warm. Sweet, milky tea was produced out of nowhere. Edith, Harold and Hugh had circled quietly and attentively, willing to do whatever was needed.

On the Tuesday morning Hugh had given Pamela the day off. 'I insist,' he'd told her after she'd spent the night in an armchair at Fred's side. 'Betty can manage quite well without you for the time being.'

Her father, too, had encouraged her to take it easy. 'You'll be no good to Fred if you wear yourself out,' he'd advised. 'Besides, you've both had a dreadful shock. It'll be much better for you to stay here in the warmth and keep each other company.'

The day had passed slowly, with Fred drifting in and out of sleep. Pamela had sat with him in the dimly lit room, observing every inch of the geometric wallpaper, every expensive, shiny ornament on the mantelpiece and each swirling tendril in the green and fawn patterned carpet. When awake, Fred had managed a few wan smiles. 'I didn't mean to drag your family into this,' he'd whispered through cracked lips.

'Nonsense.' Pamela had soothed him by stroking his forehead. 'You didn't drag us into anything.'

'But this is my battle.'

'No,' she'd objected quietly but firmly. 'This is *our* battle – Mum and Dad's, Uncle Hugh's and mine.' She'd kept quiet about the vicious note that she'd received and instead renewed her vow that he would never be alone again. 'So let's have no more talk about you leaving Kelthorpe. We'll face this together, you and I.'

As the day wore on, Fred grew more alert. Despite the stiffness and swelling affecting every joint, he insisted on sitting up. There really was no need for Pamela to watch over him and tend to his every need, he told her. He was already on the mend and yes, he would try to eat something if she promised to stop worrying. 'If I'm to stay in Kelthorpe, we must go on as if this never happened,' he insisted in the late afternoon. 'It will be our way of showing that we won't be beaten.'

'We?' she repeated tentatively. She felt a small leap

of hope inside her chest that there would be no more talk of his disappearing into the night.

Hugh's car pulled up outside the house before Fred could respond. There was the sound of quick footsteps on gravel, then the turn of a key in the lock before Pamela's uncle opened the door to the sitting room, bringing crisp, fresh air with him.

'How's the invalid?' he enquired brightly as he took off his hat and gloves. 'Sitting up, I see. Good show – very well done, my boy. That's the ticket.'

Pamela drew up another chair and invited Hugh to sit with them. He shared news of the outside world – the railway line that served the timber yard was almost repaired and business would be back to normal by Thursday at the latest. Unfortunately, it would take longer to rebuild the grain silos, though Wilfred Freeman had his men working on it night and day.

'The world hasn't collapsed without you two in the office,' Hugh said with a kindly smile. 'So there's no need for you to hurry back.'

'That's very good of you, sir.' Fred winced as he attempted to sit more upright.

'Let's drop the formalities, shall we?' Hugh sought for words that would put Fred at ease. 'I'd be perfectly happy for you to address me by my Christian name when we're not at work.' Dash it; that hadn't come out how he'd intended. 'Just call me Hugh,' he added humbly.

'Thank you, sir – I'll try.' Fred's facial muscles attempted a painful smile. 'I mean, thank you, Hugh; that's very decent of you. And thank you for offering me shelter. I'm most grateful.'

'Not at all. And I mean it: don't rush your

convalescence.' Fred had to be admired for the way he'd survived the rotten attack. A lesser man would have curled into a ball and waited to be found. But no; Fred had come round, then fought through the pain and crawled more than half a mile around the headland until he'd reached Sunrise. Hugh had heard cries for help and opened his door to a bloodied mess – a crouched figure in his porch that he'd scarcely recognized. But even on the verge of unconsciousness, the brave boy had been determined not to make a fuss. From out of the blue the thought struck Hugh that Fred was the son that he and Peggy had never been able to have: a handsome boy and decent through and through. How differently life would have turned out if that had been the case.

'I was telling Pamela: we must carry on as before.' Fred filled an awkward silence. 'I hope to be back at work next week to tie up loose ends before the holiday.'

Pamela smiled eagerly. These were the words she'd longed to hear. Her beloved Fred had resolved to stay.

'And Pamela, you must carry on as normal.' He smiled back at her and clasped her hand. 'Get back to the office and resume your evening shifts at the sector post.'

'Tonight!' she exclaimed, suddenly remembering and glancing at her watch. She had less than an hour to get ready. 'No, I won't go. I'll telephone the control centre.'

'And offer them what as an excuse?' Fred countered. 'Listen, I won't suddenly take a turn for the worse. It's perfectly safe for you to leave me.'

'Uncle Hugh?' Pamela asked for his view.

'Fred's right.' Hugh's response took her by surprise. 'I'm happy to sit with him this evening while you do your duty. Keep calm and carry on, don't you know?'

So, with a quick kiss on the cheek for Fred and a warm smile for her uncle, Pamela hurried off to her lodgings. She was amazed how good could come out of even the worst situation; her dearest wish had come true – Fred was no longer talking about running away and starting afresh. Besides, those brutes would have to think twice once they learned that Fred had Hugh Anderson's backing – her uncle was an influential man in Kelthorpe: a major employer and a member of the town council to boot. Reassuring herself as she changed into her uniform then rushed to Gas Street, Pamela was glad to find Connie putting the finishing touches to the evening's rota.

Connie greeted her with a relieved smile. 'Hello, stranger. How's Fred?'

'Not too bad, thank goodness.'

'Just so long as they haven't spoiled his film-star looks for good, eh? I take it you've gone to the police?' Connie picked up the phone, ready to make a call to report and control.

'No. You know Fred – he doesn't like a fuss.'

Connie's brow creased into a frown. 'And you two are tickety-boo?' The other phone rang so she replaced one receiver in its cradle before picking up the other.

'Yes, thanks.' Pamela's face flushed with embarrassment. 'We're grand.'

Connie put her hand over the phone. 'By the way,

just so you know: I threw that nasty note in the dustbin – best place for it, if you ask me.'

Hurriedly thanking her, Pamela went into the storeroom for her helmet and boots. She hoped for a quiet night out on patrol, checking blackouts and liaising with rescue and repair services, making house visits to post the latest government leaflets through letterboxes. Please God there would be no incidents. The cold, dark streets would be quiet – there might be a man walking his dog and the occasional messenger on a bike. With luck all would be well.

Early next morning *Sea Knight* sailed out of Kelthorpe harbour to join HMS *Intrepid* and two other trawlers that made up their small fleet of minesweepers. 'There's no need for you to wave us off,' Tom had told Connie when he'd dropped in at the sector post just before midnight carrying a small Christmas tree that he'd found in an abandoned Anderson shelter. 'In fact, I'd rather say goodbye now and get it over with.'

Connie had received the salvaged tree with a smile and had decided to bring some spare decorations from home to give the post a more festive air. Then she'd taken Tom up to the restroom and sat with him for a while. They'd talked quietly about their plans for Christmas Day: in the morning Tom would go with Connie to the hospital to visit Bert, then they would join Lizzie and Bill at number 12 for Christmas dinner – just the four of them.

'It'll be nice and cosy.' In her mind Connie had skipped the next four difficult days and looked ahead to when she and Tom could be together again. 'We'll have chicken and roast potatoes. Lizzie is a dab hand at making savoury pud from Mum's special recipe.'

'Will there be sprouts?' Tom had hoped the answer would be no. He'd pulled a face when she'd said yes; sprouts galore, sprouts until they were coming out of his ears.

Then the phone had rung – a call from the demolition team on Maypole Street asking her if she had any spare helmets they could borrow. Tom had blown her a kiss and slipped away. 'See you on Sunday,' he'd murmured on his way out.

Bill's final talk with Lizzie had taken place outside the house on Elliot Street. He'd brought her back from the Anchor on his motorbike but had refused the invitation to go in with her.

'Let's not make this any harder than it already is,' he'd implored. Separating had felt like a rope that connected two boats straining then snapping, its frayed ends falling into the water then drifting ever further apart.

They'd kissed on the pavement, not caring who might be watching. She'd forced herself to go up the steps to the front door then gone back for one last kiss that had turned into another and then another until finally Bill had broken away. 'Sunday,' he'd said, sitting astride the bike and starting the engine.

'Sunday,' she'd echoed. *Goodbye for now, my dearest love.*

Earlier, hidden away in a quiet corner of the pub after Connie and Tom had left, Bill had promised Lizzie a ring before Christmas – a ruby in a nest of diamonds. She'd shared her dreams for their wedding day. Bill had wondered where they would find pink carnations in the middle of winter. Just like a man to think of practicalities, Lizzie had teased. If Lizzie wanted pink carnations, pink carnations she would have. To and fro in the way young lovers have, holding hands and with eyes only for each other, they had been oblivious of their surroundings.

The cold light of a winter's dawn brought a dose of reality that neither Connie nor Lizzie welcomed. Their hearts were sore as they began work in the bakery, mostly silent and lost in their own thoughts. Eight o'clock approached. Connie kneaded and pummelled dough while Lizzie slid loaves in and out of the oven. They went through the motions. By the time they opened the shop *Sea Knight* had already left the harbour.

'Cheer up, you two; it might never happen.' Their first customer commented on their glum expressions as she pocketed her change.

Then Ivy Cooper called in for her cottage loaf, soon followed by Hilda Fielding for an iced bun as a special treat for her brother Cyril. Hilda chose the bun – the one with the most icing furthest to the left – then carefully counted out two pennies and one halfpenny to reach the required amount. She asked after Bert before bringing the conversation around to the recent attack on Fred. 'That young man would be wise to watch his step in future,' she opined as she popped her purchase into her basket.

Behind her counter Connie bristled at the none-too-subtle comment. 'What makes you say that?'

Hilda turned up the collar of her fur coat, ready to brave the elements. Trim and slim where her brother was slovenly and slow, she gave a knowing toss of her neatly permed head. 'There's a rumour going around that he's a German spy. I must say, I work alongside him at the control centre and I've had my suspicions for some time.'

'Have you now?' Connie bit her tongue.

'Yes, and I'm by no means the only one. Take Cyril, for instance – he saw him at close quarters when they shared lodgings on Elliot Street. Cyril told me back then that Fred was sly and secretive. It surprised no one when it transpired that he'd been classified as an enemy alien. Surely that tells you everything you need to know.'

'Yes,' Connie retorted, 'it tells me that he's one of hundreds of thousands of refugees forced to flee Germany since Herr Hitler took up the reins. I won't hear a word against Fred Miller and now if you don't mind . . .' She beckoned the next customer to step forward.

'As for his bit of fluff, Pamela Carr . . .' Ignoring Connie's impassioned defence of Fred, Hilda's crude reference was a clumsy attempt to drum up support among other customers. 'That young girl should steer well clear of Herr Muller if she knows what's good for her.'

'Next!' Connie slammed her till drawer shut.

'Hilda has a point.' A woman in a drab grey coat, wearing a brown headscarf fashioned into a turban, took sides. 'Mr Churchill is in favour of shipping 'em off to Canada.'

'*Was* in favour!' Connie pointed out. 'That was before the *Arandora Star* was torpedoed on the way to Newfoundland and hundreds of innocent souls were lost.'

'Aye, but still – you can never be too careful.' Murmurs rustled through the shop – from 'Shoot the lot' through, 'They ought to make yon lad prove he's not a Nazi spy' to, 'Live and let live'.

'Lizzie!' Connie called for reinforcements. She took off her apron and flung it down. 'Can you hold the fort while I run an errand?'

'What errand?' Entering the shop, Lizzie was puzzled by the bad atmosphere.

Connie slipped two bread buns into a paper bag. 'I want to drop these off at Pam's lodgings,' she replied in a loud voice intended to silence the rumourmongers. 'They'll do nicely for Fred's breakfast if I get a move on.'

'Well, I never!' Hilda glared as Connie grabbed her coat.

'By heck!' The turbaned woman stepped to one side.

'Good for you, love,' a small, spry woman from the fish market told Connie as she made her exit.

Connie left the shop and marched down College Road towards the harbour. She turned on to King Edward Street and took the steep hill at a rapid trot. Hilda Fielding was the limit – as bad as her brother, if not worse. Unfounded rumours spread like a contagious disease; they must be well and truly scotched.

She reached Pamela's house and knocked on the door. There was a delay before Kathleen Roberts opened it, apparently ready to set off for work at the department store.

'Is Pamela in?' a breathless Connie asked.

'No, I haven't seen her this morning.' Kathleen glanced in the hallway mirror to check the angle of her hat. 'She's probably at Friedrich what's-his-name's house.'

'Good Lord, not you too.' Connie tutted her disapproval. 'I wanted to give her these bread buns but I suppose I could leave them for Maureen instead.'

'Oh, her.' Kathleen turned down the corners of her mouth. 'Miss Misery Guts. Her room's on the top floor – feel free.'

So the shop assistant slammed the door and went on her way while Connie climbed two flights of stairs. There was no sound and the shabby, cavernous house felt quiet and chilly. 'Maureen?' Connie called as she reached the top landing. The silence seemed to intensify. 'Maureen?' she repeated as she tapped on the attic door.

It stood ajar, so Connie pushed it open for a first sight of the young mother's room. There was an iron bedstead with a lumpy mattress, bare floorboards and evidence of neglect everywhere she looked. The walls were damp, the plaster of the sloping ceiling was cracked and crumbling away to reveal the wooden eaves. But there wasn't a stick of furniture or any article of clothing here and of Maureen there was no sign.

# CHAPTER FOURTEEN

'Off you go,' Fred insisted from his sofa. 'Much as I would love to have my dear girl running around after me all day, you have a job to go to and I'll be perfectly all right here by myself.'

Pamela hovered by the door. 'I can pop back at dinner time if you like?'

'No need.' He eased himself into a more comfortable sitting position. His bruises had darkened into two perfect black eyes but the cuts on his face had already begun to heal. He'd even managed to open his mouth wide enough to eat a small amount of porridge for breakfast.

'Can I bring you something to read?'

He pointed to the book on the low table next to his sofa. 'This Flann O'Brien will keep me entertained.' *At Swim-Two-Birds* was right up Fred's street: the fanciful, light-hearted adventure story made him determined to visit Dublin with Pamela once the war was over. And after that he had *The Grapes of Wrath* and *Brave New World* to get through, both on loan from the library.

'Is there anything at all I can do?'

'Yes, you can give me a kiss.' He smiled a crooked smile, then winced.

Pamela flew across the room to do his bidding.

'Top of my head, if you please.' Fred pointed to the solitary square inch of his body that didn't hurt.

She planted the soft kiss and would have lingered longer if her mother hadn't chosen this moment to check in on the invalid.

Edith had brought two hot-water bottles from the bungalow and a host of suggestions: if in need, Fred should ring the servants' bell to attract her attention, he should wear two pairs of socks to keep his feet warm, he must not strain his eyes with too much reading.

'I'll leave you to it,' Pamela said with a wistful smile.

'I'm in good hands,' he assured her.

'Uncle Hugh will give you a lift into work,' Edith said with a nod towards the car in the drive. 'He's out there, waiting for you.'

'Now go.' Pamela's mother and her sweetheart spoke as one.

There was no word of greeting from Betty when Pamela entered the office. The secretary's silence was hostile, her glance heavy with disdain.

*What have I done to deserve this?* Pamela longed to shout, to have it out with Betty once and for all. But no; she simply went to her cluttered desk and began to type.

'Go down and collect this morning's post,' Betty barked. Or, 'Take this invoice to the main office,' or, 'We need a new packet of biscuits for Mr Anderson's elevenses. Run to the corner shop for fig rolls and be quick about it.' All served up with an impatient sigh and lashings of implied criticism.

At dinner time Pamela sat alone in a corner of the noisy, steamy canteen. Her father had been called to Hugh's office for a meeting with the company accountant so she had no shield from the not-so-covert black looks from Betty's usual crowd. At one point Keith stopped cutting up his meat to jab his knife in Pamela's direction. At another Jack laughed nastily at a comment made by Betty, who all the while had her gimlet gaze fixed on Pamela. Other workers were drawn into the conversation as they passed Betty's table. More fingers were pointed and heads shaken. Boss's niece . . . hoity-toity . . . bad company . . . should know better.

Pamela smarted under their scrutiny. Hot and trembling, she scraped back her chair and went to stack her empty plate on the metal trolley by the door. The ugly word *Kraut* was mumbled as she left the building – or was she imagining it? Misery followed her across the timber yard like a cold mist, right back to her desk, where she sat down heavily and hid her face in her hands.

'Whatever's the matter?' Hugh's meeting was over and he'd brought a sheet of scribbled notes to be typed up. He found his niece wiping away tears. 'Are you still worried about Fred?'

'No,' Pamela replied hastily. 'I'm just being silly.'

'It's Betty, isn't it?' Hugh hit the nail on the head. 'No, don't deny it. I've seen how nasty she is with you.'

Pamela stared at him in surprise.

'I'd have to be blind not to.' Depositing the notes on Pamela's desk, he went to the window and, with hands clasped behind his back, stared down on the busy yard. 'Betty likes to rule the roost,' he admitted. 'She sees you as a rival – in more ways than one.'

'It's not fair – she never gave me a chance.' Pamela was too distressed to hide the truth. 'As far as she's concerned, I can't do right for doing wrong.'

'I'll have a word with her,' Hugh promised.

'No, Uncle Hugh – please!' Pamela didn't see how this would make things better. 'Betty will know I've been telling tales.'

But he was adamant. 'I'll issue a warning.' Seeing his secretary strut across the yard with Keith in tow, he decided to take immediate action. 'Send her to me as soon as she gets back,' he ordered Pamela as he left the room. 'Personal feelings must not stand in the way of Betty doing her job properly – I simply won't have it.'

Five o'clock was slow in coming. All afternoon the office had crackled with animosity, though not a word was said following Betty's summons to Hugh's office. The furious, uninterrupted clickety-clack, tippety-tap of two typewriters rivalling each other for speed had ridden wave after wave of silence between Betty and Pamela. 'Dear Mr Wilkins, Re Account Number 457; I am sorry to inform you that the account is now closed due to non payment of invoices.' 'Dear Sir, Unfortunately we are unable to supply the full amount of American oak as per your order of the 8th Dec because of current shortages.'

Letters were folded, envelopes were licked. Hugh came in with a stern glance at Betty and more notes for Pamela to type. He told his niece that her mother had telephoned to ask her to call at Benson's music shop on her way home to pick up some sheet music that Edith had ordered. 'And she said to tell you that Fred felt strong enough at lunchtime to take a turn around the garden,' he added.

Tap-tap-tap-tap. Betty hit a key repeatedly. Tap-tap-tap-tap-tap-tap!

Escape, when it came, was a blessed relief. At the sound of the klaxon Pamela ran from the building without bothering to button her coat. A rapid calculation told her that she barely had time to call in at Benson's, then at the bungalow to drop off the music before she rushed home to get changed into warm clothes for tonight's carol singing. With luck, she might squeeze in ten minutes with Fred.

There was a snag – the sheet music was on order but hadn't yet arrived at the shop, dash it! That was five wasted minutes. Pamela hurried on. It made more sense to call in at her lodgings first, she realized. She could go on from there across the market square then round the headland to Sunrise. Key in lock, up hollow stairs (it seemed she was first home from work), off with the blue dress and into corduroy slacks and two thick jumpers, fur boots, coat, beret and woollen scarf. She launched out again into the dark night as snowflakes began to drift down. Pamela felt their icy touch before they melted on her warm cheeks. Crossing the cobbled market square then skirting the harbour, she approached the headland. Three boys in school uniform overtook her, their feet slapping the tarmac as they ran. A woman on a bike approached from the other direction. Friendly nods were exchanged. 'Mind how you go,' the older woman said.

Pamela's heart beat faster as she reached the

overhang where Fred had been attacked. The wind howled and snowflakes whirled. She heard footsteps gain on her but dismissed them from her busy mind. It was too dark to read the time on her wristwatch; still, best to pick up her pace for this final, lonely stretch of path. As Pamela broke into a run, so did the people behind. She glanced over her shoulder, saw nothing and ran on, heart pounding. *Kraut whore* – the remembered insult exploded into her consciousness as fresh as the moment when she'd first read it. She turned again to see inky darkness, nothing else. The footsteps – more than one person – had slowed to what felt like a heavy, menacing walk.

'Who's there?' Pamela called.

The wind whipped the futile, fearful question from her lips. She was ten minutes away from Sunrise and every step was fraught with danger. Under the overhang, back out into huge white flakes of dancing snow. On along the promenade, buffeted by the wind. It was almost impossible to breathe, but she must press on. Waves crashed on the shore, drowning out the sound of any footsteps that might still be following. Pamela ran towards civilization and a man walking two greyhounds, past the bombed ruins of the Royal Hotel to the safety of Sunrise and into Fred's arms.

Lizzie and Connie postponed their planned visit to the Queen Alexandra. The mystery of Maureen's sudden disappearance was an itch that demanded to be scratched without delay.

'I've telephoned the hospital for the latest news on Dad,' Connie informed Lizzie as the afternoon drew to a close. Outside the shop the first flakes of snow had begun to fall. 'The nice young nurse gave him a good report.'

'So he's still doing as he's told?' Lizzie had recently returned to the bakery after her final delivery round.

'He's being as good as gold and the doctors are pleased with him,' Connie reported. 'Then I rang Gladys Smallwood at the WVS centre, just in case Maureen had taken it into her head to sneak in there to see her baby.'

'She wouldn't risk it, would she?' Lizzie took a sharp intake of breath.

'It strikes me she's desperate enough to do anything.'

'And did she?'

Connie shook her head. 'Dragon Gladys practically breathed fire down the phone at the very idea. She assured me that nothing happens there without her knowledge and that the most recent visit to baby Susan was paid by the couple who plan to adopt her. They took in a little knitted rabbit for her cot.'

'So where on earth has Maureen gone?' Lizzie racked her brains. 'There's no one she would go to for help, is there?'

'I doubt it. I don't get the feeling that she has many friends.' Connie switched the sign on the door from 'Open' to 'Closed'. 'This is a long shot, but just suppose she's back at her mother's house.'

'On North Street?' Lizzie considered the possibility. 'No, surely not – the two of them are daggers drawn.'

'You don't think it's worth a try?' Taking off her apron, then folding it and storing it on a shelf under the counter, Connie grew more determined to follow this, their only lead. 'Honestly, Liz. I won't sleep tonight without making sure that Maureen is safe.'

'I won't sleep anyway, for thinking about Bill.'

Lizzie's candid admission drew a sympathetic sigh from Connie. 'I know, but chin up.'

It took a great effort for Lizzie to bring her mind back from dark, stormy seas to the matter in hand. 'You're right – we should pay Maureen's mother a quick visit.' There was no time to lose. If they drove to North Street, they should still be back in the old town in time to join their carol singing group for their first foray on to the streets of Kelthorpe. 'We'll have to step on it,' Lizzie urged as they shut up shop. 'But don't build up your hopes. And don't expect a warm welcome – Hans Christian Andersen's Snow Queen is a pussycat compared with Nancy Strong.'

'What do you want?' Nancy opened the door to Connie and Lizzie's knock. Her words were brusque and her head was tilted warily to one side.

'Is Maureen here?' As was her wont, Connie went for the direct approach.

Nancy's blue eyes narrowed. 'No. Try her lodgings on King Edward Street.'

'I already have. Her room is empty.'

'What do you mean, empty? She's only just moved in there.'

'It seems Maureen has moved out again.' Connie saw Nancy's suspicious expression change to one of bewilderment: her eyes widened and she grasped the edge of the door.

'We wondered if she'd come back here,' Lizzie

explained. She noticed Colin standing at the foot of the stairs at the far end of the dimly lit hallway.

Nancy took a deep breath before glancing up and down the street. A bus pulled up at the stop directly opposite and passengers alighted. 'You'd better come in,' she told them quickly.

Colin disappeared into a back room as Lizzie and Connie followed Nancy into her neat sitting room. Nothing was out of place – magazines were stored in a rack underneath the wireless, next to a maroon leather pouffe. Shiny fire tongs rested against a brass fender that surrounded a low, fawn-tiled fireplace. A round, convex mirror on the chimney breast distorted the reflection of a crimson settee and two matching armchairs.

'When did you last see Maureen?' Nancy demanded.

'Yesterday afternoon.' Lizzie kept her answer brief and to the point.

'How did she seem?'

'Upset.'

A defensive shield slid into place, blocking all expression from Nancy's delicately formed features. 'About what?'

'Come off it.' Connie stepped in with an outright challenge. 'You know full well why Maureen was upset. Having a baby at her age, then being made to give it away is too much to bear. The girl is beside herself.'

Nancy gave a short gasp of protest before crumpling under Connie's accusing stare. All her plans, every attempt to protect the family name and to hold her head high in her Church community lay in fragments at her feet. 'She told you?' she asked in a cracked whisper.

'No. We guessed.' Ever the conciliator, Lizzie tried to soften the blow. 'We could see the first time we met Maureen that she wasn't well. There was some mention of the baby that had been abandoned at St Joseph's – our conversation made Maureen dizzy and she fainted. It wasn't hard for us to put two and two together.'

Nancy shook her head and sighed. 'If only she'd stuck to the plan. It was all going perfectly well at the mother and baby home; she was looked after during her pregnancy, and once the baby had been sent for adoption she could have come home and started afresh. No one in Kelthorpe would have been any the wiser. Our lives would not have been ruined.'

'It would have broken her heart,' Connie said pointedly. As she said it, she knew that it was broken anyway.

'Maureen should have thought of that before she did what she did.' The accusatory words erupted from Nancy's mouth, twisting her attractive features and bringing a deep red flush to her face.

The mother's anger winded Connie. *Good God, where did that fury come from?*

'Mrs Strong . . . Nancy.' Lizzie appealed for calm. 'We're worried. Why would Maureen move out of King Edward Street? Where would she go?'

'How could she, after everything she'd been taught? Yes, Maureen's young but she knows the difference between right and wrong. She's had it drilled into her from an early age, at Sunday school and in her confirmation classes. She knew the disgrace it would bring.'

'Nancy,' Lizzie said again, 'what if Maureen didn't have a say in the matter? Have you considered that?'

This time the questions sank in. The dry whisper returned. 'You mean that she was forced?'

'We don't know. But it's possible.'

'No – she would have said!'

'Not if she was sworn to secrecy by the man who did this to her,' Connie muttered. 'Maybe she was – *is* – too frightened to speak.'

Nancy reeled as the fragments of her daughter's ruined reputation slowly began to reassemble themselves into a new picture. 'Surely not. The silly girl got herself into trouble with a boy she'd known at school or at the church youth club – that's the way I see it.'

Again, that phrase: 'got herself into trouble'. But Connie and Lizzie let it go unchallenged. Nancy Strong was struggling to come to terms with the new possibility as it was.

'Let's concentrate on recent events,' Lizzie insisted. 'It's clear to Connie and me that Maureen was too much in love with the baby to hand her over to the matron of the home. When she ran away with Susan she did it without thinking of the consequences. But what happened after she arrived back here?'

'I took them both in.' Nancy grew fiercely defensive, clenching her fists and flinging her arms out to the sides. 'I agreed that she could stay as long as she followed certain rules.'

Aware of Colin's footsteps creeping down the corridor, Lizzie decided to ignore his return.

Nancy continued. 'Maureen must stay in the house. She must keep the baby hidden until we'd decided what to do next. Was that too much to ask?'

So the price of a roof over the girl's head had been invisibility. But where was the love? Where was the Christian charity? Connie shook her head in disgust.

'I believed I could talk her round eventually,' Nancy insisted. 'She would see the sense of taking the baby back to Axenby and handing her over to the matron there. But did she? No, she refused to accept my advice. There were endless arguments. The atmosphere became unbearable. In the end it was mutually agreed that Maureen should leave and fend for herself, even though it risked bringing shame on all our heads.'

'Did she tell you that she intended to give up the baby?' Lizzie wondered how far ahead Maureen had planned.

'To abandon her, you mean?' Nancy's deliberate emphasis on the word 'abandon' conveyed contempt.

Lizzie gave a defeated shudder. They'd reached a dead end and it was obvious that there would be no talking Nancy round to a more compassionate view. 'And you've no idea where she might be now? Does she have grandparents or anyone else she might turn to?'

'No.' The torrent of words had run out – Nancy's answer was angry and abrupt.

'We'll go now,' Connie told her quietly. 'We're sorry if the latest news has upset you and we'll let you know if we hear anything.'

There was a scuffling noise in the hall as she and Lizzie made their way out. Nancy made no attempt to see them to the door. So Lizzie and Connie stepped out into a sprinkling of snow on the ground but to clearing skies. Overhead the stars twinkled brightly – shimmering Sirius, the Dog Star and dazzling Venus. The girls were sombre as they crossed the pavement and got into the van.

Lizzie drove in silence from North Street on to the promenade, where she spotted Colin shivering on the street corner. He stood at the edge of the pavement without a coat: a hunched, miserable figure in grey flannel shorts and long woollen socks, waving to attract their attention.

'Stop!' Connie cried when she too saw the boy.

Lizzie braked and felt her back wheels skid sideways over the thin covering of snow. Parking haphazardly, she waited in the van while Connie jumped out to speak to Colin.

'You won't tell Mam?' He cast a fearful glance towards North Street.

'Tell her what, Colin?'

'That I sneaked out to see you.'

'Of course not.' Connie was tempted to brush snowflakes from the boy's head and shoulders but suspected that the maternal gesture would send him scuttling away. 'You must be freezing. Why not come and sit in the van with us?'

He shook his head, folding his arms across his chest and clamping his fingers under his armpits, then hopping from one foot to the other.

Connie beckoned for Lizzie to join her. 'What is it? What do you want to tell us?'

'It's our Maureen.' Colin hesitated, then turned away as if he'd changed his mind about being there.

'Can you tell us where she's gone?' Connie softened her tone.

'No, and I'm scared stiff in case she does something stupid.'

'We all are.' Lizzie spoke for the first time. 'We wonder why she's run away from King Edward Street. Do *you* know someone she might go to for help?'

'What are you asking me for? She never tells me anything. We had a massive row.' The boy's mind hopped and shifted as fast as his feet.

'I heard you,' Lizzie reminded him.

'I was nasty to her.' Colin started to cry. 'That's why she ran away. I didn't mean to make her – it's all my fault.'

'No, Colin – it's not.' Connie spoke slowly and deliberately. 'Look at me. You're not to blame for any of this. You're a good lad who got caught in the middle of a situation that you couldn't do anything about. You haven't done anything wrong.'

He sniffed, then rubbed his wet cheeks with the cuff of his jumper. 'I hadn't a clue why Mam sent Maureen away in the first place,' he whined. 'Then when she came back with a baby in tow there was rows all the time. It was meant to be a secret – I wasn't allowed to mention it. I wasn't supposed to cuddle Susan or anything.'

'It must have been really hard,' Lizzie said gently.

A blast of icy wind blew off the sea. At this rate Colin would freeze to death. 'Why did you sneak out just now?' Connie steered him back on course. 'What did you want to tell us?'

Again Colin rubbed at his face with his sleeve. 'I know why she left Susan at St Joseph's,' he blurted out.

Connie flashed a quick look at Lizzie, who crouched down to Colin's level.

'Is it because there was someone at the church who would look after the baby – someone special?'

Tears welled up again and this time Colin didn't wipe them away. 'I'm not daft. I saw the way he acted: all nice to us after we got the telegram about Dad.'

'Who did?' Connie held her breath, hoping for a name that might solve the mystery of the baby's father.

Colin blinked and batted the question back. It was as if a fault on the line had suddenly cut off all communication.

Who were the regulars at St Joseph's? Lizzie raced through various possibilities but it was a large parish and she could alight on no obvious name. 'Never mind who for now. This person had been kind to you and Maureen in the past so that's the reason she left the baby at the church, hoping that he'd know what to do. And you think she might have gone back now to this same man?'

'I'm telling you, I don't know.' It was no good; the line had gone dead.

'But you didn't like this person, did you?' Connie made one last attempt to prise more information from the boy.

'No,' His face twisted in angry resentment. 'I didn't want him to be nice to us.'

'But your sister didn't mind?' Lizzie asked.

'No. Maureen liked him.'

'And you won't give us his name?' The tentative wording of Connie's question signalled defeat.

'No.' Colin punched out his reply. 'But when Mam and Maureen rowed over the baby, he was the one who was meant to find Susan and look after her. Only, it didn't work, did it?'

'No – Pamela and I found her instead.' Connie's heart sank as she realized how badly her good deed had turned out in Maureen's eyes. 'I'm sorry,' she murmured. 'We thought we were doing the right thing.'

Colin's misery mounted. 'And now look!' he cried as he backed away from Connie and Lizzie. 'It's all gone wrong. We lost Dad and now we've lost Maureen as well. She's never coming home. It's just me and Mam from now on, and I hate it and I hate you!'

Connie and Lizzie watched helplessly as their informant turned and ran wildly along the snowy street, back to his lonely, sad and loveless house.

The sky was clear when the choir gathered on Tennyson Street. There was an air of anticipation and much stamping of feet and clearing of throats as Doug did a quick headcount.

'Sixteen, seventeen, eighteen.' The choirmaster scanned the nervous faces. 'No Pamela?' He turned to Connie and Lizzie for an answer.

'Yes – here she comes now.' Lizzie pointed to the figure running up King Edward Street to join them.

'I'm sorry I'm late,' Pamela gasped. She'd dithered until the very last minute; should she go carol singing as planned or should she stay with Fred at Sunrise? If she chose to remain she would have to make a good case for not going out – the weather was too bad, it was too cold, she would rather keep Fred company. On no account must she give any hint of her frightening experience on the headland path. *I think I was followed. I heard footsteps. It came to nothing. Perhaps I made it all up.* No, it would only worry him, perhaps for no good reason.

'Go, meet your friends and sing your heart out,' Fred had encouraged. 'In any case, I'm a dull dog at present.'

'Enjoy it – it'll get you into the Christmas spirit.' As usual Uncle Hugh had backed him up.

So Pamela had left the house without sharing her worries, saying she would come tomorrow morning to sit with Fred. Now here she was on Tennyson Street, out of breath and apologizing.

Connie greeted her with a broad smile. 'You're looking a bit peaky,' she commented.

'It must be the cold.' Pamela brushed away her friend's concern.

Doug handed the collection tin to Lizzie. 'Will you do the honours?'

Lizzie accepted the tin. 'What exactly do I have to do?'

'Knock on doors and smile nicely. Rattle the tin to encourage donations. And remember, everyone: no torches. We must observe the blackout at all times.'

Doug set off along the dark terraced street, a pied piper leading his band of hearty carollers. Powdery snow glistened beneath their feet and their warm breath emerged in clouds of steam.

'Good King Wenceslas' was followed by 'While Shepherds Watched'. They sang their hearts out as Lizzie knocked on doors and was rewarded by the clunking sound of coppers and threepenny bits landing in the tin.

'Happy Christmas!' She smiled her thanks.

'Happy Christmas to you too, love,' a woman replied, her two young children clinging to her skirt and gawping at the carol singers as they went on their way.

'"Once in royal David's City".' Arnold's pure voice rose to meet the twinkling stars of the night sky. An old man stood at his door. 'By Jove, that lad's got a good pair of bellows,' he told Lizzie as he slid his pennies through the slot.

'Well done.' Connie nudged her nephew with her elbow as his solo came to an end.

They progressed slowly along the street until they came to number 7.

'We'll have no luck there,' Connie predicted. 'That's Eric Thompson's house.'

Lizzie gladly gave the run-down dwelling a miss. The next few houses were empty due to bomb damage so the choir crossed the street to stand under a lamp post and sing the remaining verses of the popular hymn: '"He came down to earth from heaven . . . With the poor and mean and lowly".'

Doors opened, coins dropped into the tin, more smiles and Happy Christmases were exchanged. The singers turned on to Maypole Street, the heart of the old town, where some of the houses were more than two hundred years old – it was a hotchpotch of styles: low, plain Georgian cottages with dates carved into stone lintels stood cheek by jowl with high Victoriana. Here Doug suggested that they pause to gather their breath.

Lizzie rattled the heavy tin in Pamela and Connie's ears. 'Not bad for a start, eh?'

'Especially when you think how folks have to scrimp and save these days.' Pamela did her best to enter into the spirit of the occasion.

Connie gave her a long, hard look. 'More trouble?'

Lizzie cocked her head to one side. *What now?*

'No, it's nothing.' Pamela pulled up her scarf to cover the bottom half of her face.

Connie disagreed. 'It's not nothing. It's preyed on my mind ever since it happened – you said to keep shtum, but do you mind if I tell Lizzie about the you-know-what?'

Noticing that Doug was about to marshal his troops, Lizzie quickly demanded to know what was going on.

'Can I?' Connie persisted.

Pamela frowned, then gave a quick nod. Lizzie's calmness and common sense might help soothe her jangled nerves.

'Someone wrote her a mean note,' Connie explained to Lizzie. 'To do with Pamela being Fred's sweetheart.'

'Don't tell her what it said.' Pamela couldn't bear to hear the vile insult spoken out loud.

'It talked about collaborators.' Connie trod carefully. 'It was nasty.'

'For heaven's sake!' Lizzie stood on the spot as the band of singers regrouped around her. 'What is the world coming to?'

'My thought exactly,' Connie agreed.

'But you asked Pam if there was *more* trouble,' Lizzie reminded her. 'Is there something else?'

'"Away in a Manger".' Doug announced the next carol and prepared to move on. An officious-looking warden wearing a white helmet approached the group to issue reminders about blackout conditions and gas masks.

'Nosy parker,' someone grumbled quietly.

'Is there?' Connie echoed Lizzie's question to Pamela. 'Have you had another note?'

'No, it's not that.' Pamela trembled afresh as she spoke. 'But I think I was followed – I'm not sure – I heard footsteps but I didn't see anyone.'

'When? Where? Who by?' As the obvious questions sprang from Lizzie's lips, Connie recalled the full contents of the original note: the coarse insult followed by the threat to shave Pamela's head and to tar and feather her, and finally the warning for her to watch out in future.

'This is serious,' Lizzie insisted. What if the note-writing thugs did to Pamela what they'd already done to Fred? 'They've obviously got it in for you, whoever they are.'

'"Away in a manger, no crib for a bed",' the choir struck up again and shuffled on. Arnold and two of his pals surreptitiously scooped snow from the top of a garden wall and made snowballs to throw at a cat sitting on a doorstep.

'Have you told Fred?' Connie demanded. 'No, I can tell by your face that you haven't.'

'I didn't want to worry him.' The explanation sounded lame but it was the best Pamela could come up with. What she kept from them was her paralysing fear that Fred would revert to his plan of leaving Kelthorpe; that she would lose him if she told him the truth.

'Tell him!' Lizzie said as Doug gestured for her to knock on the next door.

'Fred loves you – you have to face this together,' Connie insisted. 'Do it first thing tomorrow.'

'"The stars in the bright sky look down where he lay".'

Lizzie rattled her tin. *Merry Christmas*. The choir warbled on.

'I will,' Pamela promised faintly. She knew in her heart that the sisters were right – her secret had to be shared and she must accept the consequences, good or bad. It was time to stop being a hypocrite and to start being brave. She would put her love for Fred to the ultimate test.

# CHAPTER FIFTEEN

'Good riddance.' Kathleen stood with Joan and Winnie in the hallway at King Edward Street. All three girls were smartly dressed and setting off for work as Pamela opened the door of her room at eight o'clock next morning.

'Maureen just upped and left?' Joan glanced up the stairwell with a puzzled frown.

'Without saying a word to anyone,' Winnie confirmed. 'The lady, or rather the girl, vanishes!'

'There's gratitude for you.' A disgruntled Joan opened the front door and peered out. The snow had frozen overnight, making walking on the icy pavements difficult for the steady stream of shop assistants, typists and office clerks gingerly making their way to work. 'I did that girl a favour by helping her to move in here. It turns out I might as well not have bothered.'

Taking care to stay out of sight, Pamela gave a long, low sigh. Maureen's mysterious disappearance had quickly become the latest gossip fodder, with little or no sympathy on display from her fellow lodgers.

'As for the other little madam . . .' Winnie rolled her eyes heavenwards.

Pamela froze. Whatever came next she knew the criticism would be aimed at her.

Kathleen made a loud tutting noise. 'You've heard the rumours that are flying around?' she asked Joan.

'No; do tell.' Joan stepped out into the street.

'They say her ladyship's grown too pally with the German spy we have in our midst.' Winnie's voice faded as she followed Joan out of the house.

'What German spy?' Joan raised her voice in astonishment.

'You know: Fred Miller – Hugh Anderson's right-hand man, the one who works in report and control.' Kathleen delivered the juicy titbit before slamming the door behind her.

Pamela's heart sank. She felt drained and hopeless to discover how easily truth was swamped by lies. Then she gathered herself, waiting five minutes before setting off for Sunrise. On the way there she rehearsed what she would say to Fred. She would stick to the basic facts – the note and the possibility that she'd been followed. She prepared herself for his reaction. They would talk it through sensibly and gain strength from facing the threat together.

Scarcely noticing her surroundings, as she approached Sunrise her determination wavered. What if Fred were to insist on telling her parents and her uncle about the danger she was in? Her mother would be frantic with worry; her father, too. As for Uncle Hugh, he might question the wisdom of keeping Pamela and Fred under his wing and remind them that he had his own reputation to consider. Pamela's mind spun off in different directions so that by the time she reached the grand house on the seafront she was faint with fright.

She stopped at the gate to stare at the steel-grey sea. The powerful waves rolled in, their white crests breaking and smashing against the harbour wall. Heavy clouds were laden with more snow.

Fred watched her from the lounge window. Pamela looked small and uncertain, and his heart went out to her. He wanted to protect her but a familiar refrain played inside his head: what good was he in his present condition? When she turned and noticed him he raised his hand to wave but lowered it again when he saw her beautiful, anxious face.

Pamela hurried up the drive and into the house, taking off her coat and gloves in the wide hall with its stained-glass door panels. Fred was waiting for her in the sitting room – she glimpsed him through the open door, easing his stiff limbs on to the sofa and fixing a smile on his face.

Mirroring his uneasy grin, she went in and kissed him lightly on the cheek. How had he slept? Was he in less pain? Had he eaten breakfast?

'Pamela.' He stopped her with a shake of his head.

'What?' Her heart raced; he looked so serious and sad. His eyes told her that there was no room for pretending.

'I love you.'

'I know you do.' Was her heartbeat racing at top speed towards disaster? *Please God – no!*

'I will always love you.' There was not a contour on her face, not a curve of her eyelashes and lips that Fred would forget.

She sat beside him, afraid to touch his bruised body. 'Your enemies are my enemies,' she began simply.

He guessed straight away what she was leading up to. 'You received a note?'

'Yes. How did you know?'

'I had a premonition. I felt it was only a matter of time.' He waited to hear what the note said.

'I'm accused of being a collaborator.' Not good enough – she must tell him everything. 'Oh, Fred. They used terrible words. They said I was a Kraut whore.'

He closed his eyes and clenched his teeth. He would rather be beaten and kicked again to within an inch of his life – anything to save Pamela from this humiliation.

'On top of which, I may have been followed.' She spoke faintly, watching the small muscles in his jaw tighten. 'Last night, on my way here.'

'No – we can't allow this!' Ignoring the pain, he stood up and paced the room. 'We must do something.'

'I was afraid to tell you,' she confessed.

'But we must be honest. Isn't that what you always say?'

'Yes, and it's true.'

Fred stopped by the window to stare long and hard at the sea. 'The note – was it delivered by hand?'

'No, by post. It arrived at Gas Street in an envelope and with a proper stamp.'

'Typewritten?'

Pamela nodded.

No handwritten scrawl on a scrap of paper, then. So perhaps a different source from the notes he'd received. 'This is what I was afraid of.'

She joined him at the window. 'What can we do?'

'They won't stop,' he predicted grimly. 'My enemies want to get rid of me by any means possible.'

'There must be some way of finding out who's behind this?' she pleaded.

'And if there are too many of them?' When Fred turned his head to look at her his gaze was so sharp and intense that her heart jolted to a halt then thudded erratically against her ribs. 'What then?' he asked.

Pamela grasped his hand. 'I don't care if the whole world is against us,' she vowed. 'In the end people will see that we've done nothing wrong.' Fear loosened its grip as the heat from his palm warmed hers. 'We,' she repeated softly. 'Not "I" or "you".'

Her trust in the power of love moved him and he longed to believe her. But Fred knew better than most that persecution wasn't driven by notions of guilt and innocence. 'We'll see,' he said with a sigh as feathery snow began to drift to earth and settle on the lawn and hedges, covering the icy surface of the promenade and softening the stark outlines of the concrete pillboxes lined up along the beach.

'Yes, I know Maureen Strong.' Terence Ibbotson, the vicar of St Joseph's, invited Lizzie into his study. 'Why do you ask?'

Lizzie glanced around the high-ceilinged room at bookshelves supporting weighty, leather-bound tomes. She took in the neat array of diary, pens and paper on the desk and a closely patterned Turkish rug covering the polished oak floorboards. Though she knew and respected the young clergyman through her occasional attendance at church, this was the first time she'd been invited into his inner sanctum. Unbuttoning her corduroy windcheater and loosening her scarf, Lizzie sat in the leather chair indicated by the vicar while he seated himself behind the desk. Earnest and dutiful, with a shiny white dog collar, thick dark hair and lively eyes, his benign expression suggested that he was ready to answer any question Lizzie might wish to ask.

'She's my friend,' Lizzie answered. 'Unfortunately, she moved out of her lodgings without leaving a forwarding address. I'm trying to find out where she went.'

Terence leaned his elbows on the desk and made a tent shape with his fingers. 'Why? Is there cause for concern?'

'Maybe.' Aiming to be truthful without giving too much away, her answer was guarded. 'Maureen has been through a difficult time lately.'

The vicar's expression became more quizzical and he raised a long, warning finger. 'Confidences must not be breached on either side. The Strongs have worshipped at St Joseph's for many years. I know the family well, but I'm afraid it wouldn't be ethical to share personal information about any of my parishioners with you.'

'I'm not asking you to,' Lizzie assured him. She'd called at the vicarage at the end of her first round of deliveries and had been pleasantly surprised by the welcome she'd received. She and the vicar had chatted about the previous night's carol singing, then about the proposed repairs to church buildings. Then they'd moved on to the real reason for her visit. 'Maureen's brother—'

'Colin?' Terence interrupted a touch too readily. The Strong family had evidently been on his mind of late.

'Yes, Colin. He says that Maureen has close connections with St Joseph's.'

'Indeed?' The keen eyes gave her a searching look.

'Yes. It led me to wonder if anyone here has her new address.'

'I see. Would you perhaps wish me to make enquiries?'

'Yes please. I know that Maureen came here for confirmation classes; perhaps someone in her group would know where she's gone.'

'I take it you've asked her mother?' A perplexed frown appeared on Terence's smooth features. 'That would be the obvious course of action.'

'Yes, but even Nancy had no idea that Maureen had vanished from King Edward Street.'

'A mystery, then.' He took his time to size up the situation. 'You're obviously worried.'

'Honestly? Yes.' Lizzie shifted to the edge of her seat and leaned forward. 'The truth is, the last time I saw Maureen she wasn't very well. I could understand why, given what she's been through. I'm afraid it all became too much for her.'

The clergyman listened attentively before glancing out of the window at the graveyard and the church hall beyond. The snow was easing slightly and the sky was clearing. A pale sun emerged from behind the clouds. 'I see,' he said again without further probing.

'Christmas is a bad time for Maureen – for anyone – to cut themselves off from friends and family,' Lizzie pointed out. 'I really hope you can help me to find her.'

'You're right and I'll do my best. From what I know of Maureen she's an exceptionally shy girl who means well but who can be easily led. That's why her mother deemed it necessary to send her away for a while; so that she could escape certain bad influences here in Kelthorpe. Perhaps there's a new friend who we're not aware of.'

'I don't think so.' A thought struck Lizzie with some force: was Terence Ibbotson the kindly face that Colin had described with such bitterness? He certainly fitted the bill, with his clean-cut looks and mild, considerate manner. 'That's why I'm so keen to find her – me, my sister Connie and our friend, Pamela Carr, are the only allies Maureen seems to have at present.'

'Oh dear.' Terence cleared his throat. 'I'm duty-bound to mention your visit to Maureen's mother the next time I see her. I take it you have no objection?'

'Tell Nancy by all means.' Disappointed that she'd gleaned so little, Lizzie stood up. 'Finding Maureen is urgent,' she insisted a touch desperately. 'As far as we're aware, she has no money to pay for new lodgings and no job either. And she won't go back home to her mother. I know that for a fact.'

'Understood.' Terence offered to shake hands over the desk. 'I'll check our recent confirmation records and telephone you if I make any progress.'

Lizzie gave him the number of the bakery as the best and quickest way to contact her. 'Thank you for listening,' she said as he showed her to the door.

'No; thank you. And bless you for your concern about Maureen,' Ibbotson countered in the benevolent way of vicars everywhere. 'I assure you, I'll do everything in my power to help.'

*

In trouble. No better than she should be. Throughout the morning, as Connie served her regular customers, trite phrases were bandied to and fro. It seemed that Maureen's sudden disappearance had set tongues wagging. A girl like that – a nondescript, mousy little thing – who'd have thought it? And from a good family, too.

The town gossips had quickly filled in the gaps; if Maureen had been disowned by her mother, there could only be one reason for it. Remember the baby abandoned at St Joseph's? Two and two made four for all the Elsies and Emilys who sniffed out a scandal to enliven their dreary lives.

'I know what I'd do if my lass got herself into that kind of a fix,' Connie's most forthright customer commented after she ordered her usual brown loaf. 'I'd be knocking on Aggie Noble's door double quick. Aggie would soon sort her out.'

Connie frowned at the casual mention of the notorious back-street abortionist, but she slid the loaf across the counter without comment. 'Next, please.'

'I'd like two of those sultana scones, please.'

The shop bell tinkled and the gossipers fell silent as none other than telephone operator Nancy Strong joined the end of the queue.

'Ta very much. Next.'

'How much is that custard pie?'

'Threepence. Baked fresh this morning.'

Connie carried on as normal until the shop emptied out and only Nancy remained. She'd taken the usual care over her appearance: her fair hair was swept up and pinned into a French pleat and she wore the purple Sunday coat that looked smart but offered little protection against the biting cold. But no amount of carefully applied powder and lipstick could hide her distress.

'What can I do for you?' Connie asked warily. The last time she and Connie had spoken to Maureen's mother they'd been sent away with fleas in their ears.

Nancy opened her mouth but no words came out. Her whole body trembled.

*Blimey, this is serious!* Connie rushed to fetch a stool, then she flicked the sign on the door from 'Open' to 'Closed' and pulled down the blind.

Nancy sank on to the stool and began to sob uncontrollably.

Connie feared the worst. 'What's happened?'

'I didn't know who else to turn to,' Nancy said between sobs. 'God knows how, but people have found out about Maureen and the baby.'

'They didn't get it from me or Lizzie; or from Pamela either, for that matter.' Connie's guard was up as she waited to hear the reason for Nancy's visit.

'I couldn't face going to work.'

As the sobbing reached a peak and Nancy's body continued to shake, Connie's sympathies swung like a pendulum: yes, she hated to see a woman in distress but she had little patience with the family disgrace angle. Unless the worst had come to pass – the discovery of a body washed ashore at high tide, say – surely the focus should be on finding and helping Maureen not on blaming her. 'You mustn't care so much about what people think,' she insisted.

'I can't help it.' Nancy raised a gloved hand to hide her tear-stained face. 'I dread tongues wagging behind my back, blaming me and saying what a terrible mother

I've been. How can I hold my head up now that my neighbours know what Maureen got up to?'

'Listen to me.' Having gained a glimmer of understanding about what was going on beneath the careful coiffure and precise tailoring, Connie softened her voice. 'I know it's hard for you but perhaps this is the time to find out who your real friends are. People who are close to you won't judge you, believe me. They'll want to help.'

Nancy lowered her hand and looked searchingly into Connie's eyes. 'How do you know?'

'I just do.' *Take it from someone who, not so long ago, was arrested for looting, who spent time in a police cell and had to resign from her job as an ARP warden until the mess was sorted out.*

'Maureen was the apple of my husband's eye,' Nancy confessed, her gaze blurring as memories floated to the surface. 'His dear little lass – that's what Michael used to call her. After she was born I didn't get a look-in. It was Maureen this and Maureen that. Then Colin came along: a little boy for his daddy to spoil while I did all the hard work of looking after them both.'

Connie listened patiently. So was this what lay behind Nancy's immaculate get-ups and regular church attendances – a desperate struggle to be noticed and approved of?

'I do realize that I haven't been the best of mothers,' Nancy admitted. 'I've been too strict so as to make up for what I saw as her daddy's softness.'

'And now?' Connie prompted. 'It's never too late for a leopard to change its spots, you know.'

'That's just it – it is too late.' Nancy's body was

wracked by fresh sobs. 'How am I ever going to find Maureen and put things right?'

A sharp rap on the door told Connie that she couldn't keep the shop closed for much longer. 'Give me a minute,' she called through the blind to the impatient customer. 'Is that why you came?' she asked Nancy. 'To ask for our help?'

Nancy nodded miserably. 'I know what you and your sister think of me but I'm at my wits' end.'

'Listen, Lizzie intends to talk to the vicar at St Joseph's today to see if he has any clue as to where Maureen has gone.' Connie's mind worked quickly. 'The other thing we could do is find out the names of the girls who were at the home in Axenby at the same time as Maureen,' she suggested. 'If I were in her shoes I might turn for help to someone who was in the same boat as me.'

'Yes, it's possible.' Nancy sat upright and took a deep breath as she absorbed what Connie had said. There was another rap at the door. 'But what about the baby?' she asked suddenly.

'What about her?' This was a turn-up for the books and no mistake; Connie didn't hide her surprise.

'Do you know what will happen to her?'

'She'll be adopted.' Connie watched as Nancy stood up shakily and straightened the creases in her coat. 'There are no worries on that score; Susan will go to a good home in White Sands Bay.'

'I see.' With another deep breath Nancy watched Connie unbolt the door. 'And thank you.'

'Not at all. We'll keep in touch.' Connie's promise followed Nancy out on to the street, where three women with shopping baskets champed at the bit.

'About time too,' the first customer grumbled with a curious glance in Nancy's direction.

Then it was back to business as usual – a small Hovis and a teacake, a white tin loaf and a jar of lemon curd. Next, please.

Later that day, between finishing at the bakery and starting an evening shift at the ambulance depot, Lizzie squeezed in a visit to her father. She rushed into the ward dressed in her dark blue driver's uniform and breathlessly pulled up a chair beside Bert's bed. 'Hello, Dad. I've brought you some clean pyjamas and a few football magazines. And there's a bar of chocolate from Aunty Vera in one of my pockets. Here you are: your favourite – Cadbury's Dairy Milk.'

'Slow down,' he ordered. 'I get a headache from thinking about you dashing around from pillar to post.'

'Sorry, Dad. I've got a lot on my plate, what with carol singing and getting ready for Christmas on top of the usual.'

'How's your young man?' Bert sat up in bed, bolstered by pillows. There was healthy colour in his cheeks, his hair was parted and slicked back with Brylcreem and his chin was freshly shaved. 'Or should I say your fiancé?'

Lizzie beamed back at him. 'Bill is fine. He's back on minesweeping duty, worse luck, but he'll be home at the weekend.'

'Good for him.' Bert glanced around the ward as if to say to the other patients, *This is my youngest girl – as you can see she does her bit for Civil Defence, on top of running the bakery with her sister. I honestly don't know what I'd do without her*.

Lizzie raced to bring Bert up to date with events. 'Poor Pamela is in a tizzy over Fred. They've both been on the receiving end of some nasty notes and all because he was born in Berlin – notes written by ignorant people who have nothing better to do. Worse still, Fred was attacked and badly beaten on Monday evening. Pamela's Uncle Hugh is looking after him. And you remember the young girl we told you about; Maureen Strong? The girl we took under our wing. Connie and I are worried about her – I won't bother you with the details.'

'Stop.' Bert held up his hand like a traffic policeman. 'Shouldn't you be looking out for number one instead of running around after other people all the time? You'll wear yourself out if you're not careful.'

'How's that for the pot calling the kettle black?' Lizzie leaned forward to pat his hand. 'Don't worry about me, Dad. I'm fit as a flea.'

Bert grasped her hand. 'But I do worry. You say yourself that you've got a lot on your plate, and here I am: a useless article that's no help to anyone. I'd give anything to be back on my feet, at work in the bakery and at my warden's post. Instead of which, the docs won't even let me get out of bed.'

His frustration saddened Lizzie. She saw how badly her father's conscientious nature had been thwarted by this illness and how it had altered her notion of him as her uncomplaining dad who would always be there to lend his support. 'You're on the mend,' she assured him with as much confidence as she could muster. 'It'll take time but you'll get there in the end.'

'Aye, if you say so,' he acquiesced half-heartedly.

'Yes, and don't forget that I'm relying on you to

walk me down the aisle.' They must look forward with hope and avoid the pit of despair.

Bert nodded and jutted out his chin. 'In that case . . .'

'You'll be firing up those ovens before you know it.' Bill and Tom would return safely from minesweeping duties, Fred and Pam's enemies would be found and punished, Maureen's whereabouts would be discovered. One day soon the war would end. Lizzie had to believe in miracles in order to keep on putting one foot in front of the other. There was no room for doubt. She would march bravely on.

'I have to dash now,' she told Bert, gently pulling her hand free. 'Walter Adams is in charge of the depot tonight and he's a stickler for timekeeping.'

'Off you go, then.' Reluctantly letting go of Lizzie's hand, Bert watched her depart. *Oh, to be young and so full of hope.* The sight of her swinging through the door in her uniform made his bruised and battered heart ache. *Oh, Lizzie, take care. And Connie, look after your sister for me; make sure she doesn't come to harm.*

# CHAPTER SIXTEEN

At eleven o'clock on Thursday, 18 December a pair of Ju87 Stuka dive-bombers wheeled away from their successful attack on a small minesweeping convoy off England's north-east coast. The opportunist pilots headed for the nearby Kell estuary, each with a 550-pound bomb installed under his fuselage. In addition, one of the pair still carried two 110-pound bombs under its wings – four bombs in total, each in search of a target.

They flew in low, cruising at 10,000 feet, until battle commenced with a volley of ack-ack fire from ground defence teams. Grey puffballs of smoke exploded to right and left of the determined attackers while scarlet flames from the aircrafts' MG17 machine guns stabbed through the dark sky. The two veteran Luftwaffe pilots had carried out raids over every major city in the United Kingdom, so tonight was small fry. They dived down towards the fishing port of Kelthorpe at a speed of 350 miles per hour and an angle of sixty degrees, levelling out at 1,500 feet before releasing the first of their huge bombs on to St Stephen's dock, then roaring on. A cloud of thick black smoke filled the air, followed by a wall of orange flame. On the ground, firefighters on standby were held at bay by heat and choking smoke. Across town a second bomb was released, reducing the Savoy cinema to rubble, and on the hill overlooking the harbour, the Queen Alexandra Hospital survived a near miss.

The German pilots revelled in their success. One dived again, peering through the small window in the floor of his fuselage before releasing the last of his bombs over the railway station at the northern edge of town. He pulled out quickly, risking a G-force blackout before levelling out at a jubilant 12,000 feet to rejoin his fellow pilot. With wing tips almost touching, the veteran duo signalled from their cockpits – an exchange of thumbs-up – before they flew south down the east coast and on across the Channel to northern France.

On the ground, Connie liaised with the head warden of the North Street sector. David Drake was one man short and had already deployed two wardens to the train station so wasn't able to send reinforcements to the Savoy incident – Connie would have to cope without his assistance.

'Get over to the cinema, quick as you can,' she told Pamela as the sound of the Stukas' engines receded and sirens sounded the all-clear. Connie had already sent all other Gas Street wardens to St Stephen's dock. 'I received a message to say that the whole shebang has gone up in smoke. Take stock, then report back.'

Pamela set out at a run. She was pretty sure that fire services would be needed, but possibly not rescue or first aid. With luck, the cinema would have been deserted at the time of the attack. Morning ought to be soon enough for an investigation by a trained incident officer.

She was sad about the loss of her old workplace. The smooth, curved lines of the cinema with its flat roof, white stucco and wide glass entrance reminded her of an ocean liner, and it had become a significant modern landmark amidst the traditional stone terraces. Besides, Kelthorpe residents had enjoyed many happy, escapist adventures from the safety and comfort of its red, plush velvet seats.

Still, as long as no lives had been lost . . .

The scene that greeted Pamela was worse than she had imagined. In front of the demolished picture palace Jerry's bomb had opened up a crater large enough to swallow a double-decker bus. Two oak trees at the entrance to the Leisure Gardens had been uprooted and had toppled across the road. Of the cinema itself very little remained – just a mountain of smoking rubble, pools of melted plate glass and twisted girders, with a few recognizable objects in among the debris. She spotted two remarkably undamaged hinged seats and an usherette's ice-cream tray. The tattered remains of a poster advertising *Love on the Dole*, starring Deborah Kerr and Clifford Evans, fluttered towards Pamela and landed at her feet.

About to retrace her steps and report back to Connie as ordered, her attention was caught by a movement in the remains of the warehouse next door. One side wall had collapsed in flames and through the smoke she could make out a figure scrambling over the rubble. It was a young woman wearing the maroon tabard of a cinema employee, waving a white handkerchief to attract attention before sinking to her knees and sobbing.

Pamela clicked into action. She strapped on her goggles then quickly clambered over bricks, girders and broken glass to reach the woman, raising her to her feet then gently leading her clear of the building. Standing upwind of the smoke and removing the goggles, she found that the casualty had suffered a deep gash to her forehead that would need stitches. 'Was there anyone in there with you?' she asked, delving into her first-aid kit for a temporary gauze dressing.

'My manager, Mr Penrose,' the girl gasped. 'He's trapped in the cellar. Everyone else had left the cinema when the siren started.'

'I know who you mean.' Pamela's heart sank. She had no choice but to risk her own neck for the unpopular manager. 'Are you sure he's still down there?'

'Yes. There was a small gap – I managed to squeeze out but he wasn't able to follow me.'

'All right; well done. Hold steady while I clean you up.' Pamela pressed the gauze against the bleeding wound. A rescue squad would be necessary after all. She would have to send Connie a message to that effect while she herself ventured inside the burning warehouse to investigate further. Fortunately, people were slowly emerging from their houses on Valley Road to survey the damage. Pamela beckoned to the nearest group. A man wearing an overcoat on top of his pyjamas and a lad in a dressing gown and slippers came to see what help they could offer.

'I need one of you to telephone the Gas Street wardens' post,' she explained calmly. 'Please tell the head warden to send an ambulance, firefighters and a rescue team.'

'You do that, Tim,' the man ordered the boy, who immediately ran back to his house. 'My name's Ted Bainbridge, by the way.'

'Thank you, Mr Bainbridge. Can you wait here with . . . ?' Pamela waited for the injured girl to identify herself.

'Marjorie.' Shock had slowed the girl's responses.

'Wait here with Marjorie until the ambulance gets here?'

'Certainly, I can do that for you.' Accepting responsibility, the good citizen led the weeping usherette to a safe distance.

This left Pamela free to enter what remained of the warehouse. She shone her torch and picked her way through unstable debris, careful to avoid areas where small yellow flames flickered. At this point, escaping gas from a damaged main was a major hazard. If gas met flame the result would be a massive explosion. Still she must press on, directing her torch beam towards the cellar doorway and halting every time she dislodged a loose brick or a twisted piece of metal shelving. The scraping, grating sound of shifting debris struck fear into her; each time she heard it she would freeze and only move again once the noise had ceased. *Slow and steady,* she reminded herself as she inched forward. Her mind remained remarkably clear; she worked out that it would take a rescue team a minimum of thirty minutes to arrive. Ditto for the fire service. With luck an ambulance would get here sooner than that.

Reaching the cellar door at last and balancing

precariously on an unstable heap of bricks, Pamela found that it had been torn off its hinges. And sure enough, there was a gap wide enough for slim Marjorie to have squeezed through, giving Pamela access to the cellar steps. But before she went down she decided to announce her presence. 'Mr Penrose?'

Her voice was muffled and there was no reply. Pamela tried again. 'Mr Penrose, stay where you are. Help is on its way.'

A sudden shout reached her from outside the warehouse. 'Hello, in there!'

Pamela swung her torch towards the voice. Its beam was too weak to penetrate the darkness. Several shards of broken slate rattled down on to her helmet and as she ducked to dodge them she dropped her torch then toppled against the heavy door, which promptly collapsed on top of her.

'It's me – Bainbridge. Penrose is here with us; he managed to make his own way out!'

Trapped beneath the door and with the breath knocked out of her lungs by its impact, Pamela heard more heavy debris thunder down. She breathed in clouds of dust and felt the heat of flames from a length of roof timber that had fallen some six feet from where she lay.

'Miss, can you hear me?' Ted Bainbridge's voice grew high-pitched with fear.

More timbers crashed down. The fire was spreading rapidly. Pamela found she could only move her head and her left arm. 'I hear you,' she cried. Had she broken any bones? How long before the flames reached her? Was there any way of shifting the door enough for her to wriggle free?

'The manager is here with us. There's no one left in there. Get out, quick as you can!'

This was easier said than done. 'I can't – I'm stuck!' Pamela gritted her teeth and began to claw at the rubble with her free hand. The irony of the situation wasn't lost on her: she'd risked her life for Penrose of all people and, as it turned out, for no reason.

'Miss?' Bainbridge shouted. 'Hold on – I'm coming to get you!'

'No! Stay where you are,' she yelled back. The heat was intense but her goggles protected the upper part of her face and she managed to tug at her collar until it covered her mouth. If only she could dislodge more of the jagged rubble . . . She scraped and clawed until her fingers bled.

The crackling flames leaped to a second piece of timber, dancing nearer and nearer. Sweat dripped from Pamela's face. Using her elbow as a lever, she tried to haul herself out of the hole she'd managed to excavate but as she moved, the door tilted and trapped her again. She sank down under its weight, exhausted.

'Ambulance is here!' Bainbridge yelled from the street.

Pamela heard the siren followed by a screech of brakes. She raised her head to see a pair of headlights directed towards the interior of the building and two figures – a man and a woman – silhouetted in their yellow glare. 'Over here!' she called in a voice tight with fear.

'Pamela, is that you? It's me: Lizzie!' On standby at the depot, she and Walter had taken Connie's call – ambulance needed at the warehouse next to the Savoy. ARP Warden Carr already in attendance.

They'd jumped into the Bedford and raced to the rescue, not knowing what they would find. Lizzie had driven at breakneck speed through icy streets while Walter had stayed in the back, checking their stretchers and blankets before strapping on the haversack containing his first-aid kit.

They'd been greeted by the sight of a civilian at the kerbside tending to two walking wounded – a distressed girl and a middle-aged man in glasses and a torn pinstripe suit. 'One of your lot is trapped inside,' the civilian had reported hastily.

*Pamela!* Lizzie didn't pause to assess the situation. She sprinted into the burning building with Walter hard on her heels. There wasn't a moment to lose: the heat was close to unbearable and there was a danger of the whole roof falling in.

'Over here!' Pamela cried.

'Where?' Carrying his rolled-up stretcher under one arm, Walter shielded his face and peered through the smoke and dust.

'Here!' she repeated feebly. The weight of the door pressed down on her and smoke filled her lungs.

'I see you!' In a sudden burst of flame Lizzie was able to make out the shape of Pamela's helmet. She clambered over rubble towards her. 'This way, Walt.' Good God, Pamela was practically buried under a heap of bricks that had tumbled on to what looked like a broken door! 'Don't go too close,' she warned Walter. 'Not until we work out the best way to free her.'

Lizzie and Walter crouched down to examine the problem. Pamela craned her neck to see their worried faces illuminated by flickering flames. There must be no panic, no sudden moves.

'Let's go in from the left side,' Walter decided. 'One brick at a time until we can raise the door high enough for her to crawl out.'

As they worked out their plan, Pamela held her breath and prayed. She knew that one false move could bring disaster.

'I'm lighter than you,' Lizzie told Walter. 'I'm less likely to dislodge stuff on the way up. And you're stronger – you can shift the door from below.'

'Yes, you go,' he agreed.

So Lizzie picked her way up the heap, removing bricks as she climbed. Walter stayed where Pamela could see him. 'We'll get you out,' he promised as he grasped her hand. 'It won't be long now.'

She nodded. The pressure on her ribs made it hard for her to breathe but she suffered in silence and held on to his hand.

*One brick at a time,* Lizzie repeated Walt's instruction to herself. It was agonizingly slow but the danger of Pamela being crushed to death was all too real. *One brick at a time.*

Fire danced around them, roof beams and slates continued to fall.

'Not long now,' Walter said a second time, striving to keep the fear out of his voice.

Seconds ticked by. Minutes mounted.

At last Lizzie paused and took stock. 'All right, Walt – see if I've shifted enough debris for you to raise the door,' she instructed.

Letting go of Pamela's hand, he got into a position where he could attempt the manoeuvre. He heaved at the door but it didn't budge. 'No good,' he shouted up to Lizzie.

'OK – stay where you are.' She sweated as she painstakingly removed more bricks. *Don't rush and ruin everything. Take it slowly.* 'Now try,' she yelled.

Straining every muscle, Walter made a second attempt. No good again. Pamela remained trapped. Where in God's name were the fire team and the rescue squad? How long before the flames grew too intense? What were the chances of them getting out before the roof finally caved in? Fifty-fifty, Walter reckoned, as Lizzie lifted more bricks and Pamela resigned herself to her fate.

The two Stukas – among the most feared of German aircraft – had struck the Royal Naval Patrol Service convoy without warning. It had happened in the dead of night. The sea was calm and the four small ships, including HMS *Intrepid* and *Sea Knight*, had been heading steadily south on the usual lookout for mines and submarines. The planes had approached head-on, their machine guns blasting out hundreds of deadly bullets.

Tom had manned the trawler's ancient machine gun but he'd missed his mark – the sturdy Stukas weren't the most agile of aircraft but they could reach speeds of up to four hundred miles per hour and were gone in a flash. Mike Scott, their RNR sub-lieutenant, had yelled orders from *Sea Knight*'s bridge for Tom and Bill to take cover. 'Jerry will be back,' he'd predicted grimly. 'Our bloody gun might as well be a pea-shooter for all the use it is.'

And sure enough back the dive-bombers had roared, sooner than expected and this time dropping cannon shells and scoring narrow misses on both *Sea Knight* and *Halcyon*, another of the fishing boats.

Bill had seen red. Every time the Jerry blighters came at his beloved boat he took it personally – his late dad's pride and joy was under attack and she was no better than a sitting duck, waiting to be blown to smithereens.

The small craft had rocked violently in the waves created by the explosion of the submerged shells. Tom had fallen heavily against a guard rail while Bill had been sent sprawling across the open deck.

'Take cover!' Scott had warned again.

*Boom!* Within seconds the next German shell had found its target. The port side of *Sea Knight*'s bridge had collapsed, knocking the RNR man unconscious and ripping a two-foot hole in the side of the hull. She'd listed to port while Bill had crawled on all fours to take over at the wheel and Tom had done what he could for Scott, who was bleeding from a flesh wound to his shoulder. Water had rushed into the stricken vessel and the rest of the convoy had been in disarray. *Intrepid* had been the first to recover. She was better armed and had been able to drive the enemy back with a prolonged exchange of fire that eventually forced the Stuka pilots into retreat. They'd wheeled away, then flown arrow-swift in the direction of the coast.

'How much water are we taking in?' Bill had demanded from the bridge. His gut had told him that it was touch and go – *Sea Knight*'s list was worsening by the minute.

'Too much.' A glance over the port side had told

Tom that there was damage just inches clear of the waterline. 'We need to head for shore – pronto.'

The captain of *Intrepid* had come up alongside and agreed with Tom's verdict. He'd issued an order for *Halcyon* to accompany *Sea Knight* to the nearest port, while the remaining two vessels continued their patrol.

'The old girl might not make it all the way back,' he'd predicted grimly, noting that *Sea Knight*'s lifeboat had also been damaged during the attack. 'Stand by to take survivors on board,' he'd told *Halcyon*'s captain.

So *Sea Knight* had limped for home, taking in water as she went. As she approached the coast, Scott regained consciousness and learned of their dire situation. Spotting an orange glare on the dark horizon, Tom put two and two together – Jerry had unleashed his remaining bombs on unsuspecting civilians asleep in their beds. As if taking a punch to the stomach, he realized that their likely target had been Kelthorpe.

*Halcyon*'s skipper brought his vessel alongside to talk tactics. Admit it: *Sea Knight* was too badly damaged to reach the shore. Better to abandon ship while there was still time.

*Never!* Bill gripped the wheel and stared straight ahead.

'He's right.' Though groggy from loss of blood, Scott wrested back control. A decision was made for them all to don life jackets and wait for *Halcyon*'s crew to lower her lifeboat. *Sea Knight*'s crew would then jump into the drink and swim for it.

Bill watched the manoeuvre grim-faced. Waves

washed over *Sea Knight*'s deck, swamping the depth-charge rack to port. She failed to right herself and the angle of the list worsened dramatically.

'Ready – cut the engine,' Scott ordered harshly before he was suddenly swept off his feet by a savage wave. He slipped under the guard rail and into the sea.

Tom watched the injured man disappear from view, waiting with his heart in his mouth until Scott's head and yellow life jacket bobbed to the surface. The sub-lieutenant then struck out towards the lifeboat.

'Your turn,' Bill told Tom, who was gripping the guard rail for dear life.

Instinct told Tom to delay. It was highly likely that Bill would choose not to jump ship and stay with *Sea Knight* as she went down instead. 'No – we'll do this together,' he insisted.

Bill shook his head.

*Halcyon*'s skipper roared for them both to jump without delay.

Another powerful wave hit Tom, who lost his grip and, like Scott, was instantly swept overboard. Bill was alone on his boat.

Tom went under and fought a strong undertow pulling him backwards towards *Sea Knight*'s propeller. He swallowed icy water as he was dragged down. He fought. He kicked hard and rose to the surface twenty feet from the lifeboat.

'Cut the engine, you bloody idiot!' *Halcyon*'s captain roared at Bill.

Bill followed the order, then took a step back from the wheel, bracing himself against the bridge to stay upright. The engine died. The wheel spun out of control.

Tom reached the lifeboat and hauled himself over the side. Shivering and sodden, he turned to look for Bill. He saw his friend still clinging desperately to the side of the bridge as hungry waves swamped the deck. Then, with one violent, sudden motion, *Sea Knight* turned on to her side and was sucked under the surface in a swirling mass of foam. She was gone in seconds and Bill was nowhere to be seen.

Inside the burning warehouse Lizzie and Walter worked feverishly to free Pamela. Discovering a length of thick metal pole close to where she lay, Walter used it as a prop to shore up the broken door. Meanwhile, Lizzie removed more rubble to lessen the weight that was bearing down on the victim.

'Now try to move,' Walter muttered, backing off while Lizzie clambered down to floor level. Pamela strained every muscle, only to find she was still trapped.

'It's no good,' she admitted as more shards of slate from the roof clattered down and clouds of thick black smoke obscured her view. 'Don't stay – save yourselves.'

'We're not leaving without you,' Lizzie vowed. She and Walter pulled another metal pole from the wreckage and inserted it at an angle under the horizontal door. Then Walter used a heavy stone to hammer at its base, forcing the second prop into a more upright position. Slowly, inch by inch, accompanied by the clang of stone against metal, the door was raised.

'Try now,' Lizzie urged.

Pamela used her elbow to edge forward. 'Yes!' she gasped.

'That's it,' Walter encouraged calmly. 'Nice and steady.'

Every movement caused loose mortar to trickle through gaps, but she fought to release herself. 'Stand back – I can do this,' she told Lizzie, who had darted forward to help. She managed to free her shoulders, then her chest and her right arm, giving her fresh leverage to carry on easing the rest of her body out from under the door.

At last Pamela worked herself free. Without a moment to lose, Walter and Lizzie raised her from the ground then laid her on the stretcher and threw a blanket over her. Illuminated by the ambulance's headlights, they wove between flaming timbers and over heaps of rubble, carrying her out of the warehouse to safety.

Inside the ambulance Pamela insisted that there was no need to take her to hospital. She hadn't broken any bones; the worst that had happened was that her throat was sore from inhaling smoke and she'd suffered bruised ribs.

'But your hand?' Carefully Lizzie cleaned the cuts and grazes with swabs of cotton wool soaked in disinfectant.

'That's it, ladies and gents – the show's over,' Walter told the group of onlookers from Valley Road, who strained to catch a glimpse of the latest casualty. He singled out Ted Bainbridge and his son for special thanks. 'Now go back to your beds and get a good night's sleep.'

'My hand will be fine once it's bandaged.' Pamela was adamant. 'There's no point in me taking up a hospital bed for no good reason.'

Walter agreed. 'Who's at home to keep an eye on you in case of delayed shock?' he asked as he stowed the stretcher under the bench seat, then checked that Penrose and Marjorie were comfortably installed as sitting-case casualties.

'Drop me off at Sunrise,' Pamela decided. 'I'll stay at the bungalow for a day or two.'

'Good idea.' Lizzie finished applying the bandage, then took up position behind the steering wheel. She planned her route: the first drop-off would be Marjorie at the Queen Alexandra, then an uninjured Mr Penrose at his flat above Benson's on College Road before a drive around the headland to hand Pamela over to her parents. As soon as Walter settled into the passenger seat next to her, Lizzie set off along Valley Road.

They drove in silence, each wrapped in their own thoughts. Conscious of their narrow escape from the warehouse, Walter longed for his shift to end. Lizzie's attention was on the difficult driving conditions. In the back of the ambulance, their patients nursed injuries and counted blessings – scars would heal, bruises would fade and the outcome could have been so much worse.

It was three in the morning by the time Lizzie pulled into the drive at Sunrise. A quick telephone call from a phone box on College Road had given Edith and Harold ten minutes' advance warning of their daughter's arrival, and they stood in their doorway waiting anxiously. Harold rested one hand on Edith's arm as if reminding her to stay calm.

Pamela stepped down unaided from the back of the ambulance and said goodbye to Lizzie. Walking towards the bungalow on unsteady legs, she glanced over her shoulder at the big house to see Fred watching from the lounge window. Bravely she blew him a kiss. But at this moment it was her mother she needed.

Edith approached Pamela with open arms. 'My brave girl,' she murmured tearfully as she stroked her daughter's cheek. 'Come in out of the cold. The fire is on and the kettle's boiling. There's no need to talk about it unless you want to . . .'

'Mummy, don't fuss – I'm fine.' Pamela's lip trembled as she spoke.

'I know you are,' Edith said gently. 'And Daddy and I are more proud of you than we can say. Isn't that true, Harold?'

'It is.' He drew them both inside. 'We've always been proud of our dear, good girl, and never more so than now.'

Watching from the window, Fred sighed with relief as he saw the door close behind them. *Alles gut.* For now, in this brief, precious moment, all was well.

# CHAPTER SEVENTEEN

'Two and a half hours – that's all the sleep I got.' Lizzie was weary to the bone as she and Connie started work in the bakery. Lethargy had set in, and the effort of firing up the oven was almost more than she could manage.

Connie cast a concerned glance in Lizzie's direction. 'Maybe you should give carol singing a miss tonight – go straight home after work and get some shut-eye?'

'I'll see,' Lizzie mumbled. 'It'd be a pity, though – singing "Good King Wenceslas" with the rest of the crew is the highlight of my week.' The convivial gatherings helped to raise her spirits and keep her mind off Bill's dangerous mission. Sleep, on the other hand, still thrust her into a nightmare world of mountainous, icy waves and gale-force winds, of unseen mines and submarines lurking in the deep.

Connie fashioned lumps of dough into small, regular mounds before transferring each one to a greased baking tray. 'I wonder if Pamela will show up.'

'Yes – I'd put money on it.' Last night in the warehouse Lizzie had observed an unsuspected core of steel in their well-brought-up friend. 'She might not look it but she's made of stern stuff. Being buried alive under rubble won't spoil her run-up to Christmas.'

'Or being sent nasty threats in the post,' Connie observed as she thumped a fresh batch of dough. 'It makes my blood boil to think what Pamela and Fred are being put through.'

'But at least they have Hugh Anderson on their side,' Lizzie said, mid-yawn.

Connie paused to roll up her sleeves. 'You won't fall asleep at the wheel, will you?' she challenged.

'No, I'll keep the van windows open,' Lizzie promised. Too tired for more small talk, she worked on in silence until faint slivers of daylight filtered into the shop and it was time to load the van and set out on her first round of deliveries.

The foray into a wakening world forced her to be more alert. In the town square buses disgorged their passengers. Clerical workers headed up the steps of the town hall and a gang of council workmen set about resurrecting the toppled statue of Queen Victoria, intending to restore the old girl to her plinth. Driving on up the hill towards the Queen Alexandra, where she would drop off the hospital's daily bread order, Lizzie was surprised to see Doug Greenwood and Terence Ibbotson standing in the gateway to the grammar school. She pulled up for a quick word. 'Hello there – what brings you two up here so bright and early?'

Doug hurried out from the shadow of a snow-laden pine tree that overhung the school entrance and greeted her with his usual bluster. 'Good morning, Lizzie. What a pleasant coincidence. The vicar is here to conduct a school assembly. We're early, as a matter of fact. Unfortunately his car is out of action so I offered him a lift.'

'That's good of you.' A glance at the clergyman told Lizzie that he was in no mood for pleasantries. He stood with his coat collar turned up, stamping his feet against the cold and making no move to greet her.

'I take it you'll be joining us this evening?' Doug asked.

'All being well,' she confirmed. Drat – this was an ideal opportunity for the vicar to update her on the Maureen situation but Doug's presence prevented it.

'Good. I look forward to it.' Doug clapped his gloved hands to create some warmth and waited pointedly for Lizzie to drive on.

'Same here.' Pulling away from the kerb, she glanced in her overhead mirror to see the vicar join his churchwarden on the pavement before they walked together towards the WVS centre next door. *Odd,* she thought. Then again, maybe church business took them there – perhaps there was a baby's christening to arrange. Dismissing the two men from her mind, she carried on with her deliveries.

For once, Edith judged things correctly – not too much fuss and fretting but just the right amount of loving concern for Pamela. No criticism passed her lips and she resisted the urge to dissuade her daughter from carrying on with her ARP duties.

'Your mother's turned over a new leaf,' Harold said genially over breakfast in the dining room of the bungalow. 'She's determined to let you make your own decisions from now on.'

Edith brought a fresh pot of tea from the kitchen. 'It's rude to talk about people behind their backs,' she chided. Even in her lilac dressing gown and matching slippers, she was coiffed and ready to meet the day.

'Don't worry – Daddy's being nice about you.' Pamela had slept soundly after her ordeal and had awoken feeling refreshed.

'For once.' Edith raised a refined eyebrow.

'What do you mean, dear? I'm always nice about you.' As Harold got up from the table and went to the kitchen, he ran into Fred. 'Nice to see you up and about,' he remarked cheerfully.

Edith called Fred into the dining room. 'I'll leave you two lovebirds to your little tête-à-tête,' she purred, before slipping away.

'I say!' Fred glanced in disbelief at the discreetly closed door.

'I know.' Pamela gave a self-conscious laugh. 'But how long will it last, I wonder?'

Fred smiled, then shook his head at her bandaged hand.

'I'm fine,' she declared. 'More to the point: how are you?'

'Much the same,' he confessed. 'I didn't sleep well last night.'

'Not because you were worried about me, I hope?'

'No; sleep had deserted me long before I learned about your latest heroics.' There was no need to confess how afraid Fred had been when the early morning phone call had come through to Sunrise; Pamela was safe and that was all that mattered. 'I lay awake trying to put my finger on something to do with the gang who attacked me – an important detail that had slipped my mind.'

'Go on,' Pamela urged.

'There were three of them,' he explained. 'They'd all been drinking. The ringleader was thickset. I didn't recognize him but what's come back to me is that one of the others mentioned his name.'

'Which was?' Flicking through the possibilities, Keith or Jack came to the fore.

Fred hesitated – reliving the incident was painful. 'It was a nickname,' he said through clenched teeth. 'The man said, "Give it to him, Tommo!"'

Keith Nelson. Jack Watkins. Pamela had even toyed with the name Cyril Fielding. But none of these fitted with what Fred was telling her.

'Tommo could be Thomas,' Fred muttered. 'That's a common name – there could be fifty Thomases in Kelthorpe, for all we know.'

'Or it could be the surname, Thompson.' A thrill of realization passed through her. 'A man called Eric Thompson drinks at the Anchor. He's the violent type. He beat his wife and was sent to prison for attacking Connie.'

'Yes, so I recall. What does he look like?'

'I'm not sure but I can easily find out.' Pamela stood up, as if ready for action. 'Describe your man to me.'

Fred drew her back down. 'It was dark,' he reminded her. 'I couldn't see his face clearly. I only know that he was strong and heavy. His hair was dark, I think.'

'Well, that's a start.' Her excitement settled into a fixed resolution to discover more. 'Perhaps you would recognize him if you saw him?'

Fred nodded slowly. It was a possible lead, but there

was danger involved. If Thompson turned out to be their man and he got an inkling that Fred was on to him, there was no predicting what he might do. 'Give me time to think before we make our next move,' he implored Pamela. 'The situation is tricky. I have to consider you and your family's safety as well as my own.'

'Look before you leap?' she asked.

'Quite. *Erst denken, dann lenken,*' he said softly. 'Promise me?'

'I promise,' she agreed. Eric Thompson – the name lodged in her brain, where it must stay until Fred decided to act.

Lizzie was preoccupied as she drove back to the bakery. Passing the WVS centre on her way back down the hill from the hospital, she caught sight of Terence Ibbotson standing in the porch with Gladys Smallwood. Lizzie slowed down to wait for the vicar to emerge on to the street but was thwarted a second time by Doug, who turned into the WVS driveway in his black Morris and whisked the vicar away. After a few moments of indecision, Lizzie thought it worthwhile to get out of the van for a word with the WVS manager.

'Mrs Smallwood, can you spare a minute?' she said as she approached the porch.

Gladys gave a start, then smoothed over her surprise with a bland smile. 'Miss Harrison, what can I do for you?'

'As a matter of fact, I've come to talk to you about baby Susan.'

'Indeed?' The smile vanished. 'How can I help?'

'I expect you've heard the rumours that are flying around – about Susan's mother? The town gossips have got hold of a name.'

'Ah, I gathered as much from the vicar.' Gladys pricked up her ears. 'He was insistent that Susan's adoption should proceed regardless.'

'Is that so?' Lizzie stored this nugget. 'Well, I can tell you in confidence that my sister and I have been in contact with the mother and have sworn to help her – only the fact is she's gone to ground.'

'Yes, so I understand. Most unfortunate.' Uncertain about the direction of the conversation, Gladys stood square in the doorway without inviting Lizzie inside the house.

'We're on a mission to find the girl.'

'Girl, you say?' The word was picked up and turned over.

'Yes, she's very young and impressionable. It turns out that the Reverend Ibbotson knows the family well.'

'Yes; in fact, you just missed him.' Gladys released information in dribs and drabs. 'I don't suppose it does any harm to tell you what I told him – that a young girl claiming to be the mother did, in fact, turn up on our doorstep.'

Lizzie's eyes widened in surprise. 'When?'

'Yesterday.'

'Did she give her name?' Questions and answers flew back and forth.

'No, she refused to identify herself. She simply said she wished to see the baby.'

'And did you let her?'

'No.'

'How did she seem?' Lizzie absorbed the fact that Maureen was alive, thank heavens.

'In a poor way, by all accounts. I wasn't here at the time. Beryl – Mrs Bridger – was in charge.'

'Did she say where she was living?' It was vital that Lizzie squeezed out every last drop of information.

'No, there was no address. But I agree with the vicar; it's important to keep her away from the baby.'

'Why on earth do you say that?' Lizzie demanded with a fresh sense of outrage.

'Because there's no telling what the consequence might be.' Gladys followed the party line. 'If this mystery visitor does indeed turn out to be Susan's mother – I have it on good authority that not only is she in desperate trouble but she's not of sound mind.' Biting her lip and frowning, the manager wondered if perhaps she'd said too much.

*Not of sound mind.* The ominous phrase echoed in Lizzie's head. 'That's not true,' she protested.

'I merely repeat what I've been told.' Gladys pressed her thin lips together and folded her arms firmly across her chest; the sentry at the gate would say no more.

'I see. And that's it?'

'Yes, Miss Harrison, that's as much as I know.'

Lizzie retreated to her van with fresh food for thought. So her suspicion was correct – Terence Ibbotson had been less than frank during her visit to the rectory. And now here he was, casting aspersions and issuing instructions willy-nilly. *Just wait until I tell Connie and Pamela the latest,* she thought as she approached College Road.

But when Lizzie pulled up outside the bakery the

'Closed' sign was up and the blinds were down. How odd, she thought as she parked the van and looked along the street. A young woman paused to glance in her direction before entering Cynthia's hairdressers. Two men at work on the *Gazette* site leaned on their pickaxes and stared as she tried the door. It was bolted. 'Connie?' Lizzie tapped on the glass panel.

Connie had been on hand to slide back the bolt. Tom stood inside, his cap clasped between his hands, unable to meet Lizzie's gaze.

She looked around the empty shop. 'Where's Bill?'

'Lizzie, love—' Connie's voice broke down.

'Where's Bill?' she repeated. A black wave of panic rolled towards her and broke over her head.

'*Sea Knight* went down,' Tom said simply. He felt as if his insides had been ripped out but he hid his agony. Right now Lizzie was what mattered. 'Bill didn't make it.'

*No, not possible. Take it back. Tell me it's not true.*

'Late last night . . . we were hit by a cannon shell. She was holed on the port side.' Tom stumbled to a halt.

*I couldn't stand losing you* – that's what Bill had said. He and Lizzie were meant to be together for ever and ever. A ruby ring, a wedding with pink carnations. 'No,' she said angrily.

'It's true,' Connie told her. '*Sea Knight* went down and Bill went with her.'

'No. No.'

Tom and Connie rushed to support her but Lizzie pushed them away. A numbness overwhelmed her and she lost sense of where she was and what was happening. It was hard to breathe.

'Oh, Lizzie, it's true,' Connie confirmed. Tom had

come to the bakery and broken the dreadful news – two Stukas; the same ones that had gone on to drop their bombs on Kelthorpe. A direct hit on *Sea Knight* followed by a desperate attempt to sail her back to port. Tom and the RNR man had made it into a lifeboat but Bill had left it too late. His boat had capsized. Survivors of the attack had combed the area for three hours – Bill had been wearing his life jacket and there was always a slim chance – until hope of rescue had faded and *Halcyon*'s skipper had called off the search. Too cold, too long in the water for a man to survive. Bill had drowned.

Lizzie put her hands to her ears. The sound of gushing water filled her head. Everything was dark.

Connie turned to Tom, who stood gaunt and broken.

Lizzie fled. She had to get away – out of the shop then along College Road towards the harbour to face wind and waves whipping in off the sea. Bill was out there in the vast, grey, restless expanse, beyond that line where sea met sky. She ran along the jetty to its very end. He was out there and he would return. There would be a ring, a wedding dress and an adventurous life ahead. He must come back. He must.

# CHAPTER EIGHTEEN

What comfort was there? What words, what actions could soften the cruel blow?

Connie and Tom led Lizzie away from the jetty under the pitying gaze of hardened trawlermen and market traders setting up their stalls for the day ahead. The sea had claimed one of their own – a bright, popular lad who had stepped into his father's shoes and proved himself worthy. No one had a bad word to say about young Bill Evans.

Lizzie allowed herself to be led away from the jetty and back to College Road. She was dimly aware that Tom had put his jacket around her shoulders and that Connie held on to her hand for dear life. The rest was a muddle – sad faces, muttered comments, figures in shop doorways staring at her as she approached the bakery. She shivered uncontrollably without understanding why.

'What do we do?' Connie pleaded with Tom once they'd brought Lizzie inside the shop. The blind stayed down and she bolted the door.

'Wait a while for it to sink in.' Looking at the poor girl's face – so pale, with dark, unseeing eyes – he feared a total collapse. He told Connie how sorry he was. 'I'd give anything for it not to have happened, for it not to have ended like this.' In spite of Tom's strength and youth, the responsibility of being the bearer of bad news had bowed and almost broken him.

Connie was too upset to speak. She brought water for Lizzie and put the glass to her lips. She stroked her hair and soothed her as best she could.

How was it possible? Bill knew the sea, he knew *Sea Knight*. That was why the Royal Navy had asked for his help. If anyone could survive minesweeping duties it was Bill. Lizzie drew herself up and took a deep breath. Tom was wrong – her brave, bold Bill hadn't drowned.

'Better?' Connie murmured.

Lizzie nodded. No one was stronger than the man she loved – that's what the doctors had told her when Bill had been wounded carrying out his first-aider duties earlier that year. A weaker man would have bled to death, but within a short month Bill had been back on duty, riding his motorbike, trawling for fish. Jerry hadn't got him then and he couldn't get him now. 'He's still alive,' she whispered with complete certainty. 'I know it.'

Connie shot Tom a despairing glance.

'Give her time.' He bent further under the weight of their loss.

A knock at the door roused Connie. 'We're closed,' she called. 'Come back later.'

'It's me.' Pamela had set off from the bungalow to fetch clean clothes from King Edward Street. The town was buzzing with news – before she'd crossed the market square she'd learned about the tragedy: *Sea Knight* had taken a direct hit and Bill Evans was lost. Connie Bailey was said to be looking after her broken-hearted sister. Without hesitating, Pamela had headed straight to Harrison's Bakery. 'Let me in.' She tapped again, demanding entry.

'Shall I open it?' Tom asked. When Connie nodded, he slid back the bolt.

Pamela took in the scene. Lizzie sat on a stool, trembling and staring into space. Connie stood with her hands over her mouth as if holding back sobs. Tom shook his head hopelessly. 'Lizzie ought not stay here,' Pamela told Connie and Tom. 'You have to take her home.'

'She's right.' Tom was the first to respond.

'We can't leave the shop,' was Connie's first thought.

'Yes, you can, at a time like this,' Pamela insisted.

'We have to stay open for our customers.'

'Leave that to me.' Pamela wouldn't take no for an answer. How to get Lizzie to Elliot Street was a different matter. They might have to carry her to the van. Connie or Tom would drive. 'I'll take over here.'

Connie hesitated. How could Pamela run the shop? She didn't know any of the prices. Could she even work the till with her newly bandaged hand?

'I'll manage,' Pamela assured her. She would make a telephone call – someone at Sunrise would come up with a solution.

Tom crouched beside Lizzie. 'You hear that? We're going to take you home.'

'Home?' The word sounded strange to her ears. Tom's face was blurred. Why was Connie crying?

'Yes, to Elliot Street.' Tom offered his hand to help Lizzie stand.

'Why? Is Bill there?'

Connie knelt beside her. 'Oh love, no – he's not. But we can look after you better at home.'

'To Bill's cottage, then?' Lizzie asked. 'Is that where he is?'

'He's not there either.' Connie fought in vain to halt the tears that streamed down her face.

'But I can wait for him there.' Lizzie's bewildered mind settled on this course of action. 'I can light a fire and make it cosy for Bill when he gets back.'

'Let's do as she asks,' Tom murmured to Connie. 'We can stay with her until she's ready to face up to things.'

Lizzie swayed as she tried to stand and had to grasp Connie's hand. 'Come on, what are we waiting for?'

Connie and Tom held her upright. They led her out of the shop, then through a small group that had gathered on the pavement. There was much sighing and sympathy as they eased Lizzie into the van.

Home. The cottage. A fire in the hearth. Bill's maps and charts on the bookshelf, his jacket on a hook behind the door, an oil lamp in the window overlooking the harbour. Lizzie stared straight ahead. Everything would be familiar and as it should be.

By mid-afternoon Pamela and her mother had sold out of bread.

'It's hard work,' Edith acknowledged, as Pamela scooped cash out of the till into a blue canvas bag. 'How do Connie and Lizzie do this day in, day out?'

'I suppose you get used to it.' Neither Pamela nor her mother had done shop work before. Even when times had been hard, before Edith and Hugh had settled their differences and Edith had been welcomed back into the family fold, she had avoided menial work. Instead, she'd given piano lessons and relied on Harold's steady wage to get by.

'How the other half live.' With a sigh, Edith took off her borrowed apron and folded it neatly.

'Much more than half, Mummy.'

'I know – I've lived a sheltered life.' Nevertheless, Edith was pleased to have coped so well. She'd warded off impertinent questions – What's happened to the Harrison sisters? Edith Carr, what are you, of all people, doing behind that counter? – and wrapped loaves and teacakes while Pamela had manned the till. Harold had shown willing by taking orders out to regular customers. Now it was time to go home.

'You go ahead,' Pamela suggested to her mother. 'I still have to nip up to King Edward Street for some clean clothes. Tell Fred I won't be long.'

'Yes – dear Fred.' A soft expression crept over Edith's sharp features. 'You two seem to be . . . getting along very well, shall we say?'

'Mother!' Pamela warned. 'Now is not the time.'

'But you would tell me if . . . you know?' In her opinion a spring wedding would be ideal. It was the season when the mother of the bride could get away with flattering pastel shades.

Pamela handed Edith her coat and hat. 'Go home,' she said firmly.

Left to herself, she took her time to sweep the floor and tidy up. Her heart was heavy whenever she thought of Lizzie, who less than twenty-four hours earlier had risked everything to save Pamela's life, little knowing how soon sorrow would engulf her. Still, it didn't do to dwell. Later Pamela would send a message to Connie, offering whatever ongoing help was needed. Not that she felt equipped to take on tomorrow's baking – Connie would probably ask her Aunty Vera's friend Ivy to do that.

Pamela's mind ran busily through practical arrangements as she locked up the shop then headed for her lodgings. As she arrived she saw Joan alight at the bus stop and walk towards the house.

'I take it you've heard about Bill Evans,' Joan began from a distance of twenty yards. 'The whole of the town is in mourning.'

'Yes, I heard.' Pamela turned her key then stepped inside.

'There's not a girl in Kelthorpe who wasn't in love with Bill at one time or another. He was so full of life,' Joan rushed on. 'It's hard to believe – here one minute, gone the next. Tom Rose will take it badly – and your friend Lizzie, too. Oh dear, I didn't mean to make you cry.' She offered Pamela a hankie, then steered her into the sitting room. 'It's too sad for words. We should expect it by now, but we never do.'

Pamela dried her eyes, then answered Joan's question about her bandaged wrist.

'You've been in the wars, I see?'

'Yes, there was an incident last night during the air raid.'

'So it happened while you were on duty – that's all right, then.' Joan sounded relieved. 'Here was me thinking that you'd been involved in fisticuffs.'

'Oh, who with?' Joan's meaningful wink made Pamela wary.

'No one – never mind me.' Joan removed her hatpin then took off her hat before changing her mind and launching into a rapid explanation. 'Oh well, if you must know, Winnie and Kathleen have ganged up against you.'

Remembering the three-way conversation that she'd overheard, Pamela felt the hairs at the nape of her neck prickle. 'What do you mean?'

Joan needed no further prompting. 'I've picked up various bits of chit-chat. But last night I was sitting behind them on the bus. They were with Betty Holroyd; it seems the three of them are bosom pals. Yes, I know – birds of a feather. Anyway, they were gossiping and name-calling as usual. You came up in conversation. Winnie told Betty you'd be better off running back to Mummy and Daddy permanently. Kathleen said she wouldn't miss you here at King Edward Street and it would be good riddance.'

Pamela sat down heavily on the hard sofa.

'I expect you thought they were nice girls.' Joan sat down beside her. 'Butter wouldn't melt – that's how they come across. But they were downright nasty to the Italian girl who had your room before you – the niece of the chap who runs the fish and chip shop on College Road. Gina Barbieri was her name. Kathleen and Winnie weren't happy until they'd driven her out with their whisperings and catty remarks. Then they laughed about it afterwards, called Gina a collaborator – is that the right word?'

Pamela's heart sank further. 'You say Betty was on the bus with them?'

'Yes, she was egging the other two on. I've never liked Betty Holroyd; she thinks she's the bee's knees but I remember her from way back.' Joan pursed her lips. 'The less said about that the better. I didn't really think you'd been scrapping it out with Winnie and Kathleen,' she confessed after a short pause. 'I thought long and hard about telling you what I'd overheard because I knew how much it would upset you. In the end I decided that forewarned was forearmed.'

'I appreciate it. Truly, thank you.' Pamela pulled herself together and stood up. 'I'm only here to pick up a few bits and pieces . . .' Her voice trailed off. She'd been right about Betty all along. Now Kathleen and Winnie must be added to her list of enemies.

'They can be nasty pieces of work,' Joan warned. 'You'd better watch your step.'

'I will,' Pamela promised as she went upstairs to her room. It was as Fred said: lies feasted upon lies until they ran out of control.

Tom and Connie stayed with Lizzie overnight in Bill's cottage. Everywhere they turned there was a painful reminder – Bill's shoes on the bottom step of the stairs, his motorbike spanners in a metal toolbox under the kitchen table. Lizzie refused to go upstairs to bed, so they made her as comfortable as they could in an easy chair by the window overlooking the harbour. Connie used cushions to make a bed for herself on the hearth rug, while Tom retreated to Bill's bedroom, where he failed to sleep a wink. His own heart was broken over the loss of Bill, and the effort of hiding his grief made him feel as if every last ounce of energy was spent.

He was kept awake by vivid memories of his friend's final moments, hearing again the voice of the *Halcyon* skipper shouting orders above the gusting wind, seeing Bill let go of the wheel and lose his balance as

*Sea Knight* capsized. He recalled the search; how *Halcyon* had circled the area, how hope had faded well before dawn. Time and again he wondered what would have happened if he, Tom, had remained on board a few moments longer to persuade Bill to abandon ship. One idea amongst all the bitter regrets plagued him worse than any other – *I'm alive and my best friend is dead*.

In the morning Tom left the cottage to help the women who had volunteered to keep the bakery going. Bert's sister Vera was already hard at work when he arrived and Ivy Cooper was soon to join her. Tom's job would be to deliver orders. Meanwhile, Connie would try to persuade Lizzie to return to Elliot Street.

'It won't do her any good to stay here another night.' Connie's whispered conversation with Tom had taken place on the chilly harbourside in the grey dawn light. 'It encourages her to cling to the idea that Bill is coming back.'

Tom had agreed. 'But be careful – she's in a bad way.'

Connie had kissed him tenderly, then gone back inside to find Lizzie hurriedly flinging on her coat then tying a scarf around her head. 'Where are you off to?' She stood by the door, ready to block Lizzie's exit.

'Out. It's too stuffy in here. I need some fresh air.'

'It's freezing cold out there.' The irrational urge frightened Connie. 'Why not wait a while? I'll make us some breakfast instead.'

'I don't have time for breakfast.' Lizzie tried to push past Connie. 'I've got too much to do. If I don't get a move on, I won't be back in time for Bill.'

Connie grabbed her arm. 'Lizzie, listen to me. Bill was on board *Sea Knight* when she sank—'

'Don't!' She covered her ears, then took a deep breath and carried on as normal. 'I have to find Nancy Strong to tell her the latest about Maureen – she tried to see her baby, which to my mind is a good sign – it means she's alive and she hasn't given up hope.'

Sighing, Connie took up the new thread. 'Nancy will be at work,' she reminded Lizzie. 'Why don't we talk to Gladys Smallwood instead?'

'No, I tried that. Anyway, Gladys wasn't at the centre when Maureen called. I have a better idea.'

'The vicar?' Connie guessed.

'Yes – I'm sure he and Doug know more about this than they're letting on.' The desire to throw herself into the search drove Lizzie on. 'If you don't want to come, I'll go by myself,' she told Connie defiantly.

At the back of her mind Connie saw this as a way of prising Lizzie out of the cottage and persuading her back to Elliot Street. Unsure what would happen if they landed on Terence Ibbotson's doorstep without an appointment, she nevertheless went along with the plan.

An hour later their knock at the vicarage door was answered by the housekeeper – a trim, grey-haired woman with a pleasant manner, who told the visitors that they would find the vicar in the church vestry. So they made their way across the graveyard, passing the church hall: the scene of the so-called crime. Hurrying on towards the church, they came across Doug spreading salt on an icy path.

'Mind your step,' he warned Lizzie as she rushed past without greeting him.

Connie smiled apologetically. 'Hello, Doug. We'd like a word with the vicar if he's available.'

Doug looked doubtful. 'Christmas is a busy time. He's got a lot on.'

'It won't take long,' Connie promised, following Lizzie into the ancient church.

Inside, all was quiet and orderly. There was a smell of beeswax mingled with hot metal radiators. A Bible lay open on the carved pulpit, silver organ pipes towered over the choir stall and the brass cross above the altar gleamed in the sunlight.

At the sound of Lizzie and Connie's footsteps on the stone flags, Terence emerged from the vestry. He stooped to avoid knocking his head on the low stone lintel and when he straightened up he seemed disconcerted. 'Lizzie?' he began, before recollecting the tragic news about Bill Evans that had spread through the old town like wildfire. 'Ah, of course – let's sit in the vestry where it's private. Follow me.' He retraced his steps, then invited Lizzie and Connie to sit. 'First of all, may I say how very sorry—'

'I've come to talk about Maureen.' Lizzie broke in without ceremony. 'You and I both know that she recently tried to see her baby.'

Connie swallowed hard and avoided looking directly at the vicar. Instead, she fixed her attention on a damp patch creeping up the wall of the small, airless room.

Terence cleared his throat. 'I'm afraid that I really can't—'

'I saw you talking to Gladys Smallwood, so there's no use pretending that you don't know the facts about Maureen and her baby. The truth is, we all know the reason why Maureen is desperate so we must do all we can to help her.'

'Yes, quite.' The clergyman shifted in his chair. 'But you must understand – there are limits to what anyone can do, especially if Maureen has chosen to disappear.'

'She didn't choose.' Lizzie spoke calmly. 'She was at her wits' end. Surely you of all people can see that.'

Connie leaned forward in her chair. 'I'm sorry, but what my sister says is true. We've all let Maureen down, including her mother, who, by the way, now regrets sending her away to have the baby.'

'Is that so?' Increasingly uncomfortable, Terence hooked his fingers over his dog collar and tugged nervously. 'I'm sorry to hear that – Elspeth Watson, the matron of the home, is a personal friend. You can rest assured that Miss Watson is a good servant of Our Lord, providing succour to those most in need.'

*Claptrap,* Connie thought. *From what we've heard, Christian succour is in short supply over there in Axenby.*

'Picture it if you can,' Lizzie went on with the same fierce determination. 'You're an innocent girl who's been taken advantage of – for some reason you can't say who's done it to you.'

Terence frowned deeply, then resorted to clearing his throat once more.

'You find yourself in the family way without anyone to stand up for you. Then you have the baby, only to be told she'll be taken away from you and you have no say in the matter—'

'But surely that's for the best,' the vicar interrupted, as if explaining to a child. 'What kind of life would the baby have otherwise?'

'But you're her mother and you love her!' Lizzie grew animated and colour came into her pale cheeks. 'She's yours. She belongs to you. What right does anyone have to take her? So you refuse to let it happen – you run away from the home back to North Street and beg for help, only to be turned away yet again.'

The vestry door opened and Doug sidled in. 'Is everything all right, Vicar?' he asked. 'I heard raised voices.'

'Perfectly all right, thank you, Doug.' The interruption broke the rising tension in the room and Terence scraped back his chair then stood up.

But Lizzie wasn't so easily put off. 'The question is: now that we know Maureen didn't throw herself off a cliff or drown herself, what have you done to help us find her?'

'Hush!' Connie put a restraining hand on her sister's shoulder.

'You said you would look up the names of girls who went to confirmation classes with her, so have you?'

'Lizzie's not herself.' Connie was embarrassed on her sister's behalf.

'Leave it with me, Terence.' Doug stepped in. 'I'll check the registers and let you know what I find.'

'Quite. Just so. Good.' The vicar rubbed his palms together in a gesture of dismissal.

*Like bloody Pontius Pilate!* Connie thought.

Lizzie turned to Doug. 'We need to find Maureen,' she insisted, the red flush in her cheeks draining away as quickly as it had appeared. 'She's got nothing and no one except us.'

'I'll do my best,' he promised, more firmly than

Lizzie or Connie had expected. 'We pray for her safe return. And we pray for you too, Lizzie, in your hour of need.'

Left with no alternative, Connie and Lizzie made their exit from the vestry and walked down the aisle between rows of pine pews, through the porch and out into the graveyard. Cold air came as a shock and they blinked in the strong sunlight. They walked together, lost in their own thoughts. But when they reached the entrance to the church hall they came to a halt.

'Are you thinking what I'm thinking?' Connie's voice was low and hesitant as she stared at the porch and the bench where she'd discovered the baby.

Lizzie nodded. The seed of a new idea had been planted in both of their brains. 'I didn't believe our holier-than-thou vicar, did you?'

'No. All that hoo-ha about servants of Our Lord and succour, but when it comes down to it what has he actually done, besides getting Maureen shipped off to Axenby?'

'And making sure that she's not allowed to visit Susan in the WVS home. It's true – he did, besides throwing another spanner into the works by claiming that Maureen has lost her marbles.'

'Never!' Connie was shocked into silence.

'Yes, honestly, "Not of sound mind" were the exact words. And did you see his face when I mentioned Maureen being taken advantage of? I'd say it had guilt written all over it.'

Connie inhaled deeply. 'But could he really be the man we're looking for?'

'Why not? He's a vicar – in the beginning Maureen

would have trusted him. Her guard would have been down. And Colin told us a man at the church was kind to her. When you think about it, it all starts to add up.'

'I don't know about you, Liz, but it makes me feel sick – just the idea of it.' A clergyman – the last person anyone would suspect. But the new theory did explain Ibbotson's lack of action – he stood to lose everything if Maureen were found and could be persuaded to tell all. 'What are we going to do now?'

'I'm not sure,' Lizzie confessed. 'We need proof before we act.'

'We need to find Maureen,' Connie agreed.

# CHAPTER NINETEEN

Five days before Christmas and Doug's carol singers were in good voice. They stood in the doorway to the Anchor belting out 'Ding dong Merrily' for the benefit of Saturday evening regulars while Pamela did the rounds with the collection tin.

'Happy Christmas, love,' an old trawlerman said as he dropped a penny into the tin.

'". . . Gloria, Hosanna in excelsis!"' A log fire crackled in the inglenook and the landlord pulled foaming pints at the bar.

'Happy Christmas to you, too.' Pamela did her best to sound cheerful. She would be glad when six o'clock came and she could begin her shift at Gas Street.

'"And io, io, io!"'

A huddle of drinkers in a dark corner deliberately turned their backs on the singers, grumbling loudly.

Pamela decided not to approach them with the tin, but as she passed their table she heard mutterings. Had she imagined it or had one of the men uttered the harsh insult she most dreaded – 'Kraut whore'? With rising panic, she quickly moved on to the next table.

Doug raised his hand to signal the start of the next

carol: 'The Holly and the Ivy'. Pamela's hand shook and she almost dropped the tin.

'Give it here.' It was Arnold who grabbed the tin from Pamela and rattled it vigorously. '"Of all the trees that are in the wood,"' he trilled.

Pamela retreated outside to catch her breath, turning up the collar of her battledress jacket and thrusting her hands into her pockets. The evening was damp and windy, and the sky was heavy with clouds. Across the cobbled square, in defiance of blackout regulations, a lamp glowed in the downstairs window of Bill's cottage. Pamela saw movement inside the room – a woman came to the window and pulled down the blind. Recognizing Connie's silhouette, Pamela hurried along the harbour's edge and knocked on the door.

Connie answered it with a tight-lipped smile. She stepped out of the cottage and closed the door behind her. 'Lizzie is still hanging on here,' she admitted. 'I've tried to persuade her to come home but she's having none of it.'

Pamela was sorry to hear it. 'She must be heartbroken.'

Connie shook her head in despair. 'No. That's what's strange. She goes around as if nothing is wrong. This morning she had the idea of bearding Terence Ibbotson in his den, demanding to know why he wasn't doing more to find Maureen. A herd of elephants couldn't have stopped her. Now she's busy tidying up the cottage, making everything nice for when Bill comes home.'

Lost for words, Pamela was distracted by the carol singers emerging from the pub, then following her across the square. Spotting his cousin, Arnold charged ahead, shaking the collection tin under Connie's nose for all he was worth. 'Not now,' Pamela told him under her breath.

Doug brought his group to a halt at the far end of the short row of cottages. They struck up a rousing version of 'Good King Wenceslas' with the desired result – people came to their doors, coins slid through the slot into Arnold's tin and hearty greetings were exchanged.

'Ah, Connie!' Doug approached with a sympathetic smile. 'How's poor Lizzie now? She's had a terrible shock; it'll take a while for her to comprehend—'

Connie cut him short with a cool, 'As well as can be expected, thank you.'

'I carried out my promise,' he assured her. 'I went through the registers of recent confirmation classes.'

'And?' Connie grasped at the one distraction that might prevent Lizzie from drowning in grief.

'Maureen attended with five other girls and four boys.' Pulling a sheet of folded paper from his pocket, Doug handed Connie a list of names. 'I trust this satisfies your sister, because Reverend Ibbotson really is extremely busy at present.'

'And you'd rather we didn't bother him again?' The atmosphere between Connie and Doug grew as chilly as the night air.

'He's done everything in his power to support the Strong family.' Connie's defiant stare threatened to put Doug on the back foot but he came back fighting. 'And while I understand that the recent tragedy must be extremely upsetting for Lizzie, we should remember that other people's feelings are important too.'

'Whose feelings?' Connie demanded.

'I mention no names. I say only that the vicar has a duty to support everyone involved.'

Connie understood that the conversation had reached a dead end. The carol singers had galloped through 'Wenceslas' and looked to Doug for direction, while movement from inside Bill's cottage warned her that Lizzie might be about to emerge. 'Look, we're all on the same side here. And I appreciate this list.' She held up the paper before tucking it into her pocket. 'You can tell Reverend Ibbotson not to expect any more visits from us.'

'Very good.' Mission accomplished, Doug gave a click of his heels then returned to his singers, while Connie and Pamela breathed sighs of relief. The churchwarden's defence of his vicar had left them feeling uncomfortable, to say the least.

'I take it you're on duty later.' Connie noticed Pamela's uniform under her tweed coat. 'Me too. Tom has agreed to keep an eye on Lizzie for me.'

'Good. I'll see you at the sector post. But who would have thought at the start of this war that we'd be glad to be yelling "put that light out" and manning stirrup pumps on a Saturday night?' Pamela gave a wry smile.

'When girls our age should be putting on our glad rags, ready to foxtrot the night away.' Connie agreed: the times they were living through were very strange indeed.

'I've ordered a search.' Connie spoke on the telephone to Ronald Atkinson, the ARP controller at the town hall. One of her junior wardens had absented himself from duty without authority. 'Alf might have nodded off in the back of a lorry or in a handy dust-cart for all I know. We'll take a look in all the likely places.'

'This chap – is he normally reliable?' Atkinson asked.

'Yes, until an incident a few weeks back.' She hit on another possible explanation for Alf's decision to go AWOL. 'A bomb exploded on Gladstone Square and knocked him clean off his feet. He landed on top of a dead body, then had to go to hospital to get an injury to his head cleaned up. I'd say he's been a bundle of nerves ever since, jumping at his own shadow and suchlike. In fact, he's gone AWOL once before – last Monday, I think it was.'

'Then I'll definitely have to send him before the magistrate,' the controller warned. 'There'll be a statutory fine of forty shillings.'

Connie sighed and put down the phone before calling upstairs to Pamela, who sat in the restroom awaiting instructions. 'I need you to go out and look for Alf.'

'Why? Is something wrong?'

'Yes – he's done a vanishing act,' Connie explained as she began to fill out a report sheet. 'Start on Maypole Street, then move on to Elliot Street. Report back here at midnight.'

Though she didn't relish the task, Pamela set off from the Gas Street post intent on finding the missing warden. She didn't know much about Alf, her fellow junior warden, except that he worked in the fish market during the day and had an older brother in the RAF. Luckily, there seemed little chance of an air raid tonight – no reports of enemy aircraft in the vicinity had come through from the control centre and the weather was against it, with gale-force winds blowing in off the sea and bringing with them a dense covering of low cloud.

The streets of the old town were deserted. As Pamela approached Maypole Street, gusts howled down alleyways and rattled gates, blowing off a dust-bin lid and sending it rolling and clattering down the hill. She ran to retrieve it and jammed it firmly back in place. A milk float was parked near by – Pamela peered into the empty cab before moving on to investigate a ginnel between two bomb-damaged houses. At the end of the alley she found backyards piled high with broken furniture and a discarded mattress, but there was no sign of the missing man.

Pamela was about to retrace her steps when her attention was drawn to an Anderson shelter in one of the yards. It had been built to survive anything that Jerry threw at it – dug deep into the sloping ground and with its corrugated-iron roof intact; just the sort of place where Alf might be holed up. She clambered over the remains of a mahogany wardrobe, rehearsing the soothing words she would say if she found him: *Come along, Alf, let's get you back to the sector post. I'll make us a nice cup of tea and you can tell me what's bothering you.*

The door to the shelter was off its hinges but had been propped back in place. A piece of sacking had been slung across it, seemingly to keep out drafts. Pamela paused – had kids converted the abandoned shelter into a den, she wondered?

A tomcat prowled along the high wall at the back of the yard before leaping silently to the ground. A woman's high, muffled voice called the cat's name – 'Here, Ginger. Here, puss!'

Pamela removed her torch from its belt loop and cautiously switched it on, directing the beam towards the Anderson shelter's door. 'Hello, is anybody there?'

A gust of wind blew grit into her face, then caught hold of a discarded newspaper and scattered its sheets across the yard.

'Here, puss!' the cat's owner called in vain.

Pamela advanced slowly, shining her torch on the door. *Yes, most likely a kids' den*. The wind raised the piece of hessian, revealing a dim yellow light within. 'Alf?'

The light was quickly extinguished. There was no response. Silence thickened.

Someone had sought refuge in the shelter but there was no telling who – ought Pamela to return to Gas Street and request back-up? No – she steeled herself to edge forward until she could direct her torch beam through a gap into the dark interior. Slowly she made out a rough wooden bed and an upturned orange box serving as a table supporting a rusty lamp. The reek of paraffin reached Pamela's nostrils. 'Who's there?' she called.

Still she failed to get a reply. One side of the cramped space remained in shadow, but by pushing her torch further through the gap Pamela was able to angle it so that the beam picked out an old suitcase resting on the earthen floor. Recognition shot through her like a jolt of electricity – it was the self-same case that she'd lifted over the doorstep on the day that Maureen had moved into King Edward Street.

Pamela clicked into action. She shoved at the edge

of the door and shifted it to one side. Without warning a slight figure hurtled towards her but she stood her ground. 'Oh no you don't,' she said softly but firmly.

'Let go of me!' Blind panic gave Maureen strength that she didn't know she possessed. She struggled free, then started to clamber over the debris in the yard, oblivious to Pamela's entreaties. When she reached the ginnel, she broke into a run.

Pamela was hot on her heels. Their hollow footsteps echoed down the alley and as they came out on to Maypole Street, Pamela was able to gain on Maureen and catch up with her at the corner with Elliot Street. She caught her by the arm and swung her round. 'Don't run,' she said. 'There's no point.'

Maureen sank to her knees and sobbed. 'I wasn't doing any harm. I just want to be left alone.'

'I understand.' Pamela knelt beside her. 'But you'll catch your death if you stay there.'

'I don't care. I don't want anyone to know where I am.' Misery oozed from every inch of Maureen's emaciated frame. 'I want people to forget all about me.'

'We can't and we won't.' Despite the cold that seeped into their bones, Pamela didn't try to raise the girl to her feet. 'Lizzie, Connie and me – we've been worried sick. So has your mother.'

Maureen spoke through her tears. 'Why? What did Mum say?'

'She said she was sorry about the way she'd behaved and she wanted us to find out where you'd gone.'

'That can't be right.' Maureen shook her head. 'Mum's ashamed of me and I don't blame her.'

'You must ask Connie for the details. Maybe your

mother has had a change of heart. I do know that she asked after the baby.'

Fresh panic made Maureen jump to her feet, wild-eyed and terrified. 'What does that mean? What's happened to Susan?'

'Nothing – your baby is safe. Calm down and listen to me. This is what I think we should do . . .' Pamela edged towards a solution. 'It's obvious you can't carry on the way you are, so first we'll go back to the shelter to collect your belongings.'

'No – please. I feel safe there.'

'But it's *not* safe,' Pamela argued. 'First off, I promise that no one except Connie and Lizzie will know where you are until you're ready. Do you believe me?'

Slowly Maureen nodded.

'Good girl. So let's make our way to Gas Street – it's dark, so no one will notice. When we get there we'll find you some warm clothes and something to eat.'

'Why?' Maureen seemed deeply bewildered. She gazed up and down the dark street with unfocused eyes, shivering uncontrollably.

'Because the Harrison girls and I care about you, that's why. If you'd rather not go back to King Edward Street we can easily find somewhere else for you to live.' Gradually Pamela was able to gain Maureen's confidence and lead her down the ginnel to accomplish the first part of her plan. Then she walked her to Elliot Street and from there took a shortcut on to Gas Street. 'You gave me a shock back there in the shelter,' she confessed. 'I'd spotted signs of life but you were the last person I expected to see.'

'I'm sorry – I didn't mean to . . .'

Pamela stopped by the pile of sandbags under the

'Home Sweet Home' banner outside the sector post. 'Do one thing for me,' she insisted sternly before they entered the old cobbler's shop. 'Promise me once and for all that you'll stop apologizing.'

'But . . .' For the first time Maureen gained the strength to meet Pamela's gaze.

Pamela raised a warning finger. 'But nothing. You don't have to say sorry because you haven't done anything wrong. Understand?'

'Yes, miss.' The ghost of a smile crept over Maureen's pale, thin face.

Pamela smiled back. 'Come on, then – in we go. Look who it isn't!' she declared to Connie, who stood open-mouthed beside the small, brightly decorated Christmas tree perched on the counter. 'I'm afraid I didn't manage to track Alf down but I found someone just as good, if not better.'

'Why is it always so stuffy in here?' Lizzie flung open the door of Bill's cottage to be met with a blast of freezing-cold air. 'I can hardly breathe.' She voiced her complaint to Tom as she stepped outside. Her chest laboured in and out and it felt as if there were fingers around her throat trying to throttle her.

Tom waited and observed. Lizzie had been restless all evening: unable to sit and listen to the wireless and refusing to eat or drink.

'I'm going for a walk.' She set off towards the stone jetty that bordered the harbour.

Tom followed her. 'This isn't really the weather for a midnight stroll,' he cautioned.

She braced herself against the wind, ignoring an icy spray sent up by strong waves that broke against the jetty. 'It's better than sitting doing nothing. Why is time dragging? Why haven't we heard from him?'

'From who?' Striding alongside her, he dreaded her answer.

'From Bill. Why is he keeping us in suspense?' Having reached the end of the jetty, she stood and gazed out to sea.

Tom didn't answer straight away, aware that Lizzie's mind and heart were at breaking point. He concentrated instead on the heaving, rolling mass of water crashing on to the pebble shore, able to dimly make out the row of concrete pillboxes and the looming bulk of the headland.

'You were there when it happened,' Lizzie whispered, without altering her gaze.

'Yes.'

'Tell me again.' Nothing in nature was as powerful as the sea. Thousands of lost souls haunted the oceans, calling out to loved ones, their voices torn away by the wind.

'We were on patrol.' Tom began slowly, weighing every word. 'We came under attack – two Stuka dive-bombers. *Sea Knight* was holed. She took in water and we realized that we wouldn't make it back to shore. Our only option was to abandon ship.'

'I see.' Lizzie shivered as she pictured the scene.

'*Sea Knight* was done for. Bill fought to save her but it was no good. She capsized and he went down with her.'

'You saw him?' She turned to search Tom's face for the answer.

'Yes.' He knew he mustn't flinch – he must look Lizzie in the eye.

'Then he's gone? There's no hope?' *My love, my one and only.*

'None,' Tom said gently. 'I'm sorry, Lizzie.'

'What will I do without him?' Loosening her hold on the illusion that she'd clung to, she felt the world spin out of control. Sea became sky, earth gave way beneath her feet and at the centre of everything was an enormous emptiness. Where would she go? What would she do?

'You'll carry on one step at a time,' Tom promised. 'However much it hurts, you'll get through it because that's what Bill would want you to do.'

His words reached her through the lonely void. Lizzie knew in her heart that it was true. So, turning back towards the shore, they walked slowly, keeping step, storing up memories of their beloved Bill.

'I'll go home to Elliot Street,' she decided as they approached the cottage.

'Good. I'll come with you.'

A turn of the key in the lock was all it took. There would be no welcoming lamp in the window, no fire in the hearth. The house would stand empty. Tides would ebb and flow.

# CHAPTER TWENTY

It had just turned midnight when Alf Tomkins wandered into the Gas Street post. He shrugged off Connie's queries, simply saying that he'd extended his patrol around the headland, where he'd got caught up in helping a rescue team to repair a burst water main outside the railway station. It was a quiet night, so where was the harm in that?

'The harm is that it went against my orders and I hadn't a clue where you were,' she retorted. 'I had to phone the control centre to report you missing.'

Alf shrugged it off. 'Storm in a teacup. I don't know what you're so het up about.'

*See how you feel when the magistrate slaps a forty-shilling fine on you.* Connie pulled a sour face, but she had other things on her mind so she let it go. Number one on her list of priorities was to convince Maureen to come home with her at the end of her shift.

'Stay at Elliot Street for as long as you like,' she said after she'd handed over to the early morning crew, and she and Pamela provided tea and comfort to Maureen in the restroom. 'Dad's still in hospital so we have a spare bed.'

Pamela backed Connie up. 'Do you hear that? I wouldn't turn down the offer if I was you.'

Maureen shook her head. 'It's too much trouble.'

'No trouble at all. I'm just glad Pamela found you.' Connie kept her invitation low-key, afraid that at any moment Maureen would take flight for a second time. 'I've had some interesting chats since I last saw you; one of them was with your mum.'

Maureen shrank back in her chair.

'I told you,' Pamela said kindly, 'there's nothing to worry about.'

'What did she say?' Looking to Connie for an answer, Maureen gripped the arms of the chair.

'That she wants to put things right between you – those were her very words. And I believe her; I really do.'

'She's not mad at me?'

'Not any more.'

Maureen gave a long sigh and let her hands fall into her lap. Her grey coat hung open, revealing her wasted figure beneath the plain brown dress. Her dark hair lay flat against her head and her eyes looked huge in her small, scared face.

'Come home with me – please.' Wearily, Connie reached for her own coat. 'We'll all feel better after a good sleep. Then we can decide what to do next.'

An almost imperceptible nod from Maureen brought a smile of relief to Pamela's face.

There was only one obstacle and it occurred to Connie as they left the sector post together. 'Lizzie.' She clicked her tongue against the roof of her mouth. 'She's still at the cottage. Tom is keeping an eye on her but I ought to check.'

Just then the telephone rang and Bob Eddison,

the head warden who had taken over from Connie, called her back inside. 'For you,' he told her with a hint of disgruntlement. 'Your boyfriend would like a word.'

'Hello, Tom?' Fearing another emergency, Connie's hand trembled as she waited for him to speak.

'Yes, it's me. I'm glad I caught you. Lizzie's back at Elliot Street. I'll hang on until you get here.'

His voice; his wonderful, low, soothing voice! Connie longed to kiss Tom and hold him tight. 'I'm on my way. Oh, and I love you.'

Bob's bushy eyebrows shot up into his lined forehead. There was an audible tut as he scribbled away at the report he was writing.

'I love you too,' Tom said.

'Well?' Connie looked up from her newspaper as Maureen came downstairs the following morning.

Their guest wore one of Lizzie's thick sweaters over her brown dress. Her hair was brushed and a hint of colour had returned to her cheeks.

'Better,' Maureen admitted. She'd slept for a few hours, then lay awake listening to sounds in the house – unfamiliar rustlings and creaks, a tap turned on and water gurgling through pipes, soft footsteps descending the stairs.

'Tea?' Lizzie poured her a cup, then set it down on the table. Lack of sleep showed in her drawn features and the haunted, shadowy look in Maureen's eyes.

She hesitated before sitting down. One act of kindness didn't wipe away months of misery, and her mind was still plagued by doubt. 'Are you sure I'm not being a nuisance?'

'Sit.' Connie ignored the question and patted the seat of the chair next to her. 'I've been thinking – there's a spare pair of slacks in my drawer that might fit you if you wear them with a belt. And what size shoes do you wear?'

'Size five.'

'The same as you, Liz.' Connie nudged her sister into action.

Moving stiffly like an automaton, Lizzie went upstairs to fetch a pair of slippers for their visitor to wear.

'Today's Sunday,' Connie reminded Maureen. 'We can go out for a walk if you feel up to it.'

Maureen shook her head. 'Everyone would stare at me.'

'Then stare back.' Connie's advice was kindly offered and it was accompanied by a reassuring smile. 'That's what I would do in your shoes. Talking of which . . .'

At that moment Lizzie returned with the slippers and placed them at Maureen's feet. 'Here – see if they fit.'

The Cinderella moment brought a smile to Connie and Maureen's lips. 'Stare right back and hold your head high,' Connie continued. 'Remember: sticks and stones may break your bones . . .'

'But I'm nowhere near as brave as you.'

Connie narrowed her eyes thoughtfully. 'You're braver than you think,' she insisted. 'You went through nine long, hard months all by yourself, then you stood up to the matron in Axenby. That takes a ton of courage. But we won't force you to do anything you don't want to do.'

'There's only one thing I want,' Maureen confessed shakily. 'Only I'm not allowed. I tried and they wouldn't let me.'

'You mean your visit to the WVS centre?' Lizzie shrugged off her lethargy and sat down opposite Maureen. 'That must have felt like a real slap in the face.'

'The woman there didn't believe I was Susan's mother. She said at first that I was too young and then that I didn't have any proof. And in any case, what good would it do since the papers for Susan's adoption are written up and ready to be signed?'

'Perhaps it would have been even harder for you if you'd been allowed in,' Lizzie suggested.

'No – I'd give anything for one last look.'

Maureen's desperate longing to see her baby moved Connie deeply. 'I feel for you, I really do. Your heart must be breaking in two.'

'Yes, but I did the right thing, didn't I?' Maureen appealed to Lizzie. 'I couldn't give Susan a proper family – a daddy and a mummy and a nice house.'

Lizzie had no answer. Instead, she reached out to clasp the girl's trembling hand and hold it tight.

Connie stood up with a characteristic air of determination. 'I fancy a brisk walk around the block,' she announced as she reached for her coat. 'I'll leave you two to chat. Back in fifteen minutes. Bye!'

Connie timed it just right. Churchgoers were pouring out of St Joseph's as she arrived at the church gates and she quickly spotted Nancy Strong's purple coat in the throng. Nancy's back was turned and she was deep in conversation with Terence Ibbotson inside the church porch. Meanwhile, Colin hung about aimlessly in the graveyard, head down and with his hands in his pockets, the picture of bored, unhappy boyhood.

The grey, damp morning did little to dim the cheerful, pre-Christmas spirits of the dispersing crowd. Talk was all about the big day – where it would be spent and who with, what presents had been bought or made and precisely what would be eaten and drunk. Hilda Fielding and her brother Cyril said a brief hello to Connie in passing. No love lost there. Not for the first time Connie registered the difference between the ill-assorted siblings – the opposite of Jack Sprat and his wife, with Cyril almost as wide as he was high and Hilda tall and skinny as a bean-pole. Alf Tomkins came close behind; again Connie had no desire to enter into conversation – not after his recent disappearing trick and his lack of remorse. Then came her Aunty Vera, chatting away to Ronald Atkinson, followed by Ivy and a gaggle of WI friends.

'How's your Lizzie?' Ivy broke away to commiserate with Connie. 'Poor girl. It couldn't have happened at a worse time, what with her and Bill just getting engaged and Christmas coming up as well. But at least you still have your Tom, thank goodness.' The old family friend gave Connie a quick hug. 'Tell your dad I was asking after him,' she added as she hurried on her way.

By this time Nancy had emerged from the porch and was calling for Colin to join her. She walked him briskly down the path, but when she saw Connie she halted, hitched her handbag further up her arm and waited warily for her to approach.

Connie spied alarm behind the thin gauze of Nancy's black veil. 'It's all right,' she assured her. 'Maureen's safe.'

'You found her?' Nancy's shoulders dropped and she gave a long, low sigh. 'When? Where?'

'I'll fill in the details later. She's with Lizzie and me at Elliot Street. Will you come and see her?'

'Does she want me to?' Various emotions flickered across Nancy's small features, from fear to relief to hope and then doubt.

'Yes. Deep down I'm sure she does.' Connie kept her fingers firmly crossed. 'Anyway, it's high time you two made up.'

'Yes, Mam – please!' Colin tugged at her sleeve. 'But don't have any more rows – promise.'

'Very well.' Nancy nodded slowly. 'But wait a moment.' She retraced her steps to relay the news to the vicar. 'Your prayers have been answered – Maureen is safe and well.'

Terence's eyes widened in momentary disbelief, then he glanced down the path at Connie before adjusting his expression to one of benevolent well-wisher. 'That's marvellous. Wonderful. Such a relief.'

Nancy rejoined Connie and Colin. Together they hurried through the old town to Elliot Street, overtaking Hilda and Cyril on the way. Hilda would have detained Nancy to discuss the church flower rota but Connie whisked Maureen's mother onward towards number 12. By the time they got there Nancy's resolution was weakening. 'What if she won't see me? What then?' she demanded on the doorstep, her face pinched with worry as she clutched nervously at her coat collar.

'Let's find out, shall we?' Connie opened the door, then ushered Nancy and Colin into the house. Surprise was a major component in her plan but there was no guarantee that it would pay off, so she held her breath as Nancy entered the kitchen.

Lizzie was the first to react. She flew across the room and stood next to Colin while Connie edged Nancy forward. Maureen stared at her mother as if she'd seen a ghost. Why was she here? What new harsh words did she have in store? Backed up against the pantry door, Maureen waited for the axe to fall.

Nancy took a jagged breath, then spoke. 'I was afraid . . .'

Connie threw Lizzie a worried look. *Oh dear, what if this doesn't turn out well?*

Lizzie bit her lip and prayed.

Nancy began again. 'I was afraid that you'd gone for good.'

Maureen stood still and mute, desperate to make sense of what was happening.

'And I would never have had the chance to say that I was sorry for all my mistakes,' Nancy whispered. 'To admit I was in the wrong and to beg you to forgive me.'

Maureen closed her eyes in disbelief, then opened them again to see her mother in her best Sunday clothes, reaching out her hand.

'I ought not to have blamed you and worried about what people thought. I'm a small-minded, selfish woman and that's the truth.' Nancy let her hand fall to her side, a gesture of despair.

*Say something!* Connie silently urged Maureen to reply.

'I won't blame you if you want nothing to do with me.' Nancy choked over her words. 'I deserve it for what I've done. You're my daughter, your daddy's dear little lass, and I've let you both down. I'm sorry.'

'No, you didn't – it was me.' Guilt was a heavy stone that sealed the entrance to a dark cave. Maureen had lived without light for so long that she blinked in its bright rays. 'I'm the one who's sorry.'

'My girl.' At last Nancy went to Maureen and wrapped her arms around her thin body. She held her close to stop her from trembling. 'I wish I'd been stronger for you. I will be if you'll let me. I'll stand up for you and I won't let anyone hurt you.'

Maureen rested her head on Nancy's shoulder. After all these months, after the misery and the loneliness, the darkness and the doubt, there was this – her mother's arms, the smoothness of her silk scarf, the sweetness of her perfume.

'I'll make it better,' Nancy promised as she brushed away her daughter's tears.

Bert sat up in bed with his hands resting on the crisp, green hospital coverlet. The ward was busy with Sunday afternoon visitors, Connie and Lizzie among them.

'Every blinking day is a day of rest for me,' he grumbled as the girls drew up two chairs. 'Sunday is no different – just me staring out of the window at the crows in the treetops or watching the hands of that wall clock creep forward.'

'Stop moaning,' Connie told him briskly. 'You're on the mend and that's the main thing.'

'You're just like your mother,' Bert commented

without elaborating. Turning to Lizzie, he softened his tone. 'And what about you? Are you managing all right?'

'So-so,' she answered truthfully.

'Aye well, give it time – it's early days.' He studied her peaky face and decided that the subject of Bill was best skirted around. 'Just don't overdo it, that's all.'

'I'll try not to,' she promised.

Connie steered them away from the black rocks of Lizzie's grief with an account of the morning's more cheerful events. 'Nancy Strong turned up trumps,' she told Bert. 'Not before time, mind you. You should have seen young Colin's face when Maureen and Nancy hugged and made up: it was like a dozen Christmases come early and all at once. The three of them went home to North Street arm in arm, bless 'em.'

Bert shrugged. 'Fingers crossed it works out all right. I remember Nancy when she was a toddler, coming into the shop with pink ribbons and fancy lace collars, never a hair out of place – a pretty little thing but spoiled to death by that mother of hers.'

'You've got a memory like an elephant,' Connie said with an indulgent smile. 'The only mystery now that she and Maureen have made up is that we're still no nearer to knowing who was responsible for getting Maureen in the family way.'

'She wouldn't say?'

'No – she point-blank refuses.'

'And we can't force her.' Lizzie was sure of this. 'I say leave the family alone for now and give them time to come to terms with things.'

'Aye.' Bert was doubtful that all would be plain

sailing. 'Fingers crossed,' he said again. 'You two have done enough already.'

'And Pamela,' Lizzie reminded him. 'She's the one who found Maureen in the Anderson shelter.'

'But why should the father – whoever he is – get away with it? That's what gets my goat.' Connie's needle was stuck in the same old groove. 'And as a matter of fact, Lizzie and I have an idea that there's a link with St Joseph's. We could even give you a name—'

Bert held up his hand to cut her short. 'But have you got the evidence?'

Connie frowned and shifted uncomfortably in her seat. 'Not evidence exactly.'

He turned to Lizzie with the same question. 'No proof to back you up?'

'No,' she confirmed reluctantly.

'Then it's best to keep your traps firmly shut,' their father recommended in no uncertain terms. 'Don't go getting yourselves into hot water over it. No one will thank you if you do.'

Pamela dreamed of German planes flying over Kelthorpe like a swarm of flies – dozens of them droning overhead, dropping their bombs with mighty thumps, setting the dockside ablaze, tearing up railway lines and demolishing power stations. Frantic figures fled through smoke and flames, and a man stood outside a burning building crying out the names of his wife and children. 'Where shall we go? What shall we do?' an elderly woman wailed.

She woke with a start. The room was dark and silent and the chaos of her nightmare gradually receded. As morning light crept in through the chinks in her blackout blind, she managed to shake off the dreadful dream, washed and got dressed for work, then slipped silently from the bungalow to spend time with Fred.

Pamela found him in the kitchen of the big house, quietly making breakfast. 'You're up,' she said as she kissed him on the cheek. 'You must be feeling better.'

'Much better,' he assured her. He was in shirt-sleeves, with his tie hanging loose around his neck. 'In fact, Hugh has agreed to drive me into the office this morning.'

She looked in astonishment at her battle-scarred love. His bruises had faded and taken on a yellowish tinge and the cuts had closed up, but he still moved stiffly and slowly. 'Are you sure you're up to it?'

Fred handed her a cup of tea and pointed to her bandaged hand. 'If you are, then so am I.'

Pamela realized that arguing would be pointless. 'Here – let me tie your tie for you.' She performed the task gently – twisting, wrapping, then sliding the silk material with smooth, nimble fingers – then she kissed him again.

'Your uncle has been very considerate,' Fred told her. 'He says I should ease myself in by working half-days until Christmas. And he promises to use his influence at the town council.'

'How exactly?'

'Hugh will let it be known that my Home Office registration documents are in order and that he personally vouches for my loyalty to the King. Word will get around – any accusations to the contrary are completely false. You look lovely, by the way.' He stood back to appreciate the cut of Pamela's close-fitting blue dress. 'As always.'

She brushed off the compliment. 'It's good of Uncle Hugh, but remember: it wasn't town councillors who attacked you or sent me the note.'

'But perhaps they have power over those who did,' Fred countered as he tidied away the breakfast things. He'd emerged from his days of enforced isolation with a new determination to look on the bright side. 'They're Kelthorpe's big employers. Arthur Dixon runs two builders' merchants, Ronald Atkinson owns three garages and Noel Bentley has the department store. If they're seen to be on my side, perhaps the men and women under them will think twice about coming after me.'

'Yes, but will the message get through to people like Eric Thompson?' The thugs who attacked Fred probably didn't have decent jobs to lose. They were likely to be drinkers and wastrels who hung around at the pub door, fomenting hatred.

Fred finished his chore, then struggled into his jacket. 'Don't think too far ahead; if we're to get through this we must take one day at a time, keep our wits about us and try not to get into situations where we find ourselves alone.'

Pamela took on board this last piece of advice. 'I'll travel into the office with you and Uncle Hugh,' she decided.

It meant dashing back to the bungalow to finish getting ready. Her father was up and dressed when she got there, her mother still fussing and fluttering about in her dressing gown. Had Pamela slept properly, was she wearing a good, thick vest and please, Harold, make sure that your daughter has a decent dinner in the canteen.

'And what about Lizzie Harrison?' Edith asked out of the blue. 'Is she back at work in the shop or will Connie need someone to step in again?'

'Why not give her a ring?' Pamela suggested as she escaped her mother's clutches and set off across the lawn. Uncle Hugh and Fred were waiting in the car. A new day, a fresh start. With fingers firmly crossed, she ran to join them.

'He's back, I see.' Betty accosted Pamela as she took off her coat in the ladies' cloakroom at the timber yard. 'I'm talking about that precious boyfriend of yours. I just saw him getting out of Mr Anderson's car.'

Pamela kept her back turned. 'What of it?'

'I don't know how he dare show his face, that's what. No, don't say a word. You'd only stick up for him and make matters worse.'

Pamela made a point of ignoring Betty and carefully combing her hair.

'You two think you can get away with murder, but you've got another think coming.' Betty came up behind Pamela and hissed in her ear. 'And before you go crying to your uncle behind my back again – Betty said this, Betty did that – don't bother. I went off and found myself a new job, starting straight after Christmas, so there!'

'Congratulations.' Pamela turned with the hint of a sarcastic smile.

'It's at Bentley's, if you must know. I'll be in charge

of ladies' fashion, with a big fat discount off everything I buy.' Betty flaunted her success by twirling on the spot. 'No more ruining my nails on the typewriter for me and no more yes, Mr Anderson, no, Mr Anderson, three bags full, Mr Anderson. I'll be my own boss running a big department from now on.'

'Good luck,' Pamela said in the same tone as before. 'Now, if you'll excuse me . . .'

'Now, if you'll excuse me . . .' Betty mimicked as she flung open the door and raced upstairs before Pamela.

Ten minutes later they were both at their desks when Fred came in. 'Are there any new orders in this morning's post?' he asked Betty, who pointed carelessly to a pile of unopened letters and told him to help himself. 'Good Lord, your face!' she commented flippantly as she glanced up.

He took the letters away without responding.

'Fred got off lightly, all things considered,' Betty added.

Betty's catty remark nettled Pamela, but once again she bit her tongue. *Only a few more days, then I'll be rid of her,* she thought.

But it was as if Hugh's disgruntled, soon to be ex-secretary had embarked on a mission to destroy. Pamela had filed some letters incorrectly, she typed at a snail's pace and where had she hidden the new allocation of headed notepaper? At one point during the morning Hugh came into their office and overheard Betty berating Pamela for losing an all-important appointment diary.

'I have it here,' he said crisply, tapping the diary before placing it on Betty's desk then departing.

'I haven't handed in my notice yet,' Betty smirked after the door had closed. 'Won't Uncle Hugh be in for a nasty surprise!'

'When will you tell him?' In fact, Pamela didn't much care – Betty was leaving and that was that.

'Christmas Eve. And keep it to yourself, or else.'

The petty threat skimmed over Pamela's head. It was twenty minutes to dinner time, then ten, then five. At the sound of the klaxon Betty jumped up and rushed downstairs to be at the head of the canteen queue along with Jack and Keith. Her mood was jubilant throughout the dinner break, but Pamela chose a quiet corner for herself and Harold. Fred had already gone back to Sunrise.

'The lad is tired out after the morning's exertions but he got through all right,' Harold reported. 'Keith had a go at him for something or other, but Fred didn't rise to the bait.'

The day couldn't end soon enough for Pamela. Throughout the afternoon she distracted herself by envisaging a carol singing outing due to take place that evening. Fred was right: she mustn't risk making her way there alone—

'Are you deaf?' Betty broke into her train of thought. 'I said, fetch me that green folder on the shelf behind you.'

'Please,' Pamela added under her breath.

It was as if she'd lit a blue touchpaper. Betty fizzed and sparked before jumping up from her desk. 'Right, that's it! Who do you think you are, you jumped-up little so-and-so? You forget – I don't have to put up with your snide remarks and your going behind my back any more. I'm free to tell you exactly what I think of you.'

Pamela sat bolt upright, afraid of what was to come.

'You're a sly, nasty piece of work and, what's worse, you're one of those dirty collaborators who jumped into bed with Herr Muller out there without a scrap of shame.' Betty pushed papers from her desk and slammed her fist on her typewriter keys. 'Don't try to deny it,' she ranted. 'It's common knowledge that your chap is a German spy and he got what he deserved the other night. But does he learn his lesson? No. Here he is, back at work acting as if nothing happened. And you – you're a traitor to the King—'

'It was you,' Pamela said calmly. 'You typed the note and posted it to Gas Street.'

'You bet your cotton socks I did!' Wild-eyed with fury, Betty flung more papers on to the floor. 'I loathed you from the moment I clapped eyes on you, and I'm not the only one: Kathleen and Winnie can't stand the sight of you either. And you should hear what the others say at our meetings. Tarring and feathering doesn't cover it. As for Friedrich out there—'

'What others?' Pamela demanded. She felt strangely cool in the face of Betty's onslaught. At last the truth was out.

'Keith and Jack and Cyril Fielding, for a start.' Betty counted them out on her fingers. 'Then there's Eric and Walter and Alf—'

'Eric who?' *Thompson, of course!* Tommo meant Thompson; she and Fred had guessed right.

'Aha, never you mind! We meet at the Anchor, that's all I'm saying – a group of us is dead set on sniffing out a spy and giving him or her what for.'

'Eric Thompson.' Pamela kept a cool head as she stated the name of their chief suspect.

'Ha ha!' Betty scattered yet more papers. 'Not on your Nellie. That drunken fool can't see straight, let alone organize an attack on the enemy.'

'Walter who?' Pamela persisted.

Neither girl heard the door open or noticed Hugh enter the room.

'I've said enough.' Betty stood with her back to the door amongst the aftermath of her rage – papers, envelopes, index cards, blotting paper and a bottle of ink that had broken on impact and spread a blue stain over the fawn carpet. 'All you need to know is that our group won't give up until every last spy in Kelthorpe is rooted out. So tell your boyfriend to stick that in his pipe and smoke it!'

Childish, silly, petulant but nonetheless dangerous – Pamela ran out of words to describe Betty's threat.

Hugh stepped forward. 'Betty, that's quite enough.'

Betty gasped, then immediately pulled herself together. 'And you can find yourself another dogsbody,' she told her boss in a final burst of defiance. 'I've had enough of pitch pine and cranes and cutting sheds. I've gone and got a job in ladies' fashion, thank you very much!'

# CHAPTER TWENTY-ONE

Was now the time to go to Gladstone Square and report what they knew to the police?

Fred had decided to accompany Pamela into the old town and join in with the carol singing rather than risk her venturing out alone. It was a clear, cold night with little wind – the sea was calm as they slowly rounded the headland, their pace governed by Fred's injuries.

'Let's go over what we actually know.' His methodical mind assessed the situation as they walked along the harbourside arm in arm. 'I was attacked by unknown assailants and Betty has admitted that she wrote you a threatening note.'

'Yes, but Connie destroyed it and Betty will most likely deny writing it when push comes to shove.' Pamela tried to think along Fred's logical lines. 'She did mention a group that meets at the Anchor – we could inform the police about that.'

'But she gave no actual names that are worth reporting?' He glanced towards the pub, noticing the usual huddle of men lounging by the door but seemingly ignoring him and Pamela as they crossed the market square. 'Other than Eric Thompson and Cyril

Fielding, and from what Betty said, we can discount Eric.'

'And it's unlikely to be Cyril either.' Fielding was too slow and overweight to have been part of the gang that attacked Fred. 'But Betty did mention Keith and Jack as well,' Pamela remembered.

'Again – there's no evidence that they were involved. Anyway, I would have recognized them.'

'True.' Perhaps there was little point in involving the police after all. But Pamela was reluctant to let it drop. 'Betty gave the impression that it was a large group. They meet in the pub and fire themselves up with talk of collaborators and spies. She swore their members would never give up until they get rid of every last one.'

'That's how mobs operate.' Fred spoke from experience. 'History tells us that fanatics get swept along on a wave of emotion. And at a time like this, when none of us knows whether the next bomb that falls from the skies will have our name written on it, fear lies at the back of everything we do. We all dread tomorrow – whether we admit it or not.'

Snatches from Pamela's nightmare played out again in her mind – the man crying out for his family, the old woman's despairing wail amidst boom after boom of exploding bombs. Fire everywhere. 'How can you be so calm?' she wondered.

'I may sound it,' Fred replied, 'but underneath I'm as terrified as everyone else.'

Helplessness seeped into them as they reached the end of College Road. Doug's carol singers had arranged to meet tonight outside St Joseph's, a few hundred yards along the busy street. Passing the bombed remains of the *Gazette* building, Pamela became aware of people approaching quickly from behind and her hand gripped Fred's arm more tightly.

Fred heard them too. 'Don't look round. Keep walking.' The odds were that it was folk going about their normal business: dock workers hurrying home after a day's work, perhaps. But the sound reawoke memories of the attack on the headland and he braced himself. He quickly took in his surroundings – they were on a broad shopping street with buses and cars going by and shop assistants emerging on to the pavement; surely he and Pamela would be safe. But blackout was enforced and there were no street lights. Quiet side alleys led off from the main street.

Tension mounted as the footsteps behind them quickened. Silently Fred cursed the injuries that slowed him down. He was about to steer Pamela to safety across the street when two men dressed in overcoats and with their caps pulled forward emerged from the nearest alley and blocked their path. The men behind soon caught up and he and Pamela were surrounded.

Hands seized her and shoved her sideways down the deserted alley. She was wrenched away from Fred and fell to the ground, was hauled back on to her feet and pressed against the rough wall of a high building.

The men who had approached from behind had picked up broken bricks from the rubble surrounding the *Gazette* offices. Bundling Fred down the alley after Pamela, they launched their missiles. Using his arms to protect his head, he kicked out and landed a blow on an attacker's shin, then he threw himself at the thug who had Pamela in his grasp. 'Let her go, damn you!'

Five against two. Despite the hail of bricks, Pamela managed to twist free of the man who pinned her against the wall. She shouted out with all her might until a second burly man grabbed her from behind and clamped his hand over her mouth. She bit the soft flesh at the base of his thumb. Yelping then swearing, he was forced to release her. She screamed for help.

Blindly Fred kicked and punched. He took no account of the pain – he must save Pamela. As he stooped to pick up one of the broken bricks, two of the men tackled him and threw him to the ground. He landed face down in a filthy puddle and steeled himself for the blows to come.

'Help!' Pamela's cry reached the street. Several people ignored it and hurried on. 'Down here – help!'

Her frantic pleas drew the attention of two ARP wardens from the Gas Street post. They sprinted across the road then down the alley to lay hands on two of the gang and drag them into full view of passers-by. Other plucky rescuers joined in and soon the thugs were outnumbered.

Twisting on to his back, Fred delivered one last kick. The biggest of the men fell backwards in a warden's arms and was hauled away. Fred raised himself from the ground and staggered towards Pamela. He clasped her to him, and for a few moments they stood without speaking. Her breath came in harsh, dry gasps as she made sense of what had just taken place. They were alive – they had survived unharmed.

Emerging from the alley together, Fred and Pamela found that it was Eddie and Simon Fraser who had come to their rescue.

'Hold him fast.' Cool and in control, Eddie ordered the restraint of one of the attackers while his brother landed a punch that sent another assailant reeling. A swarm of civilians made sure that none of the five escaped.

Recognizing Pamela, Eddie drew her and Fred to a safe distance. He offered them water from the flask in his knapsack. 'Nothing broken?' he checked, while Simon lined up the thugs against the window of Benson's music shop.

'No, thank God!' Pamela grasped the sleeve of Eddie's battledress. She'd never been so glad to see her fresh-faced Civil Defence colleague. 'Without you, I don't know what—'

'That's why we're here – to keep order on the streets,' Eddie cut in with a cheery grin. 'You know that better than I do.'

'Someone run to the sector post and ask Bob Eddison to telephone 999,' Simon ordered. 'Tell him we need a couple of bobbies here pronto!'

Surrounded and outnumbered, all fight went out of the captured men. They swore and hung their heads, their faces obscured by the peaks of their caps. One was burlier than the rest, dressed in a heavy overcoat and with a dark scarf hiding the lower part of his face.

'Who have we here?' Eddie strode down the line to yank away the man's scarf before frowning and taking an uncertain step back.

Fred saw their attacker's face. 'You again,' he muttered. The same bull-like build, the broad, brutal, angry features . . .

The man scowled back. *So what? Your sort deserves everything you get.*

Pamela left Fred's side and approached the thug until Eddie stepped between them.

'Careful,' he warned. Then, 'Bloody hell, Alf. Are you out of your mind?'

*Alf Tomkins – Tommo.* Pamela stood in stunned silence.

He didn't blink. 'Don't look at me like that,' he snarled. 'Or you!' He turned to Fred, who had to be held back by Simon. 'They can lock me up and throw away the key for all I care, but there'll be more like me queuing up to do the job Mr Churchill wants us to do – hundreds of us.'

'And thousands more who won't,' Fred replied with complete certainty. He was no longer afraid to speak out in front of the band of helpers who had flown to the rescue. 'Look around you – these are the decent men and women of Kelthorpe who refuse to fall for your lies.'

'Says you,' came the surly, defiant reply.

But Fred had emerged from the shadows. He had risen up. With Pamela by his side and with Hugh Anderson's backing he would no longer be intimidated. A proverb from his childhood resonated through his entire body – *Lügen haben kurze Beine.* 'You can threaten me all you like.' He drew himself up and addressed Tomkins in his coolest, calmest voice. 'But in the end truth will out.'

Lizzie put one foot after another because that was what Bill would want. She joined Connie and Tom outside St Joseph's church. It was strange – her body did things while her brain was disengaged. She walked, she talked, she breathed without being truly present, and now she would sing carols too. She would drift towards Christmas and while everyone celebrated she would silently mourn.

'Well done for showing up.' Connie gave her sister's arm a gentle squeeze. 'It's a good turnout. Tom's here to swell our ranks and Nancy has let Colin off the lead at last.' She pointed to Colin and Arnold perched side by side on a wall.

At the sight of Lizzie, Colin jumped down and ran across. 'Our Maureen asked me to give this to you and Connie.' He produced an envelope containing a hand-made card. On the front was a simple drawing of a robin redbreast perching on a sprig of holly surrounded by a halo of silver glitter. Inside were the words, 'Happy Christmas from Maureen', followed by three kisses. 'It's for Pamela as well,' Colin added before scooting off to rejoin Arnold.

Connie took the card from Lizzie. 'I'm touched,' she murmured. The gesture, along with Colin's presence, signified that all was well in the Strong household.

'Watch out – Doug is marshalling his troops.' Tom noticed activity by the church gate. 'Oh no, as you were.' In fact, Terence had emerged from the vicarage and seemed intent on collaring Doug before they set off. The two churchmen talked for a while, then the vicar mingled with the carol singers while Doug made a beeline for Connie's small group.

'I hear congratulations are in order.' Pausing to clear his throat, he seemed ill at ease, casting nervous glances in his boss's direction. 'The vicar informs me that Maureen Strong is back home with her mother, thanks to you and Miss Carr.'

It was clear to Connie that Doug was acting under

the vicar's orders. 'We only did what anyone else would have done,' she replied ungraciously.

'Nevertheless . . .' Again, the throat clearing and the worried look. 'You befriended the girl at a difficult time – without judging her actions harshly where others might. She obviously trusted you and confided in you.' There was a rising intonation at the end of the sentence that turned Doug's statement into a question.

'Yes, but she didn't tell us the name of the baby's father, if that's what you're driving at.' Connie glanced at Terence and saw that his attention was riveted on their little group.

Doug made a sound midway between a cough and a laugh. 'No – quite – of course!' He stepped back, visibly relieved.

'Would you look at that!' Connie watched the warden scurry back to the vicar. 'Talk about getting someone else to do your dirty work.'

Lost in her own thoughts, Lizzie scarcely reacted and, as an outsider looking in, Tom took a more cautious view. 'I know you, Connie Bailey, and I recognize that gleam in your eye. Think before you act is my advice.'

'Did I ask you?' Connie was put out. She'd expected more support from Tom. 'You sound like Dad, but I'm hardly going to toss accusations around without getting the go-ahead from Maureen.'

'Right you are,' Tom grunted. Everyone was on edge, himself included. Emotions were running high. He was glad when the vicar disappeared inside the church and at last the carol singers were on the move.

They set off with Doug at their head, across the

graveyard and on to College Road, where they came across a queue outside Barbieri's chip shop: a captive audience, who were treated to a sweet rendering of 'O Little Town of Bethlehem' – silent stars and dark streets, hopes and fears and meek souls.

Arnold and Colin darted inside to scrounge a bag of scraps apiece from the girl behind the counter, then slowly the band of carol singers processed along the street, where shop blinds were down and wardens were out on patrol.

'Put that light out!' one yelled to an offender in the flat above Benson's music shop.

The light went off and the warden moved on.

'That's where Penrose lives,' Connie said with a frown. 'Typical!'

'"Ding dong Merrily".' Doug announced the next carol.

Tom, Connie and Lizzie sang the ding dongs, the glorias and hosannas. Arnold grasped the collection tin with greasy fingers, and the good folk of Kelthorpe came to their doors. Happy Christmas to one and all.

Next morning Connie let Lizzie sleep in. She crept out of their shared bedroom and left the house without a sound. Rest would do her grieving sister good and with a bit of luck she, Connie, could call on Aunty Vera again for some extra help in the bakery.

Dawn had broken when Lizzie woke at last. For a few blissful moments she luxuriated in the warmth of her bed and a sense that all was well. Then cold reality struck. All was not well – *Sea Knight* was lost and Bill was drowned. She groaned and sat up, swung her legs over the side of the bed and shivered as she looked at the alarm clock – almost eight o'clock. Connie's bed was empty. Panic set in.

Lizzie rushed to get dressed. There were deliveries to make. Customers depended on her. She chose clothes closest to hand – a pair of corduroy slacks and a thick Fair Isle jumper. Then she went to the bathroom and splashed her face with cold water, ran a comb through her hair and dashed downstairs. She was throwing on her warm windcheater when there was a knock at the door.

Expecting the postman with a package too large for the letter box, she rushed to answer it but found that it was locked and the spare key was missing from its usual hook to the left of the door. The knock was repeated.

'Wait a second,' she called as she opened the shallow drawer in the hall stand – the next obvious place to look.

'Lizzie?'

She froze. Her heart hammered.

'Lizzie, it's me.'

*Key!* She fumbled in the drawer. Her mind was playing tricks – it couldn't possibly be Bill's voice calling her name. Gloves, old letters and a hairbrush fell to the floor before her clumsy fingers closed over cold metal – she picked up the key and inserted it in the lock. She opened the door.

He stood on the pavement gazing up at her.

Was it a ghost? Had she gone completely mad? He wore the tweed jacket that she'd last seen hanging behind his cottage door. He was unshaven and thinner than she remembered.

'Can I come in?'

Hammer, hammer, hammer, went her heart. Her head was spinning. Perhaps she was asleep and this was a dream. She retreated to the kitchen at the back of the house.

Bill followed, watching her grope for a chair then sit down, her face white and pinched with shock. He resisted the urge to gather her up and never let her go. 'I called in at the bakery first. Connie said you were here.'

Lizzie shook her head. She hardly knew what to feel, what to think. Her mind splintered into a dozen disconnected pieces 'Impossible,' she murmured. Bill must gather the fragments and give them back to her in the proper order; explain, make it all make sense.

He sat opposite her. 'Tom told you what happened?'

She nodded. If she reached across the table and touched him, would he be real?

'We lost *Sea Knight*. I went down with her. I was wearing my life jacket.' Every thought had been of Lizzie, every action had been for her. 'When I came back up to the surface *Halcyon* was sailing off in the opposite direction.' He remembered how hope of rescue had faded in the vast dark space, against the swell and fall of mighty waves. Still, he'd clung to life.

'What did you do?' The words tumbled from her lips.

'I stayed afloat. The currents were strong – I got swept along.'

'And you're really here?'

Bill put his hand over hers. 'Luck was on my side. *Sea Knight*'s lifeboat bobbed up not far from me – it was holed and turned upside down but I managed to reach her and clamber on until a Dutch cruiser spotted me – HNLMS *Java*; a big, slow old girl on escort duties. The crew hauled me on board.'

His hand was warm and heavy. She stared at the square fingernails, felt the dryness of his skin.

'That was early Friday morning. *Java* was bound for her home port – Nieuwe Haven naval base. I didn't fancy being handed over to the Dutch authorities – I'd have ended up in a POW camp. Again I was lucky: *Java*'s skipper hated being under Jerry's thumb, so he turned a blind eye and let me slip away as soon as we docked. I spent most of Saturday under cover, looking for a friendly trawler or any other small ship to sail me back to Blighty. That was the tricky bit, but eventually I found a Dutch trawler that had been at Dunkirk. She fishes on Norfolk Banks. Her captain was a decent sort, too, so he agreed to carry me back home, no questions asked. We set sail yesterday evening and by midnight we were a few miles east of Hull, where we radioed HMRT *Guardian*, an Admiralty rescue tug in the area. She came up alongside and took me on board. We made land around dawn. That's it in a nutshell.'

*Java*, Nieuwe Haven, Dunkirk, Norfolk Banks – the words rattled around Lizzie's head. None of it mattered; fate hadn't snatched Bill from her after all.

'Say something.' He watched her closely, waiting for her to react.

'I can't,' she breathed. He'd been through so much, had come so close to death. And now he was here in the flesh, restored to her – the best gift in the world.

'Don't cry.' Bill raised Lizzie to her feet and held

her close until her trembling lessened. Days of dizzying danger had passed and here he was, standing on firm ground, holding the girl he loved. 'I came as quick as I could.' He hadn't slept, hadn't eaten, hadn't thought of anything or anyone except her.

The roughness of his jacket was real and so was the warmth of his cheek, the breadth of his shoulders and the softness of his lips. There could be no doubt. Lizzie kissed him once, twice, three times.

# CHAPTER TWENTY-TWO

Edith accepted Hugh's invitation to meet him for lunch. 'To what do I owe the pleasure?' she asked over the phone.

'Wait and see,' her brother teased. 'Meet me at the Belfry on College Road, at one o'clock.'

The Belfry stood in the shadow of St Joseph's church. The dress code for the smart restaurant required some thought on Edith's part; in the end she chose her lavender two-piece with a grey silk blouse and grey court shoes. But what lay behind the unexpected invite, she wondered, as she rode in a taxi across town. After all, it was a weekday and a mere two days before Christmas; a time when most people worked and prepared flat out.

Edith noticed the newspaper headlines on a bill-board outside a newsagent's – Mr Churchill had flown to Washington to meet Mr Roosevelt – hurrah! Another told her that the Battle of the Atlantic was still at its height – boo! She considered it a shame that this year's window displays were somewhat spoiled by networks of thick anti-blast tape. Still, perhaps by this time next year life would have returned to normal. There would be no more Christmases on the ration or families sleeping in the London Underground or closed theatres and concert halls. All being well, now that America had declared war on Japan and was intent on deploying troops all over Europe, Herr Hitler and his Nazis would soon be defeated. This Christmas, however, the British people would have to stay inside their houses and put up with *Dick Whittington* and *Any Questions?* on the wireless.

Holly and Barbed Wire – wasn't that the saying that was doing the rounds? Edith's taxi stopped outside the Belfry and she paid her fare. Inside the restaurant a waiter greeted her politely, took her coat then steered her towards a table by the window.

'Pamela – Fred – Harold!' Edith's voice rose in surprise. She looked enquiringly at Hugh, who sat at the head of the table wearing his business suit and a benign smile.

The men stood up as Edith took her place next to Fred. Harold winked at her across the table.

'None of us had any idea,' Pamela whispered. 'Uncle Hugh has arranged this behind our backs.'

'To celebrate,' Hugh announced. 'The men who attacked Fred have been arrested and charged. We'll have no more trouble from them, rest assured.'

'But shouldn't you all be at work?' Edith was in her element in the sophisticated surroundings – starched linen tablecloths, snowy-white napkins inside silver rings, swags of green satin at the windows to conceal the anti-blast tape, expensive glass lampshades suspended from the ceiling.

'Work will wait,' her brother assured her.

Menus arrived and were studied; wine was chosen. All possible boats were pushed out.

'Pamela and I have spoken to the police,' Fred informed Edith. 'It turns out that they knew of the existence of the group of fanatics that meets at the Anchor and have had their eye on its members for some time. They call themselves the Dragons, after St George and the Dragon.'

'Which speaks volumes in itself,' Harold said drily. 'The dragon came off badly in that encounter, don't you know?'

'Names include Hilda and Cyril Fielding, not to mention Betty, Keith and Jack,' Fred continued. 'And, of course, junior warden Alf Tomkins.'

'And?' Edith raised her eyebrows and darted swift glances around the table.

'Tomkins and his gang are under arrest and a police warning will be issued to the rest,' Hugh informed her. 'The landlord has banned all future meetings on his premises.'

'What about Jack Watkins and Keith Nelson?' Edith accepted a little wine. She looked to her brother for an answer. 'Will they keep their jobs?'

He shrugged. 'I don't intend to dismiss them, if that's what you're getting at. With luck, an official warning should be enough to make them toe the line.'

'The main benefit of these past few weeks is that the problem is now out in the open.' As ever, Harold opted for the cheerful viewpoint. 'Putting Tomkins behind bars will send out a clear message. And Hugh's friends on the council are aware of potential troublemakers in their employ. I'd say that, all in all, things have turned out nicely.'

'Except for some cuts and bruises and many

sleepless nights.' Edith's doubts fluttered restlessly around her head. 'Still, Fred dear, as long as you're happy . . .'

'Extremely happy, thank you, Edith.' He acknowledged each of Hugh's guests in turn and reserved his warmest, broadest smile for Pamela.

Hugh raised his glass and called for a toast. 'To Fred and Pamela.'

'To Fred and Pamela.' There was a chink of glasses.

'To us,' Pamela murmured to Fred.

As they drank there was a tap at the window and Pamela made out Connie's face peering through the glass, mouthing words that she couldn't make out.

'Sorry – excuse me – sorry!' Pamela left the table and rushed outside. 'What is it? What's wrong?'

'Nothing!' Connie's face was unreadable, distorted by excitement that could be either good or bad. She wore her shop apron and was without a coat. Passers-by cast curious glances in her direction.

'What, then?' Pamela took Connie by the shoulders. 'Come on – spit it out!'

'Bill is alive!' Connie shrieked in a delirium of joy and relief. 'He didn't drown. Lizzie's sixth sense was right all along!'

That night a thick, cold fog blanketed the town, but tomorrow was Christmas Eve and nothing could dampen Connie's spirits as she started her shift at the Gas Street post. Yes, there was the usual mountain of paperwork to get through and a storeroom inventory to be completed, but all on duty were in buoyant mood. Pamela had brought in a Victoria sponge baked with her own fair hands, to be shared between the Fraser boys and three other wardens. Tea and cake were the order of the day.

'Did you hear Mr Churchill on the wireless?' Eddie's mouth was full and he spluttered crumbs as he spoke. 'That bulldog growl of his – it gives me a thrill every time I hear it.'

'Aye, he bluffs us through the worst of it,' one of the older, more cynical wardens agreed. '"Britain expects", and all that.'

Simon grinned as he stood to attention and quoted the famous poster in full. '"Britain expects that you too, this day, will do your duty!" Mr Churchill has got our mam scurrying about collecting all the paper, metal and bones she can lay her hands on to turn into planes and tanks and what have you. To listen to her you'd think she can win the war single-handed.'

Connie and Pamela sipped their tea in silence. They enjoyed the relaxed atmosphere and the chance to take the weight off their feet. With luck, the dreaded Luftwaffe would already have called a Christmas truce and the next few nights would prove uneventful.

'Did you hear: Doug Greenwood has got his Boy Scouts to dig an allotment in the hospital grounds.' Eddie chipped in with an interesting snippet. 'They've finished painting white lines on the town roads and will move on to growing vegetables, come spring.'

'Good for them.' There was general approval for the youngsters' efforts before the talk turned to Bill Evans's return.

'Talk about a miracle!' Simon didn't know many details but voiced the general opinion. 'I reckon his middle name must be Lazarus.'

His brother laughed. 'Kelthorpe Town was mourning the loss of the best centre forward they've had in donkeys' years.'

The girls let the talk wash over them. Connie recalled the latest picture she had of Lizzie and Bill back home at Elliot Street, earnestly planning details of their spring wedding. Bliss was the best word to describe their mood – pure, unadulterated happiness. Meanwhile, Pamela basked in the memory of cheerful glasses raised during lunch to her and Fred.

The phone on Connie's desk jangled and she ran downstairs to answer it. Dorniers had been sighted a hundred miles to the south-east, heading for the Yorkshire coast; sound the alarm – the message from the town hall controller was clear and unequivocal. 'Action stations!' she cried.

There was a sudden scramble for helmets and gas masks.

'Simon, take Valley Road and the Leisure Gardens. Pamela, you patrol Maypole Street. Eddie, you're on College Road.' Connie rattled out orders as she clasped the receiver to her ear, waiting for further information. A dozen planes approached, flying in at 20,000 feet, target as yet undetermined. 'Damn and blast!' she swore under her breath as she activated the yellow alarm. 'So much for a quiet Christmas!'

Fred manned his desk at the report and control centre. His boss, Ronald Atkinson, had given him a warm welcome. He'd made a point of shaking his hand and saying how very happy he was to have him back.

'You'll be pleased to know that you won't have to

contend with Hilda Fielding or any of her nonsense in future,' he'd assured Fred. 'She's no longer second in command here. In fact, she was forced to admit that she was responsible for spreading false rumours about you and for leaving a threatening note on your desk. She's been relieved of her duties and dismissed from the ARP.'

Fred had merely nodded and said a quiet thank you. He experienced no sense of triumph; in fact, he felt oddly sorry for poor, misguided Hilda, whose star had fallen as his had risen. Ronald had put him in charge of updating the situation map and in the event of any future incident, Fred was to flag up blocked roads and damaged utilities, together with disruption to railway lines and bridges. Executive officer was his new title and he was to report directly to the controller himself.

'Dorniers!' One of the radio operators received an urgent message. 'Coming in at twenty thousand feet. Stand by!'

All sector posts were alerted. Everyone in the control centre waited for what felt like the inevitable.

'Fifteen thousand feet,' the operator reported. 'Poor visibility. Radar sighting only.'

Surely no raid would succeed in these conditions. Fred clung to a thread of hope. He knew Pamela was out on patrol, dicing with death yet again.

'Ten thousand feet.' The radio operator held them in suspense. 'Off the radar. No signal.'

A thick silence filled the airless room. Telephonists were poised to receive the first incident reports from sector posts, while plotting clerks busily charted enemy progress.

'Signal regained,' the radio operator announced. 'Change of course. Enemy aircraft now heading south towards Bruges.'

'Stand down, everyone.' Atkinson's sharp voice cut through the tension. 'Contact head wardens with the all-clear. Let everyone know it's a false alarm.'

'Too foggy.' Lizzie reported the incident to her father when she and Bill visited him next morning. 'Jerry was forced to turn tail and head for home.'

Bert sat up in bed, alert and freshly shaved. He ignored the comings and goings on the ward – nurses wheeling medicine trolleys, orderlies busy with brooms and mops – and gave his visitors his full attention. 'We've got 'em well and truly on the run,' he asserted boldly, tapping a newspaper headline about the outcome of the latest meeting between Churchill and Roosevelt. 'Who needs the Yanks anyway?'

Lizzie didn't rise to the bait. War talk wasn't why she and Bill were here. 'We'd like to fix a date for the wedding,' she declared, loud enough for other patients to hear.

Bill felt his cheeks flame red. At this rate the whole world and its bleeding aunt would know their business.

'Have you any idea when they might discharge you?' Lizzie went on brightly.

'Your guess is as good as mine.' Noting that his vague answer had disappointed her, Bert made amends. 'How long have I been here? Just under three weeks by my reckoning, though it feels more like three years.'

She did a quick calculation. 'They'll want to keep you here for another three – that takes us to mid January at the earliest.'

'Your dad will have to take it easy for quite a while after that,' Bill reasoned. Much as he longed to put a ring on Lizzie's finger, it mustn't look as if they were rushing headlong into marriage. 'We can wait until you're properly back on your feet,' he assured Bert.

Lizzie's father subjected his future son-in-law to a long, hard scrutiny. 'I'm not the only one who needs to find my feet again,' he reminded him. 'Have you thought about how you'll earn a crust now that *Sea Knight* lies rusting away on the seabed?'

'Dad!' Lizzie protested.

'He's right. And yes, sir, I have. The idea is to offer myself as crew to one of the old boys who are still allowed to fish out of Kelthorpe. The money won't be up to much but it'll tide me over until Tom and I can afford to buy a new boat. We both have savings, so it shouldn't be too long before we're up and running again.'

Bert gave a grunt of satisfaction. 'Try Norman Norris – he's getting on a bit and could do with an extra pair of hands. Or else there's Arthur Dobbs up in Raby – you could help him do up his old rust bucket; what's she called – the *Annie May*? Who knows, he might even be ready to sell her to you and at a good price, too.'

Lizzie's smile broadened as she listened. Bill would always be a trawlerman, come hell or high water. Sometimes she thought that it was salt water that coursed through his veins. But at least for now the Navy couldn't nab him and send him out on minesweeping duties. Back to the wedding! 'How about a Saturday in May?' she demanded.

Bert's favourite young nurse spooned medicine into the mouth of the patient in the next bed. 'Ooh, yes – a spring wedding!' she cooed.

A patient across the ward also gave the idea the thumbs-up.

Bert nodded. 'For what it's worth, you have my blessing. But I know you youngsters will do things your own way, come what may.'

Lizzie grew suddenly serious. 'That's not true, Dad. Bill and I want you to be happy with the arrangements. It's important to us.'

'And I am,' he assured them, wiping away a tear that had sprung from nowhere. It seemed that his brush with death had turned him soft. 'I only wish your mother could have lived to see it,' he said with a sigh. Then he rallied and was his old self again. 'Don't let what I'm about to say go to your head, young Bill, but Rhoda wouldn't have minded having you as a son-in-law – she'd have heaved a sigh of relief and said that our Lizzie could have done a lot worse.'

'And that's all the praise you're ever likely to get,' Lizzie told Bill after they'd said their goodbyes and made their way hand in hand down the hospital corridor. '"Could have done a lot worse": that was Dad giving his seal of approval.'

'I'm happy with that.' Bill was relieved to have passed muster. His pace quickened and he led her to where his bike was parked next to the bus stop outside the hospital gates. 'Now, how about that ring?' he asked after she'd hopped on to the pillion seat.

'I've seen one in the jeweller's window that you might like. A ruby with diamonds, just like you said.'

Connie was glad that Lizzie and Bill had gone to visit Bert, even though it left her short-handed in the bakery. It was important that their dad should feel included in the wedding arrangements. Tom, bless him, had stepped in once again to help with deliveries.

She worked on through the morning, surrounded by the familiar aroma of fresh baking and enjoying the winter sunshine that brightened the pavements and helped put her customers into a good mood.

'If we're not ready now, we never will be.' Vera arrived mid-morning, willing to roll up her sleeves and stand in for Lizzie for as long as necessary. 'All the presents are wrapped and I've made the batter for the savoury puddings. The little 'uns have written their letters to Father Christmas. How about you?'

'Almost there.' Connie still had to finish then wrap the Guernsey sweater she'd knitted for Tom. 'To be honest, I don't know where the time's gone.'

'That's what happens when you keep so many plates spinning all at once.' Vera's advice was slotted between serving customers. 'You and Tom should get away over New Year – just the two of you.'

'Pigs might fly,' Connie replied as the shop bell rang and Maureen came in. Smiling as she walked out from behind the counter, Connie gave her a hug. 'Look at you!' she declared. 'What a difference a few days make!'

It was true – gone were Maureen's lank locks and ashen complexion, replaced by shiny waves and a hopeful, healthy glow. Gone, too, was the plain brown dress and grey coat that Connie had always seen her in. 'Turquoise is your colour.' Connie approved of the stylish new outfit. 'Now then, what can we get you?'

Instead of placing an order, Maureen ducked her head and looked embarrassed.

'I'll be in the back if you need me.' Vera withdrew with a meaningful glance.

'What is it?' Connie pressed Maureen for an answer. 'I take it you're not here to buy a loaf of bread?'

'It's about Susan,' Maureen began hesitantly. 'Mum and me . . . last night . . . we talked for hours and hours.'

'And?' Unsure where this might lead, Connie waited with bated breath.

'We didn't talk before – you know – before I had Susan. We just argued. Mum made it plain I wasn't fit to look after a baby and, anyway, I should have known better.'

Connie knew all this but she felt that Maureen was building up to a new revelation that would come in its own good time.

'Now I've had chance to explain what happened so she doesn't think that any more – that it was my fault.'

'Whose fault does she think it was?' Connie asked carefully.

'The person – the man. I wasn't expecting it . . . He took advantage.' Maureen's confidence waned and she stammered to a halt.

Rape was an ugly word that had floated in the back of Connie's mind ever since she'd learned Maureen's story. It still seemed an impossibly crude term to use, even though there was now little doubt that this was what had taken place. *Later,* Connie thought. *There will be a time and a place to call a spade a spade.* 'Did you tell your mum the man's name?'

'No! I can't – I promised I wouldn't.' The old, defeated expression reappeared – a dark shadow behind the eyes that threatened to engulf Maureen once more. However, after a long, fraught silence, she was able to continue. 'Mum asked me if I wanted to keep Susan. If I did she said she'd help me. She won't care about the neighbours or people at church. I won't have to hide.'

*Quite the turnaround!* Connie hid her astonishment along with her doubts and fears.

'That's good, isn't it?' Maureen prompted timidly. 'Mum will be able to teach me what babies need. She'll let us live with her on North Street and buy me a pram and everything.'

'It's very good.' Maureen's naive optimism shocked Connie almost as much as Nancy Strong's change of heart. Even if Maureen were to get her wish, she had many struggles ahead. Then again, far from being weak and helpless as she at first appeared, she'd revealed hidden reserves of grit and determination.

'Mum and I want to know what to do next – how do we get Susan back?'

The direct question knocked Connie further off balance. 'I'm not sure,' she confessed. Perhaps the adoption papers had been completed by now, in which case, was it already too late? 'What I do know is that you need to act quickly.'

'But that's just it – Mum's at work today and Christmas is coming and if we leave it until after Christmas, Susan might not be there.' The shadow returned, stealing the glimmers of hope and dumping the heavy weight of misery back on Maureen's slight shoulders. 'Mum said for me to wait for her to come home tonight. I tried to but I just couldn't!' Agitated by the idea of missing her chance, she turned towards the door. 'It's all right, though. I can find my own way to the centre.'

'No, wait – I'll come!' Connie decided in a flash. She called for Vera to serve in the shop while she was gone. Within seconds she'd flung on her coat and joined Maureen on the pavement. 'I have no idea what will happen,' she warned as they ran together towards the town square. From there it was ten minutes up the hill to the WVS centre. 'Be prepared for anything; that's all I can say.'

## CHAPTER TWENTY-THREE

A coal lorry rattled over the cattle grid close to the grammar school as Maureen and Connie arrived on foot. The moor road was busy with shoppers driving and cycling into town to buy last-minute presents, and although the school had closed its doors for the Christmas holiday, there was a general air of bustle and expectation surrounding it.

Connie drew Maureen to a halt outside the school gates. Both were breathless from the effort of running up the hill. 'Stop! We have to work out how to do this,' she gasped. 'We can't just barge in.'

Maureen refused to listen. There was a wild energy about her that Connie hadn't seen before. 'They can't stop me – Susan belongs to me.'

'I know that, but the WVS people don't,' Connie argued. Deep down she feared that they were indeed too late. A picture flashed into her mind of the respectable couple from Raby taking away Maureen's baby and installing her in a light, freshly painted bedroom with a Little Bo Peep mural on one wall and a toy box containing a spinning top and brightly coloured building bricks in the corner. 'We have to explain to them why you left your baby outside the church hall in the first place and what's happened since to make you change your mind.'

Maureen pulled free and ran on towards the plain, austere building next door to the school. 'They can't stop me!' she cried a second time.

Paying scant attention to a huddle of smartly dressed men talking inside the entrance to the school building, Connie followed Maureen into the grounds of the WVS centre. There was a tall, colourfully decorated Christmas tree in a front window and inside the porch there were clusters of red balloons. Connie noted that a real effort had been made to encourage Christmas cheer among the orphans and waifs and strays unlucky enough to have ended up here.

'Yes?' A woman in the green WVS uniform answered Maureen's urgent knock. She scanned the pair of visitors – a distraught girl and her frowning companion – and was immediately on the defensive.

Connie stepped forward. 'Is Gladys Smallwood here?' she enquired without preliminaries.

'Do you have an appointment?' The plump, pleasant-faced woman ran through a speech designed to deter unwelcome callers. 'If not, I'm afraid you must make one in advance. Our telephone number is Kelthorpe 57—'

'My name is Connie Bailey and this is Maureen Strong,' Connie interrupted. 'Mrs Smallwood knows me.'

'It's all right, Edna. You can let them in.' Gladys crossed the hall and took charge. The other woman gave a resigned nod, then faded into the background. 'Mrs Lister is quite right: appointments are necessary,' Gladys said briskly as she eyed Maureen with open suspicion. 'Am I correct in assuming that this is the girl claiming to be Susan's mother? She isn't as was described to me – thin and downtrodden, if I remember rightly.'

'Maureen *is* her mother.' Connie took exception to the senior WVS woman's tactless manner. 'Surely she has a right to see her baby.'

Sighing, Gladys led them into the room containing the Christmas tree. It was furnished with a dining table large enough to seat ten people and an old-fashioned mahogany sideboard that ran the length of one wall. Framed prints of famous characters from Dickens hung on the opposite wall and two white china dogs stood guard on the black marble mantelpiece. 'There is a procedure regarding abandoned babies,' Gladys explained. 'A right way to go about things, which includes informing the police and offering proof as to parentage.'

Mention of the police threw Maureen into a fresh panic. She gave a small cry, then glanced around the room as if looking for a means of escape.

Behind her glinting, horn-rimmed glasses Gladys remained unmoved. 'Efforts were made by the officers at Gladstone Square to identify and trace Susan's mother, without success – hence the decision to go ahead with the plans for adoption.'

'Even though Maureen has now come forward of her own free will?' Connie countered as the woman called Edna entered the room to speak to Gladys. Whispered words were exchanged before the assistant retreated once more. 'You said early on that one of the hitches that could halt the adoption was if the biological mother came forward. Well, that's happening right here this minute, so the least you can do is to listen to Maureen's account of what led her to abandon Susan in the first place.'

'I'm afraid it won't make any difference – what's done is done.'

*Signed, sealed and delivered*. Connie glanced in alarm at Maureen, whose energy had deserted her and who crumpled under Gladys's implacable gaze. Her shoulders sagged forward and she wrapped her arms around her ribs as if attempting to hold herself together. 'Are all the papers signed?' Connie asked.

'And it's for the best.' Without directly answering Connie's question, Gladys held to the official line. 'Every baby deserves a comfortable home with a loving family. In this case, we've worked with the authorities and contributed to the official reports. There's no doubt in my mind that the adoptive parents are eminently suitable.'

Noises out in the hall indicated that Edna was busy with other visitors. There were imperious male voices followed by a submissive female response.

'Excuse me one moment,' Gladys said before leaving the room.

Maureen began to sob quietly. Connie put an arm around her and did her best to comfort her. 'We won't give in,' she promised.

The despairing sobs grew louder. 'It's too late – they've already given Susan away.'

Connie could only continue to hug her young friend and pray. When Gladys returned, Connie presented her most powerful argument. 'The truth is, Maureen dealt with this alone – she went through a terrible ordeal with no one to help her. It's a miracle that she coped as well as she did. Surely she deserves an ounce of your pity and the chance to see her baby daughter. You won't deny her that?'

There was a hint of indecision from Gladys and then a shrug. 'It's not up to me,' she said quietly.

'Oh, come on! You're a human being underneath that uniform. A few moments together – that's all we ask.'

Gladys shook her head. 'I'm sorry but I've been advised against it.'

'Who by?' *Of course, by the male visitors in the hall!* Connie didn't wait for an answer – she'd already jumped to her own conclusion. She thought back to the group of men observing her and Maureen from the grammar school entrance, then made another informed guess. 'Don't tell me – you've just spoken to Reverend Ibbotson.'

Again, Gladys deflected the question. She spoke to Connie as if Maureen were not there. 'Unfortunately doubt has previously been cast over the girl's soundness of mind,' she confided in a tone of quiet regret. 'From what I understand, she's prone to hysteria; prey to fantasies, and suchlike.'

'Who says so?' Connie's indignant demand echoed around the room.

'I have it on good authority.'

*Ibbotson again!* Lizzie had indicated as much. Hot fury suffused Connie's cheeks.

Gladys was unrelenting. 'The girl may have fooled you and your sister, Mrs Bailey, but her tears don't convince me – not for a moment.'

Connie was aghast. 'Are you seriously telling me that all this is a figment of Maureen's imagination, that she's made up a story about being raped and falling pregnant? Why on earth would she do that?'

The word rape – spoken for the first time – made Maureen cover her face with her hands. She stopped sobbing and was deadly still.

'So it's a case of violent attack now, is it?' Gladys hid her shock behind an unconvincing attempt to pour scorn as she flapped a hand in Maureen's direction. 'Does she say who committed this heinous crime?'

'No, but I have my suspicions.' A glance in Maureen's direction warned Connie that the stillness could be the calm before the storm. 'Take a deep breath,' she murmured. 'Slowly, count to three.'

'I repeat: there's a history to this behaviour.' Gladys's hold on the information that had been imparted grew shakier. 'Apparently this isn't the first story of the kind that the girl has made up, albeit this is much more serious.'

'For crying out loud!' Connie would hear no more. She was ready to rush from the room to challenge Ibbotson, then discover for herself where Susan was being kept when Maureen stopped her in her tracks.

'I can prove that Susan is mine.'

Connie's heart missed a beat. 'Hush,' she said softly, afraid that anything said in the heat of the moment would be used as a further weapon against Maureen.

'I can,' she insisted with unnerving calm, dipping her hand into her coat pocket and drawing out a soft, creamish-yellow object that she handed to Connie. 'It's the bonnet I knitted for Susan while I was in the home. It matches her jacket and bootees.'

'So it does!' Connie whispered. The tiny, carefully worked garment was the exact same shade of yellow.

'I took it off her before I left the box outside St Joseph's. I kept it so I would be able to remember her even when I'm old.' Maureen's explanation was heart-wrenchingly simple. 'I never want to forget her, not ever.'

Gladys sat down heavily on the nearest chair while Connie gently returned the bonnet to its owner.

'I didn't want her to be cold so I wrapped her in a warm blanket. I left a note in the box.'

'We know you did.' Connie's voice was gentle as she turned to Gladys. 'Now you see this isn't made up?'

The leader of the WVS team viewed the evidence in Maureen's trembling fingers. 'Yes, I have no option but to believe you.'

'So, for pity's sake, let Maureen see her baby.'

'And then what?' Despite her air of authority, Gladys had a deep fear of going against instructions.

'And then you must do what you can to stop the adoption,' Connie pleaded. 'Recognize that circumstances are different – Maureen's mother has had a change of heart. She agrees to take them both in at her home in North Street. Susan will be well looked after.'

'Are you certain that's the right thing to do?' Gladys clung with her fingertips to her original view. 'What part would the baby's father be prepared to play, for example?'

Connie saw Maureen retreat back into herself as she lowered her head to stare fixedly at the floor.

'How can you ask that?' Connie demanded. 'This man, whoever he is, is guilty of a vicious criminal assault. He's hardly likely to own up to what he's done.'

'Granted.' Gladys acknowledged the point but pushed her argument to its conventional conclusion.

'Then surely, without a father in the picture, it's best for the infant to go to Raby as planned.'

'No.' Maureen battled through yet another powerful whirlpool of panic to speak out. 'Those people won't love Susan as much as I do. She belongs with me.'

'I understand how you feel.' A close study of the girl's agonized expression softened Gladys's heart, and her thoughts veered off in a new direction. 'Of course, as I said before, it's not unprecedented for the natural mother to turn up out of the blue. I've seen it happen. One young woman actually took her case to the magistrates' court to prevent the adoption.'

'So it's possible?' Connie saw a glimmer of light at the end of the tunnel.

'Possible – yes. The magistrate would have to be sure that arrangements for the baby's welfare were firmly in place.'

'And would the Raby couple have to give consent?'

'Not at this stage,' Gladys conceded. 'The final papers have yet to be signed.'

The light grew brighter – it seemed that Connie and Maureen were not too late after all. Connie stripped away the ifs and buts and spoke to Gladys woman to woman. 'So please, please, can we have a few minutes with Susan – for Maureen's and the baby's sakes?'

There was a long pause filled with uncertainty then, 'Very well – I'll see what I can do. Wait here.'

Gladys was gone from the room. Maureen clutched Connie's hand and held her breath. Time seemed to stretch and the wait went on and on. Then there were footsteps and raised voices; the words, 'On no account' and 'Do you hear me?' drowned out quieter responses from Gladys.

'Right, that's it!' Connie burst from the dining room to see Terence and Doug blocking Gladys's progress across the hall. There was no baby to be seen. 'What do you think you're doing?' Connie demanded of the clergyman. She ignored Doug, who backed silently towards the front door.

The vicar looked as if he would swat Connie away like a bluebottle. 'I'm simply doing my duty,' he replied tersely. 'I explained the background of the case to Mrs Smallwood, who, however, chose to go against my wishes. I told her that on no account must she allow Maureen Strong anywhere near that baby.'

'And if she disobeys?'

'Then matters can only go from bad to worse for Maureen.' Terence spread his hands in a gesture of regret. His smooth features were unruffled, his demeanour was cool, calm and collected. 'A doctor will be brought in. She will be examined by experts in psychological ailments. The police may be involved. After that, matters will be taken out of all our hands.'

Glancing over her shoulder, Connie saw that Maureen had been too afraid to follow her into the hall. She signalled for Gladys to close the door. 'Let's be sure what we're talking about,' she went on in a more measured tone. 'You say that Maureen is unwell, that she's made up a story and persuaded herself that it's true?'

'Regretfully, yes. I'm sure there's a precise medical term for her condition. As you and I are aware, she's always been highly strung, with a vivid imagination.'

'She's nothing of the sort,' Connie countered.

'Gladys and I have been shown the proof that backs up her story. Besides, the Maureen I know has shown great steadiness and devotion to her baby. In fact, I'd say you're the one who's making things up.'

The urge to swat turned into a deeper anger. A red flush appeared on Terence's neck, set off against his pure white clerical collar. 'Fact,' he snapped at Connie, 'this isn't the first time that the girl has caused trouble in the parish. There was a boy in her communion class whom she accused of, shall we say, inappropriate behaviour. The matter was investigated and found to be without foundation. The boy's parents wished to take the matter further but fortunately I was able to dissuade them. That's when I invited Mrs Strong to the rectory to discuss her daughter's behaviour.' The vicar's account oozed smoothly from his lips, coating all present in its specious glaze.

'Who investigated the "matter", as you call it?' Connie dug in her heels.

'That's beside the point.'

*You and your damned principle of confidentiality!* she swore inwardly. 'And didn't it ever occur to you that Maureen and not the boy was telling the truth?'

Ibbotson shook his head. 'The evidence pointed to the contrary. However, during my interview with Nancy Strong I learned that her daughter was with child and was displaying all the signs of a complete mental collapse.'

*Clever!* Connie admired the sheer nerve of the man. Faced with his own spectacular fall from grace he'd had the wit to cover his tracks and shift the blame on to the helpless victim.

'My advice to Mrs Strong was that Maureen should

be moved to an out-of-the-way location, at least until after the baby was born.'

*Yes, you planned everything down to the last detail!* He'd acted swiftly to send Maureen away to Axenby and had relied on his victim's continued silence. Meanwhile, he'd boxed her into a corner by inventing a mental illness, should she ever gather the courage to speak out. 'How could you?' Connie gasped. 'Have you any idea what you've put her through?'

Shaking her head in confusion, Gladys joined Doug by the door. 'What do you know about this?' she hissed. 'Who are we to believe?'

'Leave it to the vicar to sort out,' Doug told her through gritted teeth.

'You never had any intention of helping Lizzie and me to find Maureen after she ran away from King Edward Street,' Connie counter-attacked. 'In fact, you were praying for her to stay lost. Since Pamela found her you've been on tenterhooks.'

'Come, come.' Ibbotson strode impatiently towards the door. 'You're talking nonsense.'

At last Connie had him on the run. 'Out of interest, who first decided that Maureen had made it all up? Name names. Ah no, I forgot; as a man of the cloth you're sworn to secrecy.'

The vicar turned and advanced towards her. 'You'd do well to remember who you're dealing with. Don't you realize that the whole of Kelthorpe will be against you if you continue down this road?'

'Are you threatening me?' Looking him in the eye, Connie waited for her adversary to blink. 'You'd do anything to cover your tracks, wouldn't you?'

'What tracks? What on earth do you mean?' For the

first time a flicker of panic appeared in Terence's eyes.

'If you sling the mud fast and far enough, some of it is bound to stick – that's the way men like you work. Make everyone believe that Maureen has invented the whole thing – the being nice to her then singling her out then getting her all to yourself, attacking her when there were no witnesses. Where was it – in the vestry after communion classes, after everyone else had gone home? That would have been the perfect time and place.'

As Connie's words sank in, all colour drained from Terence's face. 'You're accusing me . . . ?'

'I am.' His back was against the wall and Connie was sure that a confession was imminent. 'Maureen Strong was a young, innocent girl, and you thought nothing of using her for your own pleasure and robbing her of that innocence. Shame on you!'

'No, he never.' Maureen stepped from the dining room into the tempest of Connie's accusations. She saw St Joseph's vicar crumble under Connie's fierce gaze and Gladys and Doug hover in the doorway. 'It wasn't him,' she told Connie as she pointed to the man she had feared and loathed since the moment he'd laid hands on her. The months of terrified secrecy were over at last. 'It was him.' She singled out Doug Greenwood silhouetted against the daylight, trapped at the centre of his own web of lies.

# CHAPTER TWENTY-FOUR

'Ibbotson claims he had no idea.'

Pamela and Lizzie hung on to Connie's every word. They'd come to the bakery later that day, eager to hear Connie's explanation. The shop was closed and the shelves were empty, the floor swept and the blind pulled down.

'And you believed him?' It was a lot for Lizzie to take in.

Connie nodded. 'He swears on his precious Bible – Doug hid everything from him and poisoned his mind against Maureen.'

'Doug, of all people!' Pamela was dumbfounded. 'He seemed so . . .' She struggled to find the right word.

'Prim and proper?' Connie suggested. She couldn't pretend that she'd ever liked Doug Greenwood, not after he'd singled her out and humiliated her during choir practice, and now she felt free to pile on the scorn. 'School-teacherish? Pernickety?'

'Respectable,' Pamela decided. 'A pillar of the community, as my mother would say.'

The three girls were silent as they thought back to the first choir rehearsal, with Doug gathering the

carol singers together in St Joseph's hall, tapping his conductor's baton on the piano before leading them pedantically through 'Good King Wenceslas'. Three syllables for the king's name, not two.

'And all the time . . .' Lizzie marvelled how he'd been able to conceal his dark secret. 'Even after you found the baby in the porch, Doug never gave the smallest sign that he was responsible.'

'The man has no conscience,' Connie concluded vehemently. 'He carried on denying it even after the police arrived, spinning them the line that it was nothing to do with him, that Maureen had made it all up. He stood there bold as brass and blamed her. He carried on lying through his teeth.'

'But she had the strength to stand up to him?' Pamela was amazed.

'Yes, I was proud of her. Once she realized that the world wouldn't come crashing down about her ears if she spoke the truth, she was able to give the police details of the event, calm as anything – the time, the place, then what happened after she found she was expecting.'

'Did she go to Doug and ask for help?' Lizzie wondered.

Connie nodded. 'He said no, then proceeded to scare the living daylights out of her – laughed in her face and said that no one would believe her and anyway it was her fault for leading him on. Girls like her went straight to hell.'

'He said that!' Pamela understood the paralysing effect that this would have had on the defenceless girl. 'Not an honest bone in his body; just pure wickedness.'

'Eventually the penny dropped with Reverend Ibbotson.' Contempt entered Connie's voice. 'He saw how he'd been led by the nose – it was Doug who had turned the truth on its head. And Doug was behind the move to get Maureen sent away to Axenby. Ibbotson simply followed his advice. He admitted as much to the police sergeant, and it was enough to incriminate Doug and for them to arrest him and take him away.'

'It's a pity the light didn't dawn earlier.' Lizzie felt no sympathy for the clergyman whose gullibility had let Maureen down. When Connie told her that Ibbotson would probably pay the price by being moved on to another parish she gave a nod of satisfaction. 'But how do you think Maureen will cope when she has to appear in court as a witness against Doug?'

Connie held up her crossed fingers. 'She'll do it for Susan's sake, and her mother will stand by her, I'm sure of that.'

Nancy had been alerted at the telephone exchange and had arrived at the WVS centre as the police car had driven Doug away. She'd been at Maureen's side when Gladys had shown them to the nursery. Connie would never forget the look of joy on Maureen's face when she'd held Susan in her arms. Tears had flowed as she'd passed the baby to Nancy – three generations bound together by love.

'I don't know about you two, but I feel as if I've been through ten rounds in the boxing ring.' Connie prepared to lock up. She turned out the lights, then stood to one side to allow Lizzie and Pamela to leave the shop.

'Likewise,' Lizzie agreed.

'Down but not out.' Pamela waited for Connie to turn the key in the lock. 'Look at us – we're still standing.'

Standing tall, walking together along College Road, striding towards Christmas Day. Connie, Lizzie and Pamela had arranged to meet Tom, Bill and Fred at the Anchor prior to joining the rest of the carol singers in the heart of the old town.

'You'll have to take over as choir mistress,' Lizzie told Pamela before they entered the pub. 'We need someone to be in charge of "Ding dong Merrily" and the rest.'

'All right, I'll do it.' Much as Pamela shrank from being the centre of attention, she promised to hold the singers together for one last night.

'Lizzie has twisted Pamela's arm to lead our merry band,' Connie informed Fred as he rushed to greet them. 'Sing out of tune at your peril!'

Like the girls, the men were wrapped up in scarves, gloves and hats. They ordered, then quickly downed their drinks.

'Dutch courage,' Bill admitted to Lizzie as he emptied his pint glass. 'Will you still want to marry me when you find out I'm tone deaf?'

'Don't worry – you can't be worse than Connie,' she said with a giggle.

'Ready?' Tom was raring to go. First out of the pub, he linked arms with Connie as they crossed the market square. 'This is our last hurrah, so let's make it count.'

Lizzie and Bill followed, and Pamela and Fred brought up the rear. Fred paused to look out across the harbour towards Kelthorpe's new town at the far end of the bay. The headland was only dimly visible and the promenade was cloaked in darkness. 'One day,' he sighed.

'One day what?' Pamela asked.

'The lights will come back on.' Air raids would cease and life would return to normal. The shadow of suspicion that had hung over Fred since the start of the war would finally lift.

She kissed him then smiled. 'Come on – we don't want to be late.' Arm in arm they hurried to catch up.

The carol singers gathered at the entrance to the Leisure Gardens. The WI women had knitted and wrapped their final pairs of socks and the old trawlermen had bought in plentiful supplies of bottled beer and pipe tobacco to see them through the festive period. All were ready for the big day. Arnold was there and so was Colin, keen to rattle the collection tin and scoff all the mince pies. Colin darted up to Connie and chucked an accusation at her. 'It's all your fault!'

'What is, you cheeky monkey?'

'Maureen and the baby have come back home to North Street and they've only gone and nabbed the best bedroom. I've been put into the little room right next to the lav.'

'Poor you!' Connie allowed a wide smile to spread across her face. The Strong family were back together, arguing and muddling through – a perfect ending. 'You'll have to rough it like the rest of us.'

Sticking out his tongue, Colin dashed off to join the raucous Scout contingent while Pamela took up her new role. 'Let's begin with "The Holly and The Ivy",' she announced a touch nervously. Fred's smile encouraged her and she continued with more confidence. 'We'll save "O Little Town of Bethlehem" and "Once in Royal" until later.'

'Get a move on,' one of the old boys grumbled. 'My feet are turning into blocks of ice here.'

And so the carol singers crossed the street, giving the huge bomb crater outside the ruined cinema a wide berth, then setting off along Gas Street. '"Oh, the rising of the sun,"' they chorused as they arrived at the sector post with its blackout clock, sandbags, banner and flag.

The Fraser brothers in full ARP uniform came out on to the pavement to join in. Head warden Bob Eddison soon joined them and added his tuneless drone.

'"And the running of the deer,"' Lizzie and Pamela trilled at the tops of their voices, and even Connie joined in. Standing side by side, the three air raid girls tilted back their heads, drew air into their lungs and sang to the silent heavens. '"The playing of the merry organ, sweet singing in the choir."'

# A TRIBUTE

*My late father, Jim Lyne, served in the Royal Navy during the Second World War. Shortly before his death in 2015 he wrote this account of the sinking of his ship, the* Tanimbar, *off Malta in June 1942. This is my acknowledgement of the part he played in real events of the time.*

My flotilla of LCMs (flat-bottomed landing craft) had operated for almost two years making landings up and down the west coast of Scotland and had taken part in raids on Vadsø in Norway and on the Lofoten Islands. We knew this was all part of preparations for 'the big one'; the invasion of Europe, but of course no one could foresee when that would be.

Our vessels were unwieldy, uncomfortable and virtually unmanageable in heavy weather, however they did the job for which they had been designed, which was to get men and machines ashore where no docking facility existed. In the early days of June 1942 we were told to make our way from Inveraray to the James Watt dock in Greenock where my six LCMs were hoisted aboard a Dutch freighter with the unlikely name *Tanimbar*. My barges, together with two RAF air-sea rescue launches, were secured by heavy steel cables on the forward and midship hatches.

By the evening of 8th June we had assembled off Gourock with a convoy consisting of four other freighters, a tanker and various destroyers, cruisers etc. Our main cargo, I discovered, was aviation spirit in jerry cans and a large amount of ammunition. No one knew our destination when we sailed on the morning of the 9th, but two and a half days later as we sailed through the Straits of Gibraltar, no one was in any doubt – it had to be Malta.

The first enemy aircraft sighted were probably spotter planes and the first bombers to attack were Italian high-level jobs which made a lot of splashes but did no harm. The next high-level attacks were accompanied by low-level torpedo bombers which came in very low over the sea at mast height.

My ship was hit almost immediately. (From my position in the bow of the ship I saw the plane very clearly as he went over the mast head just before his torpedo hit.)

The *Tanimbar*, with its cargo of aviation fuel, blew up. Protected by a steel wall formed by the captain's bridge, I was one of very few survivors of the blast. The vessel sank fast and had completely vanished underwater before I had time to take it all in.

Along with two other lads (one of whom couldn't swim) I floated around for a while amongst the flotsam and eventually finished up sitting astride an upturned lifeboat.

Very few people survived that one. The convoy steamed on and vanished into the haze. We were five in number sitting astride our upturned rowing boat, but the day was fine and the water warm when out of the blue appeared a small minesweeper with scrambling nets hanging over the side, looking for survivors. I suppose about an hour and a half had elapsed since we were hit – all watches had stopped at twelve noon when we hit the water.

We quickly caught up with the convoy and over the next few days saw two more merchantmen and the tanker go down. The bombing continued more or less non-stop almost into Sliema Creek.

On the first evening after landing in Malta I was in the petty officers' mess in the submarine base in Sliema when I heard on the BBC News a report given by the then First Lord of the Admiralty, Mr A. V. Alexander in the House of Commons to the effect that 'A convoy has today successfully reached the beleaguered garrison of Malta.' Two of our six merchantmen had got through. Many men and escorting ships were lost. It made one think a bit.

I was on the island until September when, together with 51 other survivors, I embarked for Gibraltar aboard a large river-class submarine, the *Clyde*. She had a crew of 52 so things were very cramped. We took nine days to cover the 900 miles to Gib mainly because we stayed on the bottom during daylight hours and only moved on the surface at night. We went ashore at Gibraltar and eventually embarked for Scapa Flow aboard a quite severely damaged cruiser, *Kenya*.

Uneventful trip home to Scapa but a long train journey from there to Devonport then home for seven days survivor's leave.

The submarine *Clyde* was later lost with all hands in the Atlantic.

## CLASSIC FESTIVE FAMILY RECIPES

*from*

# JENNY HOLMES

These recipes have been passed down through the Holmes family line. They originated in the early twentieth century with my Yorkshire grandmother, who ran the Beckwithshaw village pub while my grandfather worked in the blacksmith's forge attached to it.

Great pride was taken in getting the Christmas cake just right. It should be made two to three months before Christmas and it should ideally be eaten with a slice of Wensleydale cheese.

The recipe for savoury pudding, an accompaniment to the festive turkey, is a delicious local speciality. Thanks are owed to my cousin, Yvonne Graham, for unearthing these recipes from the family archives!

# THE HOLMES FAMILY CHRISTMAS CAKE

225g / 8 oz butter
170g / 6 oz dark soft brown sugar
55g / 2 oz black treacle
6 medium eggs
225g / 8 oz plain flour
110g / 4 oz cherries
560g / 1¼ lb currants
340g / ¾ lb sultanas and raisins
85g / 3 oz ground almonds
1 teaspoon nutmeg
1 teaspoon mixed spice
150ml / 1 wine glass of sherry

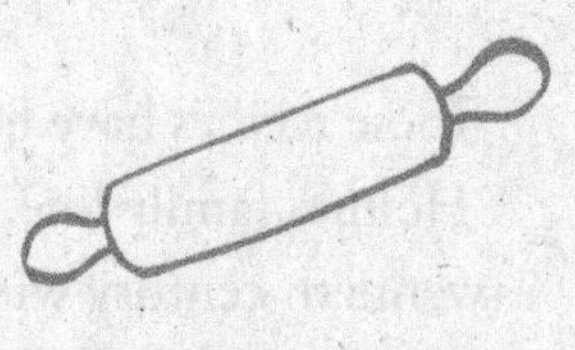

1. Line an 8-inch round tin with greaseproof paper.
2. Beat together the butter, sugar and treacle.
3. Beat the eggs and add very slowly to the butter, sugar and treacle mixture.
4. Add the flour, fruit, nuts, spices and sherry.
5. Bake at gas mark 2 / 150°C / 130°C fan for 3 to 3½ hours.
6. Pour a little more sherry over the cake when it comes out of the oven and then feed with sherry once a week until ready to be eaten.

# BECKWITHSHAW SAVOURY PUDDING

140ml / ¼ pint of milk
450g / 1 lb breadcrumbs
450g / 1 lb chopped onions
1 tablespoon salt
1 tablespoon sage
1 teaspoon pepper
110g / ¼ lb chopped suet
2 heaped tablespoons plain flour
2 eggs
Butter (for greasing)

1. Boil the milk and pour it over the breadcrumbs.
2. Mix in all other ingredients (except the eggs).
3. Leave in the fridge overnight.
4. Beat two eggs and slowly stir into the mixture to make a stiff paste. If the mixture is still dry, add another egg, but make sure it is not too sloppy.
5. Preheat the oven to gas mark 7 / 220°C / 200°C fan.
6. Grease a baking dish with butter and place in the oven for 5 minutes.
7. Add the mixture to the baking dish and cook for at least 1 hour.

*Welcome to the world of*

# JENNY HOLMES